HEX
HOUSE

AMY
JANE
STEWART

TITAN BOOKS

Hex House
Print edition ISBN: 9781835413449
E-book edition ISBN: 9781835413456

Published by Titan Books
A division of Titan Publishing Group Ltd
144 Southwark Street, London SE1 0UP
www.titanbooks.com

First edition: April 2026
10 9 8 7 6 5 4 3 2 1

A CIP catalogue record for this title is
available from the British Library.

EU RP (for authorities only)
eucomply OÜ, Pärnu mnt. 139b-14, 11317 Tallinn, Estonia
hello@eucompliancepartner.com, +3375690241

Designed and typeset in Sabon LT by Richard Mason.

Printed and bound by CPI (UK) Ltd, Croydon, CR0 4YY.

Not knowing when the Dawn will come,
I open every Door,
Or has it Feathers, like a Bird,
Or Billows, like a Shore—

EMILY DICKINSON, *Not knowing
when the Dawn will come*

for my family

*Come and find me where the
world ends and the wild starts.*

*Find me at the full stop of
everything you thought you knew.*

*Find me when you're tired and hurt
and wrong and ashamed, and nowhere
will have you, nowhere but here.*

*Find me. Come inside.
Rest your head now, angel.*

PROLOGUE

"Okay, we're ready," he tells her, looking up from the camera. He's more nervous than she's seen him before – jittery, unpredictable. He won't meet her eye. "Is there anything in particular you'd like to share? Or shall we just start the interview and see how we go?"

She bites the inside of her lip. She hadn't really thought this through, hadn't thought beyond the fact of this man and his camera on one side of a room, her on the other. "I don't know if I can talk about..." She hesitates, staring down at her hands. "I don't know if I can talk about *her*."

"That's okay," he says. "We'll go slowly." He clicks a few buttons on the camera and gives her a nod. There's a short beeping sound and the light directly above the lens glows red. She feels it immediately: that sensation of a thousand eyes all over her body, eyes from the future, eyes that know what happens tomorrow and the day after and the day after that. It makes her pulse buzz, but she can't tell whether it's with excitement or dread.

"Okay, Elly," he says. He sounds unsure, though he's smiling. "Let's talk a bit about what brought you here, to the house."

ELLY

THEN

Elly is running. She can't remember the last time she ran like this, the way you run in a nightmare: blindly, furiously, both away and towards. The baby squirms inside her but she can't stop now. What is she running from? The images are there behind her eyelids when she blinks: a bone-white dress, Ethan's hand gripping her wrist, her mum sitting in the pews, smiling a little too widely.

The night air is cold as old stone. This morning already feels like another life. The wedding had taken place in a church with a looming bell tower and toppled gravestones across the lawn. Elly's mum had requested that: the village church, where all the women in her family had been christened, got married, eventually been laid to rest – the place where their lives had been punctuated with import. *It's what your dad would have wanted*, she'd said the day before the wedding, drinking white wine in the kitchen, *if he were still here.*

If Elly's dad were still here, he might have been the one

to notice, the one to pull her aside and say, *You seem a little quiet, pet, has something happened? Are you sure this is what you want?* He had met Ethan properly only once: the first time Elly brought him home for dinner. Her dad was already ill by that point, but not yet ill enough for the hospital. She remembered that they'd eaten spaghetti carbonara and homemade garlic bread. Ethan had made clever jokes about the stock market and complimented their buddleias. Afterwards, feeling giddy, Elly asked her parents what they thought of Ethan. Her mum said, *He's so well spoken.* Her dad said, *His shoes are very shiny.*

Elly's mum walked her down the aisle, and with every step Elly tried to ignore the feeling in the bottom of her stomach, like a burnt piece of paper curling. When her mum kissed her on the cheek and handed her over to Ethan, resplendent in his charcoal suit, eyes glittering like dark stones, he held her so tightly it was as though he knew she was a hair away from running.

Well, she's running now. Now, when it's too late. The muscles in her thighs feel like liquid, but she presses on.

Elly can't remember much else of the ceremony, only that saying *I do* into the silence of the church had felt both as natural as opening a door and as final as pulling a trigger. The way he'd smiled at her – like she'd finally done something right – made her pulse hop, like a spring hare trapped under her skin.

They held the reception at the village hall. It smelled like old trainers and wood polish. Ethan had scoffed when she first suggested it, had wanted some fancy bar in Edinburgh, but Elly couldn't let it go. She needed the reception to be somewhere her dad had been before, somewhere he was familiar with. That felt important. Ethan shrugged and acquiesced when she told him that, and she was relieved not to have to push the matter further. Elly's mum had made the red-and-white gingham bunting, had spent many nights swearing at the sewing machine, trying to get the stitches perfect. Everything had to be symmetrical, neat, tied up in a bow. When she and Ethan walked in as a newly married couple, people threw confetti at them and thrust phones into their faces for pictures. *Smile*, Ethan said in her ear, squeezing her hand so that the bones rubbed together. *Come on. It's our wedding day.*

They ate ham hock terrine slathered with piccalilli, poached salmon dressed in lemon and dill and sitting on top of buttery new potatoes, a lemon meringue tart and ice cream to finish. Suzanne had made the tarts for her at the bakery. Elly had asked for them specifically, because they were her dad's favourite, because the decision on dessert was something she could control. At the reception, she took bite after bite, tasting nothing. Ethan's arm was a familiar weight around her shoulders, and she met his every smile with one of her own. *Steady on*, he said as she chewed on flaky pastry, *there's eating for two, then there's just being greedy*. Elly put down her fork.

During the disco, her cousin's kids stalked around the cake table, stealing strips of icing, using their tiny white shirts as napkins. Suzanne passed her a wrapped, bottle-shaped gift. Elly said, *Is it a can-opener*, and Suzanne laughed, pulling her into a perfumey hug. They used to spend every day together at the bakery but had barely seen each other since Elly left. *Help me*, she wanted to whisper into her friend's ear, *I don't know if I've done the right thing*, but Suzanne pulled away. Her mum danced to ABBA with a vigour Elly hadn't seen in years, not since her dad died, maybe even before that, swaying with her Aunt Judith and singing the lyrics to 'Dancing Queen'. When she came over to Elly's table afterwards, her skin was flushed pink and slightly damp. She reached over and kissed Ethan first, clasping his hands in both of hers. Her eyes were shiny.

I'm just so pleased you're going to take care of her now.

Ethan smiled. To Elly, she said, *I'm so proud of you.*

She beamed so bright, her happiness blinding as a lens flare. To stop herself from crying, Elly thought about her dad's hands – large and wrinkled and caked with dried clay from his pottery wheel. She opened her mouth and thought about all the things she wanted to say.

I'm sorry I'm so sorry but I honestly don't think I can do this I know how much this means to you after Dad and you think Ethan's funny and charming and clever and yes he is all those things and I love him but I don't understand him and sometimes I think he does things just to hurt me and I'm worried it's going to get worse and at the altar he held my hands too tight and I know it sounds silly and I know I really ought to be happier but—

Instead, she smiled and said, *I'll be okay now, Mum. You don't have to worry about me anymore.*

Elly stops in the woods to catch her breath, one hand on her stomach. The baby is still. Everything has started to look the same in this light. All around her, the night is the colour of bled ink and smoke. She keeps moving. She just has to keep moving.

As the reception wore on, she'd found herself not wanting to leave, to stay with family, in safe company. Most of the guests were hers. Elly looked around at her friends and tried to remember when she'd last spent proper time with any of them, the last time Ethan hadn't given her some reason why she shouldn't. They smiled at her from across the village hall, far enough away that they wouldn't be able to hear her if she said something. Their politeness was unbearable – the way they'd dressed up nicely, said congratulations, and were waiting until it was an acceptable time to leave. Smiling back at them felt like standing in a dark room, grasping towards the light. She willed them to notice, to see her, to take her into the corner and say the right combination of words that would have made it all right for her to confess how she was feeling, but what would those words even have been? She was marooned in a place beyond language now, a place she could no longer be reached.

It was difficult to breathe suddenly, difficult to swallow. Elly stood up without knowing where she was going, only that she needed to be away from the loud music and the dancing bodies, from the smiles that kept flashing up in front of her, belonging to people who seemed to expect one in return. She found herself in the toilets, which were quiet, cool and empty. Bracing a hand on either side of the sink, she studied her reflection in the mirror and tried to see a bride on her wedding day. All the pieces were there, but they seemed to add up to a different whole. Her white dress and veil felt sterile and seeped of colour; the blush on her cheeks made them look freshly slapped rather than rosy. Her face didn't look like her own. How had she let it come to this? It had all seemed so inevitable – events rolling on with a fierce momentum towards a foregone conclusion – that she sometimes thought she couldn't have stopped it at all. But that was just an excuse, she knew. That was just her being weak. Elly started to cry, wondering if she needed saving, wondering if it was too late for that now.

The door to the toilets opened and a woman in an orange dress entered. Elly straightened, wiping her face. The woman didn't go into a cubicle but instead approached the sinks and started running the tap, her long fingers flexing and curling under the water. Elly sniffed in a way she hoped was discreet, rubbing at a smudge of mascara on her cheek and watching the woman from the corner of her eye. Could she tell that Elly had been crying? The thought of it getting back to Ethan made her breathing quicken. Whenever she'd cried in front of him, he'd always comforted her, but she'd sensed a flicker of something else behind his concern. She wished it was as simple as irritation or impatience, embarrassment even. But there was a tightness in his jaw, a heavy-liddedness to his gaze, which made it feel more like a thirst he didn't know what to do with. Like he wanted to hold her in his palms and close his fingers around her.

As Elly watched the woman in the mirror, she realised she didn't recognise her. She couldn't remember seeing her during either the ceremony or reception, and yet there was something familiar about her face, something she couldn't place. Perhaps she was a relative of Ethan's, someone she'd once seen in the background of a photograph. The woman met Elly's eye in the mirror, and her expression was so careful and serious that it made the hairs on Elly's forearms prickle. She had dark skin that looked weathered, lived-in, yet smooth. Her black hair was cropped in a nest close to her head, the curls shining like the surface of a pond at night. The woman kept on looking at Elly for longer than was polite, eyes moving from her tear-stained face to her wrists, where the sleeves had ridden up to expose a newly forming bracelet of bruises. Elly looked down at them, too, thinking about the altar and the strength in Ethan's fingers as they'd pressed into her skin, then shoved her sleeves back down. She thought about making some kind of excuse for it all, but the frankness of the woman's gaze stopped her. *She sees me*, Elly thought, with a sudden clarity and something close to relief. *Maybe she sees all of it. Maybe I don't have to explain.*

"You probably feel like it's too late now," was the first thing the woman said. Her voice echoed off the bathroom tiles. It had a soft, melodic quality, like the call of a bird heard in the seconds before sleep. "But it isn't."

Elly wiped her nose, suddenly aware of how pathetic she must look, eyes bleary and mascara smeared. "Sorry, what was your name?" she asked, still facing the mirror. "Today has been a bit of a whirlwind."

"You're frightened of that man," the woman said, ignoring Elly's question, nodding towards the bathroom door. The sounds of the wedding reached them from underneath it, persistent as smoke: the thumping bass of a pop song, the delighted shriek of a running child. "You're frightened of the man you just married. I think you're right to be."

Elly's pulse fluttered, a startled creature, her eyes

9

flickering down to her wedding ring. It was shiny and tight around her finger. "I'm married," she said simply. It felt like the only thing that mattered. The weight of those two words pressed down on her shoulders like a pair of hands, keeping her rooted to the spot. "I... I don't really know what you mean. Why would I be frightened of Ethan? Everything's fine."

The woman inhaled, the lines around her eyes deepening. She looked to be around Elly's mum's age, maybe older. "Maybe everything is fine. Maybe it isn't." One of her hands found the small of Elly's back, pressing gently. She lowered her voice to a whisper, leaned in close. "Do you want to wait and find out?"

Elly stiffened. The woman's hand felt cold even through her dress. She flinched away from the touch, realising, suddenly and intensely, how strange the situation was. The thought of this woman knowing the truth about Ethan made her want to protect him, to divert the conversation in another direction. Turning, she asked, "Who did you say you were again?"

The woman smiled, but there was no warmth to it, just a tired kind of knowing. "Only a messenger."

"A *messenger*," Elly repeated.

"I know somewhere. Somewhere you could go."

Elly felt it straight away: an electricity in the room, the fizzing current of something changing and rewiring. Possibilities emerging. "What?" She still felt defensive, but her voice came out as a squeak.

The woman glanced to the bathroom door then back again. "Have you ever heard of Hex House?"

The tiny hope that had bloomed in Elly's stomach

withered. Hex House. It was a thing of teenage Ouija board sessions, of whispered stories around campfires, of truth and dare. *I dare you to find Hex House and come back with your head still attached*. She and Suzanne had gotten lost in the woods more than once trying to find it as children. When was the first time she'd heard the story of that old house, supposedly hidden somewhere amongst the trees, home only to mad women and monsters? She couldn't remember, it had just always been there, tucked away in her mind next to werewolves and witches. A local legend in a place where nothing really happens, that's all Hex House was. It wasn't *real*. This woman was talking about a myth and offering it as a solution.

Elly started to laugh, but the woman's face remained still, impassive. "It's just a story," Elly said. "No one's ever actually been there."

A beat of silence. "I have," the woman said, and her voice was trembling, spilling over with so much unsaid meaning that it made coldness creep across Elly's scalp. She searched the woman's expression for any trace of humour or deceit, but found none. Was she insane? The baby wriggled in Elly's stomach, jabbing an elbow into the space between her ribs and making her wince, as if warning her to move. Elly swallowed thickly. She needed to go and sit down, to rejoin the party before she was missed, but she couldn't seem to get her legs to obey her.

"The house saved my life," the woman was saying. "It's saved many lives, too many to count, so now I spend my time looking for other women who might need it. I've been keeping an eye on you for... quite a while."

Elly shifted on her feet, feeling as though she'd been

11

set a test that she was rapidly failing. Something about the woman's intensity, the way her eyes shifted quickly from left to right, made Elly question how stable she was. Perhaps there was something seriously wrong with her – maybe she needed help. That thought made Elly feel cornered. It made her want to run. "I need to get back to my wedding," she said. "And I think maybe you should leave."

"Listen to me," the woman said, her voice deeper now. "You can only find Hex House if you need it. That's why no one knows where it is. Why no one believes it's real."

"That doesn't make any sense."

"I can't explain it all to you now, Elly." With a shiver Elly thought, *She knows my name.* "But if you look for it, I promise you'll find it. You'll be safe. *She'll* protect you." The woman swallowed and Elly watched the muscles in her throat contract, relax. Something about that movement was too fluid. It didn't look quite right. "He will never find you there."

"But he's my husband," said Elly.

The woman clicked her tongue, a slight shudder rippling through her body. It reminded Elly of something wet shaking out its feathers. The woman might have said something else, but at that second the door to the toilets opened, making them both spin around. One of Elly's little cousins came stumbling in with cake smeared around her face. "I feel sick," she proclaimed, and disappeared into one of the cubicles.

The woman turned back to Elly, a hotness to her now, an urgency. "It's the woods you need." Her voice was almost a hiss. "Just keep going and don't stop. The house will find you."

She gave Elly's arm a final squeeze and then left, leaving Elly standing alone and shivering, listening to the sound of retching from the toilet cubicle.

Later, Elly and Ethan departed for the cottage he'd rented for the occasion, on the outskirts of the village. He carried her over the threshold, performing the ritual with a tight-lipped glee. The cottage itself was small, brickwork dripping with light from candle sconces. The fireplace was stacked with fresh wood. Ethan would start a fire and soon things would start burning, moving onwards with uncontrollable momentum. Elly was still in her long, white dress and she ran her fingers over the fine lace at her wrists. At the altar, Ethan had pressed that lace so hard that it made a net of her skin. That grip had felt like a warning, a claiming.

It's the woods you need.

Just keep going and don't stop.

Elly had looked for the woman for the rest of the reception but couldn't find her. When she asked Suzanne if she'd seen a woman in an orange dress, she'd shaken her head. And then it had been time to leave.

To distract herself, Elly clicked on the old Roberts radio. It started playing Eva Cassidy's 'Fields of Gold', one of her dad's favourites, a song she'd listened to on repeat in the long months after he died. The sound was quiet and tinny but it was still enough to make her eyes burn, until Ethan reappeared behind her and clicked off the radio.

"Do we really need to listen to that tonight? It's so depressing."

13

Was that the moment she decided? Elly considers it now as she reaches a wide clearing in the woods, cold air harsh in her lungs. Was that the loose brick that brought the whole house toppling down?

"But I love that song," she'd said. "You know I love that song." Maybe Ethan didn't like the way she said it, because he gripped the tops of both her arms and pushed her down so that she was forced to sit on the bed. She blinked up at him. "Stay," he whispered, with a wilting kind of smile. This was a game he liked to play, as though it were fun for them both. He kissed her in the place where her forehead met her nose. "God, I love you so much."

He went to bring in their cases and Elly sat in the silence, picking at her hem, which had started to fray. She'd still been hopeful when she'd picked this dress. It had reminded her of the sepia photo of her parents on their own wedding day, beaming in the same church doorway, squinting into the sun. Her mum had worn a similar style: high-necked, demure, traditional. In the photo, her father held her mother's arm like she was a prize he couldn't believe he'd just won.

Elly shifted on the thick floral bedspread. She was a married woman now. Married. *He's my husband*, she'd told the woman in the bathroom, and it had felt like the truest thing in the world, and the most inescapable. Of course Ethan was her husband. From the first day, standing in the bakery and looking at his hair dusted with snow, he was always going to be – if only because he'd decided, and because Ethan was very good at following through on things he'd decided. The cottage seemed to grow smaller around her, candles burning low. Resting her hand on the swell of her stomach, Elly could almost convince herself that this really was the best thing for everyone, and that the meeting with the woman in the bathroom had never happened. She and Ethan were a solid unit now; they shared a last name. Being married was an invisible act of binding that would make them new. It would strip away all their stains and make her worthy. It would make him love her better. It had to.

Elly turned to the window. The world outside was soaked in twilight, but she still knew it by heart. She'd been living with Ethan in Edinburgh for the last six months, and coming back home for the wedding, nostalgia had settled on her like a coat of dust. The village's quaint houses and fallow fields were as familiar as the landscape of her own body. Its quiet streets were peppered with significance: the wooden bench on the Green where she and Suzanne drank smuggled vodka from a thermos as teenagers, the little bakery on the high street where she'd worked since she was sixteen. To the north were the woods, then the hills: silent monoliths standing in the background of her every memory.

Ethan returned with the bags. The cottage walls felt thick and too close. Elly's mum would be at home now, tucked up in bed, falling asleep soundly in the belief that her only child was happily married. It seemed impossible that Elly could be just a stone's throw from her, and yet still feel this loneliness that seemed too big to hold inside her body. Suzanne and the others might have gotten a taxi into Edinburgh, to a bar with 2-4-1 cocktails. Maybe they would toast Elly and talk about how much they missed her, how they hoped they'd find partners as witty and charismatic as Ethan one day. Elly reached for her clutch bag and pulled out her phone but couldn't think of one person to call. *It's your wedding night*, she imagined whoever picked up saying, *why on earth are you calling me?* She wouldn't have an answer. She could never find the words.

"Isn't this nice?" Ethan said, sitting beside her on the bed. "Just us, finally?"

Elly leaned her head on his shoulder, tried to make herself relax. His smell was so familiar. *This is nice*, she told herself. *This is nice.*

"You looked so beautiful today," he said, kissing the top of her head. He murmured the words into her hair. "You've never looked so lovely."

She let herself melt into him, closing her eyes. Had she really felt afraid of him, just a few minutes ago? Had she really cried in the bathroom at her own wedding? It was dizzying, sometimes, how quickly things could seem one way, and then shift to become something else entirely, like the turning of a kaleidoscope. Her dress was starting to itch against her skin, the material straining uncomfortably across her belly.

"I'll go and get changed," Elly said. She made to stand up, but Ethan's hand clasped at her wrist, an anchor snagging her in the rocks, bringing her back down.

"Didn't I tell you to stay?"

A quick, cold feeling – everywhere, like an ice sheet forming across the skin.

"It's just a bit tight."

"But I want to look at you wearing it a while longer," he said. "So you can wait."

Another turn of the kaleidoscope, a new reality grinding into shape.

He hadn't always been like this. And this wasn't what he was always like. This was just a facet, a layer – but it was a layer that seemed to find the sunlight more and more.

Elly sensed Ethan's hands move. She was always hyper-aware of his movements in these moments, the rest of the world dulled and only him turned up in intensity. He raised his left hand to her mouth, his thumb on one side of her jaw and his fingers on the other. She thought he might caress her. Instead, he squeezed, pressing her cheeks into her teeth and forcing her lips open. His right hand found the back of her head, lacing through the hair and gripping it so that he could tilt her head back. Elly watched him with wide eyes, wishing she knew what any of this meant, wishing she was the kind of person who wouldn't accept it, that she was the kind of person he would never even think of doing this to.

Ethan got to his feet, bringing her up with him. Not forcefully, but without compromise. He walked into her, so that she had to step clumsily backwards. Her back found the stone wall. Still squeezing her face, he kissed her hard on the mouth. "I've wanted to do this all day," he said when he pulled away. "It's all I've thought about."

Elly forced her body to relax into his. She'd read in a women's magazine once that the key to enjoying intimacy was just to tell yourself you're enjoying it, even if you're not. The brain can trick the body into all sorts of things. But his chest was too heavy and his mouth was too warm and all she could think about was him saying, *Stay, stay*, and how she'd just submitted, like a puppet. What would her mum have said in that situation? Suzanne, or even the woman in the bathroom? It was mortifying to see herself through their eyes, pitiful and compliant.

With a light touch on his chest, Elly pushed Ethan away. "I want to go and get changed," she said, with more conviction than she felt. "I don't want to wear this dress anymore."

She saw straight away what those words did to him, how they pulled his brows down and made his eyes darker. He looked at her for a long moment and Elly wished she could snatch the words back into her mouth. She already knew that they wouldn't be worth whatever came next.

It happened quickly – the hand snaking around her throat, applying pressure. In one fluid movement, Ethan pulled her towards him then slammed the weight of her body backwards, so that her head snapped hard against the stone wall.

That sound. Dull, like distant thunder.

Elly's vision fractured, as if it had never been made of anything more than glass. A high-pitched ringing exploded in her ears.

He hurt me, she thought, stumbling to one side. That thought was the one bright spot in a world that had become dark. *He's never actually hurt me before. Not like this.* She was aware of some boundary having been crossed, some invisible but unignorable pact having now been signed. Ethan seemed to know it, too. He pulled away from her, as if her skin burned him.

"Oh god," he whispered, not looking at her face, but at her stomach and then the wall behind her head. "Oh god, Elly. I didn't mean to."

She put her hand to the back of her head, and it came away wet.

Ethan disappeared into the bathroom, locking the door. Elly stayed where she was, holding her stomach, getting smears of blood on her white dress. The sound of a tap running came from the bathroom, filling the small cottage. She felt as though she were underwater, swimming desperately upwards on the last of her breath. Upwards, towards the light.

Slowly, she smoothed down her dress, breathed in.

Later, Elly will wonder where the courage came from. She will wonder about the nature of conviction, the tangibility of it, how it fits inside the skeleton, hiding under muscle, dormant until it's needed.

She slipped her feet back into her satin shoes. She opened the front door and thanked it for not creaking. The air met her with a cool kiss, creeping under her dress, pulling up goosebumps. Stepping out of the cottage, she left the door wide open behind her, not wanting him to hear her close it. She walked down the quiet lane and didn't turn back. The lane snaked through a park and then past a row of houses, their dark windows like watching eyes, before bringing her back into the heart of the village and onto the high street. Elly walked with her head down beneath the glow of familiar streetlights, heels clicking on the pavement. Past the village hall, the pharmacy where she used to pick up her dad's prescriptions, the bakery where Suzanne would be in just a few short hours to start the ovens, creating a flash of fire and warmth in the loneliness of the early morning. The streets seemed to recognise her, carrying her quickly, kindly, silently. The back of her head throbbed. She placed her hands on her stomach to stop them from shaking and kept walking. Down the street, past the church where she'd been married just this morning. Onto the path leading into the woods.

The house will find you.

Her thoughts chased each other around her head. What on earth was she doing? Why was she out here in the cold and dark? Was she mad?

She ignored them all and kept walking.

Elly had spent plenty of time in the tangle of woodland that edged the village, but she knew that the woods themselves went on for miles, an unknowable, sprawling mass on the map. How long would she need to walk? *Walk where?* She didn't dare answer that question. Elly wished she could have someone to spill it all into. She wished they'd understand her, believe her, without words.

She could go to her mum's. Or Suzanne's, just round the corner. But she couldn't face their questions or opinions, their concerned expressions and soft words. She briefly considered a pub a few towns over, where no one would know her. They'd still be open. She could drink something fizzy and a stranger with a kind face might say something like, *You look lost, are you alright?* But she couldn't do that in a wedding dress with bloody fingerprints on the bodice.

The hills rose up on her left, three of them in a row like a trio of sisters with their heads together, their unseen eyes watching her in the dark. She'd grown up in their shadow, had known their moss-slicked and rock-scarred faces since she was a little girl. She used to play hide and seek here with Suzanne, breath short in her throat, like something far worse than her friend were chasing her. All those bored afternoons, giggling about Hex House and mad witches in the windows, all the while believing there was nothing there to find. Elly felt it again, that awful tightening behind the knees, the prickling of the scalp – and stopped to look around. But there was nothing there but the night-time world, barely disturbed by her presence. Ahead, the trees grew thick and wild in the foothills, creating a long throat into the blackness, carving out places to hide. Elly didn't give herself time to think. She let the woods swallow her up, and then she started to run.

It's only now, after running so far and for so long, lungs throbbing and surrounded by tall birches and beeches, that Elly begins to panic. How did Ethan react when he realised she'd gone? The fear floods in quickly, like the sudden shock of waking up. She can't understand why she's out here, when her new husband is at the charming cottage he's rented for them, worrying about her. He hadn't meant to hurt her. Of course he hadn't. He'd looked horrified and guilty and now she'll have made him feel even worse. Running away – it's what children do. She's married now. Married women stay.

The footpath has long since disappeared. Something squelches in Elly's shoe, and she knows it's blood. She's come too far. She's always lived in the countryside, in the rugged borders between places of note, but only now thinks how there is so much wilderness that she's never even seen, wilderness that's always been here while she lived a life of pavements and wine and engines turning over. She starts to hear things: pursuers, things with hunt in their heads.

A woman in the woods alone is never the beginning of a story. It's usually the end.

Just keep going and don't stop, the woman had said, but how much further? Elly forces the thought down somewhere deep. Of course, she isn't *really* looking for Hex House – that would mean she's losing her mind, surely. She wonders for the first time whether Ethan has seriously hurt her, if it's a hospital she really needs. *The baby*, she thinks. *I need to think about the baby*. As if in response, there's a fluttering in her abdomen. She's still getting used to this, the soft susurration of another body twisting inside her own. Elly tries to steady her breath and keeps walking. After a couple of minutes, she stumbles over a tree root and curses. She's getting tired, clumsy. The truth is that she doesn't know where she's going, only that the things the woman in the bathroom said – *You're frightened of the man you just married. I think you're right to be* – changed something in her. Ethan smashing her head backwards into the cottage wall *changed* something in her. Now, she doesn't know how to change back.

The landscape no longer looks familiar. It's getting colder. This is madness – she should turn around. Maybe it would be fine. She could tell Ethan that she'd needed some air after all the festivities, that was all. She could apologise and hope that he would accept it. She'd make cheese scones for breakfast in the morning, top them with salty slithers of bacon. They'd laugh about this tomorrow, golden butter dripping from their chins.

Elly turns and starts to walk back in the direction she's

come from, but she's tired, so tired, and eventually she sits down on a patch of moss to rest. The woods seem to hold their breath, waiting to see what she might do next. She twists the wedding ring on her finger but doesn't take it off. Her dress glows white in the gloom, creating a halo around her. She tries to think of it as a circle of protection, but it feels more like a beacon, making her vulnerable. Palms atop her belly, she wonders if she's already a bad mother.

Nearby, things rustle and squirm. Raptors, toads, nightjars. The woods are never still. Elly can see her own breath making shapes in the twilight, a secret language. She eases off each heel and abandons them to the undergrowth, imagines them being swallowed up by the soil, then keeps walking.

How long does she walk? An hour, maybe two. She can't stop thinking about cheese scones, about lemon meringue tarts. Surely, she'll stumble onto a road soon. She shouldn't hitchhike but maybe she would, just this once.

But no roads appear. There are only the woods – cold, dark, endless.

Just as she starts to feel desperate – really, truly, desperate – Elly becomes aware of a different sound, like air being sucked out of the hills. It's all around her, inside her. Her heart beats hard in her chest, as though it's trying to escape her body. Then, a soft tinkling noise, like silver bells beckoning, and something moving in the canopy overhead. She staggers backwards, breathless, her hands on her stomach.

When the tree falls it is sudden, but also slow – graceful, like a woman fainting. Breath hot in her throat, Elly watches it settle into the ground, its new resting place, gently rocking. Her eyes are drawn to what's behind it, to something that wasn't there before.

There's a house.

It's very large, and very old, its grand style somewhere between a farmhouse and a country manor. It's surrounded by lush gardens of roses and wildflowers. Purple wisteria grows up its honey-stone walls, crowding around the leaded windows as if trying to find a way inside. The house has an irregular shape, the building folding and protruding like complicated origami, pocked with little terraces and clusters of chimney pots. It has a pointed gabled roof, and the front door is wide open, leaking light all over the path. It is incredible. It is impossible.

Elly watches and waits, shivering, her arms still wrapped around her belly. She has the curious feeling she's being watched. She waits until a woman appears, as Elly had somehow known she would. The woman smiles and raises a hand.

"Would you like to come inside?" she asks.

SIOBHAN

NOW

Siobhan sits alone, drenched in the dark of the cinema. This darkness is a safe smother, its fullness pierced by the glow of the screen. She can breathe better in here, surrounded by so many warm bodies, than back at the flat where she never allows the bedside lamp to go out. Whatever happens on the cinema screen, the lights will always snap back on. Siobhan finds that more comforting than she should.

She'd slid into a row after her shift on the box office and cheered with everyone else as the velvet drapes drew back, like red lips framing a howling mouth. The Horror Film Festival at the Showroom always draws an eclectic crowd. All around Siobhan are stitched Frankenstein foreheads, vampire teeth shoved up into gums, faces splattered with fake gore. They jeer as terrified final girls run from pursuers and laugh throatily when first blood is spilled.

She scrapes her fingers around the bottom of a popcorn tub swiped from the concession stand, searching out the burnt bits, finding only whole kernels hard enough to crack a tooth. The film is Spanish, surreal, the debut of a young director with a fondness for showing the whites of eyes in close-up. The camera crawls through a Madrid apartment in a heatwave, its sun-bleached walls dripping as though swollen with sweat, balcony doors thrown open to a stifling city at dusk. The protagonist – a young woman with dirty feet and doll-like eyelashes – is safe, for now, having outrun her masked predator through the streets. She sits on the sofa with her knees drawn to her chest, watching the balcony doors. Should she shut them and just suffer the heat? Will he find her here?

There's a violent burst of strings as a large black bird comes hurtling through the open apartment doors. The woman screams and the cinema screams with her, then guffaws almost confrontationally, fear pulled from underneath them like a rug. Siobhan's hands are white-knuckled around the popcorn tub. The camera stays zoomed in on the bird, catching frenzied snatches of its beating wings, snapping beak, outstretched claws.

Siobhan closes her eyes. It'll be over in a minute.

But she can still hear it: the panicked squawking of the bird as it circles the apartment, looking for an exit, the girl's repeated screams in Spanish: *Fuera! Fuera!* Siobhan's palms are clammy and her skin is starting to itch, hot and furious, as if it's on the brink of rashing. She can still see those wings – veiny and fanned, like lungs turned inside out – on the back of her eyelids. She needs fresh air. She needs to get out.

Siobhan grabs her backpack and stands, knocking her popcorn bucket to the floor, and shimmies past the row of seated knees without apologising. Their owners boo and twist their necks to see around her. Only one looks up as she makes it to the end of the row. Only one watches her with interest as she runs up the central aisle and bursts out of the screen door.

Siobhan takes a lungful of cool air. It's almost too quiet out here after the boom of the cinema's surround sound. Both screens are currently mid-movie, so she's alone in the narrow corridor with its diamond-print carpet and vintage movie posters. She slumps against the wall, looking up at the image of Raquel Welch, perfectly poised beneath a pterodactyl in her scrappy bikini, and takes a bottle of wine from her backpack. The wine is warm, but since when has that stopped her? She drinks half of it in one go like she's chugging a Diet Coke, suppressing a gag at the vinegary after-bite. The cheapest bottle always feels the best. The taste is like a punishment, the bitter hangover even more so. From inside the screen, there's a billowing cheer. Siobhan grimaces. Maybe the murderer finally got in.

She's taking a second swig when the screen door opens and someone comes out. She turns away and waits for them to pass, but they don't, even though there's plenty of room.

"Siobhan?" A familiar male voice makes her look back around. "I thought it was you."

He's barely changed in the years since she's last seen him, though he's perhaps a little greyer at the temples. He's wearing a shabby but well-fitted black blazer over a *Jaws* T-shirt, suggestions of tattoos poking out at the wrists, dark jeans and beat-up leather ankle boots. Behind his heavy-rimmed glasses, his pale eyes glitter. He must be in his fifties now but still manages to appear boyish. He looks eager, she thinks. There's something hungry about him. She's always thought that.

"Hi," she says stiffly, then hesitates, unsure what to call him. She settles on, "Professor Jameson," although she never even called him that during her degree.

"Oh god," he says, laughing too loudly and brushing the back of his neck with his palm. "No need for any of that nonsense. Besides, you graduated, what – five years ago now? Just call me Owen."

"Four."

"I'm sorry?"

"I graduated four years ago."

"Oh! Okay, right." His laugh contains many notes, like a radio jingle.

From inside the cinema comes a shrill scream. The audience cheers. She pictures them as a single mouth, wide open and laughing.

Owen looks at the door as though he can see through it, and then says, "You weren't enjoying the film?" Siobhan shakes her head, and he nods in agreement. "It was a bit derivative, I have to say. I expected a bit more subtlety." When she doesn't answer, he changes the subject. "So, you're working here now?" He inclines his head to her burgundy polo, the word *Showroom* scrawled in gold font over the right breast pocket. It's impossible to miss the quirk in his eyebrow.

Siobhan wonders for the first time what she must look like to him, her eyes still blinking from the dark, old eyeliner smudged, a half-empty bottle of cheap wine clutched in her hand. She thinks about putting it back in her bag but doesn't. Owen looks down at the bottle, then back at her face. He's still smiling. "Yeah," she says. She could add that she's only part-time, but there's no need to justify herself to this man. He has no personal stake in her; he isn't someone she needs to impress. She doesn't really need to impress anyone anymore. That's a freeing thought. He's still looking at her and Siobhan hasn't felt this studied in a while – it makes her feel raw, plucked clean. She maintains eye contact as she brings the wine to her lips and finishes it. She means it as a sort of challenge. *Judge away*.

Owen shifts a little, boots squeaking, but he keeps his eyes on her. His nostril twitches, like it used to when someone said something he didn't agree with in class. His idiosyncrasies are returning to her like the lyrics to a song she'd half-forgotten, but they're out of order and out of context. His throat sounds dry as he says, "You *are* still making films though? Directing?"

"Not really."

"No?"

Siobhan swallows. Everything suddenly feels too big to say, so she says nothing, hoping he'll sense her discomfort and drop it. He doesn't. The silence simmers, stretches, starts to strain.

"I've moved on, I guess." Siobhan pushes herself off the wall and begins to wander down the corridor. After a second, she senses Owen follow her, as she'd suspected he would. In the foyer, Keith is emptying the popcorn machine with his usual focused precision, and the air smells like grease and stale butter. There are a few drinkers at the cinema bar, the word 'Showroom' blinking in red neon behind the bottles of spirits, reflecting off their glasses. The cinema styles itself as vintage, which really only means the tickets are a bit more expensive than the local chain, and it shows black-and-white films on Sundays. Siobhan's eyes snag on a smear on the glass of the box office. She'll have to clean it first thing tomorrow. If she goes home now, the only thing waiting for her between this moment and that one is the hollowness the flat seems to adopt in the dark hours, the way the silence swallows everything. There's been too much of that, recently. How long before those feelings start to consume a life, how long before they become the axis on which the whole thing turns?

"Do you want to go for a drink?" she asks, turning to Owen.

He blinks then clears his throat, trying to hide his surprise. "A drink?"

She nods. His eyes crease a little and she can see him weighing it up – how inappropriate would it be? How much does he really want to go for a drink with this dishevelled, unpredictable creature in front of him?

"Just one?" Her voice goes instinctively higher as she says it. She shrugs in a way that softens the defensiveness of her crossed arms.

"One drink." Owen smiles. His hand smooths his hair. "It would be good to hear how you're getting on."

He holds the door open for her so that she has to step under his arm, vaguely embarrassed. He smells of aftershave, the clean, simple kind that's usually expensive. They step out into Edinburgh's Friday night as it's flickering into life, the bars beginning to fill and ooze their glow onto the pavement. The city smells faintly of smoke, of petrol, of yeasty malt breezing over from the distilleries. It's only October, but cold enough already that visible breath curls from Siobhan's mouth as she pulls her hoodie up to her chin.

They walk side by side, a new awkwardness taking shape in the space between their bodies. Siobhan has the acute sensation of being alone with him despite the busyness of the pavement. Her skin prickles in response. They meander along Princes Street and up the Mound, speaking only in stilted snatches, before descending Victoria Street and into the Grassmarket. There's a more direct route to get where she's going, but it feels good to walk. Walking gives her a distraction from the images that had sent her running from the cinema screen. Black feathers. Sharp beaks.

Owen gestures to a pub on their right – The Last Drop. "I guess you know why it's called that?"

Siobhan does. The Grassmarket was where the city did most of its hangings until the late eighteenth century, its flat central square providing a prime viewing location. She's always had a soft spot for Edinburgh's filthy history – the body snatchers Burke and Hare, the plague of 1645 that wiped out half the population – so she suspects she probably knows more about The Last Drop than Owen does, but she lets him explain anyway. He veers towards the pub, but she keeps walking, and again, he follows. She wants to choose where they go. She wants to drink where she always drinks. Owen struggles to keep up with her, making polite interjections every few minutes that she doesn't quite hear. After passing through the Cowgate, the traffic on George IV Bridge rumbling above their heads, they reach Holyrood 9a: an upmarket bar and gastropub that's far too expensive for Siobhan to frequent as much as she does. But it's where she and Theo had come to celebrate her graduation, sitting at a window table and gorging themselves on gourmet burgers and pint after pint of craft beer with racehorse-like names. And so, she finds herself continually drawn back here, to sit at the crowded bar and stare at the window table. It's always taken.

Without protest, Owen follows her inside. She's aware of his body behind her – not exactly broad but broader than hers – and remembers the girl from the film, running barefoot through the streets of the Spanish capital, losing her tormentor's face in a crowd of thousands.

Inside, Holyrood 9a is busy and warm, all dark wood panelling and low light. They manage to grab a spot in a tucked-away nook, opposite a fireplace topped with fat candles, melted wax dripping from the mantel.

"I'll get this," Owen says, leaning in close to her. He gives her a conspiratorial smile. "Bottle of wine?"

"Sure." Siobhan takes her seat in the chocolate-leather booth, watching Owen at the bar. He's turned to the side so she can see him in profile – the long nose with a bump where his glasses rest, the brow that overhangs his eyes slightly, like cliffs brooding over the sea. He's still wearing a faint smile, though no one is looking at him. He exudes a self-conscious kind of affability, as if everything about him has been purposefully designed to be non-threatening. He'd taught her Critical Debates module in third year, and she remembers now how he'd never quite been able to control the dynamic of the room. It was just too easy to talk over him.

A few minutes later, Owen returns with the wine – red, French, expensive-looking – and two glasses. He pours them both a generous measure, the liquid tarry and viscous.

"Are you still teaching?" she asks. It's disconcerting, somehow, to hear the question come out of her mouth. To remember that she is an adult capable of polite conversation.

Owen nods. "Still at Edinburgh. Programme Director now, actually." He raises his glass then lowers it. "No way of saying that without sounding like a wanker."

Siobhan smiles. She takes a generous glug of wine and feels it fur her teeth, staining them dark. When she puts the glass down it's already empty.

"So," Owen says, refilling it, "the last I heard, you and your brother had that incredible documentary commission. What was his name again? Hugo?"

"Theo." Saying his name is like pressing a bruise.

"How is he?"

"We don't really talk anymore."

Owen leans back into the leather, swirling the liquid in his glass, holding it by its stem. He hasn't taken a sip yet. "I'm sorry to hear that. You made a good team, I heard."

Siobhan shrugs. The last time she saw him, Theo's clothes were covered in blood and he had mud tracked up his bare calves from running through the woods. *I don't even know who you are anymore*, he'd screamed at her. "Creative differences," Siobhan says, shaking her head to rid herself of the image.

"The commission though," Owen says, blowing air out through his lips. "I was so pleased when I heard about that. You really deserved it. What was it – six months on-location filming? A year?"

Siobhan keeps her eyes on the table, on the complex grain of the wood, its whorls and half-faces. She feels like she's in an old silent movie, waiting prone on the tracks for the train to come.

"The cult!" Owen says loudly, slapping his free hand on his thigh. "I remember now, out in the middle of nowhere. All very top secret and mysterious. You can tell me all the gory details now though, right?"

"No," Siobhan whispers, too quickly. Owen blinks, raised eyebrows betraying his surprise. Under the table, she forces her fingernails into the flesh of her thigh, gasping as one of them bends all the way back. She doesn't know what she'd expected, inviting him out for a drink – of course he would ask about this. "And it wasn't a cult," she manages to say. "It was..." *Go on, Siobhan. What was* it? "It doesn't matter. The doc didn't really come to anything, anyway."

"That's a shame," Owen says carefully. "I get it though. Sometimes the stars just don't align. I'd still love to see that footage, if you're ever happy to share. I don't know if you remember, but I co-founded a production company a while back. We're always on the lookout for fresh ideas." He takes a long, deep sip of wine. "And to be honest, you always stood out to me, Siobhan. Distinctive style. Uncompromising."

Siobhan's stomach tightens. It always does when she receives a compliment, though it's been a while. There'd been a time when she'd been led to believe that she was a different sort of person, an exceptional one, even, after she graduated. She'd won an award for her short film based in a domestic violence shelter, the same one where she'd lived with her mum and Theo for a year when she was three. After that, professors and peers alike seemed in a rush to tell her that they'd been the ones to sense her potential early. People can be possessive over talent, and she'd felt like a prize to be fought over. There were job offers floated, emails constantly landing in her inbox about projects that might be a good fit for her and Theo, who'd graduated a couple of years before. Siobhan had basked in the golden glow of things starting and gaining momentum with little effort on her part. This, she'd thought, *this* is the way my life is going to be now. I'm going to be a filmmaker.

Then, of course, came the letter. How had they gotten her address? She's always wondered, not that it matters now. Her name on the envelope was blotted in places, as if it had been written out slowly, the ink pooling from a proper fountain pen. Siobhan couldn't remember the last time she'd received a letter that wasn't a utilities bill, and seeing the scratchy handwriting felt strangely intimate, as though the sender were standing in the room with her and looking over her shoulder, their breath on her neck.

We have a special opportunity for you, Siobhan. Here at Hex House.

Hex House. She'd laughed when she read that, thinking, fleetingly, that it must be a prank. A jealous course mate maybe; someone who hated all the positive attention she was getting. But there had been something about the letter that felt true, somehow – earnest.

We know about your work. We would like to invite you to stay with us.

The letter had seemed to throb in her hand, to demand an answer, though there was no return address. She read it over and over, sitting at her desk at home, training her eyes to focus on each word and not skip ahead.

You're very special.

You're exactly what we need.

How easily that simple flattery had reeled her in, spiked her curiosity. But it was the ending of the letter that had really cemented what she did next. That strange, out-of-place turn of phrase that had made her feel cold all over.

Would you like to come inside?

She often wishes she could go back to that moment. Scream *No, no, no.* Rip up the letter. Throw it away, forget about it. Become a different person entirely.

"Siobhan?" Owen prompts.

The door to the pub opens and lets in a gasp of cold air, bringing her back into herself. She doesn't want to talk about any of it anymore. She wants to be here, now, in a dark room with expensive wine and a man who may or may not want her. She's flush with alcohol, lazy in a bold sort of way. Each movement feels predestined and out of her control. She puts down her wine glass and places one hand on either side of Owen's face. He flinches only slightly. His skin is warm, the suggestion of stubble breaking through. His eyes widen for a half-second, then glaze over with something else and Siobhan recognises it instantly for what it is: the first flickering of desire. She knows now, and so does he, what they have the potential to be to each other. She might as well have said it out loud. She might as well have carved it into the table with a knife.

"Stop talking," she says instead, barely loud enough for him to hear, and she sees that desire grow brighter. This is another one of those moments, she knows, when one thing slides into another; a moment she'll look back on as one she should have handled differently. Her life seems full of them. "Go and get me another drink," she says, and takes her hands away.

Later, Siobhan wanders alone through Edinburgh's knotted streets. She hadn't let Owen walk her home, wanting him nowhere near the flat, so had led him in the opposite direction instead until she was too tired to make conversation anymore.

"This is me," she lied, when they got to the top of Leith Walk. "My flat's just round the corner."

Owen swayed a little, looking past her. "You're sure? You'll be alright? I can come with you the rest of the way."

She shook her head but did let him take her number, watching his clumsy fingers as he keyed in her name, the way he had to concentrate hard through his semi-drunken haze. Then she strode away from him down Leith Walk, knowing she'd have to retrace her steps once she was confident he'd gone. When she turned around, he was watching her walk away. He raised a single hand in a wave she didn't return.

Now, she crosses North Bridge, stumbling only slightly. The sky is cobalt, blistered with stars straining through the city smog. Trains departing Waverley roar beneath her feet and the gothic tenements of the Mile rise up to her right, their windows like a thousand eyes peering from their stone sockets. Edinburgh Castle looms above it all, quiet and dark. Sometimes she wonders how it's possible to stay sane with a city like this looking back at you, never letting you out of its sight. She wonders if she ever felt this way before Hex House, like everything was a barely veiled threat, like there were ghosts living inside her – tangled in her hair, wrapped around each sinew – teeming at her edges to get out.

She lives in a tiny one-bedroom in a tall, narrow building off the Mile. The arched entrance and cobbled courtyard give it a faded sense of elegance, but the light in the stairwell hasn't worked in months and it perpetually smells of piss, of stale smoke. Edinburgh is a grand old dame, but she's got rotted teeth and her bones are fit to snap.

Her flat is at the very top of the building, stuffed into a misshapen corner. It's all awkward angles that won't fit any furniture and windows that barely open, but it's what she can afford. Siobhan turns the lights on in the order she prefers – overhead living room light, lonely kitchen bulb, then the bedside lamp. The flat simmers in the gloom. She has the sense, as she often does, that someone has been here while she was out, wearing her dirty clothes and wiping their tongue around the top of the milk. She wonders what Owen would have made of all this had she brought him back here: the one sofa sagging under unwashed laundry, the empty bottles lined up on the windowsill and around the bin like trophies. Maybe he wouldn't have cared, and they'd be in the bedroom already. In the bedroom, where there is a small desk with a drawer that locks. In that drawer is a laptop, and on that laptop is a folder called 'Hex House'. Siobhan is always aware of that folder, as if it's a siren, singing softly to her, but she won't give into it. Not tonight.

Instead, she pours herself a measure of tequila and drinks it quickly. She wrestles her dark, coarse hair into a bun on the top of her head. While she's changing for bed, she pauses to check, as she always does, the scar that sits between her belly button and pubic bone. It's a furious red-pink against her olive skin, even all these years later. She drags one fingernail over the shape of it, across its ridges and furrows, just deep enough to hurt.

She's falling asleep when it starts to rain. The rain is always loud up here, the building's pointed roof just a few metres above her head. It's soft at first, a pitter-patter that soaks the tiles. In the early hours it turns thunderous, raindrops the size of pellets hammering the roof like they're trying to get into her skin, to make their way inside her. In the space between wakefulness and dreams, Siobhan imagines they're the bodies of birds. One by one, they fall dead and heavy from the sky, skeletons smashing against the houses.

ELLY

THEN

Elly is watching a woman rolling a plum between her palms, its waxy skin the colour of a bruise. The woman has one fox-like eye, and the other is scarred shut, the skin flat where a bulge should be. She holds still for a moment, and then squeezes the plum in one hand until there's a wet sound. Juice leaks out from between her fingers. She smiles and Elly feels as though an egg has cracked in the pit of her stomach.

"That's what it was like, when it popped." A quick tongue darts out from between the woman's neat teeth and she catches a drip of amber juice before it hits the table. "I think about it *all* the time."

The woman is called Margot, and she has soot-coloured curls and skin so pale you can see the veins right through. She has a northern accent and talks quickly and loudly, as if time is always running out. Sometimes, the words collapse into each other and Elly struggles to understand her, but by the time she asks Margot to repeat herself, she's already moved on.

They sit with around thirty other women at a very long oak table, eating breakfast. They take all their meals in the narrow room the guests call the refectory, which juts out from the back of the house and runs the length of the garden. It's made almost entirely of glass and is crowded with tall, fern-like plants that brush against their faces while they eat and make the whole room smell like damp earth. This morning, the sun suffuses the glass and casts the women's faces in buttery light. It makes their keen eyes glitter, picks out the purple of their bruises and the white of the bandages around their arms. Those bandages – Elly can't stop looking at them. Why do so many of the women have wounds? The women themselves seem unfazed by their injuries, reaching across the table to pass spoons and plates, stretching and yawning, leaning against one another lazily. There is an easiness to their touch, Elly has noticed, as if they are all very familiar with each other's bodies.

The table is covered with sticky spoons left in pots of preserve, jugs of milk growing warm and starting to spoil. A cornucopia appears on the table each morning: tart green apples vivisected and sprinkled with sugar, freshly baked loaves of bread studded with seeds, stoneware bowls full of steaming porridge. The women also eat a surprising amount of meat – so much *meat* – at every meal. They tear into tender strips of steak, they chew on kidneys stewed with mushrooms, they peel the fat from bacon with their fingers.

Hex House is a myth, Elly tells herself, multiple times a day. *It is a hole on the map where no one has ever been. Hex House isn't real.*

And yet, here she is.

The minutes pass, and then the hours, and here she is still.

Elly looks down at the pulpy mess in Margot's hand and tries to remember it's a plum. "I almost feel sorry for you," Margot tells her dreamily, "that you've never felt it before."

Elly lets herself imagine it: the wet pluck of an eyeball from a socket. It makes bile creep up the back of her throat. She shudders.

"You're easily scared," Margot is saying, nodding, matter-of-fact. "Like a little mouse."

"My angel." A deep voice from behind them, smooth as coffee shot through with honey.

Haina.

Haina, with her dark eyes and steady stare. Her hands are in Margot's curls, brushing them gently back from her face. "Shall we let Elly eat her breakfast in peace?"

"Sorry, Haina." Margot raises her hand to her mouth and starts to lick her sticky fingers. She looks like a cat, finally fed. The juice drips onto her faded Coca-Cola T-shirt.

Elly feels Haina's palms land on her own shoulders. Their warmth is palpable, even through her T-shirt. When she looks up, Haina is smiling down at her. "Have you been made to feel welcome, Elly?"

Elly nods. It's the truth. The other women have welcomed her like a lost sister since she arrived two days ago. Margot showed her the bed in the dormitory where she'd sleep, gleeful that it was the one beside her own. Janine, with her shorn head covered with silvery scars, brought her some spare T-shirts, which Elly gratefully accepted though they smelled of sweat and dirt. Lakshmi showed her where the bathrooms were and then asked if Elly wanted to borrow her lipstick, a dark damson shade almost worn down to the nub. Isla and Iona – the red sisters, the other guests call them, on account of their fiery hair – immediately wanted to talk about the baby, looking at her stomach with darting, quicksilver eyes. Their plaits are braided so close to their scalps that they pull the papery skin at the temples taut, giving them permanently startled expressions. Each day, they ask if they can touch her belly. They squeal and clutch each other when the baby kicks.

Haina is still watching Elly. Her eyes are the colour of carob, two shining beetles embedded deep in her skin, which has a Middle Eastern warmth. Her lips are full, bud-like, her nose long and sharp at the tip. Elly has watched the way Haina glides through rooms, elegant as a ballerina but with more ferocity than flourish, beautiful in the same way that a blade is beautiful. There is something uncompromising about her, something urgent, though her composure is as calm as a still pool. Two days and forever ago, when Elly had found the house – or when the house had found her – she'd seen Haina standing in the doorway and been struck by a thought that hasn't left her since: that she should never give this woman any reason to be disappointed in her. That night, when Elly had arrived with a dirty, tear-streaked face, her bones so heavy she could barely stand, Haina had led her into a circular room with stained-glass windows and old books lining the walls. She wrapped Elly in a blanket, sat her in an armchair by the fire and pressed tea into her numb hands. *Run*, part of Elly's brain had screamed. *Run, now.* But she'd done enough running, and the room was so warm, so comforting, the

43

woman in front of her wearing an expression so welcoming and concerned that it had all come spilling out: Ethan, the wedding, the baby, the blood on the cottage wall, all of it. As she spoke, Haina held Elly's hands in hers, pulled her close. She stroked Elly's hair and cooed in her ear, *You're safe here, my angel, he will never find you*, and Elly had felt as though she were melting, as if her body had finally been given permission to surrender.

The sun was coming up when Elly said, "I just don't understand how I'm here."

"You're here because you needed us. The house – the house always knows."

"We'll have our first session today, Elly," Haina says now. "After lunch. If you feel ready for it."

Elly nods, biting the inside of her cheek. She's heard about the sessions from the other women: an hour of one-on-one time with Haina, every week. The guests talk about the sessions in revered tones and with a strange, dreamy look in their eyes, though no one has actually told her what she should expect to happen. *We're very lucky that we have Haina to teach us*, is all Margot will tell her. Elly has been half-hoping and half-dreading the invite would never come.

Haina grins at her, revealing a row of gleaming, slightly crooked teeth. That smile takes Elly by surprise, momentarily dazzling her. "You're going to fit in so well here with us," Haina says. "I can tell."

It's incredible, how those words make Elly feel as though she's glowing from the inside out. *You could belong here*, she tells herself, slipping the new reality over her skin. *This could be your home.*

When she blinks, Ethan's face is there: the spray of russet freckles across his nose, his full mouth and knowing eyes. She can almost feel his hand on her face, the softness of his skin and the cool grip of his fingers. When the back of her head connected with the stone wall it had felt, just for a second, like he'd erased her completely.

I thought I told you to stay.

She blinks him away again, but her mum replaces him, along with a stab of guilt. She wonders how she reacted when Ethan told her Elly was missing. Are they out combing the woods for her right now? Does her mum have nightmares of finding her bloated body in the river? What kind of a daughter does that to her mother? The cooling porridge in her bowl tastes like lead.

Haina never stays for the whole of breakfast, and so far, Elly has never seen her eat anything. She only sips a small cup of espresso and watches the other guests. Sometimes, she pulls them in close to her, like a mother comforting a child. She whispers in their ears; she raises pastries to their mouths and catches the crumbs. The room grows quieter as she stands and leaves, then resumes its low-level hum. Margot leans her head on Elly's shoulder, sighing. She smells vaguely sweet, like cupcake icing.

"You'll be one of us so soon, Little Mouse," she says. "Isn't that nice?"

One of us, Elly thinks absently. Is that what she wants? To be one of them? She looks around the table again. Some of the guests have already left the refectory for morning chores, but the room is still fairly full. On the other side of Margot, Iona is rebraiding Isla's hair, singing a quiet song in an unfamiliar language. Her fingers are quick and pale as they work. Across the table, Janine's gaze is fixed on the butterknife laid askew on the plate in front of her. Her eyes look far away as she runs a hand over her bald head, this way then that, agitating the bristles over and over. Lakshmi watches her carefully, and after a moment, squeezes her arm. Janine seems to break out of her trance and puts her hand on top of Lakshmi's. "I went away again, didn't I?" she says.

Margot has raised her head from Elly's shoulder and is gnawing at the remaining scraps of meat on a pork rib. When she's picked it clean, she dips it into a jar of honey, sucking the sticky liquid from the bone.

"How long have you been here, Margot?" Elly hears herself ask. She feels too light, unrooted, as if she no longer belongs to a body. Even her voice doesn't sound like her own.

Margot's eyebrows dip into a frown. She turns the sticky rib over in her hands. "I don't know," she says after a long moment. "A long time."

"Don't you want to go home?" No answer. "How long will you stay?"

At that, Margot smiles. Her one eye seems to twinkle. "As long as it takes."

Before Elly can ask what that means, raised voices across the table draw her attention. Janine has started to cry, the sound like an engine trying and failing to start. Lakshmi is whispering to her, holding both of Janine's arms down, keeping her hands in her lap.

"I need to, just for a minute," Janine says in a rough, hiccupping voice, struggling against Lakshmi's grip. Her cheeks have turned a ruddy purple.

Lakshmi shakes her head. "You know what Haina says," she tells Janine. "No hexing at the table."

Hexing?

Elly watches as Janine begins to calm, her eyes squeezing shut as her breathing slows.

"Well done, angel," coos Lakshmi. "Don't think about it. Just be here now, with me."

Beside Elly, Margot has stopped sucking on her rib, leaving it pale and abandoned on her plate. She's wrapped her thin arms around her torso. "Poor Janine," she murmurs.

"What happened to her?" Elly asks. "What brought her here?"

Margot gives her a look so sharp it steals the breath from her throat. "We don't ask about before, Little Mouse," she says, voice low. A warning.

Elly doesn't know what else to do but nod, but when Margot stands up to leave the breakfast table, Elly reaches out a hand to hold her wrist. Margot flinches, looks down at her in surprise.

"What is this place?" Elly whispers. Yesterday at breakfast, she'd barely been able to speak, let alone ask questions. Now, she can't go another second without at least attempting to slot all the pieces together, to make sense of this fever dream. "I don't understand it. I'm trying to... I just want to understand. Why are we here? What *is* Hex House?"

At that, Margot's expression melts, her frown becoming a smile. "Hex House is a refuge for the lost," she says, louder than she needs to. Something about the words feel familiar, practised. She isn't looking at Elly anymore, but around the room at the other guests, as though commanding an audience.

"A home for the wayward," Iona calls back, making Elly jump.

"A sanctuary for the melancholy," someone else says, and before Elly can figure out who, another woman has shouted, "An asylum for the mad!"

They all laugh, as if this is hilarious, as if this is a completely normal thing to say, and then on it goes, round and round, every guest taking their turn to contribute. There's a singsong quality to their voices, each woman seeming to know her place in the chorus.

When it comes to Janine's turn, her voice is quieter than the others, shakier, but there's no mistaking her words. "Hex House is a home," she whispers, and all the women fall silent.

Yesterday, Haina had assigned Elly to the kitchens.

"Your baker's hands," she'd said, one sharp fingernail trailing the grooves in Elly's palm, "they'll be a great help to us."

Elly makes her way there now, down the hallway with its cream wainscotting and faded floral wallpaper. It's a relief to be out of the refectory with all of those strange voices, the food on the table starting to spoil and give the air a cloying smell. The hallway is quiet – she guesses most of the other guests will already be working at their morning chores, tending the gardens, tidying the dormitory, mending clothes. Her chest feels strange, tight, but she loosens slightly at the sight of the kitchen coming into view at the end of the hall. Kitchens have always felt

48

like safe places to Elly. Cooking, baking in particular, makes her feel calm and useful – the putting together of humble things a tonic for the unpredictability of everything else.

The kitchen at Hex House is the largest one Elly has ever been in, but it's somehow still homely: the counters made from oak, the tiles underfoot a warm terracotta, hazy sunlight flooding in from large arched windows looking out over the gardens. There are huge wooden beams overhead, hung with pots, pans, strings of fat garlic bulbs and dried herbs. Fresh produce spills from every cupboard, and there's a larder stocked high with preserves, tins of tomatoes, jars of rice. Even though the day is warm, there's a fire crackling in the grate. The range cooker is lit, too, but somehow the room doesn't feel too warm. It's cosy, comforting, wrapped up in the smell of fresh bread. The range is framed by a brick arch with a complex tile mural underneath. Elly spent a lot of time staring at that mural yesterday, while peeling potatoes. It seems to depict the house: the ornate windows, the wisteria growing up the walls, the crooked chimneypots, they're all there. But there's a surrealistic quality to it, too, the flowers not to scale, instead stretching up around the walls like fingers, making it look as though the house is sitting in someone's palm. Beneath the house, roots reach deep down into the soil, while overhead the sky is filled with birds, birds with golden wings and eyes that seem to glitter with knowing.

When Elly arrives, Grace, who runs the kitchen, is kneading dough with her rough hands. It gives and gives, pliable as a body without bones. Behind her is Keiko, whose eyes hide behind a thick, dark fringe. So far, Elly hasn't heard her speak. She watches as Keiko hacks at a watermelon with a cleaver, sending gritty pulp spraying across the countertop.

"That arrived this morning," Grace tells Elly in place of a greeting. Her northern Irish accent is strong and musical. She nods to something large on the counter next to her, wrapped loosely in stained fabric. Elly glimpses white feathers. "Chicken. Big one. Okay to pluck it?"

Elly gingerly puts a hand on top of the fabric. It's emanating warmth. "It came just now?"

"Yes," says Grace without pausing her kneading. There's a peppering of irritation in her tone. She doesn't seem one to entertain curiosity. Still, Elly has to know.

"Who brought it?" She gestures around the kitchen, at the overflowing fruit bowl and the fridge packed with cheese and meat. "Who brings all of this?"

Grace doesn't look up. For a long moment, she doesn't say anything at all, and Elly wonders if she heard her. Grace continues to work the dough, her calloused fingers pushing and stretching. Those fingers – they're twisted oddly, as if they've been broken and reset all wrong. It looks painful, the way Grace forces them into the dough, over and over. What happened to this woman, before she found Hex House? *We don't ask about before*, Margot had warned her, so Elly makes herself look at Grace's face instead. There's a hardness there, the skin mottled and lined, as if she's spent a great deal of her life outside. Grace picks up the dough and throws it back down. It hits the counter with a wet slap, sending up a plume of flour. Keiko flinches, then returns to her watermelon. Grace finally looks up at Elly, frowning. She feels like a schoolchild about to be scolded.

"Who do you think brings it?" Grace says with an impatient huff. "Women. Former guests."

"But why?" Elly asks. She's surprised at herself – usually she shrinks from the slightest hint of confrontation, hates to make anyone else even slightly irritated or uncomfortable. But the sense that she's stumbling through a dream is starting to fade, and in its place is the need for answers. Some, at least.

Grace smooths the grey-blonde hairs that have escaped her bun with the back of her hand. "Some women leave the house, but they never really *leave* it, you know. It lives in their bones, like." She cracks her swollen fingers, one by one. The sound is like twigs snapping. Elly winces, but Grace's expression betrays no pain. "There are a lot of them out there," she continues, "a kind of... network, I guess. Haina calls them the *flock*. They help out where they can, bring food and leave it on the doorstep. We never see them. They do other things for Haina, too – search for women who might need the house, that kind of thing."

Elly thinks about her wedding, about the woman in the orange dress. *We've been watching you for... some time.* She swallows thickly.

"Now," Grace says, voice gruff again, her head inclining towards the chicken. "I'm not planning on serving that with feathers on. It's already been scalded. Get to plucking."

Elly chews the inside of her cheek. She's never plucked a chicken before, but Grace has already turned back to her dough and Elly is reluctant to test her patience any further.

Slowly, she lifts the sheeting. Beneath it, the chicken's white feathers are turning grey with damp, its limp neck twisted and thin, glassy eyes staring at nothing. Its body is deflated, uncanny. She pulls tentatively at a feather on one of the wings, and it gives, sliding out clean. Elly watches the hole where it came from as something clear and fatty oozes and trickles out. She takes a step back, suddenly lightheaded. There's a movement inside her belly then, a nauseous rolling, like the baby is recoiling. Elly retches, turning so that she's leaning back against the counter. Trying not to be sick, she closes her eyes and counts her breaths, forcing her mind somewhere else.

One. Her dad's hands, covered in clay. *Two*. Her dad sitting out in the garden, drinking coffee. *Three*. What would he think of her now?

A gentle touch at the back of her neck. She looks up to see Keiko wearing an uncertain smile, offering a glass of water. She has the most flawless skin, Elly registers distantly as she accepts the glass.

"Thank you," Elly whispers.

Keiko raises both hands to chest-height and beckons inwards. Elly stares at her, still feeling faint, trying to focus on Keiko's young, serious face.

"Sign language," says Grace from behind them. "She's saying, 'You're welcome'."

Keiko smiles again and then returns to her watermelon. Elly takes a long sip of water. Her sweat has made hair stick to her temples and forehead. When she looks at Grace, she's frowning, pale eyes narrow. Her gaze settles on Elly's stomach, and Elly reflexively places her palms there. The skin beneath feels tight, itchy. It's starting to stretch, she knows. The thought makes her feel as though she's pitching forward into something, and there's nothing she can do to stop herself from falling.

"Maybe that's enough plucking," Grace says. "Come and take over here instead."

Elly does what she's told, running her hands under the tap before sinking them deep into the softness of the dough. Her breathing starts to regulate. This – this is better. It makes her think of all those early mornings in the bakery with Suzanne before the sun had even come up. She tries to conjure her friend's loud laugh, her mild Scottish twang. *What on earth are you doing, you mad thing?* she'd say, if she could see Elly now. But it's no good thinking about Suzanne, about her dad, about any of them. Not until she figures out what the hell she's doing here, not until she decides what she's going to do next. She just needs a day – two. Her eyes burn as the dough stretches and folds under her fingertips. Beside her, Grace's quick hands pluck, pluck, pluck at the chicken. Soon, there's a mound of feathers on the counter. It looks like another animal entirely now, one with no eyes, no bones.

After a couple of hours of quiet, steady work, the preparations for dinner are complete. The sun beams into the kitchen, making apricot slices of light on the floor. Other guests begin to mill in and out after their morning chores, helping themselves to the plates of cheese, meats and fruit Keiko has set out for lunch.

"You need to eat, Little Mouse," says Margot, appearing next to her and holding up a grape to her lips. There's dirt embedded deep under her fingernails from working in the garden. "For your session with Haina."

Elly accepts the grape, chews on it absent-mindedly. She'd pushed her impending meeting with Haina to the back of her mind all morning, but now she feels nerves start to creep in. She wishes someone would just tell her what to expect. She catches Lakshmi's eye as she leans against the range, nibbling on a fig.

"Don't be frightened," she tells Elly. "Just try to be... open. Think with your body, not your brain."

"What do you mean?" Elly asks, but Lakshmi just shrugs, swapping her fig for a slice of rare beef, dripping fat and blood down the front of her shirt.

Elly doesn't go straight to Haina's study. She needs to wander for a moment or two, settle her nerves. She leaves the kitchen and follows the hallway towards the large, curved staircase. Like the rest of the house, it's grand but fading: the stair runner threadbare in places and secured by tarnished brass rods, the thick banister crafted from worn cherry wood. She emerges out onto the landing, the dormitory in front of her and the bathroom at the far end on the left. There's another staircase, which Margot told her leads up to a couple of attic rooms and the roof terrace, but Elly turns right instead. She follows the landing to where it ends at a large, circular window with a stained-glass trim. With the midday light streaming through it, the panels cast the carpet in shimmering jewel tones: the aquamarine of tropical pools, sparkling yellow like the inside of a lemon. There's a window seat built into the sill, upholstered in soft fabric. Elly climbs up onto it, feeling instant relief in her lower back and pelvis. She is still getting used to the way the baby presses down on her from the inside, as if it would prefer that she always lie down, bones to the earth. There's a little shelf built into the wall next to the seat, topped with an empty mug and a stack of pulpy paperbacks. They all have yellowing pages and faded covers, sensational titles like *Lake Terror* and *Darkwater Canyon*. The cover art mostly shows red-lipped women screaming at unseen things in the shadows. It's a strange thing, to see books here. Do the women on the outside bring them? The *flock*? Elly flicks through one and notices that someone has underlined words and sentences, added their own notes in the margins. *I have never been the kind of girl boys write songs about*, she reads. She traces the words with a fingertip, wondering about the hand that wrote them, wondering if that woman had once felt as she does: adrift in a strange sea.

Elly replaces the books on the shelf and looks out of the window, which offers a view of the front of the house, the winding path that leads from the woods to its front door. The woods – they don't look as dark and impenetrable as they had the night she arrived here. What would happen, Elly wonders, if she just walked out of the front door and back into those woods? What would happen if she just kept walking? Surely, that's what she should do. You can't just up and leave your life – she has responsibilities. She has a husband. But as hard as she tries, she just can't imagine it: walking back into the village. Slipping her hand back into Ethan's. She tries to play the scenes in her mind but it's like she's watching a film, a film where the main character has no face. At the very least, she needs to meet with Haina first, understand what Hex House is, why she's here. With effort, she swings her legs off from the window seat and makes her way downstairs.

Haina's study is a large room off the main hallway, immediately to the left of the entranceway. Elly knocks gently on the door.

"Come in," Haina calls through the wood.

The study looks different in the daytime. The night she'd arrived, it had felt so comforting she could cry, all soft surfaces and dark warmth, red as a heart's chamber. Now, it's filled with afternoon light that picks out the carmine and gold of the Persian rug in the centre of the room, illuminates long, deep grooves in the floor. Elly wonders what could have made them, what kind of animal, but she can't dwell on it, because Haina has turned from her large mahogany desk.

"Come and sit down," she says.

Elly does as she's told, crossing the room to take a seat in the velvet armchair positioned across from Haina's. She rests her hands over her belly, feeling the baby turn inside her stomach. Haina smiles warmly. Her hair is pure black, even with the sunlight shining directly on it. The rest of the guests wear a rotating selection of second-hand clothing from the communal bin in the dorm – faded slogan T-shirts, jeans with holes at the knees, American collegiate sweaters – but Elly hasn't seen Haina in anything but loose-fitting linen dresses in shades of orange: umber, vermillion, marigold. She thinks distantly that the cut of them looks expensive. Haina leans forward in her chair and laces her hands underneath her chin.

"So, Elly," she says, her voice low and rich. "These

sessions are a time for us to get to know each other. For you to learn a little more about what we do here at Hex House, and for me to learn more about you, and what you might need."

What do I need? Elly asks herself, eyes on the swirls of the rug at her feet. *I need to understand why Ethan wanted to hurt me so badly. What it was about me that meant he couldn't stop himself.*

I need to find my way back to him.

"Some sessions we'll spend just talking," Haina continues. "Others will be more... practical in nature."

"Practical?"

Haina waves a hand. "It'll all make more sense as we go, the longer you're with us."

Elly's throat grows dry. She clears it painfully then looks down at her hands. "And what happens if I..." She trails off. She's hyper-aware of Haina's eyes on her forehead, unblinking. She imagines them burning two perfectly symmetrical holes into the skin.

"If you want to leave?" Haina offers, after a silence that stretches on a second too long. Elly nods, still not meeting her eye. "I understand that impulse, Elly. I do. Almost all the women feel it, at some point. Perfectly natural. But I suppose what I would say to you is," she pauses and leans so far forward that Elly can see the flecks of gold in her eyes, "why are you so keen to return to the thing that broke you?"

Despite the warmth of the day, despite the heat of the fire against her skin, Elly goes suddenly and completely cold.

"Hex House is for *you*," Haina continues. "It's a place to rest, to heal. To rediscover yourself – your *true* self.

By the time you're ready to leave, you'll be stronger. More resilient." Haina lowers her voice to a whisper. "No one will ever be able to make you feel small ever again."

There's a tightness in Elly's chest, and she realises she's been holding her breath. How would it feel, to be the kind of person Ethan couldn't bully? Someone with whom he'd always be the care-free, self-deprecating person he'd seemed to be when she'd first met him?

Someone he would never tell to *stay* and know without question would obey him?

There's another question she wants to ask Haina, one she *needs* to ask. *But I can leave, if I want to?* The words are there, poised on her lips and ready to drop, but she can't put breath behind them. Doing so would feel too much like receiving a generous gift, an unlikely chance, something from nothing, and throwing it back in Haina's face.

"Sometimes during these sessions," says Haina, "things might get... *difficult*. Challenging, perhaps. You don't get any stronger by having your hand held, and so you can expect to be confronted with some harsh truths. Growing can hurt. But no matter what happens next, there's one thing I need you to remember."

Elly feels the skin on the underside of her thighs prickle, the tiny hairs rising.

"We all love you," Haina says gently. "You have the love of the whole house."

As if in response, the sounds around them seem to suddenly grow louder: the crackle and rasp of the fire, the muffled voices in the garden beyond the window, the omnipresent creaking of the house's old bones as it settles deeper into the earth.

"Shall we start, my angel?" Haina asks, leaning back in her chair.

Elly wonders, not for the first time, whether she tripped and fell in the woods, whether she hit her head on a tree root and is lying inert in a hospital bed somewhere. She wonders if she contracted hypothermia and her body is hooked up to a life support machine, surrounded by wires and being pumped full of drugs at every hour. There are, after all, so many ways that the woods can kill you. Perhaps Hex House is simply the last wild imagining of a brain in the final moments of its life.

And yet.

And yet, she digs her fingers into the soft velvet of the armchair; she breathes in the scent of burning wood and old paper. This morning's orange juice is still furring her teeth. It is all so incredibly, undeniably real.

Inside her belly, the baby shifts and wriggles. In a matter of months, or perhaps even weeks, whoever is growing inside her will exist on the other side of her skin. A tiny person who knows nothing yet of her ineptitude, the multiple ways she's already failed as a mother. Before she leaves Hex House, she has a chance to make herself worthy of them.

"Okay," Elly says. She clears her throat, then says a little more loudly, "Let's start."

Haina offers one of her disarming smiles. There's not a hint of surprise in it. The light shifts a little outside the window; there's a dimming as a cloud covers the sun. Elly shivers.

"Just when I was starting to think you were too much of a coward," Haina says, so quietly that at first, Elly thinks she must have misheard. Haina is still smiling, as though they're being watched without sound, as though she's keeping up appearances.

"I'm... I'm sorry?"

"Elly Carmichael. Never says no. Never rocks the boat. Brought up on warm milk and compliments. It's no wonder is it, really? About Ethan?"

Haina's face has changed. The soft look in her eyes is gone, replaced by a cold steeliness that makes Elly's stomach lurch. "Ethan loves me," she hears herself say.

"Ethan *broke* you," Haina sneers. "Because he could. Because you let him. You wear it all over, like a wounded puppy."

Elly hates herself for the tears that sting the backs of her eyes. She hates the way she can't stop her hands from shaking in her lap. "You told me... you told me you understood. I don't—"

"God help that baby," Haina spits, interrupting her. Each word is a poison arrow, burrowing deeper beneath her skin. "In this world? Having you for a mother?"

She gives Elly one last derisive glance, then spins back to her desk. She picks up the papers she'd been working on before as if Elly isn't there and starts to shuffle them, quick and decisive.

"I've changed my mind," she says. "You can go."

Elly's vision is blurry. The patterns on the rug transform themselves into faces, hanks of hair, laughing mouths. She doesn't know what just happened. She's never been hit in the face but wonders whether it feels like this: the sudden, stinging shock of violence.

"You're dismissed," Haina says, voice brusque.

Elly can't get her muscles to move. They're gluey and heavy, like she hasn't used them in months. Haina is turned away from her as if she already knows everything Elly might say in her own defence, and has decided none of it is even worth listening to. The way she'd looked at her, so confident that she was the one in control – it had reminded Elly of Ethan. It's unbearable to feel like that again, at the complete whim of another person, being told what to do, where to go. She stares at the back of Haina's head, the gloss of her impossibly black hair. She's aware of a new thought, unfurling itself like a creature from hibernation.

She wants to grab a chunk of that hair and rip it from Haina's head.

"No," she whispers, the word out of her mouth before she can stop it.

Slowly, Haina turns in her chair. The look in her eyes is withering. "Excuse me?"

"No," Elly says again, louder now. "I am not dismissed. You're going to explain to me what's happening."

For a moment, neither of them speaks, and there's no sound in the study except the rustling of the fire. Elly is warm all over, as though she's burning. Her hands itch. She watches every inch of Haina's face for clues, noting the way her dark eyes flicker down to Elly's lap and then back up. She doesn't expect the wide smile, the hushed anticipation in Haina's voice when she speaks again.

"Elly," she whispers. "Look."

Elly glances down at the hands lying in her lap. Only, they aren't her hands anymore. Her arms are still her arms, her wrists are still her wrists, but there's a lightening at her palms where the warm skin has become something soft, furred. Where there had been fingers, there are now glossy fronds, intersecting like a fan. It takes Elly a long second to see them for what they are.

Feathers. Five of them, white dappled with brown, like footprints through snow, long claws curling from the tips. When Elly screams, those feathers quiver and twitch, as if they've only just remembered that they're alive.

SIOBHAN

NOW

The email arrives the morning after Siobhan has drinks with Owen.

She's insulated in the queasy fuzz of her hangover, not quite part of the world yet. She stands yawning by the sink, one hand clutching the cool stainless steel of the draining board and the other pouring boiling water over lumps of old coffee at the bottom of a cafetière. There's a window over the sink, tall and thin, crowded by plants she never remembers to water. Past their brown and curling leaves, the city sprawls like an ancient body finally given permission to recline. Tiny people shuffle down its veiny streets, cells in constant motion.

The coffee is so hot that it takes the top layer off her tongue. Siobhan feels like a different species, cloistered up here in the quiet. She longs, suddenly, to be amongst crowds, to be one of those bodies, driven by a purpose and somewhere to go. The email flashes up on her phone, innocuous until she opens it. She bites the inside of her cheek as she reads.

Hey Siobhan,

I hope you don't mind me reaching out. My name's Zara Doherty, and I'm a journalist. I work for SunWolf Productions here in Edinburgh, and we're currently putting together a new documentary that I'd love to discuss with you. The working title is: *Hex House: Coven or Cult?*

Apologies if I've misunderstood the situation, but I've been led to believe by an anonymous source that you were working on a documentary about Hex House a few years ago. Is that true? I heard the doc ultimately didn't pan out for you, so I just wanted to touch base and see how you'd feel about working together on this, or even coming on as co-director. We've got a great budget for the project at SunWolf, and everyone is really excited about the doc and keen to get your expertise on the team.

This is a real passion project for me, and I think it has the potential to be huge. Obviously, everyone's heard of Hex House. It's got real enduring appeal. Together, I reckon we can get to the bottom of this whole thing and debunk one of the biggest urban legends out there.

Also, and this is maybe a bit unorthodox, but my source also asked to pass a message on to you. She wants you to know that Haina is dead. My apologies if this is upsetting news, but my source was very keen that you should know as soon as possible.

I appreciate all this might be a little confusing, so I can share plenty more if we were able to speak in person.

Looking forward to hearing from you soon.

Zara x

Siobhan swallows.

Haina is dead. Haina is dead. Haina is dead.

She leans back against the sink, Haina's name ringing in her ears. It's a name from another life; a name she knew when she was a different person. She rereads the email until the words become shed snakeskins, unfamiliar, without meaning. How neatly she's been able to push that life aside, to almost convince herself that she'd made it all up: Haina, Elly, all of it. Seeing Haina's name, she feels it tugging taut – the thread connecting this life to that other, impossible one. She puts her fingers to her throat and is almost surprised to find that there's no hand there, squeezing out the breath.

Haina is dead. She can't let herself think about what that means.

Siobhan swallows. SunWolf – the biggest production company in Edinburgh. Following graduation, it was the place everyone wanted to land a job, Siobhan included. She reads the email a final time, then hits delete.

The second day of the Horror Film Festival at the Showroom is dedicated to Hitchcock. Women appear at the box office in lime-green dresses, plastic crows attached to their arms, chests, faces. Some have had real fun with the gore, their peck marks scarlet and oozing. Siobhan looks only at their eyes as she serves them their tickets, the way they glitter with the heady anticipation of being frightened.

"Jesus, Siobhan," says Sylvie, who's manning the other till in the box office. A French accent clings to the curves of her words like a silk slip. "You're making the whole booth smell like a bar."

Siobhan raises her forearm to her nose and sniffs the skin. It's clammy and tart, like something souring. She taps the glass that separates them from the customers. "Thank god for this, then."

Sylvie gives her a tight smile. Red lipstick stretches over her teeth, which are startlingly white against her dark skin. "Just don't let Keith smell you." She shrugs. "If you care at all about keeping your job."

Sylvie is Parisian and young, younger than Siobhan, with an acerbity Siobhan admires and the kind of serious-ness that only comes from intense, innate ambition. She's still in the first year of her undergrad degree but already has an impressive portfolio of short pieces online. Siobhan has clicked through her website more than once, usually in the middle of the night, growing more agitated with every well-judged and well-produced clip. She never knows whether to feel envious or proud or something else entirely.

In a quiet moment between customers, she asks Sylvie, "Do you have Owen Jameson for any of your classes?"

Sylvie is smoothing her tight curls into a low pony. She

nods, removes the claw clip from between her teeth, and says, "Yeah, Documentary. Why?"

"What do you think of him?"

Sylvie rubs at an invisible mark on her pristine polo with her thumb. "I dunno, he's fine? Quite a generous marker apparently, so maybe I'll like him more at the end of term. But I do get the feeling he's a bit of a... creep. Like if he was standing close to you, he'd try and smell your hair or something."

A teenage couple approach the box office, wrapped in bloodstained shower curtains, their hair slicked back to look wet. They glance between Sylvie's and Siobhan's tills and choose Sylvie's. The girl giddily requests two tickets for *Psycho*.

Siobhan leans back in her chair and pulls out her phone. Two new messages. The first is from her mum, asking how she is, and has she done a proper food shop recently, and would she like a delivery of some basics, you know like potatoes and some bananas? Does Siobhan know bananas are full of potassium and make a great breakfast, that they have plenty of calories but good ones, not like alcohol? Oh also, and no big deal, but Theo is popping round this weekend, would Siobhan consider stopping by to say hello?

Siobhan stares at the message then clicks on the next one. It's from Owen.

Come round tonight, it says. *I'll make you dinner. Here's the address.*

It's no surprise to learn that he lives in the New Town, Google Maps revealing a flat on Heriot Row. She thinks about going there and wearing something low-cut and watching him try not to look at her. Would it be fun?

He'd probably make some elaborate pasta dish and she'd have to say things like *love the sauce* and compliment his vintage record collection. She's exhausted at the thought, but then she thinks about the alternative: going home, sitting in the gloom, trying not to look for Zara's email in her trash folder.

"Sylvie," she says, when the couple have moved on to the concession stand, "what are you doing tonight? Want to go out?" They've been out before. Not often, and mostly work drinks, but enough so that it's not weird to ask.

Sylvie blinks. "I'm going to the theatre with some friends," she says. Siobhan waits for the invite that doesn't come, then returns to her phone.

I'll be there, she types to Owen.

Two minutes later, he replies. *Bring wine!* Siobhan stares at the winky-face emoji and wishes she was already drunk.

She doesn't often have reason to come to this part of town and had forgotten how sleepy it is. There's not much to it but street after street of stately Georgian townhouses in elegant arched configurations, locked parks for residents only, dog walkers emerging to side-eye her bag clanking with bottles. The pavements are so clean. Even the pinking sky looks washed, scrubbed at.

Owen buzzes her into his building and she steps into his stairwell. It's airy, tiles buffed to sparkle underfoot, scented by a fresh diffuser on an antique dresser. Who thought to put that there, she wonders, who took time out of their day to do it? When she gets to the top level, he's already waiting at the open door. She almost turns around at the sight of his tightly tied apron, but there's nowhere better to be tonight. His cheeks are flushed and his hair is ungelled. He looks homey, healthy, like someone's well-meaning husband.

"You made it." He beams, as if surprised, as though she hadn't texted him just ten minutes ago to let him know she was on her way. He reaches out one arm, perhaps for a kind of side hug, but Siobhan meets his outstretched hand with a bottle. He looks down and she relishes the way he tries to hide his disappointment. She'd chosen the cheapest she could find, a bottle without even a grape variety on the label, simply block letters reading 'red wine'. Just to see what he'd do.

"Wow," he says. "Never tried this one before." He grins again and steps to one side to let her in.

Siobhan walks down a spacious hallway and into an impressive kitchen, all butcher's block counters and abstract art above the Aga. The room is warm; it smells of butter and melting cheese. Colourful children's drawings are pinned to the stainless-steel fridge, 'Uncle Owen' scrawled unevenly on each. There's an enormous window at one end of the room, bigger than she is tall. She's drawn to that window; it pulls her over. Through the slightly steamed glass, Edinburgh's dusk lights blink back at her. Beyond the city is the sea, and in the other direction, the quiet villages and towns to the south. Somewhere lurking in all that loose countryside, somewhere on no map and with no address, is a house that until this morning, she'd almost convinced herself couldn't really exist.

Haina is dead.

Whoever Zara's source was, they must be legitimate to know Haina's name. Siobhan wonders which of the guests might consider talking to another filmmaker after what happened last time, or whether it's someone she's never met, someone who only arrived at the house once she'd left.

No. No point in thinking about any of that tonight.

Siobhan takes a seat at the island, where Owen has laid out neat little dishes of olives and nuts. He appears behind her to peel her leather jacket from her shoulders. He drapes it on the back of her chair then returns to stir something bubbling on the hob. "Hope you like fettuccine Alfredo."

Siobhan stabs an olive with a toothpick. "I don't know what that is."

"Oh, it's just pasta. With cream and Parmesan."

On the wall, next to his head, is a magnetic strip from which hang more knives than Siobhan has ever seen in one place: great big cleavers and mean little blades like scalpels. He sees her looking at them and clears his throat like he's about to make a joke. Before he can, Siobhan says, "You cook a lot?"

"More enthusiasm than skill, I'm afraid, but yes. Though I rarely have anyone to cook for."

Siobhan rolls the olive around on her tongue. It's so salty it makes her mouth pool with saliva. Owen turns back to the stove, stirs the pot, picks up a bunch of parsley then quickly puts it down again. He'd seemed so confident when he'd messaged her this afternoon – sure and assertive. Now he doesn't seem to know where to look or what to do with her. She's out of context in here. Something essential about her is at odds with his bookshelf of curated cookbooks and the fresh sourdough loaf by the toaster. He knows it and she knows it. It makes her feel bold.

"I'll pour the wine," she says, reaching for the bottle.

"Ah! Of course, sorry, I should have done that. What a shoddy host." He reaches into a high cupboard and brings down two glasses. They're impractically large and sparkling. She wonders if she imagines that his hand is shaking slightly as he sets them down in front of her. She pours for them both and they clink their glasses just a little bit too hard. "Cheers," she says.

He leans against the island, loosening a fraction. He sips the wine, barely disguising his wince at the taste, then says quietly, "You know, I wasn't sure whether you'd come."

"No?"

"I didn't know if it was a bit, you know... weird of me, to ask."

"Why would it be weird of you?"

Owen holds her gaze for a long second, as if her words are a knot to untangle, a test to pass, then looks away with a contained laugh. "Oh, you know. You used to be one of my students."

"Used to be."

He shrugs, wipes his hands on his apron. "I just hope it isn't inappropriate. I would never want you to feel uncomfortable."

"It can be hard to know where the lines are," Siobhan offers, keeping her voice flat.

Owen hesitates, clears his throat. "Obviously if I was still teaching you, I would never—"

"Do you think it's inappropriate?" Siobhan interrupts. She swivels on her stool so that she can face him, and her knees brush the front of his apron. "Do you not want me here?"

The thick knuckle of his Adam's apple bobs up and down. It's dizzying, to know she can make a grown man this nervous. "Of course I want you here."

The room has started to feel a little too warm. A bitter smell is coming from somewhere, and Siobhan glances over his shoulder at the hob. "I think something might be burning."

Owen blinks, as though she's woken him from sleep-walking, then slams his glass down so hard on the island that the wine sloshes up and over the sides. "Shit, the sauce."

It's almost endearing to watch him panic, muttering to himself as he scrapes the bottom of the pan and turns up the extractor fan until it's too loud to talk over. Siobhan gets the sense that things are constantly slipping out of his control, that it might even be a source of insecurity for him, this inability to keep his composure. She leans back, sipping her vinegar wine.

"Right," Owen announces theatrically a few minutes later, once he's plated up. His cheeks have grown ruddier and his forehead looks damp. "Bon appétit." He sets a steaming bowl of pasta in front of her. It's piled high and topped with parsley. She could probably live off a serving this size for a week.

"You'll have to excuse the burnt bits." He takes a seat opposite her on the island. As Siobhan takes her first mouthful, she wonders how long it's been since she had a hot meal. Probably the last time she was at her mum's. At home, she lives off cereal and coffee, the occasional instant ramen, leftover popcorn from the Showroom. The pasta is thin and silky, the sauce almost indecently decadent, thick with cream and Parmesan, only a hint of burnt bitterness. The liquid splashes her cheeks, her white T-shirt.

She feels Owen's gaze on her as she eats but they don't talk, listening instead to the tinkling of forks against plates and the low rumble of the radio Siobhan hadn't realised was on. An old Van Morrison song is playing, one her mum loves, one she says reminds her of Siobhan and Theo's dad before he drank.

When she can't take another bite, Siobhan sets down her fork and raises her glass to Owen. "You can make that for me every single day."

"Gladly." He grins. Then, after a pause, "I like having you here. I like being in your company."

"All I've done is eat."

"Maybe I find you intriguing. Mysterious."

Siobhan fights the urge to roll her eyes. She tops up their glasses. "If you tell me I'm not like the other girls, I'm leaving."

"Sorry, I know you're far too smart to patronise," he says. "I wouldn't mind getting to know you better, is what I mean."

He removes his apron and hangs it carefully on a hook by the oven. Underneath, he's wearing a navy-blue shirt, a discreet designer logo at the cuff. He is the type of man who cares about keeping his shirts clean, she notes, composing her growing litany of him. The type of man who gets irritated when the sauce burns. She wonders what all the clues might add up to. She watches him sweep crumbs from the island into his hand then into the bin. He wipes the corner of his mouth with a napkin.

"What do you want to know?"

He tilts his head from side to side like a metronome, clicking his tongue. "Why aren't you making films anymore?"

"Straight for the jugular."

"Is it a sore subject?"

Siobhan swallows, swirls the wine in her glass. What's the point in lying? "Something happened. When Theo and I were making that documentary." *At Hex House*, she says in her head. "I suppose I couldn't face it after that."

His eyes are on her, on the twin arches of her collarbones, the way their knife edges press upwards into her skin. She waits for him to ask what happened, but he doesn't, so she says, "We found something out about the woman who ran... the cult. She was doing something to the guests there."

Why are the words tumbling out like this? Zara's email. *Haina is dead.* Reading those words had felt like finally letting a wound bleed, just a little.

"*Doing* something to them?" Owen's voice has grown low, serious. Maybe he can sense it, too – the presence of something new in the room with them, breathing against their necks.

She could tell him everything. What's stopping her now? Haina is gone for good, and freedom from the pressure of keeping this secret is only a matter of words away. She tries to think about what Owen will do, if he'll believe any of it. She'd kept the details of the commission vague with anyone who asked, knowing what their reaction would be. Will he shut down the second she says Hex House? Laugh at her, tell her it's nothing but lore designed to scare children? Perhaps he'll think she's seriously unwell and attempt to comfort her, console her, all while subtly edging her out of the door. The words are heavy bullets on her tongue but they're impossible to fire. Instead, she says, "She was doing something... unethical. Theo and I disagreed on how to handle it. That's why we don't talk anymore. It's why I can't even pick up a camera." She swills the bitter liquid in her mouth and swallows. "It's pathetic, I guess."

Owen is quiet for a long moment. The kitchen has grown cooler, and the cream is congealing on their abandoned plates. "Sounds like it would have made for a hell of a documentary." They lock eyes for a second, and he looks away first. "Come on. Let's go and sit somewhere a bit more comfortable."

He shows her into a high-ceilinged living room with walls of warm orange. It's low-lit and cosy, soft carpet underfoot. One wall is taken up entirely by books – *The Story of Cinema in 50 Palettes*, *The Stanley Kubrick Archives* – one by a flat-screen TV, and another by framed vintage film prints. Siobhan peers into the lens of James Stewart's binoculars on an enormous poster for *Rear Window*. She feels Owen come up behind her. He takes a long time to speak.

"I don't want to be too forward," he whispers. "But this can be whatever you want it to be. You're in control here. I hope you know that." His words come out so easily, as if he's long perfected their ambiguity, as if he's said them before. Maybe many times. She turns to face him. "What do you want, Siobhan?"

What does she want? It's been a long time since she's

been asked that. She wants to be drunk all the time with no consequences. She wants Theo to talk to her again. She wants to feel nothing and everything, to be nowhere and everywhere. She wants to be the version of herself she was before Hex House. She wants Owen to touch her and she wants to never see him again. She wants to stop dreaming about the beating of wings.

"I want to stop being afraid," she says eventually.

Owen reaches out his index finger to brush a strand of dark hair from her face. "You don't have to be afraid of me."

"Not you." She expects her voice to shake, but it's steely. "I'm afraid of myself."

He flinches slightly, and she wonders what he sees in her face. She wonders if fury shows through the skin and what colour it might be.

"Am I really in control?" she asks quietly. "Am I in control of this? Us?"

"Of course."

"What I say goes?"

"If that's what makes you feel comfortable."

"Okay then. Undo your top button." Her stomach is fizzing as she says it. He laughs, and she smells parsley and wine on his breath. "Now," she whispers, and something changes in his face. Something ignites.

He holds her eye, undoing the button with one hand, quick fingers. The skin underneath is paler than his neck, dark hair creeping up from his chest.

"And the next one," she says.

He does so, and the next, and the next. She catches the slight hitch in his breath that he's trying to hide. He stands facing her, a smile waiting at the edges of his lips. His arms hang limp at his sides. He looks vulnerablé, unprepared.

"Close your eyes," she whispers.

He hesitates and makes a sound of resistance that's almost a word. Then he closes his eyes.

Siobhan looks at him, pristine shirt half-undone, cheeks flushed with expectation, eyelids quivering. She leaves the living room, leaves him standing there. She goes back to the kitchen and smears two fingers around the edge of his pasta bowl, collecting a dollop of thick sauce. One finger she places in her mouth, relishing the cold saltiness, the other she smears onto the sparkling surface of the island.

Just before she closes the front door behind her, she hears Owen call her name.

ELLY

THEN

Elly is screaming. She's never heard her voice sound like this before, like it could rip a hole right through fabric. Across the room, Haina is saying something to her, something that might be consoling or explanatory or useful, but she can't make out the words. All she can do is scream and look at her hands that are no longer hands.

White feathers, sinewy cartilage underneath. Sharp points; creature-like claws.

She stands up, bringing one of her hands to her face in reflex. It slices a shallow cut into her cheekbone, the pain clean and quick. She staggers towards the door, but Haina is faster. Reaching it before Elly, she turns the key in the lock and pockets it, sealing them inside the study. Haina puts one hand on each of Elly's shoulders and Elly feels as though her skin is crawling; as though it's too hot to stay on her bones. When her throat grows too hoarse to keep screaming, she falls silent. There's a strange and slow leaching away, like something abandoning her, something seeping between the cracks, leaving her shaking.

"That's it," Haina is saying, voice soft and soothing. "That's it, my angel. It's all okay now, just breathe a little."

Elly opens her eyes. Her breath hurts her lungs, as though they're scorched. She barely dares, but she forces herself to look down, only to find that her hands are her hands again. They're small and bony, her wedding ring shining on her left hand. She blinks.

"I don't understand," she whispers. Then, with a sudden clarity, "I'm going insane."

"The opposite," Haina says, taking one of Elly's hands in her own. "You're finally seeing the truth."

Elly lets herself be led back to the armchair, as if her body no longer belongs to her. She can still feel the echoes of her screams in the small room and wonders who else in the house heard them. A thought strikes her, making her skin prickle.

Even if they did hear her, no one came to help.

She sits but stays perched on the very edge of the armchair, in case she needs to run again. There's a faint queasiness in the pit of her belly, the disorientating sensation of just having woken up from a long sleep. The light has changed again, falling sideways across Haina's face, casting half of it in shadow. Elly wonders how long she's been in this room – and distantly, but with a distinct sense of alarm, if she'll ever be allowed to leave. She balls her hands into fists and then releases them, over and over, not quite trusting them not to betray her again. Haina lets her settle, making notes in a journal on the desk. For a while, there's only the sound of the fire and the pencil scratching across paper. Elly wonders if Haina is writing about her, about whatever it is that just happened. She's starting to think that Haina has forgotten she's even in the room until she turns and meets Elly's eye.

"You probably want to know where this house got its name."

"What..." Elly stumbles over her words, unsure how to get them to obey her. "What happened? What did you do to me?"

"Most people think a hex is a kind of curse," continues Haina, ignoring her, "cast by someone who's been wronged. And you know, they're *almost* right." She pours herself a measure of something dark and rich-looking from a decanter on the desk, offering a tumbler to Elly before thinking better of it, glancing at her belly. "The word has lost its way over time. Lots do, you know. What 'hex' really means, is something, *someone*, very powerful. The form someone takes when everything about them has been broken and they're ready to build themselves again." She inclines her glass towards Elly. "You just got your first glimpse of your hex. What you might be able to become."

Elly's gaze snaps back to her hands, and she's relieved to still find them their own.

"Don't be afraid, my angel," Haina whispers. "Don't resist it."

Hex, a voice chimes, somewhere deep inside her. *Hex*.

Haina finishes whatever was in her tumbler in one gulp, then slaps both of her palms against her thighs, a sudden movement that makes Elly blink in surprise. Haina reaches into her pocket, fishes out the study key then presses it into Elly's hand. It's small and gold. "Time's getting on. We'll meet again for our second session next week."

Elly guesses that she's dismissed – really dismissed, this time. Haina has turned away from her, and Elly studies the way her hair twists together into a plait, a triplet of snakes, before standing. She makes her way to the door and lets herself out, leaving the key in the lock.

Has even an hour passed? Everything out here already looks different, vaguely threatening: the winding staircase leading up into the dark, the patterns in the floral wallpaper that could be simple swirls or hands reaching out to touch her. The sounds of the house surround her, the same as any other house: the muttering of voices, the creaking of floorboards, the clattering of pipes. But this house is not like any other, she knows that now. There's something deeply, awfully wrong with it.

Or there's something deeply, awfully wrong with *her*.

Elly knows she should leave. She could walk right out the front door. Coming here in the first place had been an act of desperate madness, of cowardice. She thought she'd find solace, comfort, or at least safety here. She isn't quite sure what it is that she has found. Her feet are numb as she climbs the staircase. The few things she owns are in the shared dormitory. She'll collect them, and then she'll leave. She'll go home and she'll forget all about this place. She'll forget all about the way her hands had looked: mottled and feathery, like human skin never should.

There are around forty beds in the dorm, twenty running along each side of the room, one row facing the other. When Haina had told her she'd be sleeping in the dormitory, Elly had pictured iron bedframes and stiff white sheets like something from a Victorian hospital, but this room is warm and cosy. Shabby chandeliers hang from

81

the high ceiling, and colourful rugs cover the hardwood floor. The beds are large and wooden. Some are empty and stripped but most are topped with bedspreads, blankets and patterned pillows. Many are neatly made while others look only recently vacated, cuddly toys abandoned in the rucked-up sheets. Every bed has its own bedside table. Left alone to settle yesterday, Elly had examined each one, trying to piece together an idea of the owners from their contents: packets of cigarettes, old books, notepads, lipsticks with blunted ends, tampons, sweet wrappers, half-eaten slices of cake, half-drunk cups of tea. She'd dreaded the first night, sleeping amongst all those strange bodies. To her surprise, she'd fallen asleep quickly, but noises in the dark had woken her: muffled chittering, the sound of nails on wood. A rhythmic scraping on the roof above their heads, like something trying to get inside.

When Elly gets to her bed, she reaches for the bundle of things in her side table. Her silver watch and pearl earrings she puts in her pocket, and her dirty wedding dress she presses to her face, breathing in the smell of the woods – earth, cold air, sweat – and the lingering after-breath of perfume. It makes her think of her wedding day. It makes her think of bruises and crackling songs on the radio and running, running, running. There's no point trying not to cry. What will Ethan do when he sees her? She can already hear his voice, sharp as gravel. She can feel his hands. Maybe he won't be able to hold himself back this time. Maybe she deserves whatever's finally coming to her.

A soft creak behind her makes her jump. Elly turns to see Margot, soil streaked across her forehead, wild hair restrained by a tie.

"There you are, Little Mouse! I've been looking for you." Her high voice makes her seem so much younger than she looks. She chuckles. "So lazy, hiding out in here."

Elly doesn't say anything. She folds her wedding dress carefully, placing it beside her on the bed.

Margot frowns. "What are you doing, Little Mouse?"

"I'm sorry," Elly says, because she doesn't know what else to say. "I'm leaving."

Margot stands silently in front of her, her single greenish eye peering up from under dark eyelashes. She looks like Elly has struck her. "Leaving? But didn't you just have your first session?" She sits down on Elly's bed, bouncing a little so that it creaks. "Isn't it just wonderful? I *told* you it would be."

"Wonderful?" Elly's stomach feels hollow, and she puts a hand to it. She longs to feel the familiarity of the baby moving, to let it comfort her, but for now it is still. "This is crazy, Margot. All of it. What is this place? What are we *doing* here?"

Margot screws up her face, deep wrinkles appearing on her nose, hiding the faint freckles there. "Don't like that word. Crazy. Haina says you shouldn't say it."

Elly feels like a feral dog backed into a corner, taunted, just as she had in Haina's study. She has to get out of here. She has to get out of here *now*. "Maybe I don't care what Haina says," she whispers, surprised at how combative her voice sounds.

Margot's eye widens. She lunges sideways and claps a hand over Elly's mouth. The shock of it makes Elly fall backwards but Margot has her other hand on her shoulder, maintaining her grip, bringing her close. She's frightened,

Elly thinks. She's terrified. There are tiny red veins on her eyeball, spidering their way across the white. "Stop that right now," Margot hisses. "No talk like that. Haina won't like it." Elly wriggles but Margot holds her tight. "Do you promise?" It's only when Elly nods that she releases her hand, slumping back on the bed. There's something defeated about her, as though it's drained all her energy to speak. "Sick of clearing up the mess," she mumbles. "Go on, then – try to leave. Go back into the world a lamb. See what it does to you. Don't come crying to Margot." She blows out an exasperated puff of air, shrugs, and leaves Elly alone in the dorm.

Elly watches the empty doorway for a while. She can still feel the ghost of Margot's palm on her lips, the way her pupil had almost seemed to quiver when she said, *Haina won't like it*. She feels heavy but forces herself to move – zipping up the hoodie she's wearing, leaving the dress where it is on the bed, and making for the doorway. No one pays her any attention as she descends the staircase and walks back down the hallway. There's a gentle hubbub from the kitchens, and a few more guests are lounging in the parlour room, playing cards. She can hear the faint tinkle of piano keys. Haina's study door is shut, and Elly stares at it for a second before moving away. Outside, the day is hot and bright and the women in the gardens are hard at work, brows sweating and backs bent as they prune the rose bushes, weed the twisting borders, trim the grass. They look so normal, but do they all know? Do they all *change*, too, behind the thick panelled door to Haina's study? No one looks up as she makes her way down the path and into the woods.

Elly feels relief almost immediately as the house retreats further and further behind her, the trees offering a cool shade from the heat. The sun is still high in the sky. If she walks quickly, she could be at her mum's house – radio always on, wellies by the door – before evening. The thought makes her stomach feel strange, like there's a hook buried deep, starting to loosen.

But what will she say, when she gets there? How can she possibly explain where she's been, why she left?

Don't think about that now, she tells herself. *Just keep walking.*

When she'd run through the woods, she'd arrived at the house relatively unscathed. The skin of her bare feet had been almost unbroken, as if the woods had welcomed her, carried her. Now, twigs catch at her forearms and leave forked scratches, like bloodied lightning. She trips over protruding roots, and nettles give her red welts when she brushes past them. She feels unwanted, like an intruder, but forces herself onwards; crossing streams that shimmer in the sunlight and climbing over fallen logs grown over with lichen, no idea whether she's going in the right direction. The woods are filled with the sound of birdsong, and she strains to hear the steady whooshing of cars. She keeps waiting for a trail to appear, or another walker, or the outlines of buildings in the distance. After a while, she stops to rest against a thick oak trunk. It would have been a good idea to bring some food with her, or at least some water. She's starting to feel woozy and detached, her muscles weaker with every step.

Elly has been walking for another hour when she sees it. The pointed roof emerging from between the trees, the pretty gabled windows, the door left open to let the sunshine in and the women milling around the gardens like worker ants. It looks as inviting as it had on that first night: a mirage, an impossibility conjured from nothing.

No. It can't be. The woods look the same from every angle – she must have gotten disorientated and walked in a circle. Elly backs away without taking her eyes off the house, half-expecting it might follow her in retreat, then sets off again in the opposite direction.

She walks and walks. There's a blurriness to her vision now, as if everything is only half-formed and undecided. She stops at a stream to splash her face and then carries on. She doesn't know how far she walks. The sun is starting to dip when the house appears from between the trees again. There are no women in the gardens now, and light is spilling from the kitchen window, along with the homely smell of something cooking.

"No." Her own voice makes her jump, makes her stagger backwards. "No, no."

Back in the woods again. Stumbling, feet on fire. The sky is a mellow blue streaked with coral, the sun disappearing, the air cooling. Elly picks up a stick from the ground and snaps it into a point, carves an X into the dirt at her feet. She walks on, making Xs at regular intervals. She won't get lost. Soon, she'll find a road.

She doesn't come across any of her Xs. It's dark by the time the house appears again. The lights are on in all the windows. She can hear the low hum of voices and she's so tired that she can barely stand.

Elly limps towards the house and when she's close enough, she watches the faces through the glass panes of the refectory. The guests inside grin as bowls of food are passed around and shared. The dough she kneaded earlier has become a proud loaf that's being sliced and buttered, consumed by many mouths. The room is candlelit, flickering gently, in and out of focus. Someone is singing. Elly has the peculiar sense that she's looking in at someone else's family, at a scene forbidden to her. She shivers with jealousy. Inside her belly, the baby twists. She's hungry, so hungry. The exhaustion goes as deep as her bones.

"Elly," comes a voice from the open front door. Elly turns, blinking back tears. She's overwhelmed by the house, by Haina standing in the doorway again, calling out to her, just like on that first night. The glow from the hallway seems to sit upon her skin, making her look golden. Elly already knows that nowhere else has light quite like that. "Won't you come inside, my angel? It's getting cold."

Elly doesn't say anything. She wraps her arms around herself, casts one last glance back at the woods, and then follows Haina inside.

The house is a different animal at night. Elly walks behind Haina into the low-lit parlour, where the women are now draped over chairs and drinking, spilling out into the garden with their cigarettes, others wrapped up in one another in shadowy corners by the slow-burning fire. Elly eats the slice of bread Haina has given her slowly, watching Janine and Lakshmi dance in the centre of the room, bodies hot and close. Everything is abundant: the piles of food on plates, the bottles topping tables. The room quivers in the light of coloured lanterns, casting everyone's faces in shades of amethyst and emerald.

Music thrums from a record player, throbbing bass and whispering guitar, low and suggestive, and Elly feels aware of her every limb. She doesn't know where to look. There's an edge to the atmosphere, as if the night is on the brink of turning feral. It smells of sweat and spice and something sweet, slightly burnt.

"I trust you won't try that again?" Haina whispers in her ear, stroking her arm. Elly flinches and stares at Haina, but her smiling face doesn't match her threat. She leaves Elly's side and disappears into the crowd.

A moment later, Margot appears and nuzzles into her shoulder like a hungry cat. When she squeezes Elly's arm, it only hurts a little bit.

"Knew you'd come back, Little Mouse," she whispers. "Once the house wants you, it wants you."

The night unravels like a spool of dark thread. Elly gives in to her fatigue, sinking heavily into the cushions of the sofa. She lets Margot slip a plump segment of tangerine between her lips. She listens to the tinkling of piano keys, the icy voices of the red sisters as they sing an old Gaelic song. Then, sometime after midnight, Elly becomes aware of a new quiet. Everyone is looking at Haina, who has climbed up onto the coffee table in the middle of the parlour. As the guests notice her, one by one, they fall silent. Haina presses one hand to her chest, smiling benevolently. Her voice is calm as the sea on a windless night.

"My angels. I have a very important and exciting announcement to make." Her voice has no problem filling every inch of the room. Elly pictures it seeping into the weave of the upholstery, forcing its way into shadowy corners. Beside her, Margot is tapping her palms against the outside of her thighs, like she can't stay still, like there are insects crawling beneath her clothes. "Many of you will know how fiercely I guard our privacy here. How important it is that we're protected from everything going on... *out there*." Those two words seem to hurt her tongue. "It's only by untethering ourselves completely that we can really begin to heal."

On the night she arrived, one of the first things Haina asked Elly was whether she had a mobile phone. Elly had left hers back on the bed in the cottage; hadn't even thought to take it with her in the molten second she'd decided to run. She's heard from some of the other guests that Haina took their phones and stamped on them with the heel of her boot until they were mangled. It's one of the things that gives Hex House its intense immediacy, she realises now. No one's attention is divided. There's nothing else to do or think about other than what's in front of you. There's no intangible world to escape into. There is no other place. Only here, only now.

"That being said," Haina continues, "those of you who've been here a while will notice that we've had fewer arrivals recently. Our newest guest aside." Heads swivel to seek out Elly, and she finds herself pierced by many eyes. She keeps her eyes trained ahead, on Haina. "Despite the best efforts of the flock, most of the people who need us aren't finding us, and I've been thinking hard about why that might be. And I think one of the reasons, perhaps the biggest reason, is that people *out there* don't understand what Hex House is, or what it can offer. Some of you have told me about the rumours. They won't believe in it. And those that do, don't think that this is a safe place. They don't know how much it can help them. And what good is this sanctuary if the people who need us misunderstand who we are?" She pauses, her hand still braced on her chest. Her eyes are large and watery, and Elly wonders how long Haina's been here, for her to care this much. "So," she says, brightening a little, "I've made the decision to invite two outsiders into our midst. *Filmmakers*." She says the word as though it's an exotic fruit. "Over the next few months, they'll be staying with us and making a documentary about the important work we do here. Eventually, they'll broadcast our mission to those who might benefit from it."

The room starts to simmer with uncertainty, maybe a little panic, hushed whispers passing back and forth. Beside Elly, Margot's leg taps have become slaps. Elly reaches out a hand to calm her and finds her skin clammy, cool to the touch. The idea of filmmakers, *here*, their cameras and microphones amongst all the candles and roses, is surreal. Elly remembers how her hands had looked today and bites down on her tongue, hard. There's a shape to this place that Elly doesn't understand yet. How much can Haina really mean to show the rest of the world?

Haina raises a hand, and the room falls silent again. Elly tastes saltiness in her mouth and realises she's bitten her tongue hard enough to bleed. "I understand that it'll take some getting used to," Haina says, more gently now. "I realise that it might even feel frightening at first, to open up the walls of this sanctuary, just a little. Please know – anyone who doesn't wish to be on camera can ask for their identity to be hidden. I have selected these filmmakers especially for their affinity with the house, their sympathy to our ethos and what we do here."

Near the back of the room, Grace has raised her hand. Her thin lips are set into a hard line.

"Yes, my angel?"

"When will they get here?" Grace's voice is different here than in the kitchen, where she sounds authoritative and sure. Now, it is small, contained.

Haina beams, teeth gleaming. "That's the best part of all. Our new friends will be here with us within the week."

SIOBHAN

NOW

Siobhan walks quickly down Leith Walk towards her mum's flat. There's something prickly about Leith that Siobhan has always loved: the sweaty pubs with the same hollow-faced men staring out of the windows day after day, the graffiti on the sides of the yoga studios. A march out of town and towards the shore, Leith feels like a different world to Old Town Edinburgh, a surly cousin lurking on the outside of a party, smoking.

The air has a bite and it's drizzling, a thin static of rain dampening her face. The other people on the pavement seem lethargic and oblivious today and Siobhan has to elbow her way past them, growing more fractious the further down the street she gets. She's wearing a battered navy rain jacket of Theo's, one he grew out of as a teenager and let her have. The zip is broken and there's a hole in the left pocket. She wears it every time it rains.

Every few minutes, her thoughts return to Zara's email, lurking in her trash folder. Four years ago, she'd decided that the only way to survive was to convince herself that Hex House had never happened. But Haina is dead – Haina, whose striking face often returns to her unbidden, sending her teetering off-balance for days after – and that changes everything. She can feel the claws that have been buried deep in her skin for so long start to come loose. She could rid herself of it, unburden herself of every awful detail. There are so many consequences to telling her story that feel like routes down a foggy road – she can't see where they might go, or what she might be freeing by putting what she knows out into the world. She follows her thoughts around in circles, trying to pin them down, all the way down Leith Walk.

Her mum Nora has lived in the same poky flat above a drycleaners since they left the shelter. Theo will already be inside now, almost certainly unaware she's coming, and Siobhan pauses at the main door to collect herself. She chews on a hangnail, ripping off a little too much skin. It stings. She's starting to feel clammy under her clothes, thinking about the last time she saw Theo. Running. The woods. Hex House getting smaller and smaller until it was nothing, nothing at all. Theo screaming at her, each word pointed and hurled to hurt.

Fine, have it your way. But I'll never speak to you again. That's the deal.

He had stalked away from her, the woods consuming him with no effort at all, and Siobhan had stood still and alone for a very long time. Eventually, she'd retraced her steps back to the house and found only trees, endless trees. They felt so insistent and absolute that she'd looked down at herself and expected to see not her body but a gnarled trunk, for the woods to have claimed her as punishment. She looked for hours. She never found her way back to Hex House.

Siobhan had tried to go and see Theo in Glasgow about a year later. She'd turned up drunk outside his flat, jabbed repeatedly at the buzzer, slurred her name into the intercom box like an apology. He sent his flatmate Joe down with a ten-pound note and a folded piece of paper she was too drunk to read. Joe drove her to Queen Street Station where she fell asleep on the platform and got nudged awake by a cleaner in the early hours of the morning. Before boarding the train, she remembered the paper in her pocket and took it out. Theo's handwriting – the careful capitals, the looping 's's – made her stomach feel warm, but the words cut at her insides.

Just leave me alone Shiv. Remember the deal.

She hasn't tried to contact him since. Sometimes she dreams about him, but he's always screaming at her. He's always leaving.

Siobhan lets herself into the main stairwell and makes her way up to the second floor. Stepping inside her mum's flat is always like going back in time: the twinkling sound of the bead curtain as it parts, the way the light falls across the hallway in the afternoon. She knows that in the bedroom down the hall, the one she shared with Theo, the faded Green Day and Sum 41 posters will still be Blu-Tacked to the walls, that inside the kitchen cupboards will be the same Nutella jars repurposed as water glasses, and that on the lounge bookcase there will be no books but rows and rows of *Dallas* VHS tapes, proudly displayed. Siobhan slips out of her trainers. She can hear Nora humming in the kitchen as something spits and crackles in a frying pan. She makes her way instead to the living room, where she's almost surprised to find Theo, surprised to find that he is, in fact, real, that he didn't disappear for good that day in the woods. He's curled up on the sofa watching an old episode of *The OC*, wearing a grey sweatshirt and black jeans. He's turned towards the TV and doesn't see her straight away, so she has a moment to observe him uninterrupted, to indulge in the details that have been forbidden to her for so long. At first glance, even though it's been four years, he looks no different: dark hair curly and unkempt, tortoiseshell glasses framing melancholy eyes, a long, slightly crooked nose she could draw in her sleep. His lean body is folded in half as he concentrates on the TV, back rounded and one arm looped around his knees. But the more she looks, the more she can see the subtle changes: the way he's filled out slightly around the shoulders, the silver watch around his wrist she never would have thought he'd like. He's twenty-seven now, she realises. He's gotten older. Maybe he's a different person entirely. He's acquired four years of memories and tiny bursts of happiness and aching lonely moments that she has no idea about, and maybe never will. Her throat feels tight and a small sound escapes her, making Theo turn towards the doorway. When he sees her, he straightens, eyes widening like she's a burglar. His feet swing from the sofa and onto the floor, as if he's considering making a run for it.

"Theo," Siobhan starts, but he's no longer looking at her.

"For fuck's sake, Mum," he shouts as he gets to his feet. "You promised you wouldn't do this."

"Just five minutes, Theo. Please." Siobhan hates how her voice sounds – there's a needling quality to it, the shrillness of desperation.

Theo pushes past her as though she isn't even there, out into the hallway. Siobhan watches him reach the kitchen in three strides. She hasn't seen him in this flat for so long and had forgotten how much space his tall body inhabits. The idea that the three of them lived here once, spending every day together, feels almost magical now. It feels like a fairytale childhood she's dreamed up.

She follows him silently into the kitchen. Nora stands at the stove, tending to sausages. When she sees Theo's expression, the way his face has drained of colour, she sighs and turns off the gas. Her dark hair is twisted into a bun on top of her head, thick kohl around her eyes. Siobhan has only seen her mum without make-up a handful of times and always hated how fragile it made her look, with her small eyes and pale lips. She much prefers her like this, brownish-red liner framing her cupid's bow, almost cartoonish. Brash, bold. She's wearing the apron Siobhan and Theo had bought her one Christmas, the characters from *Dallas* printed on the front.

"Hi, Shivvy," Nora says, ignoring Theo and giving Siobhan a light squeeze on the arm. Siobhan catches a whiff of her perfume – sweet vanilla, soft jasmine. "Thanks for coming."

"*Mum,*" Theo hisses, incredulous, one hand raking through his hair. "Are you serious? I've told you a thousand times. I do not want to speak to Siobhan."

"What about what I want?" Nora says. Her voice is level, calm. She has obviously prepared herself for the onset of this particular storm. "I want my two children to speak to each other. It's been long enough."

Theo splutters something incomprehensible and then seems to think better of even trying. He still won't look at Siobhan. "Whatever. I'll just go."

He stalks back down the hallway, and Siobhan hears the front door open. She reaches it just in time to catch him at the top of the main stairs.

"I've changed my mind," she tells him, breathless, lightheaded, desperate to delay him for even a couple of seconds. To keep looking at him just a little while longer. "I'm going to talk about it. All of it."

Her words are enough to make him pause, one foot on the first stair. There's a terseness to his face, which he turns sharply to one side, as if he's trying as hard as he can to ignore her. "What?" he growls eventually, hands white-knuckled around the banister.

"Someone reached out, about a documentary," Siobhan says. "I'm going to talk about Hex House."

Theo stares at her now. Siobhan can't quite meet his gaze – she didn't even know his face could look that unkind. One of his sleeves is rolled up, and she can see the scar from where she'd dared him to hold a lighter to his skin when they were little. Neither of them had known it would burn. "Why?" he says quietly. "Why now?"

Siobhan bites at the inside of her lip. "Haina is dead." She remembers Zara's email, the pointed way it closed. *I'll share more when we meet.* "Maybe you were right. When we left, we should have told someone. After Elly…"

"Stop it," Theo snaps. There's something simmering about him now, on the brink of tipping over.

"Theo, just listen to me…"

"Don't you dare talk about Elly."

"You didn't own her," Siobhan bites back. "She was my friend, too."

A long, heavy moment of silence. Siobhan can hear Nora moving around the flat and wonders what she's overheard. She's never told her mum anything about Hex House, and to the best of her knowledge, neither has Theo. That was part of the deal. *Mum can know nothing.*

"Don't pretend she was your friend," Theo growls. "Don't fucking do that."

"Just come over to mine," Siobhan says on an outbreath. She feels like all the energy has been squeezed out of her body; it's an effort to stay upright. She sags against the doorway. "We can talk about all of it. It's so stupid, not talking. I feel like you've *died* half the time."

Theo scoffs and rubs a hand over the shadow of stubble around his chin. "I haven't changed my mind," he says, and takes a few steps down the stairs. "I want nothing to do with you. But by all means, go and talk to some stranger about all of it now that Haina's dead and you're finally brave enough. You're only four years too late."

He descends the stairs out of sight, and Siobhan watches the blank space where he'd been standing. She hears the main door slam. Her blood is sluggish in her veins. She closes the door to the flat and retreats inside, finding Nora still in the kitchen. The hob has been switched back on and the whole room smells like grease and meat.

"Went well, did it?" Nora asks drily, poking the sausages back and forth.

Siobhan slumps down at the kitchen table, running her

hands over her face. She suddenly, fiercely, wants a drink. No, five. "I don't know what you expected," she grumbles. "He hates me. I tried to tell you."

"He doesn't hate you. You're his sister."

"I don't think that matters."

"I wish you'd just tell me what happened. I wish you'd help me understand. I feel like I'm breaking apart with the two of you not speaking."

Me too, Siobhan almost says, but stops herself at the last minute. Outside, the drizzle has turned into a downpour, droplets pelting insistently against the sash window. It's open a crack, and Siobhan gets up to close it.

"Leave it," Nora says, quiet but firm. Siobhan had almost forgotten. Nora always likes more than one escape route: an unlocked door, an open window. There's nothing to run from anymore, but of course, that makes no difference. Siobhan sits back down at the table. She watches the rain, thinking of Theo walking, head down, to the station, then boarding a train back to Glasgow. This very second, he's getting further and further away from her. For him, it's probably never far enough.

Nora puts a plated sausage sandwich in front of her. Siobhan's stomach turns.

"Eat it," Nora warns. "All of it. You look like a waif."

Nora sits down and they eat in a comfortable silence. The sausages are hot and salty but they taste like dust in Siobhan's mouth. In her head, she composes the text she'll send to Owen when she leaves.

Let's go for a drink.

You said I'm in control of this.

You can't say no.

"How's the cinema?" Nora asks.

Siobhan abandons her half-eaten sandwich. "Fine. The money's okay."

Nora nods. "And you've still got some savings?"

"Of course."

"Good. That's important. And you're not..." Nora trails off, biting her bottom lip, and Siobhan knows the exact conversation they're about to have. She could recite it word by word. It hangs all around them in the air, a cloying smoke closing in.

"I'm not drinking, Mum," says Siobhan.

"You know why I ask."

Siobhan feels a hot flare of fury, as much as she tries to stop it. "Yeah, well, don't. I'm nothing like him."

The words are loud and sharp. Nora flinches, eyes darting away. Siobhan hates that look, that flash of unbearable vulnerability; a fleeting glimpse of long-hidden scars. She hates being the cause of it even more. She gets up and goes to stand behind Nora. Leaning over, she rests her chin on the top of her mum's head and wraps both arms around her.

"I'm sorry," she whispers.

Nora clasps both of Siobhan's wrists, pulling her in tighter. They stay like that for a while, one body concertinaed over the other, listening to the starting and stopping of the rain.

Back home, Siobhan decides against texting Owen. She'd rather drink alone tonight. She takes a cold bottle of wine from the fridge and fills a pint glass, drinking half of it before she feels ready to open her laptop.

She restores Zara's email from the trash and reads it a couple more times. In the quiet and still of the flat, she lets herself wonder, really wonder, what it could possibly mean that Haina is dead, and what that would mean for Hex House. Haina *was* Hex House. She was the bricks and the mortar and the fire in the hearth. All of those women who idolised her – would they leave now, too? Where would they go?

Siobhan's head feels full and loud, as if there's a long-dead carcass inside being swarmed by flies. These kinds of images often appear to her when she's drunk: once-living things in various stages of decay. Festering flesh. Rot.

She's finished the full pint of wine before she starts typing a reply to Zara.

I need you to tell me who you've been speaking to and what happened to Haina. Then we can talk.

S

She fires off the email before she can talk herself out of it, then leans back like the air's been knocked out of her. After about an hour, Zara's response arrives.

Siobhan,

Thank you so much for getting back to me. I'm sure you're busy, so I really appreciate your time.

Sorry, I can't reveal my source, even if I wanted to. She signs her name 'Willow', but I know that's not her real name.

In her last letter, she told me Haina was very unwell for a very long time. Over the last few years, apparently more and more of the guests lost faith in her, and they left the house (she used the word 'escaped'), and it had a profound effect on her health. Willow seems to be tracing it all back to something that happened when you were still at the house. Hopefully you know what I mean, because honestly, I don't know what to make of it all.

Hesitant to put any more in an email at this stage – I can explain everything when we meet. How does Tuesday, 11:30 at Black Medicine Coffee sound? I'm just so excited that you'll consider talking to me.

Can I be frank? This is a huge story. I'll do it with or without you, but together, I really believe we can blow this whole fucking thing apart.

Let me know if you're in.

Zara x

Siobhan refills her glass from a fresh bottle of wine and shuts her email. She stares at the screen, vision beginning to blur.

Her fingertips are shaking on the touchpad as she finds the documents icon and navigates to the folder titled 'Hex House'.

She hasn't opened this file in four years, but tonight it's a magnet, its pull too strong. Her stomach churns as she skims the video clips inside, hundreds of them, ranging from a couple of seconds to a full hour-long. The thumbnails are too small to decipher details, but she can still make out the looming shape of Hex House in some, ivy creeping up its walls, and the faces of some of the women in others, their expressions frozen as they talk directly to the camera. Siobhan knows that in many of these clips will be Haina, staring down the lens like there's an enemy hidden in the machinery. There'll be Elly, clear-eyed and meek, one arm wrapped protectively around her belly. Siobhan opens the first clip in the list before she can stop herself.

It's the house, the first time she and Theo ever saw it. The camera glimpses it through a thicket of trees, the shot lingering over its warm honey stone, the heavy wooden door, the ornate windows. They were about to give up, Siobhan remembers. She and Theo had been searching the woods all morning and had half-convinced themselves it was all a hoax: the letter begging Siobhan to come, the cryptic directions that followed, all of it. But then a nearby tree had come crashing down and suddenly there it was, where it hadn't been before, an impossible structure in all that greenery.

"Theo."

Siobhan's breath catches like an animal in a trap when she hears her own voice on the film, just out of shot. Her blurry finger appears in the right of the frame, pointing to one of the windows. "Quick, zoom in." She can hear the feverish excitement in her voice. It makes her queasy.

The camera obeys, finding the second window from the left on the bottom floor of the house. Behind the glass is a pale face that hardly looks like a face at all. In the place of a mouth is something long and distended, and there's a mottled coating over the skin, dark, textured. From behind the lens, Theo whispers, "*Fuck*." In the next second, the face disappears, leaving only the black mouth of the window. The clip ends abruptly.

Siobhan slams the laptop shut. Her cheeks are wet, and there's an awful feeling in her gut: a stirring, a revolt. She barely makes it to the bathroom before she vomits, clutching at the toilet bowl as her stomach scrapes itself clean. Her eyes are screwed shut as she slowly gets her breath back, the regurgitated wine bitter on her tongue. She already knows she'll dream of it tonight: that face in the window, pale and strange. Maybe in her dreams at least, she'll turn around. She won't go inside.

If she could have that moment again, she'd tell Theo to drop the camera. She'd tell him to run.

ELLY

THEN

Since she tried to leave the house, Elly has lived in a constant state of numbness, of liminality. She feels as though she's trapped inside the walls of Hex House, but at the same time, she no longer has any desire to escape them. It feels almost like inhabiting a body that's unwell. Uncomfortable, but inevitable, like there's simply nothing to be done.

The events that took place in Haina's study – the grotesque transformation of her hands, the impossible becoming possible in one snatch of breath – seem softer and more palatable as the days go on. The urgent fear becomes replaced by a sort of enquiring, the stirrings of curiosity. What happened is no less strange, after all, than a sanctuary in the woods that no one can find unless they need it. She lies awake in the dormitory at night, listening to the women murmuring in their sleep, staring at the branches just visible from the window, and thinks about what Haina told her: that she'd seen the first glimpse of her hex, of her true potential. She compiles a list of questions to ask Haina over breakfast, or when she sees her around the house, but the opportunity never seems to present itself. Haina is always in conversation with another guest, walking quickly somewhere with an espresso cup in her hand, a blur of orange linen, or locked behind the door of her study. Elly is surprised to find that she is looking forward to her next session. She prickles with the idea of it, but as much as she watches the goosebumps speckling her forearms, the skin there never changes.

Grace furrows her eyebrows when Elly asks her one morning in the kitchen what it all means. Whether the transformation could possibly be real, or whether it's only in her head. She looks at Elly as if she should know better than to ask, setting down the knife she's using to remove the head from a fish. "For god's sake, why do you think we're all here?" She wipes her hands down her apron, leaving wet, pinkish streaks. "You're not special. Just get on with it."

"But why does it happen?" Elly can't help but ask. "Are we still... *us*?"

Grace looks at her plainly. Her eyes are set deep in her face but still manage to look fiercely blue in every light. "I am sixty-two years old, Elly," she says, "I have been at this house for four years. I have never felt more like myself in all my life."

She refuses to answer any more questions and shoos Elly away to make the stock for the lunchtime soup. When Elly asks Keiko, she just shrugs and looks down into the flour she's spread out on the countertops, glossy black hair covering her face. She puts her forefinger into the flour and starts to drag it around, forming a rough shape. Elly watches, a hard lump in her throat, as the shape clarifies itself into the pointed tips of wings.

"You ask too many questions, Little Mouse," Margot tells her one night at the dinner table. She chews on a piece of liver and pulls out a knob of gristle from between her teeth. "Trust yourself. Trust Haina."

Elly *wants* to trust Haina. She wants this wise, confident woman to be the answer to everything, to fix it for her, to help her save herself. She just doesn't know what that looks like yet. She doesn't know what she might have the potential to become if she stays here, and the thought makes her feel almost dangerously buoyant, as though the slightest gust of wind might carry her far, far away.

The first time Elly hears the filmmakers' voices, she's in the kitchen, sifting flour into a bowl to make shortcrust pastry. It falls like snow from the sieve. It's hot in the kitchen and she sweats under her apron, but the work gives her purpose, keeps her thoughts from straying too far. As long as she's in the kitchen, being useful, nothing can be too strange or wrong. Her pelvis aches as she works. Every day it's as though there's less space for her to exist inside her own body. The baby is pushing her stomach up into her chest, forcing her hips outwards. The kicks are getting more frequent, and sometimes they're so strong they take her breath away. She finds herself wondering if the baby can break her ribs, shatter her pelvis, break her from the inside out. It would be worth it, she reasons, if the baby would survive. She'd give up her body a hundred times for that. These are new thoughts. As the baby becomes bigger, it becomes more real. *I am more of a mother every day*, she thinks to herself. *Somehow, I have to make myself worthy of this life inside me.* She's concentrating hard and so is barely aware of the front door clicking open, of Haina saying something in her low timbre as she approaches down the hallway, getting louder.

It's the man's voice that gets her attention, makes her freeze. Every part of her is on alert. "We saw something when we were outside," he says. His voice is young, cloaked in a soft Scottish accent. He sounds polite but there's a wariness there, too, some grit mixed into the silt, textured as a coastline. Elly senses the other women's bodies stiffen at the sound. She can hear their thoughts buzzing in the air, a sudden swarm. *A man a man a man.* Perhaps it has been years since they last heard a man speak. "Some kind of... animal? In one of the windows?"

The hairs on Elly's forearms rise, like they've been summoned by electricity. *Some kind of animal.* She doesn't hear Haina's reply, only the tone of it, and it's a tone she's never heard her use before: light, breezy, almost coquettish. Then they appear in the open kitchen doorway: Haina first, leading the way, followed by the man – lean, boyish, a bulky camera propped on his shoulder. Behind them is a tall, skinny woman with messy hair and keen eyes that cast all around as though everything she can see belongs to her. They pause by the doorframe and Haina says, "These are our kitchens. You'll meet our guests later. For now, let's continue your tour."

The man peers briefly inside, his eyes landing on Elly's

for half a second. She doesn't look away. Then the three of them are gone again, heading back down the hall.

Grace is motionless, staring at the now-empty doorway. It is one of the only times Elly has seen her still, not busying her hands with a task. Keiko pauses with her knife poised above a scarlet tomato. The blade shakes slightly.

"The filmmakers," Elly hears herself whisper. No one replies. Grace gives her a stern look, as if she's broken a rule by stating the fact out loud, then returns to her chopping board.

Into the silence comes the woman's voice from further down the hall, louder than the man's, more confident. "Fuck," she says. "This place is like stepping back in time. Theo, are you getting all this?"

They hear the door to the gardens open, close. The house is quiet again. Something has already changed, Elly can tell. Some delicate balance is being recalibrated with every second that passes.

The filmmakers are seated in the refectory when the rest of the guests enter for dinner that evening. They sit at the head of the table, flanking Haina. The light outside the windows is waning. Someone has lit all the candles, and their reflections dance in the windowpanes. Elly, Grace and Keiko spent the afternoon preparing rich beef pies, the joint cooked long and slow so the meat was falling off the bone. They bring them to the table now in heavy cast-iron pots, serve them alongside fresh bread and tiny potatoes swimming in butter.

The women keep their distance from the filmmakers,

and the refectory feels much quieter than normal. There's only the clearing of throats, the scraping of chairs along the wooden floor. Elly sits beside Margot at the opposite end of the table to the newcomers, taking in their details with surreptitious glances. The woman seems the younger of the two, but perhaps only by a couple of years. She looks to be in her early twenties, likely around Elly's own age. She and the man have the same olive skin and dark eyes, the same sharp, watchful features. The man wears glasses and rounds his shoulders in his seat, as if he's trying to make himself smaller. Perhaps he feels all their eyes on him, hears the thoughts the women don't need to speak.

You are a man. What are you doing here?

The camera sits on the table in front of him, vaguely threatening, like a dog no one is quite sure won't bite. The woman seems less self-conscious, or just less aware, of the atmosphere in the room. She engages in fluid conversation with Haina, her voice a little too loud. She meets the eyes of the women as they enter, not smiling exactly, but something close to it. Every now and again, she says something to the man, and he responds by nodding and jotting something down in his notebook. To Elly, she looks like the kind of person who would think nothing of cutting into a queue; the kind of person who would be able to talk herself out of any resulting reprimand.

No one touches the food. When everyone has taken their seats, Haina gets to her feet, clasping her hands in front of her heart in the way she does before she addresses the group.

"My angels," she says. There's a warm, unspooling sensation in Elly's stomach whenever Haina calls them that. *My angels*. At first it had felt jarring, but now it makes her feel as though she is part of something. "Let me introduce Siobhan and Theo. They'll be spending the next few months with us to make their film."

"Documentary," the woman named Siobhan corrects her. Margot scoffs. Elly's pulse stutters. She has never heard anyone correct Haina.

Haina's wide smile doesn't change. "Documentary," she repeats. "They're as eager as we are to demonstrate what a sanctuary Hex House is from the rest of the world. Please make them feel very welcome while they get settled over the next few days." She looks down at the filmmakers. Her hand lands on Theo's shoulder and he flinches slightly. "Is there anything either of you would like to say?"

Theo pushes his glasses up the bridge of his nose, his small smile like an apology. His gaze skips over the cooling bowls of food as he says, "Just pretend we're not here. Don't feel any pressure to act in a certain way. We want to capture things as they are."

"Be authentic, natural," adds Siobhan, nodding. "Also, we're looking for a couple of volunteers who wouldn't mind doing some to-camera interviews – simple stuff, what brought you here, what you think about the house."

Elly feels some of the women around her bristle. *Simple stuff*. She doesn't know many details of the women's stories, but she doubts anyone around this table would define what brought them to Hex House as *simple*, or would feel comfortable unravelling it all in front of the camera and examining the threads.

"Excellent," Haina says, clapping her hands together. "Let's eat."

The table rumbles into hesitant action and slowly, chatter starts up. Elly helps herself to a slice of pie. A skin of grease has formed over the top of the potatoes while they've been sitting. Her eyes return to the head of the table. Siobhan whispers something to Theo, then elbows him in the ribs. He pushes her gently and she laughs, her mouth wide open, full of food. There is an easiness to both of them, to the way they interact, that gives away the invisible stitching of family. Something about it makes Elly's stomach ache. Haina speaks more to Theo than she does to Siobhan, pressing into him and giggling, squeezing the top of his arm.

"It's been so long since we've had a man in the house," she hears Haina say at one point. "It's been such a long time."

Theo smiles uncertainly, leaning away.

"Don't like this," mumbles Margot beside her. Her plate is empty.

"It'll be alright, Margot," says Elly. "You don't have to speak to them. Pretend they're not here, like he said."

Margot says nothing. Her fingers are splayed and running up and down the length of her thighs, making ripples in the faded blue denim.

"Come on, you should eat something." Elly piles some vegetables onto her plate, but Margot doesn't touch them. Throughout dinner, she ignores Elly's attempts at conversation and mutters to herself under her breath, barely looking up. Elly can only pick out the odd phrase.

"Not safe here anymore, Little Mouse," she says. "Not safe."

112

For a couple of days, no one really speaks to the filmmakers. Life at Hex House unfurls in its familiar routine – breakfast, chores, lunch, downtime, dinner, evening in the parlour, and eventually, bedtime. Sometimes, while Elly is working in the kitchen, baking loaves and laminating pastry for croissants and carving endless joints of meat, she forgets all about them. They sleep separately to the rest of the guests, in an attic room overlooking the garden. But then she'll catch a glimpse of one or both of them, cameras pointing at faces from a distance, drinking up the house's secret details, committing it all to tape. It's strange, the things they deem important enough to film: a butterfly landing on the upturned face of a coneflower, the red sisters scrubbing the hallway floors, singing to each other, the messy covers of the just-vacated beds in the dormitory. Sometimes, Elly notices Siobhan alone, no camera in hand, just observing. Perhaps she means to be inconspicuous, but her height and the confident way she moves mean she always draws attention. Watching her, Elly feels like the interloper. Theo is more stealthy, more able to slip by unnoticed. Sometimes, she won't even realise he's in the room until she hears the soft bleep of a camera as it stops recording, and when he meets her eye it's with a sheepishness, a wordless apology. Will her mum ever see this footage? she finds herself wondering. Will Ethan? Will they glimpse her in the background, jump forward, pause the TV? At least then, she reasons, they'll know she's okay. That she left them, but she's okay.

The signs of acceptance come slowly, subtly. Elly notices Janine smile at Theo when he walks past her one afternoon in the hallway, rubbing a hand shyly over her

113

shorn head once he's gone. Over breakfast one morning, Lakshmi passes Siobhan a bowl of porridge. Margot is still fractious, but at night she whimpers in her sleep, rather than screams.

On the morning of Elly's second session with Haina, she finds herself fidgety at breakfast, barely able to touch her food. She pulled a grey Harvard sweatshirt out of the communal clothing bin this morning and now it feels too heavy and too tight, straining over her swelling stomach. She's been waiting for this, for the opportunity to be in a room alone with Haina again, to ask questions, to begin to understand. But now she only feels a creeping sense of dread, a fear that makes tea taste bitter in her mouth. She looks down at her fingers wrapped around her mug. Her gold wedding ring catches the light. Last night, she'd tried to remove it, only to find her pregnant fingers too swollen. It feels now like a tiny manacle, slowly cutting off her blood supply.

As the guests start to leave the refectory for chores, Haina gets up from the table. She lays a heavy hand on Elly's shoulder as she passes, giving her a silent nod. Elly's skin tingles at the point of contact. She takes a deep breath, then follows Haina down the hallway and into the study.

When the door is locked behind them and Elly is seated once more on the velvet armchair, running her hands the wrong way along its surface, Haina says, "One moment." She's writing some notes on her pad, seemingly in no rush. Outside the window, birds trill in the bushes and the women's chatter is a low hum as they prune, plant and water. Elly can hear Margot, squealing over the colour of a dahlia. After a minute or two, Haina turns to Elly and says, "I imagine you have some questions about what happened in our last session?"

Elly almost laughs. *Some questions.* "I've been struggling to understand..." she says eventually, "what happened to me. What it means."

Haina's expression doesn't change. "What do you think happened to you? What did it feel like?"

Shifting. Shedding. Body getting lighter and thoughts quieter, a feeling pure and hot in her veins. "I don't know. I felt... annoyed, I think." *Annoyed at* you, she almost adds. *At the way you spoke to me like I was nothing.*

Haina smiles. "I think you were more than annoyed. I think you were angry."

Elly shifts in her seat. "Maybe."

"Do you often get angry, my angel?"

"In what way?"

"Well, in any way. In your day-to-day life, do you tend to feel angry? Or does that seem like something you're not allowed to feel?"

Elly bites at her nail. Anger doesn't feel like something that's particularly relevant to her. In an argument, she's much more likely to cry than to shout. If she had ever become angry with Ethan, in the way that he did with her, so often and so effortlessly, what would have happened? The thought makes her shrink into herself, back pressing into the armchair. "I don't know how to answer that," she says. "I'm sorry."

"Why are you sorry?"

"Because I don't think I'm doing this right."

Haina pauses, then braces both hands on her knees, leaning forward towards Elly. "You're doing it perfectly. Last time, I tapped into your anger to get you to respond.

And do you know something? It takes most guests two, three, even four sessions for their hex to start to appear. Yours appeared in your first session. Do you know what that tells me?"

Elly shakes her head.

"That you're a lot angrier than you think you are, Elly." Haina says this with such conviction that it makes the hairs on Elly's arms stand on end. "I think anger sits right under your skin. I didn't have to go deep to find the seam, and that seam is rich. It's fruitful. We can work with it."

Elly swallows. Her throat is itchy, dry. *Is* she angry? She searches for the feeling within her body, chasing it through her veins, trying to pin it down. She doesn't find it but becomes aware instead of a pressure – a vibration that, now she thinks about it, is constant, a thing that's with her always. It gets louder when she thinks about her dad dying. It's almost deafening when she thinks about Ethan and their wedding day, the softness of his voice as he told her to *stay*. If she concentrates, she can feel the expression on her own face changing, her jaw setting, her body sitting up straight. There's a new clarity to her vision.

"We can use that anger," Haina is saying now. She stares squarely at Elly, eyes burning, and Elly forces herself not to look away. "It's not a bad thing. It's not an ugly thing. It can be beautiful, if you let it."

Elly bites at her inner lip. There's a sore there that she's been agitating for days now, feeling it get bigger and more swollen. The room is quiet, bar the fire and the soft ticking of the grandfather clock in the corner. She risks a glance down at her hands, which are still her own. "Can everyone in the house change in the same way as me?"

Haina nods, but she looks disappointed by the question, as if she'd been expecting Elly to say something else, something more interesting. "Well, their own version of it, anyway. Everyone's hex is slightly different."

"And when they eventually leave the house, do they... stay that way?" She remembers the woman in the bathroom at her wedding, the way she'd seemed almost supernaturally graceful. "Can they always change into their... hex?"

Haina shakes her head. "No, not usually. It's the house that gives them the power to do so. By the time they leave, they don't need their hex anymore, and they don't often feel the need to speak of it. You'll understand all that soon enough." Haina smiles and Elly's pulse flutters. She senses layers of meaning underneath the words that she can't begin to guess at yet. "There are some that carry the house with them. They choose to stay part of our flock, to help us, and so they can always find the house. And, yes, there have been very, very few who choose to stay in their hex form always. When there's nothing else left for them otherwise." She pauses, as if wondering whether to go on. Whatever she finds in Elly's face seems to give her permission. "There was Violet. A long time ago now. I shouldn't have favourites, my angel, and really I don't. But some of my guests are very special. Violet's hex was..." She trails off, looking at the sky out of the window. "She was spectacular. There was just no question she would stay that way."

Elly wants to ask more questions about that, but Haina has closed the journal on her desk, seemingly ready to move on. "Shall we see if we can wake yours up again today?"

Elly thinks about saying no. Every instinct insists that she should. The word is hanging from her lips. She could shut the door on whatever unknown thing has started to lurk at the edges of her consciousness, its shape unseen and unknowable, that hot feeling in her veins Haina has told her is anger. It's so tempting to stay on the path, not to stray into these particular woods, to tell herself that she hasn't a hope of surviving if she did. When she really thinks about it, she knows this is the thing she's afraid of, the thing that keeps her small: the belief that she is somehow weaker, less adequate than everyone else. Since she can remember, she's felt as though she's missing some key component, some internal scaffolding that makes things just a little bit simpler for other people, helps them move through the world with a fraction more ease. That suspicion makes it easy to think that to be controlled is to be taken care of, and to be taken care of is what someone like her needs. That she's too inept to survive without it.

She could stay on that path. Or she could choose to tip forward and fall wildly into whatever *this* is, into whatever Haina is offering her, into whatever forced itself upwards and outwards from her skin the last time she was sitting in this study. She could choose to keep going through the woods, and into the dark.

"What do we need to do?" Elly asks quietly.

If Haina is pleased with her response, she doesn't show it. She smooths out a wrinkle in her linen dress, which is the colour of terracotta tiles. It sits above strong-looking knees pockmarked with scars. She clasps her hands together and lays them in her lap, formal.

"How do you feel about pain?" she asks eventually.

Elly blinks. "Pain?"

"When you're in pain, where does your mind go?"

"I... I'm not sure."

Haina nods, her mouth an unreadable line. "I think we should find out."

She reaches down, turns the key in the desk, then slides out a drawer and pulls out a knife. It is unremarkable, with a worn plastic handle, but the blade looks sharp. The metal catches the light when Haina places it in her lap. Elly doesn't take her eyes from it, even as Haina starts to speak.

"When we're in pain," she's saying, softly now, cautious, as if trying to coax a frightened animal into movement, "we can respond in one of two ways. We can let the fear take over, retreat inward to protect ourselves. Try and find the fastest way to get the pain to stop."

Elly watches as Haina picks up the knife and lifts the hem of her dress so that it reveals an inch of golden thigh. Without hesitation, she places the edge against the skin there, presses down hard, and drags it cleanly across. Blood rises quickly to the site of the cut, keen and hot.

"What are you..." Elly starts to say, but Haina holds up a hand to silence her.

Watching the cut, watching it redden and start to ooze, Elly's mouth goes dry. Suddenly, she doesn't want to be in the same room as Haina, someone who uses a knife as softly as they'd use a feather. It makes everything feel unsafe, uneven, in flux. Still, she forces herself to stay in the chair, to watch. Haina's chest is rising and falling more rapidly now, and there is a dampness spreading out from under her armpits, staining the linen. Her rich complexion is drained of colour.

"If we respond to pain like this, with fear, then we respond with weakness," she says, and her voice is hitching and high, like Elly has never heard it before. Her wound is bleeding quickly in response to her increased heart rate. "If someone hurts us and we're afraid, then we've already lost, my angel. They own your fear. They own *you*. But if we respond to pain in a different way, if we replace that fear with anger, well," her eyes sparkle, a smile on her lips, "we can get an altogether different result."

Elly watches as Haina's breathing begins to slow, to resume its steady rhythm. Her eyes lose their wideness, so the whites are no longer as visible, just the cool, steely black. There's an energy in the room: cold, still. When the flesh of Haina's forearms starts to quiver and rupture, Elly finds that she isn't, in fact, afraid. She's barely even surprised.

Yes, she finds herself thinking instead. *Yes, show me.*

The skin on Haina's arms begins to break apart, creating hundreds of tiny holes. From inside each one sprouts something dark and soft. Once free of the boundary of Haina's skin, the buds elongate into feathers, long and silken, the colour of amber. Every time Haina breathes, they bristle, like each one is filled with a thousand nerve endings, like each one is linked to her heartbeat by intricate and ancient wiring. The room smells like the deepest part of the forest, mulch and rot and carrion. Elly looks at the cut on Haina's leg, which is barely more than a red line now, hardly bleeding. It isn't possible, but she almost thinks that it's healing, stitching itself back together.

When Haina speaks again, her voice is a sheet of ice. "Do you see? Do you understand?"

Elly nods. Haina grins. The immediacy and intensity of that grin makes Elly breathless. Haina's arms are changing again now, the feathers retreating underneath her skin, the animal smell fading, everything resuming its usual form and shape. Haina cracks her neck from one side to the next, then blinks a few times, rapidly, as though she's almost surprised to find herself in her study. She picks up the knife again. This time, she grips the blade in her fist and holds the handle out to Elly.

"Your turn," she whispers.

Fifteen minutes later, Elly emerges from the study. Her muscles don't feel like her own – they're too loose, barely contained by her skin. Standing on the other side of the closed door, she runs her fingertips over her wrists, remembering how they had looked just minutes ago: sleek, avian. It had felt so different from the first time. She'd still been afraid when she saw herself changing, had still felt as though she'd somehow fallen outside of the natural way of things. But this time, she'd felt something else, too. A lack of resistance. She'd felt able to push open the door a crack, and to welcome it in – a thin trickle of fury.

I'm so angry, Elly had whispered, and Haina had said back, *Good, my angel. You should be.*

There is a white bandage wound around the crook of her right elbow. The blood is blooming through. Elly is so busy studying the pattern it makes, like the tiny handprint of a newborn, that she doesn't realise she isn't alone in the hallway. It isn't until she hears a quiet beep, so incongruous in the quiet of the shady hall, that she looks up to see Theo standing over by the staircase. He is holding a small camera in one hand, held up to his face, pointed in her direction. Elly looks directly into the black eye of the lens, into the nothingness there, and then at the single eye of his that she can see. It is wide and green and questioning. He doesn't lower the camera. She doesn't look away. The feeling of being watched, of being recorded – the idea that this image of her is being preserved and that it might be watched in a different time, in a different life, makes her skin tingle all over. It isn't an unpleasant feeling. She *wants* to be seen like this, she realises. She no longer cares who might see her. She simply wants to be witnessed in this rare moment of strength.

Elly looks back into the lens as she slowly unwraps the bandage from her elbow. It falls away, reveals the wound underneath, already smaller than it was in the study. Theo takes a step closer to her and then adjusts a dial on the side of the camera. It makes a whirring sound as it zooms in. Elly stands still, offering up her bloodied skin. She feels fiercely seen, acknowledged. Neither of them speak. She can hear Theo breathing, the quickness of it, the slight hitch. Elly fights it, the sudden urge she has to remove the rest of her clothing, too, piece by piece – to let his camera drink her in for what she is. After a moment, she rewraps her arm and walks away from him. There's a beep, soft as a sigh, as the recording stops.

SIOBHAN

NOW

On Tuesday morning, Siobhan enters the hubbub of Black Medicine Coffee and orders a double espresso. The café is dark and atmospheric, all exposed stone walls and intricately carved wooden furniture. It's close to the university campus and popular with students, so there's only a tiny table left in the corner when Siobhan arrives. She grabs it, glad for the view of the door. She's arrived early for this very reason – so that she can watch Zara enter and not the other way around. This meeting is all she's been able to think about for the last few days, working the box office with Sylvie and wandering the aisles of Tesco, trying to buy something other than wine. She's talked herself in and out of attending more times than she can count.

It's just a conversation, she reminds herself now, sipping at her espresso, grateful for its heat and unapologetic strength, the way it assaults her tastebuds. She's only here to find out what she can about Haina. It doesn't have to be anything more than that, not if she doesn't want it to be.

When a young woman comes into the coffee shop wearing an orange beanie, Siobhan slumps down further in her seat. *I'll be wearing an orange hat*, Zara had told her in her last email. *Besides, you can't really miss me.*

Siobhan knows now what she meant. Almost every visible inch of Zara's skin is covered in tattoos: snakes coiled around both wrists, a spiderweb across her collarbone. Her hair is dyed a deep, artificial red and piercings glisten in her eyebrows, nose, lips. She's short, curvy, with a presence that demands attention. From her place in the queue, Zara scans the room. Siobhan wills herself invisible and Zara appears not to see her, or know what she looks like, so she's granted a couple of extra minutes to observe. Zara smiles at a baby gurgling at her, widening her eyes and sticking out her tongue. She checks a smart watch on her wrist, frowning before her face becomes neutral again. At the till, she orders something with a long name, extra hot, leaves a tip in the jar. When she's collected her drink, she stands at the front of the coffee shop and looks around again, no sign of nerves or discomfort in her face, just anticipation. Reluctantly, Siobhan raises a hand to wave her over. Zara's face breaks into a smile so warm and genuine that Siobhan feels momentarily wrongfooted. She can't imagine ever being that pleased to see anyone, let alone someone she'd never met.

"Great to meet you, Siobhan," Zara says, approaching the table and offering out her hand to shake. She has a strong Yorkshire accent. Siobhan's gaze snags on a tattoo just below her thumbnail: a staring eye. She takes Zara's hand, feeling ridiculous and overly formal. Zara sits down and removes her jacket, revealing a bright yellow halter-neck beneath a heap of layered necklaces. It's cool in the coffee shop, and she obviously isn't wearing a bra, but Zara doesn't seem to notice or care about the way her nipples strain against the fabric.

"Thanks so much for meeting me," Zara is saying. "Everyone at SunWolf is really excited. Did you have to come far?"

"No," Siobhan says. She thinks about offering more information, then decides against it. She's feeling surly. She holds the power here and she's keen now to wield it, to make things difficult. Zara's smile doesn't fade. She takes a long sip of her coffee and leans back in her chair. She doesn't seem in any rush. Under the table, her legs are spread out wide. She takes up space without apology, seemingly at ease with the moment and whatever it might contain. Siobhan thinks she was probably like that once, too.

"How did you find your source?" she asks Zara. "And how did you get my email address?"

"Oh yeah, sorry," Zara says, laughing. It makes her look younger and Siobhan briefly wonders how old she is. Twenty-eight, maybe thirty. "I probably should have explained that. Let me give you a bit of background to the whole thing. I don't know if you've heard about the HexHeads?"

"The *what*?"

"It started out as an internet forum, really, but it's a whole community now. Hex House conspiracy theorists. Mega fans."

"Mega fans," Siobhan repeats flatly.

"People who really, *really*, want the house to be real. They post supposed 'sightings', blurry pictures of faces between trees. A few say they know someone who's been, friend of a friend, cousin's best friend's dog, you get the gist. They arrange meet-ups in the woods down in the Borders to hunt for the house, share links to any new rumours, that sort of thing. There's even a HexHeads podcast. It's pretty popular."

"That's fucking weird," Siobhan says, draining her espresso.

"Yeah, I guess it is a bit." Zara laughs again – she's so quick to laugh, Siobhan thinks – and shrugs. "Anyway. I'm a total HexHead." She must sense Siobhan's hostility, because she rolls her eyes in a way that somehow manages to be both self-deprecating and dismissive. "Some of them are real nut-jobs, let me tell you. But we're all allowed our obsessions, right? And a sanctuary for women in the wilderness that no one can find? Come *on*. Ever since I heard of it, I knew there was a story there, that there was so much more to it than some Atlantis-style conspiracy theory. I pitched it to SunWolf last year." A brief pause. "I'm so glad that they've been receptive to the idea, that they saw the potential in it."

Siobhan imagines Zara sitting with a bunch of other beautiful young people – and perhaps a few stern-faced, older men – talking about how much money Hex House might make for them. *You think you know what you're getting into*, she almost says out loud, *but you have no idea*.

"A couple of months ago, things were drying up a bit. We were in the early research phases but not really getting anywhere. I had no idea about you or your documentary, and I didn't have any sources. All my leads came to nothing.

But then someone reached out to me. Willow. Via *post* of all things." Zara laughs into her drink, shrugging. There's something slightly forced about her nonchalance. "Apparently, she's still inside the house. Using some kind of network to get the letters out."

Siobhan's breath catches in her throat. She bites down on the inside of her cheek, hard.

"People have pretended to be at the house before, obviously, on the HexHeads forum," Zara is saying, "but their posts were usually pretty transparent: hyperbolic, vague on the details. Plus, I doubt Hex House is the kind of place with a high-speed internet connection, you know? Willow's letters are just... *different*. She's so specific. She writes about what the women eat, what they wear, what they do all day. It's bizarre. She's never included an address, so I can't write back, but she just keeps on sending them. So much information, so much detail. It doesn't feel feasible that she could make it all up. Whatever Hex House is, I feel like she could really be there." Zara's speaking quickly, her voice high and excited. "She told me all about Haina." Zara pauses. "And all about you."

Siobhan stares down into her espresso mug. She feels suddenly warm, and regrets the old fleece she'd shrugged on this morning.

"It wasn't hard to find out more about you, and your email address, once I had your name," says Zara. "You should probably tighten up your internet security a bit. There are weirdos out there, you know."

"You don't say."

Zara gives her a wry smile. "Touché. Anyway. From what Willow has told me, I think Hex House is so much more than some cult in the woods." Her smile fades. "I think it's the place where missing girls go."

Siobhan holds her gaze, fighting the instinct to bolt.

Zara leans over the table, and Siobhan can smell coffee on her breath. "Were you really there, Siobhan? At the house? Is it actually real?"

Siobhan wishes she could give any other answer but the truth. She wishes she were nothing but a HexHead, obsessed with the idea of escape. She doesn't answer Zara's question. Instead, she says, "What does Willow want? Why is she writing to *you*, telling you all this?"

Siobhan doesn't miss the way Zara's expression alters, darkening slightly before she recovers. Eventually, she says, "Now that Haina's gone, I think she's tired of keeping all the house's secrets."

Siobhan's mouth is dry. When she swallows, it's as though there are stones in her throat. The house's secrets have been drowning her since the day she left.

"She told me that you recorded loads of footage when you were at the house," Zara is saying, her tone light, expectant. "Is that true? You've got evidence it exists?"

"I'm not just going to hand it all over to you," Siobhan snaps, "if that's what this is about."

Zara shakes her head, one hand landing softly in the middle of the table as if she'd been about to reach for Siobhan's, then thought better of it. "Of course not. I just want us to work together, is all." Zara takes a long sip of her drink, the mug knocking against her lip piercing, a delicate clinking sound. "I just want to know what you saw. I bet it was some wild shit."

Wild shit, thinks Siobhan. *That's one way to put it.*

Zara is older than Siobhan, but all she can think is, *You child. You have no idea.* She wishes she were alone so she could pick at the scar on her abdomen, rip open the barely healed skin.

Zara casts a glance over her shoulder, then lowers her voice. "Willow also mentioned a girl called Elly Carmichael." Siobhan feels everything inside of her still. "She said something awful happened to her when you were at the house, and that's why you left. She said you might have… proof."

Siobhan blinks. It's as though the world is tilting. The rest of the coffee shop – its warm lights, its safe noise – seems to fall away, as if it had only ever been an illusion in the first place. It's no longer Zara sitting opposite her, but Elly – Elly pregnant, young, almost unbearably fragile. When she blinks again, Elly disappears.

"Are you alright, Siobhan? You look a bit pale."

"I'm fine."

"We don't have to…"

"I'm sorry," Siobhan murmurs, stumbling to her feet and sending her chair clattering to the floor. A few heads turn in her direction, frowning. "I can't do this. I thought I could, but I can't."

Zara stands, too. "Siobhan, wait…"

But Siobhan is already making her way out of the coffee shop, she's already at the door, she's already out in the cold air. She breaks into a half-jog without looking back, not wanting to give Zara a chance to catch up with her.

A wild wind has picked up and it fights against her as she makes her way over North Bridge, into the tangles of people walking down Princes Street. Every face she passes is so blank, so unknowing. She wants to pry open each mouth and make them swallow her secrets, so she no longer has to carry them all. She wants to smash open their skulls and examine the contents; to remember what it would feel like to not know.

When she gets to the Showroom, she changes into her black slacks and burgundy polo in the toilets. The face in the mirror stares back at her, blank and pale. There's a smudge near her chin that she rubs at unsuccessfully. When was the last time she had a shower? She forces herself to take a deep breath then leaves the toilets and sidles into the box office booth next to Sylvie. Today, Sylvie's curls are slicked back, and she's wearing magenta lip gloss. She looks poised, regal. Siobhan wants to reach out and touch her little finger to the surface of her lips, just to disrupt the perfect lacquer. Sylvie frowns at her and checks her watch.

"You're early," she says.

Siobhan shrugs. "I'm early all the time."

"No, you're not. You've literally never been early. Keith gave you a disciplinary last month for lateness."

"Maybe I've turned over a new leaf."

Sylvie rolls her eyes and returns to her phone. The cinema is quiet. The Horror Film Festival ended last week, and now they're back to regular showings, booming action films with next to no dialogue, swooning rom-coms starring ageing film stars from the 90s. Siobhan feels edgy, her body thrumming with excess energy. Keith passes by the box office holding a dustpan and brush. His hair is gelled up into improbable spikes, a spray of stubble across his weak chin. He gives Siobhan a surprised nod.

"You won't get paid for the extra hour, you know,"

he says. He turns to Sylvie. "Had some really great customer feedback about you, Sylvie. *Kind and personable*." He gives her a beatific grin. "I'd have to agree."

"Thanks, Keith."

Sylvie waits until Keith has moved on before whispering, "*Fuck*, he's weird. I cannot wait to get out of this place."

"You're leaving?" asks Siobhan.

Sylvie rolls her eyes. "Hopefully. Applied for a job at SunWolf, just waiting to hear back." She eyes Keith, checking his hair in the mirrored bar, and shudders.

Siobhan pulls at a loose thread on her polo, staring at Sylvie's perfect lips. The hollowness in her belly starts to yawn wider. She'd been desperate to work at SunWolf once, too. Before that letter from Haina, before Hex House. *It can only be you, Siobhan. Would you like to come inside?* If she had never opened that letter, would she be working at SunWolf now? Probably. Would she have immaculately made-up lips and own an Apple Watch and drink green smoothies instead of endless bottles of wine? Would she hate herself any less? It's possible. She thinks about the offer in Zara's original email. *I just wanted to touch base and see how you'd feel about working together on this, or even coming on as co-director.*

"Good luck," she manages to say. "I'm sure you'll get it."

Sylvie either doesn't notice the way Siobhan's voice is as limp as a balloon with all the air let out, or maybe she doesn't care. A customer approaches the box office and Sylvie turns to serve them. Under the desk, Siobhan digs her nails deep into her scar. She presses and presses until she feels the release of blood.

At the end of her shift, Siobhan turns left instead of right, heading into the quiet of the New Town. It's almost 9 p.m. and the streets are already deserted, like a film set that's closed for the night. She's at Owen's door before she can even think to text him and check he's in. She rings the buzzer once. Twice.

His voice crackles over the intercom half a minute later. "Hello?" He sounds slow, sleepy.

"It's me."

A long pause. "Siobhan?"

She says nothing. The buzzer sounds to let her inside.

He's waiting for her at the open door again. His hair is wet and he's still pulling on a grey T-shirt when she gets to the top of the stairs. She glimpses a slice of his torso before it's covered up by the fabric: tanned, a long line of dark hair, the beginnings of a paunch just beginning to show.

"Sorry," he says, self-consciousness emanating from him along with the smell of something fresh and citrussy. "I was in the shower. I didn't know you were coming. Did we arrange...?"

"No." She thinks of the coffee shop, of Zara's questioning stare. Sylvie's smug smile, the job at SunWolf she'll probably get, a glittering future half a breath away. "I just wanted to see you. I... I needed to see you."

Instantly, his face changes, the edge of his lip quirking and his eyebrow raising. It strips away his wariness and leaves him raw, receptive. She can almost hear his heart beating faster. It is so easy, Siobhan thinks, almost too easy. It's ridiculous that she should have this much power over him, and that he should just let her have it. She remembers how she'd left him last time, half-dressed and vulnerable in his own home. Whatever he says next, she knows, will tell her how he really felt about that. How much more she can push.

"Well, who am I to deny you?" He gives her a wide grin and gestures for her to come inside.

His flat is less orderly than last time, but still clean, cleaner than Siobhan's flat has ever been. She walks past the kitchen and the lounge and straight to the room at the end of the hall, his bedroom. It's minimal and modern, white sheets and nothing on the walls. She perches on the edge of the bed. It smells of him in here. She imagines his head on the pillow, tossing and turning in a nightmare. Owen watches from the doorway, leaning against the frame. His T-shirt is damp at the collar where his hair has dripped, making him look sweaty.

"Do you mind me turning up here like this?"

"Not at all." He eyes her carefully, as if afraid to make any sudden movements. "Is everything okay?"

"Not really." She looks away, towards the bedroom window. She can see all the way to the water. "I feel good here, with you. I don't really feel good anywhere else."

He crosses the room to sit next to her. The heat of his body radiates across the space between them. "You can come here whenever you want," he whispers. His hand is at the hem of her polo, hesitant. "I've been thinking about you so much." At first, he just runs his fingers over the stitching, pinches the scarlet thread that's come loose. He narrows his eyes, as if it's suddenly the most interesting thing in the world to him. When he looks at her face again, it's with a question hidden in his features, in his slightly parted lips, in the unevenness of his breath. A bead of water has collected at the tip of a lock of hair and is about to fall. She can see the pulse in his neck, quick quick quick. He looks like someone hanging on to the rags of his composure.

Siobhan raises her arms to let him lift the polo over her head. He places it gently next to them, and it is a scarlet stain on the white bedspread. She half-expects him to fold it. Instead, he buries his head in the place where her neck meets her shoulder, his want making him clumsy. His mouth is hot and warm. He gnaws at her like he's starving, and it sets her teeth on edge. It feels like he'll leave her with an open wound. When was she last touched like this? She can't remember, only that it was months ago, only that she was drunk, so drunk the other person probably should have known better. She lets Owen push her body back so that she's horizontal on the bed, his mouth still at her neck. She looks at the ceiling, at the elaborate details in the cornicing, as he works his way down over her collarbone, avoiding her breasts for now, landing at her navel. He stops with a short intake of breath, and she knows he'll have reached her scar. She looks down to find him peering at it with furrowed eyebrows, the sprawling winged shape of it, the way the skin congeals and overlaps in lumps. It's covered in barely formed scabs, drying blood. His mouth hovers above it, as if he can't bring himself to move in one direction or the other.

Go on, Siobhan thinks, *look at it. Tell me what you see.*

"You don't have to say how you got it," Owen says eventually. Something about the gentleness in his voice makes her suddenly furious. She doesn't need concession from him. She doesn't need permission to keep her own secrets.

She props herself back up on her hands so quickly that he flinches. She reaches for her polo and pulls it back over her head.

"Siobhan, I didn't mean to…"

"Shut up," she snaps. The cruelty in her words seems to shock him. She loves how it drains away all his self-satisfied kindness, leaving in its place something closer to fear. His desire feels like a petal in her hands.

"Are you sorry?" she whispers.

"If I hurt your feelings, or made you feel self-conscious, then…"

"I said, are you sorry?"

He holds her gaze. She can feel it then: an inevitable grinding towards something new, something dark, something she can't quite name yet.

"Yes," he says eventually.

"Say it."

One of his hands had been braced on the bed between them, as if he were trying to make a bridge. Now, both fall into his lap, useless. "I'm sorry."

It doesn't feel as good to hear the words as she'd hoped it would. Because of course, it's not Owen she needs to hear them from. Siobhan sags back against the headboard, shoves the heels of her hands into her eyes and swims in the fuzzy blackness behind her eyelids before opening them again.

"There's a girl in your Documentary class," she says. "Sylvie Fournier."

A pause. "That's right. You know Sylvie?" She can hear the caution in his voice, the trepidation.

"What do you think of her?"

"She's… nice, I suppose? Attentive. A good eye."

"So, you think she's talented?"

"What is this about?"

"Just answer the question."

Owen repositions his weight on the bed. He's no longer meeting her eye. "Yes, Siobhan," he says with a sigh. "I do think she's talented, actually. Why?"

Siobhan wraps her arms tightly around herself, probing the gaps between ribs with her thumbs. Her scar is throbbing, as if being looked at woke it up. She can't think of a single place in the world she wants to be.

"Shall I bring you some food?" Owen asks, more softly now.

Siobhan doesn't know whether she's hungry or not. She only feels tired. She peels back his duvet so she can slip underneath, and the sheets are deliciously cool against her skin. "Okay," she mumbles. "And some wine."

When he's gone to the kitchen, she presses her face into his pillow and inhales deeply, taking in the simple scent of him: soap and scalp. She feels like she should probably cry, like it would help release some of the pressure between her ears. Instead, she lies face down, smothers her face with the pillow, and lets out a long, silent scream.

ELLY

THEN

Elly stays in the shower for longer than she needs to, until the skin at her fingertips begins to wrinkle and her focus blurs. The house's shared bathrooms are in a high-ceilinged room with walls of old stone. Inside are a row of stalls, the cisterns ancient and clanking, and a freestanding bath in the corner. It must have been grand once, but the porcelain is cracked now, the brass feet tarnished. The individual shower cubicles are newer, with opaque glass doors and slate tiles, but still, the water splutters irregularly from the showerhead, icy one minute and burning the next. Elly barely notices. She runs a solid bar of soap slowly over her skin, filling the air with sweet orange and the bite of sage.

When she comes out, she finds Siobhan standing by the sinks, rubbing lotion into her skin. The oval mirrors are steamed, dripping with condensation, and the air around her dances with moisture. Siobhan is wearing a dressing gown, wet hair swept up and off her face by a towel. Her face is free from make-up, and she looks younger than usual, a little softer.

"Hey," she says when she sees Elly. She grins as confidently as someone wearing a sleek suit rather than a thin towel. "Have you seen this?"

She gestures to the floor, which is covered by an inch of water. One of the pipes running into the sinks has burst and is leaking all over the tiles.

"This place is a health and safety hazard," Siobhan is saying. "Last night I put a foot through a floorboard in our room. Don't think Haina's ever heard of redecorating."

Elly frowns. She's experienced similar things in the house – doorknobs coming off in her hand, chairs wobbling dangerously underneath her – but in the face of Siobhan's criticism, she finds herself wanting to defend it. She wonders if Siobhan knows the truth about the house yet, what happens to the guests behind the closed door of the study, and hopes she doesn't. "Haina's doing her best," she says. "It's an old house."

Siobhan shrugs, kicking up the water like a child in a puddle. Elly's making her way out of the door when Siobhan says, "Wait." She peers at Elly strangely, with a little too much intensity. "I recognise you."

Elly's hair is wet and cold around her shoulders. She shudders. "I'm sorry?"

Siobhan bites her lip and tilts her head to the side, then lets out a little laugh, clicking her fingers. "God, it's you. You've been all over the news." She watches Elly's face carefully. "But obviously you wouldn't know that."

Elly feels as though someone has knocked the wind

out of her, stolen the air right out of her lungs. "No," she whispers. "I wouldn't know that."

"Elly Carmichael, isn't it? Yeah, I've seen you. I mean, I guess you're lucky that people care enough to look for you – I don't think it's the same for everyone here. But, man, you're everywhere. *Much-loved pregnant wife and baker, went missing on her wedding night.* Hollywood stuff. Your husband's giving loads of interviews, appeals and shit. Crying in every single one. He gives me the creeps a bit, to be honest. If you weren't standing right in front of me, I'd probably think he was involved. No offence." She whistles, looking at Elly from head to toe, as if she can't quite believe that she's real. "Holy shit. You've just been *here* the whole time, and they can't find you. How is that even possible?"

Elly swallows. She can't take in anything Siobhan is saying, nothing after, *I guess you're lucky that people care enough to look for you.* She pictures her face on the news. She wonders which photo they would have used but doesn't know why that matters.

Ethan. Ethan is looking for her. She'd known he would be, but to have it confirmed makes her eyes burn.

She thinks back to a morning in his flat, a few months ago now. He'd made an espresso then climbed back into bed with her, head nestled between her shoulder and chin. He smelled of coffee and shampoo, of potential, of the day starting. She'd only just started to feel the baby move at that point, each kick was still a surprise, and she'd reached over to grab his hand and hold it to her bare stomach. She'll never forget how his face looked when the baby kicked under his hand – so vulnerable, broken wide open with hope. She's taken so much from him, she thinks now, standing in the bathroom doorway. How could she have taken so much from him?

"You alright?" Siobhan asks.

"No," Elly murmurs. "I don't know."

"It must feel fucking insane," Siobhan says, nodding, as if she understands completely. She unwraps her hair from the towel, letting it fall in dark tendrils around her face. When she looks back at Elly, it's with a new focus. "Hey, what would you think about doing a couple of interviews to camera? I'd love to get your perspective. Why you came here, why you've stayed, how it feels to have people out there looking for you."

"What? No." The bathroom is hot and muggy. It feels as though blood is rushing too quickly through Elly's veins. To be spotted moving around the house in the background, even to face the camera wordlessly, as she had in the hallway after her session with Haina – that was one thing. To be interviewed, to speak, to have to explain herself – that was something else entirely. "I'm sorry, I just can't. What if they... what if they saw it? How could I possibly make them understand?"

Siobhan waves a hand, as if none of this really matters. "We could blur your face, change your voice, if you really wanted us to." Her gaze wanders for a second then she looks back, eyes crackling. She reaches out to grip Elly's upper arm, making her flinch. "No, wait. What if we did show them who you are? What if you used the documentary as a way to, you know, communicate with them? Let them know you're okay, and that they can stop looking for you? You could tell them that you're safe, but that you're not going back." Then, after a pause, "I guess

140

you're never going back? I mean, how *could* you?"

Elly feels the wooden doorway digging into her shoulder. It hurts, but she needs it to keep her standing. *Is she going back?* She hasn't let herself think that far ahead. She doesn't know if Hex House is the kind of place you can stay forever, or if she'd even want to. But if she doesn't go home, she can't think of a single other place she might go.

"I think I saw your mum on one of the appeals, too," Siobhan is saying, thoughtful now. "She looks a lot like you, doesn't she? She seemed, I dunno, a bit *broken* by it all. The working theory is that you've been abducted or murdered or something." Siobhan shrugs again, almost nonchalant. "I don't know. I won't tell you what to do. But if it was *my* mum, I'd at least want to tell her I was okay."

Elly thinks about her mum sitting alone at the kitchen table, surrounded by the offcuts from the bunting she'd made for Elly's wedding. She pictures her leaving her phone on loud, constantly checking it and waiting for it to ring; lying in bed during the loneliest of hours, thinking the worst of things: Elly, beaten and broken in a ditch. Elly, face-down in the river. She screws her eyes shut. It's useless, trying not to cry. It only ever makes it worse.

"Shit," Siobhan says on an outbreath. "I really wasn't trying to upset you. If you let us interview you, well, it could work for both of us, is all I'm saying. Just think about it."

Elly wipes away the wetness on her cheeks and sighs, feeling heavy, feeling as though her bones are made of ancient stone, being dragged deep to the earth. "I'll think about it," she says.

The guests usually spend the downtime between lunch and dinner relaxing, and it's often the time Elly feels that the house is at its fullest, in its most natural state. Some of the women play the piano in the parlour. Lakshmi, with her long, graceful fingers, is the most skilled, playing complicated melodies with an almost lazy ease. Some have their private sessions with Haina, while others mend holes in the communal clothing or knit things for the winter months: chunky scarves, patterned mittens, woolly hats. Elly likes to wander the gardens, lying out on the sun-soaked stretch of lawn or watching the bees from the rickety bench by the back door. Sometimes, she reads one of the battered paperbacks from the nook on the landing. Time can move slowly in these hours, and Elly finds herself wondering how she filled her afternoons before. But of course, in the before time, there had been a phone that was always pinging with messages, a job to go to, a Netflix account with new viral shows every week. There is next to no technology in the house, bar the old record player in the parlour, and Haina had told Elly on her first day that this was intentional. *How do you heal from the world if it's right here with you?* she'd asked, almost confrontationally. Elly had felt flattened into her seat by Haina's vigour. *How can you expect yourself to evolve, in the midst of all that noise?* She hadn't understood it fully at the time, but after speaking to Siobhan, she thinks she can appreciate Haina's approach a little more.

It's the lack of technology that makes it so incongruous when she hears it – the tinny whine of recorded voices. It reaches her as she passes the parlour on her way out to the gardens after lunch. The day is warm but not as oppressive as the ones before it, the leaves on the trees starting to hint at their decay, only just beginning to turn warm shades of gold and orange. Elly craves the fresh air, the breeze, but the noises coming from the parlour make her pause. Theo is sitting on the sofa with his laptop, surrounded by a small group of women: Lakshmi, Margot and Janine. Elly hears Haina's voice from the computer. He must be playing them some of the clips he's recorded around the house.

"There's me!" Lakshmi squeals, jabbing her finger at the screen. Her dark ponytail swings wildly. "Wait, pause it. Do I really stand like that? I look so... hunched."

"You look fine," says Theo. Elly doesn't miss the way those words make Lakshmi look away, colour seeping into her cheeks.

"Do you have any of me?" Janine asks, reaching over Lakshmi to take control of the keypad.

"I think so. Wait a minute." Theo concentrates on the screen.

While he searches, Lakshmi notices Elly in the doorway. "Elly, come and see. You're in loads of these."

Theo looks up at Elly, surprised. He gives a shy kind of laugh, as if he's been caught doing something he shouldn't.

"Am I?" she finds herself asking. Does she want to be? She remembers coming out of Haina's study, dazed, almost drunk with the possibilities of what she'd seen. She'd stared down the barrel of a lens, daring Theo to see her, to really see her. The memory makes her feel self-conscious now.

Theo hesitates, then shrugs. "You're in some, yeah."

"Haina won't like this," says Margot. She's leaning away from the rest of them, not looking at the screen, her arms wrapped around her knees.

"That's right," a voice says from behind Elly, making

143

her jump. She turns to see Haina standing in the doorway, watching them. Her face is severe. "That footage isn't for your eyes, my angels."

Margot has skin the colour of bone, but now it pales even further. "Sorry, Haina," she says, voice barely audible. Janine and Lakshmi edge away from Theo, as if they'd never wanted to look at the laptop in the first place. Theo blinks and rubs at his chin. For a long moment, no one says anything at all. The air feels pulled taut. Elly marvels at it: Haina's ability to change the mood in the room with one withering look, one vague warning.

"Theo," Haina says eventually. "Will you join me in my study for a moment?"

Elly watches Theo's face, and she knows that he feels it, too: Haina's unignorable gravity. The impossibility of saying no to her. "Sure," he says.

He looks back over his shoulder as he follows Haina out of the parlour, meeting Elly's eye. For a split second, he makes a face – pulling his lips to one side, frowning in exaggerated worry. It's so unexpected, so silly, such a welcome dose of relief dissolving the tension in the room, that Elly finds herself smiling.

That night, Haina announces to the guests that they will be gathering on the rooftop after dinner. Elly has never been up to the roof before, and she feels nervous as she makes her way up the narrow, winding staircase from the attic with the other guests. They emerge out onto a flat terrace built into the roof at the back of the house, only just big enough to fit all of them standing close together. It looks out over the gardens and the woods beyond. It's a struggle to remember that somewhere over the treeline, the normal world still rolls on – a world that still believes Hex House is a fairytale and that Elly is a missing person.

The sky is the purple-streaked, powdery blue that comes just before dark. Haina takes her place at the front of the crowd, closest to the stone wall separating the roof terrace from the sky and the drop below it. Siobhan and Theo stand close to Haina, Theo holding the large camera on his shoulder, Siobhan just behind him, peering into the viewfinder. She gives him constant direction, changing the angle, the height, the focus. Elly stands near the back of the group with Grace and Margot, wondering what they're all doing up here. When everyone has assembled, Haina brings both hands to her chest to address them.

"My angels." That feeling in Elly's stomach again, like the fizzing of fireflies. "This is a very special occasion indeed. It's been a long time since we've been lucky enough to experience what you're all about to witness." There's something different in her voice tonight. Elly senses anticipation, excitement. "But those of you who have been here for a while will remember seeing someone take their First Fly."

Many of the guests look around blankly, but others – Grace, Margot – grin, gasp, clutch each other's hands. Elly can feel something peculiar under her skin, like the blood's broken free of the veins. First *Fly?*

"When a guest takes their First Fly successfully, it shows me that I've taught all I can teach. It shows me that, soon, they'll be ready to leave our sanctuary and take their place in the world again. For some, it might only take a matter of months, but for most, like Lakshmi here, seven years is the time it takes to gain the courage to try."

Lakshmi steps forward from the crowd to stand beside Haina. She's beaming with so much effervescence that she's almost blinding to look at. She tightens her high, dark ponytail and straightens her cotton dress. Her hands are clearly shaking.

Haina turns to Theo and Siobhan. "I've battled with myself over whether to share this with you, and with the rest of the world," she says. "But if people out there are to know what Hex House truly is, to *understand* it, well, then you simply have to see. There's no other way." Her smile becomes smaller as she says, in a lower voice now, "Whatever happens, keep the camera rolling."

Theo nods gravely. Elly wonders what Haina told him in her study, whether she would have reprimanded him for letting the women use the laptop. But then, Theo isn't a guest. What would be the consequences of him not listening to her? Elly doesn't know exactly what they would be for her, either, only that there would be some. Next to him, Siobhan's smile is so wide it makes her look almost feral. She says something to Theo, and he steps closer to Lakshmi, carefully lining up the shot. Elly can glimpse it through the viewfinder: Lakshmi's glittering eyes, the open, darkening sky behind her, the stretching yawn of the woods and their gloom.

Haina turns to Lakshmi. "Do you want to take your First Fly tonight?"

"Yes," Lakshmi says, loud enough for the crowd to hear. "I want to do it tonight."

Haina smiles at her and retreats into the crowd,

leaving Lakshmi standing alone by the stone wall. She looks vulnerable suddenly, set against all that open space. *First Fly*, Elly thinks distantly, *surely can't mean what I think it means.*

"I am so proud of you, my angel," Haina is saying to Lakshmi now. Then, to the rest of the guests, "She has the love of the whole house, doesn't she? Show her that she does."

Elly doesn't expect what happens next: the group responding in unison, a chorus of voices calling out the same words once then repeating them, over and over, until they start to lose their meaning.

May your hex protect you.

Then, quiet. Elly can hear the thumping of her heart. She whispers it to herself. *May your hex protect you, Lakshmi.* The baby wriggles in her belly, restless, as if it, too, knows that something is about to happen. She feels Margot's hand slip into hers and squeeze tight.

"Are you ready?" Haina asks Lakshmi. Lakshmi nods. Her hands are balled into fists at her sides. Haina turns and gives the crowd a slow nod. At first, Elly doesn't know what this means, but into the silence that follows, the other guests start to hurl new words: these ones loud, pointed, cruel.

"You're disgusting, Lakshmi."

"What did your father used to call you?"

"The runt?"

One of the guests throws something round and hard at Lakshmi. Is it fruit? Who brought fruit? Whatever it is hits her squarely on the jaw, causing her head to snap back.

"You're filth."

"Not worth the dirt on our shoes."

Someone spits. Someone else starts to boo. There's

hissing coming from the back. The crowd has taken on the character of a mob, teetering on the edge of fever.

"You made it so easy for him to hurt you."

"You're nothing. You're less than nothing. You're pointless."

Elly is so busy looking around, searching the crowd for the thrower of each insult, that she's stopped watching Lakshmi. It's only when the crowd grows quiet again, their silence arriving as quickly and unexpectedly as their fury, that Elly realises what's happening, what it is that they've done.

Lakshmi has started to change.

Her shoulders are rounded forward, hiding her face, her whole body quivering. From the hunched summit of her back, two blade-like bones explode outwards. The sound is like rocks hitting water from a height. They curve inwards like whalebones, growing first a layer of fleshy gristle, then a covering of obsidian feathers. Impossibly smooth; liquid velvet. Elly wants to reach out and touch them, until she sees the sharp talons erupt from their ends, and from Lakshmi's toenails, tearing through the leather of her shoes. *What could they do to a person?* Elly wonders. *What could they do to soft, human skin?* Her dress rips at the seams as the flesh on her legs and abdomen warps, settling finally into a rippling silken down, its sheen a furious violet. Then, her face. God – that face. A hooked nose of shining black, the mouth a howling hole, sharp teeth embedded in soft, pink flesh. Her eyes are still Lakshmi's, but they are burning with vigour; they are awful and searing and furious and Elly can barely stand to look at them, but she knows nothing on earth could make her look away.

Is this what's waiting for her? Is this monstrosity what she can expect to find on the other side of her anger? Elly feels dizzy, staggers back a little. It's only Margot's hand in hers, squeezing tightly, that keeps her rooted in the moment, standing upright.

"Holy shit," she hears someone say. A man's voice. Theo is staring open-mouthed at Lakshmi, the camera lowered from his shoulder, dangling impotently by his hip. "What the hell is happening?"

Beside him, Siobhan appears shaken, too, but she recovers more quickly. "Keep filming, Theo," she hisses, hauling the camera back up to his shoulder. "Keep fucking filming."

Elly can once again see the shot through the viewfinder. She can see Lakshmi, or what was Lakshmi, standing in the centre of the frame, her eyes shining in the dull twilight. It's through the camera that she watches Lakshmi tilt that awful head back and let out a scream that feels as if it pierces every organ and bursts every blood vessel in her body. She sends it hurtling upwards into all that sky, and in response, birds erupt from the surrounding trees, flapping rapidly away as though they're being chased by a predator. All the while, Haina looks on, proud as a mentor, protective as a mother.

Lakshmi shakes out her enormous wings – *Because of course that's what they are*, Elly thinks, *wings* – and turns to the stone wall. She climbs atop it, her claws wrapping themselves around the ridge. Elly feels her stomach drop, a sickness brewing in her gut. There is nothing left now between Lakshmi and the hard ground below. Nothing but air.

"May your hex protect you!" the guests shout, the

149

words running into each other and overlapping, until it becomes one bellowing voice that feels loud enough to tear down the sky. They cheer, holler, clap their hands above their heads. They watch Lakshmi with something like awe, like she is a wonder. It gives Elly whiplash, the way their mood has morphed from derision to reverence. "May your hex protect you!"

It happens quickly, what comes next – though Elly will always think later that there should have been a way for her to stop it.

When Lakshmi leaps from the roof, Elly feels as if she has jumped, too: every muscle in her body contracts, and she bites down on her tongue so hard that her mouth fills with blood. There's a whooshing sound as the air hits against the veiny undersides of Lakshmi's outstretched wings, and then she disappears beneath their sight line. A moment of awful, hushed quiet – then she appears again, wings beating, sending her higher, higher, higher. She can barely make herself believe it, but of course, Lakshmi is flying. She doesn't look like a bird, but she doesn't look like a woman either – she's a creature in between, clawed, lithe, powerful, tearing through the sky as though it belongs to her alone. It appears almost like she's dancing rather than flying, using her feet to propel her forward, turning her body over in sweeping arcs. The crowd is frenzied, wild, their stamping feet a hurricane. Beside Elly, Margot's cheeks are wet with tears, her single eye is wide and staring; she is laughing. It's almost dark now, but Elly can still make out Lakshmi's form as she nears the treeline, turns, and begins to arc back towards the house.

"Lakshmi!" the women shout in broken and beautiful

voices, more bursting with hope than any voice Elly has ever heard. "May your hex protect you!"

Elly looks to Theo's viewfinder again. The shot is somehow even more unreal than what's unfolding before her eyes: the sky a more violent blue, Lakshmi's shape even more stark and impossible. Theo zooms in so that he has a clearer image, and so it's through the viewfinder that Elly sees Lakshmi first start to struggle. It's because she's watching through the camera that she is one of the first to notice. With every few beats of her wings, Lakshmi sags a little, as though she's weakening. Theo pans upwards slightly to her face: the white of her eyes and her wide-open mouth. He starts to say something to Siobhan, but Elly can't hear him over the racket, and Siobhan barely seems to be listening to him. Lakshmi tilts dangerously to one side, falling two or three feet before righting herself again.

"Wait," Elly says, to no one in particular. "There's something wrong."

But no one hears her. Everyone is half-mad with their cheering and screaming. No one else seems to realise what's happening, no one but Theo. He's trying to put the camera down but Siobhan won't let him – she keeps it upright and pointing straight at Lakshmi. She's shouting something at him, jabbing her finger repeatedly at the viewfinder. Theo's eyes search the crowd, landing on Elly. He must recognise the panic in her expression because she sees, rather than hears, her name on his lips. She opens then closes her mouth uselessly, and they both turn their heads back to Lakshmi. They look back in time to see her falter, to let out a horrible, nightmare-haunting screech and then fall from their view, plummeting to the earth below.

SIOBHAN

NOW

Siobhan pauses the video. On the screen is the empty sky – so close to black – the camera trained on the spot Lakshmi had been just a few seconds earlier, before she fell. She should shut the laptop now, delete this clip, delete the whole fucking thing, because she knows what happens next. But she hits play anyway. She deserves to watch, to be forced to live this horror a second time.

In that moment, it had felt like the seams of everything she knew had been ripped open, like the earth had collapsed beneath her, as if it had never been anything more than a trapdoor all along. Theo was screaming – she can hear it on the tape – screaming like an animal, tearing at his hair as if he was about to pull it right out of his head. She tells herself that she only took the camera and walked to the edge of the stone wall so that she could preserve the truth of what happened. That's the only reason she tilted it over the wall to film the lawn below, the only reason she zoomed in on the prone figure there. That figure no longer had a fantastical beak and wings with a span larger than the height of a grown man, but was nothing more than a small naked woman with a dark pool of blood underneath her, her right leg hooked at an angle it should never reach. Siobhan had turned the camera around then, to the haunted faces of the women, who stood strangely silent. The last frame of the clip is Haina. Haina's face, blank and emotionless, staring back into the lens. Siobhan thought it at the time, and she thinks it again now: Haina doesn't look frightened or panicked.

She looks disappointed.

Minutes later, Theo dragged Siobhan to the attic room, locked the door behind them, and looked at her in a way he never had before. It was like something inside of him had bent so far that it had snapped. The intensity of his fear was blinding, flooding the room. She could almost smell it. He started rushing around, shoving cameras into bags and slamming laptops shut.

"We have to go," he kept saying, panting, like he couldn't get enough air into his lungs. "We have to get the fuck out of here and get that girl some help."

Every few seconds, he'd sit down, frenetic activity replaced by quiet sobs. "Fuck," he whispered. "What the hell is this place? How was that even possible?" Then he was pacing again, his eyes desperate.

Siobhan could do nothing but stand with her back to the door. She was numb and shivering. It was only when Theo started shaking her shoulders that she returned to herself, that she was able to pin down the fracturing of her thoughts.

"We can't leave, Theo," she told him, watching his eyes

widen in response. "Do you have any idea what we just got on tape? Bird women who fly through the sky? Jesus Christ. This documentary could *make* us, Theo. We have to stay." Her voice sounded shaky and strange, but she believed the words with everything she had. This was the reason she'd been brought to Hex House, she knew now. In this moment, she had to choose between being afraid or becoming someone unforgettable, exceptional, and she already knew her answer. "Whatever's happening in this house, we have to be here to witness it."

Theo shook his head, studying her eyes, as if he couldn't quite recognise her. "How can you even *think* about the doc right now? That girl..." he whispered raggedly, before trailing off.

"We'll tell everyone, Theo," Siobhan said quickly, laying a steadying hand on his shoulder. "We'll expose what's going on here. But don't we need all the evidence first?" She sucked in a breath, mind reeling. "Just imagine what else we might film, if we stay."

Theo didn't respond. His shuddering exhales were the only sound in the room. Eventually, he said, "Are you really naïve enough to think Haina is going to let us leave with that footage? A woman falling from the sky? She could *die*, Shiv, don't you understand that?" Siobhan flinched, but he didn't seem to notice. "Jesus. No one in their right mind would ever set foot in this house."

A knock at the door had startled them both, sent them jumping backwards. Siobhan opened it to find Haina, holding out two cups of tea. Theo didn't move, so Siobhan accepted them both, watching Haina enter the room and sit down on the edge of Theo's bed. She was careful and calm, Siobhan remembers now, moving as though through water. She was so measured.

"What you saw tonight," Haina said, meeting both of their eyes in turn, "was very unfortunate. It's also very rare."

"Is that girl... Lakshmi..." Theo wrapped his arms tightly around himself. "Is she still alive?"

Haina nodded. "She is. The women here are very strong."

"Are you going to make us delete the footage?" Siobhan heard herself ask, feeling Theo's gaze snap to her, incredulous.

Haina slowly turned her head. "And why would I do that?"

"Surely no one would ever come, if they saw. If they knew."

For the first time, Siobhan saw a hardness in Haina's eyes, the glinting of something furious. "Everything that happens at Hex House is natural. It's beautiful. It's ancient. The whole world out there might be terrified of our true potential, but we're not. We have nothing to hide." She stood and crossed the room to Siobhan. "I need them to see. They have to see." She lowered her voice, picked up one of Siobhan's hands and cradled it in her own. Siobhan's skin tingled at the touch. "*You* have to see."

"She needs medical help," said Theo from the corner, still visibly trembling.

Haina watched him carefully. "Her state is too precarious to move her, I'm sure you can see that. We will take care of her. Here. Don't worry – Lakshmi is exactly where she needs to be. This is the safest place in the world."

Theo barked a harsh laugh, but Haina didn't flinch.

"This place is *fucked up*," he hissed. "They'll come for you. The police." Even as he said the words, he seemed to recognise their futility. He deflated a little, swearing under his breath.

Haina dropped Siobhan's hand and moved to Theo. Gently, she pulled him in close, and to Siobhan's surprise, Theo let her. His face rested on Haina's shoulder, turned towards Siobhan, his expression stunned and eyes watery. Haina stroked his back, fingernails drawing slow circles. She was tactile with all the guests, but with Theo, something felt different. There was nothing comforting or maternal about it. Siobhan looked away, skin bristling.

"Those who *need* us will find us," Haina whispered. "Anyone else will simply find themselves lost in the woods."

Siobhan feels cold all over, like she'll never be warm again. She exits the video player and sits shaking on the sofa. She's shivering so much her teeth are smashing together, so hard it hurts. She doesn't know how long she sits there. She doesn't know how long it is until her phone rings.

Zara's name appears on the screen. Siobhan stares at it for a long second before it makes sense to her. Zara has called multiple times since their meeting at Black Medicine Coffee, but Siobhan has ignored each one. She doesn't know what makes her answer this time – perhaps only the sudden, desperate need not to feel so alone in the flat, to rid herself of the image of Lakshmi's broken body, Haina's dispassionate gaze.

"Siobhan," Zara's northern lilt chimes down the phone, "thanks so much for picking up."

"What time is it?" Siobhan says. She feels disorientated, exhausted.

A hesitant pause. "About 10 p.m. Why? Are you alright? You sound a bit... shaken."

Four hours. She's been watching clips of Hex House for four hours. After a while, the laptop screen had seemed to melt away, and it was as if she were there again, walking the corridors with their peeling wallpaper and vases of flowers on every surface, brushing her fingers along the velvety roses outside the parlour window. The camera crawled its way through the house, drinking in everything with its single eye, and the time elapsed between this life and that one had dissolved into vapour. She could almost smell the fresh bread cooking in the kitchen, hear the creak of the floorboard on the landing as the guests came and went from the dormitory, see the way the sunlight refracted through the stained-glass window on the landing. The light in that house. It made her feel weightless once. Like anything was possible, like she could live forever.

"Siobhan?" Zara's voice down the line, questioning and insistent. "Look, I'm really sorry about the other day. I pushed you too far, too fast – I can see that now. I shouldn't have asked you about... well, you know."

When Siobhan swallows, it feels like pure bile.

"Would you be willing to meet me again? Just to chat. I won't press you, I promise."

"Can I come over now?"

"I'm sorry?"

"Can I come to your flat?"

Siobhan rubs her hand along her lower abdomen, feeling the ridges of her scar bristle against the fabric of her T-shirt. If she doesn't have company, if she doesn't have a real person's face to look at and voice to respond to, she's going to tear it wide open.

A long pause. "It's late."

"Please," Siobhan says.

"I'll come to you," Zara says eventually, haltingly, then adds, "if you want me to, sure, of course. I can come."

Once she's given Zara the address and hung up, Siobhan takes a deep breath in, relieved she won't be here alone all night. If she had to guess, she would say that Zara would be the kind of person to have well-watered house plants on every surface, framed feminist art prints, all line drawings of breasts and vulvas. There was probably organic handwash by the sink. Maybe a purring cat sleeping on an artisan throw.

Siobhan looks around her own flat, trying to see it through Zara's eyes: the woven rug that had been there when she moved in (sometimes she imagines all of the people-dust trapped inside all the fibres, all the eyelashes and hairs and tiny fragments of nail); the fridge containing half a bottle of wine and an expired yoghurt; the unmade bed covered with sheets she can't remember washing. This flat is a display of her most intimate failings. It's where she keeps all her broken parts. The thought of bringing Zara here feels a bit like showing her the inside of her mouth, the softening places where the cavities hide. She thinks about tidying up, putting some of the washing in the machine, clearing the sink of its debris, but can't summon the energy. Instead, she clicks on the radio, pours the last of the wine and listens absent-mindedly to tinny trance tracks until the buzzer rings.

She opens the door to Zara bundled in a bright orange

teddy coat, gold hoops dangling from her stretched lobes, so large Siobhan could fit her fist through them. Her rounded cheeks are flushed red with cold. She's drawn on thick eyeliner in two symmetrical flicks and wears a pair of shining Doc Martens. In one hand, she holds a bottle of vodka – the cheap, perfect kind that burns on the way down – and in the other, a plastic bag filled with takeaway cartons. Siobhan can already smell greasy noodles, sweet and sour sauce. "Just in case you didn't have anything in," Zara says. "And you sounded like you needed this." She holds up the bottle as she follows Siobhan inside.

Zara takes a seat on the sofa. If she has an issue with the way it sags underneath her, or the pile of clothes teetering on the arm, she doesn't show it. She unpacks the takeaway boxes while Siobhan rinses plates and glasses and brings them through to the coffee table. She pours them each a generous measure of vodka, watching Zara heap their plates high with chow mein and spring rolls.

"Cheers," Zara says, picking up her glass.

"To what?"

Zara shrugs. "To whatever. To vodka."

They clink glasses. Siobhan starts to feel calmer when she's drained hers, when the spirit wraps itself around her senses and dulls them, files off all their edges. They don't speak for a while, so Siobhan can hear the fierce wind that's picked up outside. The flat's old windows tremble in their frames.

"Thanks for giving me another chance," Zara says eventually, through a mouthful of food.

Siobhan doesn't touch hers. "I don't want to talk about Hex House. I can't, not tonight."

"That's fine," Zara says quickly – too quickly. "We can talk about whatever."

Siobhan watches her taking delicate sips from her glass, wincing each time. Her nails are long and painted dark red. She finds herself looking at the small eye tattoo she'd noticed last time, staring out at her from just below Zara's thumbnail, always watching.

"I like that tattoo," she finds herself saying. "The eye."

Zara holds out her hand to look at it, bending her thumb so that the eye appears and disappears from Siobhan's sight. "I got this one for my little sister," she says. Her voice is small and tight. "She died, a while ago."

The polite thing to say would be, *I'm sorry*, but Siobhan has never felt helped or particularly reassured by that sentiment, so she says nothing.

Zara rolls up her sleeve, exposing skin crowded with artwork: snakes, mermaids, moons and delicate flowers. "I feel like when you're a journalist, you use other people's stories for your own means," she's saying. "It's exploitative. It's pretty fucking selfish. I've always felt really aware of that. I think that if you're going to benefit from using someone else's story, then you should at least carry some of its weight. So I started getting something tattooed on me for each one." The way she speaks doesn't seem to seek validation or response, but there is a smugness to it, as if she's proud of this particular principle and likes what it says about her. She taps her finger to a tiny teddy bear on her bicep. It has simple, cartoon features: two beady eyes, a single curved line for a smile. "I went freelance pretty much straight after graduating, and this was from the first story I ever worked on. Way before SunWolf. It was for a podcast about people who'd been missing for a long time, decades, sometimes. Jared Peach, that was his name. He'd be... thirty-five, I think, now. He went missing on a trip to Portstewart beach when he was four. His mum has been looking for him ever since and can't really think of him as a man, as ever being taller than her, ever growing facial hair. I think she's still expecting to find a little boy with ice cream smeared around his mouth and sand on his knees. She keeps his bedroom exactly as it was the day he went missing: water beaker on the side, Lego scattered across the floor, teddy bear on the pillow." She rolls down her sleeve, laughs gently. "I'm a giant sketchpad. My parents used to call tattoos 'devil marks'. When I'm sad, I think about how horrified they'd be if they could see me now, just to cheer myself up a bit."

"You don't talk to them?"

"Nah. I had kind of an intense childhood. Me and my sister moved up here as soon as we could, but she... she didn't last long."

The words hang heavy in the air and Siobhan has the feeling that if she were to prod Zara for more details, even gently, it would all come tumbling out. She's the kind of person who likes to talk, it seems, who is generous and loose with their words. Perhaps it helps her, to say these things out loud. But Siobhan doesn't ask. She tops up their glasses and listens to the wind hurling itself against the window.

"You haven't touched your food," Zara says.

"Not really hungry."

"Right. Well, keep some in the fridge, then. You might want it tomorrow and I can't be bothered to take it home."

Siobhan knows how she must look to Zara. She's noticed it while studying her reflection in the mornings, wrapping her body in a towel after a shower: her thinness. She wonders whether her cheeks have always been so hollow, her ribs so sharp-looking, the circles under her eyes so stormy and dark. She wonders how long it'll be until she simply fades away.

"Siobhan," Zara says eventually, "why did you want me to come here tonight?"

Siobhan stares at the old water rings on the coffee table. "I just didn't want to be alone with it all." She clears her throat, doesn't meet Zara's eye. "I don't know how much longer I can hold it all in."

"You don't have to hold it in." Zara puts down her glass and shifts closer to Siobhan. She smells clean, like pine and citrus, and a little bit like fried noodles. "We can tell the story in any way you want to tell it."

"I don't know how to," Siobhan whispers. "I don't know where to start."

Zara nods. She tucks her bright red hair behind her ears, then leans back into the sofa. She's moving slowly, as if she's handling something made of delicate porcelain. "Starting's the hardest part, I reckon. But it'll get easier. I use a room in the university library for all my interview recordings. It's small and safe and no one else would hear us." *Surely SunWolf has a studio*, Siobhan thinks absently. She wants to see it, to glimpse the life she might have had, a life Sylvie is about to step into – but she doesn't have the energy to press the point. "We could meet there tomorrow and have a chat. You could just see how you go. We'll obviously pay you for your time, give you a production credit." In a lower voice, she adds, "You could let me hold some of that heaviness for you. You deserve that, after all this time."

Siobhan doesn't think she does deserve that. She doesn't deserve Zara's soft voice and her kind words and her careful approach. She doesn't deserve to be brought food, for someone to care about whether or not she's eating. What she does deserve is to have to live it all again, to be forced to look at it for what it is, to own her part in the whole awful mess. She owes it to Elly, to Theo – she owes it to all of them.

"You don't know what you're getting yourself into," she tells Zara. "You should just walk away now."

Zara holds her gaze. A long moment passes. "I can't," she says quietly, and Siobhan senses weight behind the words, a tangled web of meaning she can't unravel tonight.

Siobhan drains her glass. "Fine. Tomorrow."

The next day, Siobhan wakes to a hangover that is fierce and raging, a riptide in her stomach. After Zara left, she'd finished the vodka and fallen asleep on the sofa, the edge of the cushion pressing a deep groove into her cheek. The half-empty takeaway boxes are still sitting open on the coffee table leaking smells of fat and grease, and she has to swallow down vomit as she boils the kettle for coffee and splashes cold water onto her face. The flat feels hollow and quiet again and she almost wishes Zara were still here; Zara, who talks to fill silences and chews with her mouth open. The oven clock tells her it's 11:29 a.m.

She'd arranged to meet Zara at the university at 1 p.m., so she has time to drain the contents of the cafetière and make another before she needs to leave. She uses the bitter, cooling coffee to swallow two ibuprofen before showering quickly and pulling on an old pair of jeans, holes at the knees and loose at the waist, and an old hoodie of Theo's. Before leaving the flat for the university, she checks her phone to find two new messages. The first is from her mum, recommending a documentary from a young Italian filmmaker on Netflix: has she seen it yet, might it provide her with some inspiration maybe, get her back into things? The second is from an unknown number. As she reads it, her mouth goes dry and the coffee spikes through her veins, making her pulse hammer.

Shiv, it's Theo. This is my new number. I've written and deleted this text ten times already and I really actually don't want to send it, but I need to know about this new documentary. I need to know what you're going to say. This doesn't change anything, I'm not interested in having you in my life, but we need to talk about this first. Let me know when you're free.

Siobhan rereads the text a couple of times, puts her phone down on the coffee table then picks it up, reads the message again. Her fingers are trembling as she types her reply.

I'd love to talk. I'm free anytime. I can call you now?

His response comes a minute later. *Probably better in person. I don't feel comfortable talking about this stuff on the phone. Can you come to Glasgow this week? I'm swamped at work but we could have a drink.* Siobhan stares into space. He works in advertising or something now, Nora had said, for some big agency with Nespresso machines in the office and company retreats to Venice. Online content creation, something like that. She wonders whether he can bear to look down a camera lens anymore, or whether it's only her who is that weak. A second message arrives before she has chance to respond. *Or maybe just coffee. Shiv, I need you to know I haven't changed my mind. After we talk, I don't want to meet again.*

Siobhan rubs her fists into her eyes, a dull headache starting to form. She types, *That's okay, I love you*, then deletes it and replaces it with, *I get it. I'll come on Thursday.* He doesn't respond after that, but she copies his number and saves it in her contacts. She does it more slowly than she needs to. Typing 'Theo' into the name field feels like new skin closing over a wound.

The sky is a bleak white and there's a dusting of snow across the top of Arthur's Seat as Siobhan makes her way to the university. It's November now, the heart of the autumn term, and so the campus is busy with students. It's always obvious which ones are freshers, books clutched to their chests as they mill between classes. Siobhan hasn't been back here since she graduated, and she'd almost forgotten how it felt: the safe cloak of academia, the reliable structure of terms and exams and coursework to lean back on. The last time she'd been here, she'd barely even heard the words Hex House, never as anything more than a story, a fairytale, a joke. It's obvious to her now how clearly she has demarcated her life into before and after. Everything before the house has a rosiness to it. She wishes she could slip between the years and find herself as a fresher in this very courtyard. She'd say that life can be so much more unforgiving and awful than she knows. She'd tell herself to take all that heady ambition and aim it as far away as possible from Hex House.

Instead of going straight to the library, she finds herself heading for the film department. She remembers a time when her life was composed of seminars and lectures, long, leisurely hours talking and thinking about the craft of film, analysing colour palettes and learning how to make things that might matter. Siobhan takes the stairs to the staff offices, walks the slim hallway and peers into the open doors at the brimming bookcases, messy filing systems, lecturers typing away at keypads. She stops when she sees the sign reading 'Professor Owen Jameson – Programme Director'. His door is closed, but there are voices coming from inside: Owen's, and another – younger, female, presumably a student. Siobhan had a one-to-one with him in this office once, towards the end of her degree. He'd told her to watch some films by an obscure Ukrainian filmmaker who'd also done a lot of work in women's violence shelters, and she remembers nodding, yes she would, knowing all the time that she wouldn't, because her project was already finished and she didn't want to make any changes to it. She'd been arrogant, had believed that she'd already seen all she needed to see, knew all she needed to know. Impatience is what she'd felt, sitting in that office. She'd found Owen dull and the room too hot, had been keen to stride forward into whatever came next. Now, she waits outside with her heart beating quickly, leaning her head close to the door so that she can pick out snippets of conversation.

"... is really a representation of desire, and simultaneously a rejection of the domestic," Owen says. His voice is different in this context: deeper, more authoritative. Siobhan tries to reconcile it with the man who burned the pasta sauce and kissed her neck like a teenage boy, but the voice won't fit the image. He's more capable here.

"That's really interesting," the girl is saying, and Siobhan imagines her scribbling in her notepad, trying to keep up. "I hadn't thought of that."

Owen says something else that Siobhan can't hear, and their conversation rumbles on for a few more minutes. Then, the sound of a bag being zipped, the squeak of a chair. The voices grow louder as they approach the door.

"Thanks, Amber. Really exciting stuff. You know, you should think about applying to my production company when term ends. You'd be a real asset."

Siobhan's stomach churns. She steps back as the door opens. A short girl with a thick fringe and thin lips comes out, adjusting her backpack and giving Owen an awkward wave as she sets off down the hall. Owen stays in the doorway and watches her, eyes flickering down her body. Siobhan clears her throat. He turns to her. His eyes widen but he recovers quickly, his smile warm and without reservation. His cheeks flood with colour. He's always giving himself away, Siobhan thinks. Does he know that? Owen coughs then looks again down the hallway behind her, seeming relieved to find it empty apart from Amber's retreating back.

"Can I come in?" Siobhan asks.

Owen hesitates. He's wearing a simple white shirt, dark jeans, glasses. Understated and dignified. "Okay," he says eventually. "I don't have long though."

They enter his office, and Siobhan shuts the door behind them. She sits down in the seat that's still warm from Amber and glances around the room, which is small and narrow. Above the desk are mounted shelves, loaded with what looks like a dangerous number of books. There's a series of Star Wars prints on the wall opposite, and next to his computer is a framed picture of two dark-haired children Siobhan assumes are his niece and nephew. Owen takes a seat in front of the desk and begins to clear away the papers in front of him. Siobhan glimpses the name 'Amber Stevens' on the top of a marked essay.

"The female characters in this film are subject to the male gaze," she reads flatly from the first paragraph. "Wow. Amber is a *savant*."

"Don't be mean," Owen says, but he's smiling. "To what do I owe the pleasure?"

Siobhan shrugs. "I was in the area."

He furrows his eyebrows quizzically, but then a ping from his computer makes him turn. Siobhan watches his eyes run back and forth over the screen. "Hmmm," he says softly, hand on the mouse. "Two seconds. I just need to respond to this."

Siobhan leans back and watches him. She likes seeing him here, his practised fingers skating across the keys, skin healthy and tanned against the whiteness of his shirt, biting his lip as he concentrates. He had said she was in control, that the shifting thing between them could be whatever she wanted it to be, but she wonders if that still

168

applies in this environment. While he's still typing, she stands. She uses her knee to nudge his chair so it moves a little, away from the desk and towards her.

"Siobhan," Owen says, laughing, still trying to type, but he goes quiet when she places a knee either side of his hips and climbs up so that she's sitting astride him. His eyes fix on hers then wander down to her lips. "Wait," he says, but Siobhan kisses him, the way she wants to this time, firm and hard, pressing him back into the chair. He hesitates for a second then responds, one hand on each of her hips, pulling her into him. Outside the door, footsteps approach then recede. The sound seems to wake him up.

"Siobhan," he says again, this time pushing her shoulders away. "We can't do this here." His mouth is red and almost sore-looking where it pressed against hers. She wonders whether it'll bruise.

"Fine," she says. She dismounts his chair and returns to her own, inspecting her ragged nails, as if bored. There's a flush of anger rising up her neck, hot and urgent.

"It's not that I don't want to," he whispers. "Believe me. It's just," he gestures to his computer, the stack of papers on his desk, "I've got meetings to go to and essays to mark. Student tutorials to arrange."

Siobhan looks over Owen's shoulder, out of the window, where the bare branches of a large tree are just visible. She's envious, suddenly, of those students and their tutorials and all the things they have coming next. She wonders how many of them will go on to have shiny careers, job offers at Owen's company, or at SunWolf.

"You should arrange a tutorial with Sylvie Fournier," she hears herself saying.

Owen had been cracking his knuckles against his knee, but now he stops, peering at her. "What? Why?"

"Because she's talented, remember? You said so, the other day."

Owen opens his mouth then closes it again, shaking his head gently. "Sylvie hasn't asked for a tutorial, Siobhan. Why do you keep bringing her up? Is there something going on?"

Siobhan shrugs. "Sylvie's my friend, that's all. I think she might benefit from your guidance."

"I don't really understand what's going on, Siobhan. Talking about Sylvie with you feels a bit... inappropriate, to be honest." He bites his lip. There's a tiny bead of blood where the skin's been ripped off. *I'm still in control*, she tells herself, and it makes her fingers tingle where they're wedged under her thighs. *Even here.*

"What's inappropriate about it? Don't you have tutorials with every student on the module at some point?"

"Well, yes, but usually..."

"Has Sylvie had one yet?"

"No, I don't think so."

"Well, then. There's nothing inappropriate about offering some extra support."

Owen pauses, sighs.

"It would make me happy. Really happy."

She can see how powerful those words are. They tighten everything about him. "If I offer Sylvie a tutorial," he says carefully, "can I take you out for dinner next week?"

"Sure," she says.

Owen hesitates. "Fine," he eventually concedes, holding both his hands up as if Siobhan is aiming a gun at him.

"There can't be any harm in it." He swivels back to his desk, writes a two-line email and clicks send. The computer emits a quiet little 'whoosh' as the email is fired into the ether. "Happy?" he asks, when he turns back to her.

"Very," says Siobhan.

ELLY

THEN

Elly lies in bed, not sleeping. The house won't let her. Screams from the parlour below rip their way into the dorm like stray bullets, making the women bolt upright in their beds. Then, silence, which is almost worse. Occasionally, she can make out the soothing voice of whichever woman whose turn it is to watch her. A few beds over, Elly can hear Janine whimpering, her hands clamped over her ears. *May your hex protect you*, she whispers, over and over, in a voice like stretched elastic.

From the tiny attic room above their heads, snatches of Theo's and Siobhan's raised voices trickle down through the floorboards. Elly only catches the occasional word. *Help. Documentary.*

Lakshmi.

It had all happened so quickly. One second Lakshmi was there, airborne and mighty and unstoppable, and then the next she was gone, wrenched from the sky back down to earth. Elly remembers what happened next in fevered snatches: Siobhan, peering over the side of the wall with the camera, zooming in. Haina, not moving, Theo screaming. Grace, Janine and a couple of the others sprinting towards the staircase, thundering back down into the house, out of the doors, onto the lawn. Elly had made it downstairs in time to watch Lakshmi being carried inside and laid out on a blanket in the parlour. The whole room filled with a sour smell, like old meat, like a body turned inside out.

Every time she closed her eyes, she could still see it: the single dribble of blood from the corner of Lakshmi's mouth, the way the hard ground had torn up the skin and muscle of her leg and torso and made them into something new, something awful. Just hours beforehand, Lakshmi had giggled at the sight of herself on Theo's computer screen, told Elly, *You're in loads of these*, like they were teenage girls flicking through a photo album. Through the crowd that was gathered in the dark parlour, Elly could hear Lakshmi gargling something.

Haina. Haina.

But Haina wasn't there, and a few minutes later, they heard the door to her study slam. It was left to the women to pour whisky into Lakshmi's open mouth, to press wet flannels into her wounds and whisper soft words into her hair.

"We have to take her to the hospital," Elly said to no one in particular.

Grace had shot her a cold look. "She stays here," is all she said.

Now, above her head, Siobhan and Theo have gone quiet. There's another voice. Haina. What could she possibly be telling them about what happened tonight?

And what will the filmmakers do with the footage they captured? Theo had looked terrified, but Siobhan... there'd been something else entirely written into her face. Something like fascination. Something like *hunger*.

Elly rolls over in bed so that she's facing Margot, who's also awake, wide-eyed and staring at the ceiling, the cover pulled up to her chin. In the dim light, she looks tiny and child-like.

"Margot," Elly whispers, and Margot turns to face her. "What happened tonight? Why did she fall?"

Margot's mouth is downturned, as though she's about to cry. "She failed her First Fly, Little Mouse. She isn't ready to leave yet, see? She didn't have full control of her hex, or she wouldn't have fallen." She turns back to the ceiling and lets out a long, sad breath. "But didn't she look so beautiful," she says dreamily, "didn't she look so beautiful when she flew?"

Neither the filmmakers nor Haina appear at breakfast the next day, and the door to the study remains closed. Lakshmi, still laid out on the sofa in the parlour, is quiet now. Her breathing is shallow. One of the women always stays with her, dressing her wounds and keeping them clean, while the rest of the guests attempt to go on as normal. *Hospital*, Elly keeps thinking, ever more distantly, *she needs to go to the hospital*, but she knows it's useless. How would they even get her there? Would they ever make their way out of the woods, or would the house just keep reappearing, again and again, like it had the last time she tried to leave? Every time she sees Lakshmi's inert body, crumpled and rattling with broken breaths, she knows that to move her would be to kill her. And so, like the rest of them, she carries on with life at Hex House.

The mood in the kitchens is strained as Elly, Grace and Keiko prepare that night's dinner. Elly chops carrots and leeks, fries them with butter, trying to find solace in the repetitive tasks. But by dinner, she still hasn't seen Haina, Siobhan or Theo, and it makes her stomach clench. Once she's finished eating, she fills a plate with cuts of meat and bread and takes it up to the attic. There's not much up there apart from boxes and dustsheets covering broken bits of old furniture. Elly eyes the rickety iron staircase that leads up to the roof and turns in the opposite direction, towards the small door leading to a room in the eaves. She can't hear anything from inside, so she knocks gently.

"Come in." Theo's voice is raspy, as if he hasn't spoken in a while. Elly pushes the door open. The room is small, but efforts have been made – by Haina, Elly assumes – to make it comfortable, even luxurious. The drapes at the window are velvet and the bedsheets are made of vermillion silk. The only light comes from a computer monitor positioned on the desk in between the two beds. Every other available surface is covered with equipment: cameras, microphones, laptops, charging packs, hard drives. It all looks so incongruous against the ancient beams and wooden floor that Elly pauses abruptly, almost spilling the contents of the plate.

"Oh, hey," says Theo, jumping up from where he'd been lying on the bed to switch on the lamp. He seems surprised to see her. He looks down at the plate in her hands, and says, "You brought me food?"

But Elly isn't really listening to him, because her eyes have snagged on the monitor. It's open on the video player, paused mid-clip. Lakshmi, in the final seconds before she fell, her mouth twisted open in a scream.

"Shit, let me close that." Theo leans his long body over the computer and makes a series of quick clicks. Lakshmi disappears. "I just can't stop watching it. I can't... I can't get it out of my head. Sorry."

Elly blinks, trying to rid herself of the image. "Where's Siobhan?" she asks.

Theo runs a hand over his unruly curls. "Needed to blow off some steam. We had a bit of a disagreement last night."

"I heard."

"Shit. Sorry."

Theo takes the plate from her and places it on the side table. He sits on the edge of the bed and gestures for her to do the same. Elly hadn't realised how tired she felt, how aching her legs and her hips were, until she sinks down onto the mattress.

"What happened last night," Theo is saying, not looking directly at her, "Jesus. That was so insane. I just don't understand it – any of it."

"Me neither," Elly admits.

"What is happening here, Elly?" Theo asks quietly, looking around at the walls as if there might be hidden eyes there, watching him. "This place is fucking *dangerous*, right? That poor girl, I don't even know if..." He covers his face with his hands before carrying on. "I told Siobhan we've got to leave. We've got to warn someone about what's happening here. It's not right."

Elly listens to him voice all the thoughts that have run through her mind since Lakshmi fell, even since she arrived at Hex House. She knows how reasonable they all are, how true. And yet, although she doesn't know why, and although it doesn't make any sense at all, she feels a tiny kernel of resistance. There's a tiny part of her that wants to say, *But didn't she look so beautiful? Didn't she look so beautiful when she flew?*

"Siobhan says we have to stay. She wants to finish the documentary. Says it's important that we show people what this place is and what it does." Theo laughs suddenly, and it's a sharp, cool sound. "I thought there was no way that Haina would let us use that footage, but it's like she wants it to get out. It's almost like she's proud of it. She…" He swallows, hard. "She scares me sometimes."

Elly sits still, listening. She thinks of Haina's gentle hands and deep voice. *There's nothing to be scared of*, she almost says, but doesn't.

"I don't know though," Theo is saying. "Surely, I have to tell the police? Rather than just staying here and filming everything? We could be in danger. All of us."

"The police could never find us," Elly says before she can stop herself. She doesn't know where the words come from, only that they're true. Theo seems to know it, too, because his expression is different now. He looks tired, defeated. She imagines that Haina has told him the same thing.

"Do you think you'll stay?" she asks.

"I don't know," he says on an exhale. "Maybe Siobhan will. I'm not sure… I'm not sure if I can."

There's an unexpected spasm of panic in Elly's belly

at that thought, that Theo might leave. She wants, she discovers, for his camera to see her again, to feel strange and powerful in the face of its gaze. She has never felt as solid or as real as when she was standing in front of the lens, letting him see her, really see her.

"What if I did the interviews?" she asks, and he looks up.

"What interviews?"

"Siobhan asked me if I'd do some interviews to camera. Would you…" She stumbles, feeling foolish, clumsy. Theo is staring at her, waiting for her to continue, so she forces the words out of her mouth. "Would you stay to interview me?"

The words feel heavier than they should, as if they're soaked in water. Elly lets them hang in the air. Eventually, Theo says, very quietly, "Would you like me to?"

Fifteen minutes later, they're in the refectory. It's empty of guests, but with the disruption of Haina's absence and caring for Lakshmi, no one has cleared the plates. Theo sets up his camera amongst the debris, the chunks of half-eaten bread and meat gristle, glasses smeared with the imprints of lips. The candles are still burning, making it feel warm. Elly fidgets in her seat while Theo lines up the shot, checking the lighting, moving candles closer and then further away again. She only relaxes when he peers through the viewfinder and she feels herself being observed, appraised, appreciated.

"Okay, we're ready," he tells her eventually, looking up. He looks more nervous than she's seen him before, not meeting her eye. "Is there anything in particular you'd like to share? Or shall we just start, and see how we go?"

Elly bites the inside of her lip. She hadn't really thought this through, hadn't thought beyond the fact of Theo and his camera on one side of a room, her on the other. "I don't know," she says. "I don't know if I can talk about her. About Lakshmi."

"That's okay," he says. "We'll go slowly. You'll have to be patient with me – usually Siobhan does all the interviews, but I'll do my best." He clicks a few buttons on the camera and then gives her a nod. There's a short beeping sound, and then the light directly above the lens glows red. Elly feels it immediately – that sensation of a thousand eyes crawling all over her body, eyes from the future, eyes that know what happens tomorrow and the day after and the day after that. It makes her pulse buzz, but she can't tell whether it's with excitement or dread.

"Okay, Elly," Theo says. He sounds hesitant, though he's smiling. "Let's talk a bit about what brought you here, to the house."

A cool trickling underneath her skin. "You want me to talk about Ethan?"

Theo frowns. "Who's Ethan?"

"My husband."

Something flickers across his features, fleeting and unreadable. "Right. Well, yes. Let's talk about Ethan."

Elly lets a breath pass through her, turning to the side so that she can look out of one of the refectory windows and into the garden. The rose bushes and oak trees are nothing more than shapes in the gloom. She's thought often about the day she and Ethan met, especially in the run-up to the wedding. In the last moments before falling asleep, she'd fantasise about what she might have done differently to change the outcome of that first day, the day that determined everything that came after. Perhaps there were words she could have said that wouldn't have appealed to him, a colour she could have worn that he wouldn't have liked so much. Sometimes she likes to pretend she took her lunch half an hour earlier and so didn't see him at all, or perhaps only glimpsed his retreating form on the street as he walked away from the bakery. Instead, she starts to tell Theo what did happen, the truth, the finely tuned sequence of events that led her to now, to this room.

Four years ago, December, a colder one than anyone could remember. In the village, icicles clung to the drainpipes, impending skewers above everyone's heads. Snow edged the pavements. A thick coating of glistening grit ran down the centre of the high street, which was quieter than usual, except for the odd person bundled up in a coat, barely looking up. Elly was working with Suzanne, and the warmth of the bakery was a sanctuary from outside. Customers lingered longer over the scones and upside-down pineapple cakes, buying more than they usually would. When a stocky man with reddish hair dusted with snow entered the bakery, 'Last Christmas' by Wham! was playing. Elly will always remember that.

What did she think of him, at first? Not much.

She remembers that he smelled nice, that he brought the expensive smell of aftershave into the bakery with him, the scent of elsewhere. She remembers that he was wearing a tailored coat and a striped cashmere scarf. He had a taste for the finer things – she'd learn that later. He had a certain set of standards. She'd smiled at him, asked him what he wanted. She might even have said something like,

Isn't it so cold out there, just to be polite. Maybe he could see it, even then: her inbuilt need to please people, to break herself down into tiny pieces so that others might find her easier to consume. Ethan had looked at the cakes and tarts behind the glass as if he had no idea what any of them were. Later, he would tell her that he'd glimpsed her in the window (*You looked so sweet, that red jumper against your blonde hair*), and decided to come inside without even knowing that it was a bakery. In the end, he ordered three strawberry tarts, two scones and a seeded loaf. The way he was unsure as he said, *Maybe that*, and, *Add two of those, please*, was endearing. She'd thought then that he was the kind of man who found it easy to be vulnerable. They chatted a little bit – she told him she'd lived in the village all her life, he told her he was down from Edinburgh for the weekend to walk the hills, get some headspace, you know. He didn't ask for her number until everything was bagged up and paid for. Elly could feel Suzanne watching them from the back room, barely repressing a snigger. He asked politely and with a smile so warm she didn't feel like she could say no. When he left the bakery laden with things he didn't need (and, she would find out later, didn't even eat), he'd been blushing, and Suzanne had said something like, *Well he's a bit wonderful, isn't he*, and Elly had let herself think that yes, maybe he was.

She didn't see any other side to him for months, maybe half a year. And when it did emerge, it was a creature skulking out from the shadows, testing to see if it could survive the light. When had she first felt that tipping feeling in her belly, like everything was sliding out of alignment? Maybe the first times were too subtle for her to remember, but the one that comes to her now, the one she tells Theo about, is the first time she met his brother, Martin. They went to a steak restaurant in Edinburgh. It had white tablecloths and a wine list bigger than the menu. Some of the steaks cost the same as the wage Elly made in a day. Elly and Ethan arrived first, and Ethan was fractious as they waited for Martin at the table. He kept suggesting they had a drink at the bar instead, not seeming to like the idea that his brother would know he'd kept them waiting. The next minute, he'd change his mind and fiddle furiously with the napkin, barely talking to Elly. She couldn't understand his anxiety, but when Martin arrived soon after, things began to shift into focus. Martin was the elder of the two, the more classically good-looking, tall with dark hair and broad shoulders. He worked for a bank in London, a bigger and more well-known bank than the one where Ethan worked, and was only up in Edinburgh to wine and dine clients.

"Bit of a shoddy wine list, isn't it?" he said to Elly, before holding his hand out for her to shake.

He was pleasant enough. He asked Elly whether she'd eaten here before and what her favourite cut of steak was. But Ethan was quiet and surly from the off, giving the dinner an edgy atmosphere. When Martin asked Elly what she did for work, Ethan said quickly, "She's a chef." The kind of look he gave her made Elly feel like prey pinned down by an animal's paw.

"Well," she said, looking from him to Martin, wondering if she was missing anything, "I wouldn't say chef, exactly. I just work in a bakery."

Elly can still see it now: the way Ethan's face seemed

to drain of life, his grip tightening so hard around his fork that it turned his knuckles white. There was a long, awkward moment before Martin started to laugh. It wasn't mean, not exactly, but it was very close.

"Fuck's sake, Ethan." He laughed, jabbing his brother in the side with his elbow. "Do Mum and Dad know that? They'll never let you hear the end of it. A bakery, Jesus Christ." He shook his head, then seemed to remember Elly was there. "No offence, Elly."

"None taken." She'd wanted to sink as far down as she could in her seat. "I love it there."

"Well, good," Martin said. "That's good."

For the rest of the meal, Ethan wouldn't speak to her, would barely look at her. Every bite of steak seemed to take forever to grind down to nothing. Luckily, Martin had enough to say for all three of them, launching into lengthy speeches about Formula One, Bitcoin, the Bauhaus movement. Over dessert, he asked Elly whether she'd ever been to the Guggenheim.

"Don't bother," Ethan said, sticking a fork into the centre of his chocolate fondue and letting the sauce come spilling out, "she won't even know what that is."

Elly stared at him, waiting for a joking smile or wink that never came. Martin looked between them with a wry smile, but even he'd started to look uncomfortable. "Actually, I went when I was a teenager," she said eventually. "My dad was a sculptor." To Ethan, she added quietly, "You know that."

It wasn't until they'd said goodbye to Martin at the station and climbed into a taxi that Ethan finally turned to her. At first, Elly thought he was going to apologise for his brother being so rude, or for his own odd mood all evening, say something like, *I'm so sorry, I get a bit weird around my brother, you can probably see why.*

Instead, in a voice as cold and precise as a scalpel, he said, "You're going to stop working at the bakery, and you're going to get a proper fucking job."

When Elly says this, Theo looks away from the viewfinder and straight at her. It shakes her a little, brings her back into the room. "Jesus," he whispers quietly. He leans all the way forward in his seat, as if he wants to reach out and touch her. She half-wishes he would – finds herself wondering whether his hands would be calloused or smooth, how they'd feel against her skin. It sends little jolts through her. It's an effort to remember she'd been talking about her husband. She knows how it makes Ethan look, the story she's just told, but the guilt she expects never arrives. There is so much more she could say, so much more that she wants to say: how his chides had turned to barely veiled insults about her job, her appearance, the food she made; how he'd sometimes go silent for days at a time, until she found herself apologising for anything she could think of that might have provoked him. The way he'd pull her close then gut her with his words, so she was never sure of the ground she walked on. *You're just lucky I'm so patient, Elly.*

But Elly's muscles are heavy now, her throat scratchy. She doesn't know how long she's been talking. "Can we stop there? I'm tired."

"Sure." Theo coughs, sitting back and clicking a button on the camera. The red light above the lens turns black.

She's just dozed off into a light sleep when Margot shakes her awake. Her eyes are pale moons in the dark lake of the night. "Wakey wakey, Little Mouse. It's your turn to watch Lakshmi."

Elly rises reluctantly out of bed, the vestiges of her dreams clinging to her like leeches. Ethan in the bakery, snow in his hair. It all feels too close now, after talking about him with Theo. She pulls on a loose hoodie over her pyjamas, slow and stumbling, sensing the other bodies in the beds watching her. As she pads downstairs barefoot, Elly realises that this is as quiet as she's ever heard the house: in the absence of voices, of music, of doors opening and closing, there's only the occasional bird call and the creaking of the foundations, the house murmuring in its sleep.

In the parlour, Lakshmi lies still under a tartan blanket. Her lumpen form looks so small and insubstantial, as if she might fade away at any moment. The room is low-lit by table lamps, the French doors open a crack to let in a breath of air from the garden. Elly kneels beside Lakshmi and watches her chest rising and falling slowly, wondering how it is that she's still alive. Her face is wan and drawn, sheathed in a thin sweat that glistens in the cleft above her upper lip, sweat curling the hair at her temples and forehead. Her right cheekbone is swollen, bruised, and there are bandages across her visible chest. Elly guesses that there are many, many more beneath the blanket. Lakshmi groans and Elly takes one of her hands. The skin is cool, clammy.

"You're going to be okay," she finds herself whispering. "I promise."

Lakshmi's lips tremble and part. They're chapped, on

the brink of bleeding. She whispers something and Elly can smell her stale breath.

On the table beside the sofa, there is a glass of water with a straw, a flannel and some spare bandages. Elly dips the flannel into the water to wet it and then squeezes a drop or two onto Lakshmi's lips. She imagines the drops snaking their way deep down into her body, seeking out the broken places.

"I'm sorry," she says, although she isn't quite sure what she's sorry for. That Lakshmi fell? That she can't leave the house now? That whatever happened to her meant she had to come to Hex House in the first place?

When Elly looks up, Lakshmi is smiling at her. She reaches out a hand to touch Elly's cheek, brushing away a tear she hadn't known had fallen. "No sadness," Lakshmi whispers. "I was flying, didn't you see?" She squeezes her eyes shut, wincing. "I wish he could have seen me. I wish he could have seen what I can do."

Elly nods. She can't stop the tears now. She doesn't know who Lakshmi's talking about, knows it isn't her place to ask, so she says nothing. When Lakshmi opens her eyes again, they're filmy, dull, devoid of lucidity.

"Is my dad here?" she whispers. "I want my dad here."

"He's coming," she offers, hoping it's the right thing to say. "He'll be here soon."

That seems to calm her. Lakshmi settles back into the cushions, closing her eyes again. Elly lays her head on the sofa arm, keeping Lakshmi's hand in hers. She doesn't realise she's fallen asleep until Lakshmi squeezes her gently. When Elly looks at her, there's a little more colour in her cheeks.

"You can go now, Elly," she says. Her voice creaks like an old floorboard. She beams. "Haina's here."

Haina is standing in the doorway. She is as tall and serene as always. Her dark hair is unplaited and loose over her shoulders, and she wears a nightgown of orange silk. She isn't smiling.

"I can stay with her," Elly whispers. "I don't mind."

Haina crosses the parlour towards them. She stands behind the sofa so that she can reach down and cup one hand around Lakshmi's chin. She addresses Elly without looking at her. "Go to bed."

Something feels different in the room now; there is a heaviness, a tightness. Elly does as she's told, knees aching as she gets to her feet. Before she leaves the parlour, she turns to look back at Haina and Lakshmi. Haina is still standing over the sofa, peering down. Her eyes are dark. Lakshmi looks up at her, smiling softly, a child ready to submit to the comforting arms of a mother.

SIOBHAN

NOW

After leaving Owen's office, Siobhan makes her way to the library. Without really knowing why, she's brought her laptop with her, and her bag feels heavy as she walks. She feels the laptop's thrumming presence at her back. It's already 1:30, and she's late to meet Zara, a fact evidenced by the three missed calls on her phone. Still, she can't make herself hurry as she enters the library's revolving doors.

The library feels larger and fuller than she remembers it, the bottom floor crammed with people studying and chatting in groups. At the barriers she remembers that she doesn't have a card and can't get in. It makes her feel prickly, like a fraud. She asks at reception for the guest pass Zara has left for her, then makes her way up to the first floor. It's quieter up here, only a few headphoned students plugged into laptops, surrounded by empty coffee cups and crisp packets. Off the main floor with its stacks and shelves is a slim corridor, home to a number of individual study rooms.

Zara jumps up when Siobhan walks in, then quickly

sits again, as if trying not to let her relief show. Today, her bright hair is curled and loose around her face. The room is cosy and plain, windowless. There are various pieces of equipment set up already on the table: a laptop, a couple of mic packs, a small camera on a tripod.

"Hope you don't mind me saying, but you look like hell," Zara says as Siobhan takes a seat.

"You're the one who brought the vodka," Siobhan says. She can still feel her hangover clinging to the edges of her senses. Staring into the camera lens, her skin begins to itch. She shuffles and looks away – she'd rather Zara think she was bored than nervous. She is used to being the one doing the recording, she realises now. It doesn't feel right to be on the other side.

"Like I said last night," Zara is saying, "we'll just chat. There's no pressure."

Haina is dead, Siobhan reminds herself as she nods. *Haina is dead.*

Zara turns her attention to the camera. There's a beeping sound, then Zara gives her a thumbs up. "Maybe we could start right at the beginning," she says. "What did you know about Hex House, before you were offered the commission?"

"Not much," Siobhan says. Her voice sounds dry and gravelly, so she clears her throat. "Just rumours and silly stories. Kids at school used to talk about it like it was the Bermuda Triangle or something. A place to go missing. Some people said it was where women went to learn black magic and curses. I had a friend who was convinced girls turned into monsters there, monsters who hunted you if you told lies. I never believed in any of it. Not even as a kid."

"Until?"

"Until that letter. Haina…" She stops, not quite able to believe that she's just said Haina's name out loud. She digs her fingernails into her palms. "Haina told me she wanted someone to tell the house's story. Somehow, she knew about the film I made as part of my degree. She said I would understand what the house was, what it was trying to do. She didn't mention bringing Theo, but I wouldn't have gone without him."

"I've seen your film, about the women's shelter," Zara says, "it's very powerful. Very raw." Siobhan feels a bristling under her skin, something she takes a while to recognise as a stirring of old pride. "Am I right in thinking that it's a personal topic for you?"

Siobhan swallows. She hadn't expected to talk about this, about Nora, about her dad. "I lived there for a year after my mum left my dad."

"Where is he now?"

"Dead." A beat of silence. "Drunk driving."

Zara takes a sharp intake of breath. One hand rests softly on her chest. "I'm so sorry."

"I'm not."

"Are you happy to continue?"

"Sure."

"Do you know why Haina wanted to make the documentary, at that point in time? It seems strange. A house, hidden away for decades, some even say centuries, cloistered in a forest where no one can find it. Then suddenly, Haina decides it should be all over Netflix. Did that strike you as odd?"

"She wanted to help more people," Siobhan murmurs. "At least, that's what she said."

Something flickers in Zara's eyes: a suspicion, a journalistic instinct. But for whatever reason, she moves on. Her voice is tentative, tiptoeing. "According to Willow, the woman who was at the centre of your documentary was the same one who went missing in the Borders on her wedding night. Elly Carmichael. She was all over the news a few years ago. Is that right?"

Siobhan nods, staring into the lens.

"Willow says that something happened to Elly while you were at the house. She says…" Zara trails off.

Siobhan closes her eyes, and Elly is waiting for her there in the blackness. Elly's fragile voice and spun-silk hair. Elly, gentle as a lamb, baby in her belly. Elly, who she has betrayed every day of her life since she left that house. What does it mean, to speak her name into her air now? What will it call into being? Siobhan's skin creeps to think of it, but that's why she's here. She's here to finally look Elly's ghost in the eye. "Yes," is all she can manage to say, her voice barely more than a croak.

"Can we talk about that now?"

Siobhan opens her mouth, but nothing comes out. She feels as though her tongue is bolted to her soft palate, writhing like a fish out of water.

"Don't worry," Zara says quickly. "We have plenty of time. Let's move on." She flicks through a notebook in front of her, looking for something, pinning the page down with her finger when she finds it. "Did you also know someone called Lakshmi Khan?" Siobhan nods again. "Willow told me about her, too. That she fell."

Siobhan scoffs, an empty, humourless sound. "That's one way of putting it, I suppose."

"How would you put it, Siobhan?"

Siobhan meets her gaze now, maintains eye contact. Here they are, at the meaty centre of everything, at the crux of what Hex House is and what it does to the women who find themselves there. Can she really speak it? Should she?

Haina is dead. Haina is dead.

Once she starts, the words flow surprisingly easily. These words have been waiting, she realises, waiting all this time to rip a hole right through the silence. "The women change, at Hex House. They become something that isn't quite a woman anymore. Something that's both more and less. Haina makes them into something. She... transforms them."

The words seem to pull the air from the room. They curl themselves around the table legs and climb up the grained wood, find Siobhan's ribcage, the lean muscle of her neck. Start to squeeze. Zara is still looking at her blankly, and it dawns on Siobhan that she doesn't understand, or maybe she doesn't even believe her. How could she? What can Siobhan possibly say to make her see? What words could come close to the awful, incredible, terrifying creatures the women became?

"I'm not speaking metaphorically," she says limply, and Zara narrows her eyes. "The women's bodies. They change. They become monsters."

"Monsters?"

Gnarled hands. Clawed feet. Wings that could crush a man. "I can show you," she says eventually.

Is she doing this? Is she *really* doing this? No one has ever seen the footage apart from her and Theo, and even he doesn't know she still has it. She thinks about getting up and leaving, but her body won't listen to her, is already unzipping her bag and bringing out her laptop. Zara watches her carefully as she places it on the table, opens it, clicks open the video player. There it is, the clip still paused from the night before. Siobhan can't look at it. She turns the screen towards Zara, who hesitates, and then presses play.

Siobhan tries to tune it out: the sound of the women hollering insults as Lakshmi stands on the rooftop and begins to change. She watches Zara's face, watches as it drains of colour, watches as her mouth grows slack and drops open. The beating of wings, women's voices, cheering. Then, the screams. The silence that came after. The camera, Siobhan knows now, will be trained on Lakshmi's broken body. Zara's hand is covering her mouth, her eyes are wide and unblinking. She pushes the laptop away, as though it might infect her.

"No," she says, breathless, "oh my god, no. Willow, she told me that the women, they change... but I never thought..."

The camera is still rolling, recording every second. Siobhan finds herself standing up and turning it off. For a long time, neither of them says a word. Siobhan digs her fingers so deeply into her scar that the pain takes her breath away. When she looks at Zara, at her face which has turned greenish, she almost feels guilty. *Now you know, too*, she thinks grimly. *Now you're in this with me*. Zara doesn't know it yet, but every day she lives with this knowledge it will exact a punishment from her, will take its pound of flesh.

Zara hasn't looked directly at Siobhan since watching

the clip. It's only when Siobhan reaches over and shuts the laptop screen that she finally meets her eye.

"It's real," Zara whispers eventually. She looks a bit dazed, haunted, like she's coming round from a nightmare. "Hex House. It's *real*."

Later, back at the flat, Siobhan pauses in front of the bathroom mirror. She watches herself hiding behind the smears and toothpaste flecks. There's a haziness to her, like she's the ghost in a film. Sam in *Ghost*. *The Woman in Black*.

Siobhan peels up the hem of her T-shirt to inspect her scar. Her clawing at it in the library has had an impact: the scabs are gone, replaced by a vivid red seam surrounded by just-dried blood. Not only that, but the scar is oozing something, a sickly yellow liquid, greasy and viscous. Siobhan wipes a little of it onto her finger and holds it to her nose. It smells putrid, like something that should never come out of a human body. Siobhan wipes haphazardly at the scar with some toilet tissue. When she can't look at it any longer, she goes over to the sofa, where the takeaway cartons still litter the coffee table. Taking a bite of stone-cold chow mein, she opens her laptop again, even though she'd promised herself she wouldn't. She tells herself that each clip she watches will be the last, but still she clicks on thumbnail after thumbnail, powerless in the face of Hex House's magnetism, even now. Many of the clips are hard to watch, but just as many are mundane, snippets of everyday life in the house: guests singing to each other in the parlour, trying on clothes, eating together around the dinner table. These clips are comforting, somehow.

Siobhan has started to miss the house when she's not inhabiting it through the screen, she realises, as much as she doesn't want to admit it. Every second she isn't immersed in its details, she wants to be. She needs to be. It feels more real than her reality, a richer and more textured world than the one she now inhabits. When had it started to pull her in again? To sink its teeth into her, so deep that she could never hope to pull them out?

The next clip in the list is of Elly. So many of them are. Theo and his camera seemed always to find her: Elly smiling shyly at breakfast, Elly lying on the bench in the sun like a cat, proud belly towards the sky. After Theo showed Siobhan the first interview he'd done with Elly, it became obvious to both of them that she would be the focus of the documentary, the heart of it, the story around which everything else would revolve. There was something so fragile about her – as if you could crush her beneath your thumb with the smallest amount of pressure – that made her compelling to watch. She also seemed to have some kind of intimate connection with the camera, to know exactly when to look and when to look away. So many of the other guests performed awkwardly for Theo's gaze, but never Elly.

In this clip, she is looking at herself in the dormitory's full-length mirror. She smooths her dress down over her bump so that she can feel the size of it, and then turns to the side to appreciate it from different angles. She doesn't seem to know that Theo and his camera are there until she catches the glint of the lens in the mirror. She turns, grinning.

In the next clip, Elly is in the kitchen. When Siobhan thinks of her, she is always in the kitchen, in the warmth, standing at the wooden countertop with dough under her fingers. Theo zooms in on her hands, pale and fine-boned, as they sweep flour across the surface. By this point, she isn't wearing her wedding ring. Keiko and Grace are in the background having a quiet conversation the camera can't quite pick up. Haina enters the shot, a sudden flare of orange. She embraces each of the women in turn, dances with them around the kitchen to an old song on the radio. She grips Elly close, laughing with an open mouth, spinning her round and round. Whenever Haina entered a room, it seemed to bloom into technicolour. In the clip, Haina releases Elly, who looks back at the camera with flushed cheeks and a heaving chest. She smiles at Theo in a way that makes Siobhan's heart constrict.

The bond between Elly and Theo – when did it start? Maybe it was that first interview, while Siobhan was stalking the gardens after their argument, trying to make sense of what had happened to Lakshmi and why her first instinct had been to commit as much of the girl's broken body to camera as she could. Or maybe it had started before that. It seems so obvious now, watching the clips, how they felt about each other. But Siobhan had been less tuned in to it at the time. Or, she simply couldn't have cared less. Elly had been a subject, fodder for the camera, her story nothing more than a way to add depth and dimension to the documentary. Watching the footage now, Elly so vital and shimmering, it's easy to forget what happened next.

Siobhan shuts the laptop again. Some unreachable place inside her is itching. The only thing that'll help, she knows, is a drink. She checks the fridge but it's empty, and so she shrugs on a denim jacket and shoves her feet into trainers, leaving the warmth of the flat for the cool Edinburgh evening. She wanders down the Mile without really knowing where she's going, only that she needs to move. She finds herself down on the Cowgate, the long, dark street lurking under George IV Bridge. It used to be the road farmers would use to bring their cows to market, a thick highway of dung and noise. Now, it's home to a strip of bars and basement clubs. Everything in Edinburgh is coated in layers of existence like this: everything restless and changing and unfinished, like skin that constantly regenerates. She walks into a nondescript bar without bothering to read the name. The floor is dark and sticky; it smells of cheap beer and urine. It's only ten thirty, but it's already getting busy. From the floor beneath comes the thump of techno music. At the bar, Siobhan orders a vodka tonic, drinks it quickly, then orders another. The drinks don't work as fast as she'd like – she's fidgety as she sits alone with her elbows on the bar. A skinny man with a moustache peers at her and asks to buy her a drink. She lets him. He tries to start up a conversation about the music downstairs but Siobhan ignores him. Still, he buys her another drink, a shot.

By this time, the alcohol has finally started to work its magic. Siobhan feels it hit against her senses, like a hammer into metal, transforming them into a more manageable shape. Hex House and its details fall away. Elly's clear eyes and quiet laugh recede into the blackness. Maybe Siobhan drinks something else, or maybe she just imagines that she does, and then she's being led by the skinny man down a steep set of stairs into the basement club. The music is so loud it rattles her teeth, the tangle of bodies so tight that she has to push in between them to find a space on the dance floor, every inch of her body seeming to connect with every inch of theirs. She can barely make out anything but bass, it's so loud. Siobhan lets it move her bones. The skinny man tries to push himself against her but it's easy enough to push him away, to reclaim the space he took as her own, to sway and move until her feet ache and her scar starts to throb. If only she could always feel like this, this far away and detached from everything real. She'd be okay, then, she thinks. She'd really be okay.

When she can barely breathe for the closeness of the club, she stumbles back out into the main bar, and then out onto the Cowgate. It's busier now, clouds of smokers standing outside the clubs, spitting and shouting and shoving each other. She makes her way back to the Mile, looking for a reason not to have to go straight home. She can't bear to be alone in the flat again. That's why Sylvie seems almost god-sent when she appears, walking quickly from the direction of the Parliament. She's so tall that she stands out wherever she is, legs long and graceful, back slender. Tonight, she walks quickly and with purpose. Siobhan has rarely seen her outside of the Showroom, and realises just how stylish she is, how put-together in her fitted black coat and silk dress the colour of red wine. Sylvie hasn't seen Siobhan yet. She wonders what she must look like, sweat-slicked from the club, drinks spilled down her old hoodie. She falls back a little into the crowd and follows Sylvie from a short distance away as she takes a shortcut down Fleshmarket Close. Siobhan wills herself invisible as she sticks to the shadows twenty steps behind, but Sylvie is wearing large headphones, and she doesn't turn around.

You should be more careful, Sylvie, Siobhan thinks. *Pretty girl like you. You never know who might be following you.*

Sylvie crosses onto Princes Street. It's easier to hide here, the crowds thicker and more fast-moving. She keeps on walking through town to George Street, with its wide pavements and upscale restaurants. Of course, this is where Sylvie would come. Of course, this would be her natural habitat. Siobhan hangs back and watches Sylvie go inside Melody Blossom, a sleek cocktail bar with an elaborate floral arch curling around the door. It has large windows, so Siobhan has a good view inside. She watches as Sylvie removes her headphones and greets someone at the bar, a young woman wearing a pristine camel blazer and high boots. She wonders what cocktails they might order, what obscure ingredients they'll contain, how much they might cost.

Siobhan stays outside the window for a long moment, watching, and then pulls out her phone. Her scar is throbbing – she should sit, she should go home – but instead, she fires off a text to Owen.

Did you have your tutorial with Sylvie?

He replies after a couple of minutes. *Hey. Yeah. It was quite useful for her actually – she's got some great ideas. Cheers for suggesting it. Still on for dinner tomorrow night?*

It's strange, the feeling that spreads out in the bottom of her stomach. She feels caught out, punished, but at the same time, it's intoxicating. She feels like a wife who's caught her husband watching porn – there's a betrayal to it, but a fascination, too.

She types, *Good. I'm at Melody Blossom on George Street. Come and meet me?*

Wouldn't have thought that was your kind of place? She waits until he texts again. *Okay, sure. On my way.*

Hurry up.

Siobhan calculates that it'll take him about fifteen minutes to walk from his flat to the bar, but he turns up in a taxi barely five minutes later. She has to duck behind a phone box so that he doesn't see her. She watches as he shuts the taxi door and makes his way inside. Only when she's confident he won't see her does she look back through the window. Owen is standing at the bar, scanning the room for her. Sylvie stands on the opposite side of the room with her friend.

Her phone pings. *Here. Where are you?*

She doesn't answer. She feels heady, unpredictable, light on her feet. After a minute, she texts back, *I'm not there, but Sylvie is.*

She watches as he opens the message. He frowns. She wants him to look around, but he doesn't, he just keeps looking down at his phone. *How do you know that? Why aren't you here?*

Siobhan watches as Sylvie's friend leaves the bar in the direction of the toilet.

Go and talk to her, she types quickly, fingers shaking on the keys. *Go and say hi.*

Owen looks up from his phone again, searches the bar. There's something more desperate about him now. He seems upset. She sees him notice Sylvie, her perfect skin, the red sheen of her expensive dress, the careful way she's done her make-up. What kind of man is he, if he doesn't want that for himself? He looks down again at his phone. His text is a simple word.

Why?

Siobhan's fingers hover over the keys. *Because I want you to.* Then, she adds, *Because you told me I was in control.*

Owen rubs a weary hand over his face. What will he do? Will he come out here and find her? He sends her one last text, *This isn't fun, Siobhan*, and then heads down the bar in Sylvie's direction. He touches a hand to the small of her back, and Sylvie turns. She's holding a martini glass. Siobhan squints to better see her reaction. Is she pleased? Is she creeped out? Owen leans in close to whisper something in her ear and she doesn't pull away. She looks up at him, laughing, one hand half-covering her mouth. Siobhan turns away from the window and sets off down the street, trying to understand why she feels so electric, why she feels like her every nerve ending is burning.

ELLY

THEN

Elly wakes in the morning to find another body in her bed. Margot must have crawled in with her during the night and is now curled up tightly against her back. Her dark hair is almost completely covering her face.

"Margot," she whispers. "Time to wake up."

Margot squints against the shafts of sun filtering in from the window. Her eye is puffy and swollen, as if she's been crying.

"What is it? What's happened?"

"Lakshmi." Margot sniffs, pulling down the sleeve of her jumper to wipe her nose. "She's gone."

"Gone?" Elly blinks at her, still waking up, unable to process the words.

"She died," Margot whispers, voice breaking. The words are so stark they make Elly's stomach lurch.

"No, she was okay last night. She looked... *better*."

Margot shakes her head, propping herself up to sit.

"No, Little Mouse. Haina said. Haina was with her. She just… she just slipped away. No more pain now."

Elly bites down on her lip, feeling sick. She thinks of Lakshmi, the way she'd gazed up at Haina from the sofa as if she were looking up at an angel. The dorm is bathed in morning light the colour of egg yolks. The other women are just beginning to stir. Everything feels too normal, too wholesome. A woman can't possibly be dead downstairs.

Haina tells the rest of the guests about Lakshmi over breakfast. She stands at the head of the table as she addresses them, and Elly thinks distantly that she looks healthier and more vital than she has ever seen her, her hair shining and eyes sparkling, as she delivers this news about death.

"Lakshmi has already been laid to rest, my angels, to spare you the torment," she tells them, and Elly feels as if her whole body is numb, like the nerves have simply given up, fizzled out. Beside Haina, both Siobhan and Theo sit white-faced, barely looking at each other. "She's in the garden now, where you can of course visit her, if you wish to."

Later, Elly will wander the gardens and come across a steep bank near the pond at the back of the house. There will be a long and wide patch of recently overturned earth. Above it, a simple plank of wood, into which has been carved the outline of two wings alongside Lakshmi's name. Elly will stare at it for a long time. She will think about Lakshmi's family and wonder where they are. She'll think about the way that, even after seven years, even after whatever he must have done to her to make her run, Lakshmi still asked for her father at the end. She will be concentrating so intently on Lakshmi's grave that it will take her a long time to notice the other planks of wood, so many of them, stretching away from her in a line.

That evening is the Autumn Equinox, and it's decided that the feast they had planned will still go ahead, despite the events of the night before. In the kitchens, Grace has Elly and Keiko coating fleshy ham shanks in brown sugar and mustard, preparing enormous salmon sides, soaking ripe plums in brandy and blackberries in sloe gin for dessert. The long oak table is carried out from the refectory and into the gardens, so the guests can dine under the light of the moon. Elly tries to lose herself in the labour, but it's more difficult than usual. Keiko is red-eyed as she works, and Grace barely speaks except to give them orders.

Haina summons Elly to her study in the late afternoon for her third session. Elly lingers for a long time outside the closed door, not able to stop thinking about Lakshmi, about the indescribable form she'd taken on the rooftop. The things that happened to her own body behind this door had felt like potential before – they'd felt like strength. Now, they feel like stepping off the edge of the roof, just as Lakshmi had, and waiting to fall.

"Come in, Elly," Haina calls, making her jump. She hadn't realised she'd knocked.

Elly takes her usual seat across from Haina at the desk. There's something even cosier about the study today; it smells like candlewax and spice, and the fire in the grate is just the right temperature.

"How are you feeling, Elly?" Haina asks, leaning forward in her chair. Her dress is the colour of a flame. "I know the last few days must have been difficult for you. There's so much you don't understand yet."

"Will you tell her family?" Elly finds herself asking. "Or the police?"

Haina's eyebrow quirks, just for a second, before her face resumes its placid expression. "Why would I do that?"

"Don't you think you… should? If she's missing, they should know. There'll be records to update, and—"

"Elly," Haina says firmly, interrupting her. "You need to listen to me when I say this. No one *out there*," she inclines her head sharply towards the window, to the world beyond Hex House's gardens, "had Lakshmi's best interests at heart. When she was a child, her father beat her so badly that one of her ribs punctured her lung. Social services were called. Do you know what they did? Nothing. Do you know why?"

Elly shakes her head.

"Because Lakshmi's father was a police officer. Only, he decided that he didn't really care much about the law, not if it stopped him using his daughter as a piece of meat to pummel."

Elly listens dumbly. She feels as though her scalp is crawling.

"People come to this house for so many reasons, Elly." Haina sighs. "They've been abandoned, abused, forgotten, tormented. They don't feel at home inside themselves; they don't feel at home anywhere. Some have been through things you can't even begin to imagine. That pain – it unites us. We don't owe the world anything. We could

205

tell Lakshmi's family, we could leave her body somewhere they'd find it, but for what? Lakshmi turned her back on all of it when she found us. She would have preferred to die a hundred times in here than live a hundred lifetimes out there."

Elly's head buzzes. She has so many questions but she can't wrangle the words into coherent sentences. She wonders whether it's illegal, what Haina has done: burying someone in the middle of the night, telling no one beyond these walls. Not the authorities, not her family, who, no matter how corrupt their characters, might still be searching for Lakshmi.

But Haina has already moved on, is shuffling the papers on her desk into a neat pile. "Are you ready to begin?" she asks, and Elly doesn't feel like she can say anything other than yes. Her body prickles in anticipation of violence, of the skin opening and the blood running, but Haina makes no move to fetch the knife from the drawer.

"Let's see if you can summon your hex yourself today," says Haina. "Some people never learn to find it themselves. They always need a threat to coax it out into the light. But I have a good feeling about you, my angel." Elly wonders at that, at what could have given her that impression. "Close your eyes," Haina whispers. "Try to feel it."

Elly does so, swapping the soft light of the study for the quiet dark behind her eyelids.

"Concentrate," Haina says gently. "What do you see?"

At first, Elly sees nothing but fuzziness, how she imagines the static between radio stations to look. But slowly, like ice beginning to melt, the images seep in. She sees the woods at night, but from the air, from the point of view of something

206

soaring high above the treetops. Her senses feel keener – she can smell the warm-blooded things below, prey running, seeking out the hiding places. She can see the intricate swirls of organic matter in the dirt. She can hear voices, very far away. It's irresistible, the power of it all.

"That's it," Haina is saying. "Sink into it. How do you *feel*?"

Part of Elly tries to resist, but it's impossible not to tune in to the internal life of this creature – a creature that feels completely separate from her, but simultaneously as if it inhabits her completely. It is strong and it likes to use its muscles; it likes to carve up the sky with its wings. It likes to assert itself, it likes to feel large, furious, instant. It's hungry, she realises. It is so, so hungry.

"It wants to hunt," she says.

"Very good," Haina says, and Elly can hear the smile in her voice. It is intoxicating, to please her like this. "What does it want to hunt?"

Elly thinks about the forest below her, all of the tiny hearts beating, all of the little skeletons with their strips of flesh that would be so easy to peel away. Does she want any of those? No. She wants something bigger. She flies on, until the treetops are swapped for the pointed roofs of houses. Elly makes her creature – her *hex* – fly higher, so that she won't be spotted by the figures walking in the streets. She recognises these houses. She knows the topography of this particular place by heart. It feels familiar in her bones a minute or two before she recognises it as the village she grew up in. There's her mum and dad's house, with its triangular garden and the roof slates that need replacing, a job her mum will probably never get round to now. There's the church she was married in. How long ago now? A month? A lifetime.

There's nothing here, she realises. Nothing to satisfy her appetite. And she is so, so hungry.

"Keep looking," says Haina.

Elly flies on. She skirts the top of the hills so closely that her claws scrape along the dirt, tearing up the grass. She flies over a choked-up motorway, busy roundabouts, congested carriageways that belch car after car into the centre of Edinburgh. Does she know where she's going? Of course she does.

"Ah," Haina whispers. "You've found him."

She's hovering over Ethan's flat in the New Town. She descends so that she can see inside his window, into the living room where she's spent so many evenings sitting with him, trying to convince herself she liked her life. He is on the phone. He is *smiling*.

Elly's mouth starts to pool with saliva. There is something wicked pulsing with her every heartbeat, charging up her bones, making her wings ache with longing.

"What are you going to do about it?" Haina asks, in a voice like a prayer.

Elly lets herself picture it. Ethan's supple body beneath her powerful claws, ripping the arms from the torso, shredding the meat of his thighs. She could smash *his* head against the wall, watch it open in all its spectacular colours. She almost cries out with the pleasure of it, with the heady sensation of her hex having fulfilled its need.

Elly's eyes snap open. "No," she gasps, gripping onto the arms of the armchair. "Please, not that."

It takes a long time for Haina's face to come into focus

again, for Elly to recognise the expression on her face for what it is. Fury.

"*Please not that?*" she spits back at Elly. "After how he treated you?"

"He's my husband," Elly says. She doesn't know why this is the only thing she can think whenever she feels like she needs to defend Ethan. It feels like the truest thing. Sometimes it feels like the only true thing.

Haina's eyes are dark. They burn. "Think about it, Elly," she says, and her voice is lower now, steadier, which is somehow even worse than her anger. "What do you think this is all for? Why do you think we're here?"

Elly can't answer that. She can still feel it: how the earth had unrolled beneath her when she was airborne, how good it felt, how strong she'd been. The body she's in now is so weak in comparison. It's a liability, so aching and frail and encumbered. She can still feel it on her tongue and in her fingertips and stretching across the taut skin of her collarbone: how much she'd wanted to show herself to Ethan. *Look at me now*, she'd wanted to scream in his face. *Look at what I can do to you.*

As darkness falls, the guests take their seats outside for the Equinox feast. Festoon lights have been hung between the trees and lanterns swing from branches, casting the garden in hazy light. The table has been piled high with food, jugs of dark wine set next to mismatched glasses, wildflowers spilling over the lips of vases. The night is cool but not cold, and the harvest moon glows orange when it appears from behind the clouds, watching them all. All of it together has an effect on the mood of the house – Elly feels the other guests loosen, relax. They eat and eat until their stomachs strain. After dinner, the French doors to the back of the parlour are thrown wide so the music from the record player can reach them. The guests disperse from the table to lounge on the grass, to chase each other around the garden, yipping at each other's heels, howling and biting necks when they find each other. The red sisters have found a skipping rope and each hold an end as the other women take their turn to jump. They swing the rope in perfect unison, hooting with laughter whenever anyone's legs get whipped. Elly isn't surprised to see Siobhan and Theo hunched together over a camera, talking. Siobhan points at the table, the moon, the empty wine glasses, and Theo nods without looking at her, aiming the camera this way and that. At one point, Haina approaches them and speaks only to Siobhan. Siobhan's expression – it's so similar to the way Lakshmi had looked at Haina, the night she died. Almost like devotion, almost like love.

Elly finds Margot sitting alone on the grass, twirling one curl around her fingers. She sits down beside her, and Margot smiles weakly, taking Elly's arm in hers. "Hi, Little Mouse."

"Is everything okay?"

Margot shrugs, sniffling a little.

"Are you still worried about the filmmakers?"

Margot considers this for a second, then shakes her head. "Nothing I can do about it." Then, she places both of her hands on Elly's rounded belly. "I had a baby, too," she whispers.

Elly remembers seeing Margot's silvery C-section scar one night while they were getting changed. She had made herself look away. "You did?"

"I wasn't supposed to." The look in Margot's eye is detached. She takes her hands from Elly's stomach, looks up at the moon. "Everybody told me not to. But I had a baby and she had hair the colour of coal and skin like cream. Her skin was the softest thing I ever felt. I gave her away. I think that's where I went wrong. I gave her away." The words hang in the air, which is smoky from a small campfire some of the guests have started nearby.

Elly shifts a little closer to Margot. "Maybe it was the right thing. At the time."

Margot starts to tap her thighs against her palm, only gently, and Elly doesn't stop her. "The right thing," she says on a soft outbreath. "I think doing the right thing split me straight down the middle, let the dark in. Sometimes I don't want to be here at all. I just want to be with my baby."

They don't speak for a long time. Eventually, Elly takes one of Margot's hands in hers and presses it to her lips. "I'm so sorry," she whispers. Margot sniffs and shakes her head, as if she can shake away whatever images are crowding there, making her eye cloudy and dark. She looks so young, too young for the life she must have led to end up here.

They watch the guests around the campfire. Some of them are taking turns jumping over the flames, their eyes wild and glazed with wine, while the others look on, clapping. In the flickering light, it takes Elly a while to realise that they've taken their hex forms, or something close to them. Their faces are their own, but their naked bodies are covered with feathers that flare across their exposed midriffs, breasts, strong thighs.

"They're hexing," Elly says. There's a strange feeling in the pit of her belly – an aching, a pull.

Margot makes a little noise in the back of her throat. "Not usually supposed to, not like this. But Haina won't mind tonight."

Elly searches for Haina and Siobhan but can't find them anywhere in the gardens. From where she's sitting, she can see that the light in Haina's study is on.

It's getting late, already close to midnight, and some of the guests are retreating inside. Only a few are left scattered around the table: Keiko, starting to clear up the used dishes and glasses; Grace, smoking, her chair turned so she can face the treeline and the woods beyond. Then there's Theo, sitting next to a visibly drunk Janine. Her face is wet with tears, and her body drapes against his. She looks up at him with eyes wide and searching, as if he might be able to hold all her sadness for her. She hasn't stopped crying since she found out about Lakshmi, but there's an edge to her tonight, a hunger in the way her hands cling to Theo's T-shirt. Elly wonders how Theo must feel in this house full of women – how he feels when the intensity of their desire is turned on him. Does he feel like a king, or like prey? Theo turns and catches Elly's eye, and she looks away.

That night, Elly dreams of flying. She dreams of the swoop and glide. She circles high above the house, and when she comes to land, it's next to Lakshmi's grave. In the dream, she digs down deep into the earth and finds no body. Then she's in the forest, winding through the thickness of the canopy. In the dream, her belly is aching. It is rounded and swollen and distended. She hops across the forest floor to find a place to hide, a quiet place where the predators won't smell her. There's a huge pressure on her furred abdomen, and she pushes and squeezes and channels her life force into it. She looks down to see that her baby is a round, smooth egg.

When she wakes the next day, it's with dirt under her fingernails and leaves in her hair. Margot sits next to her on the bed and picks them out one by one, tender, monkey-like. "You went wandering, Little Mouse," she says softly. "It's a good sign."

Over the next week, Elly does three more interviews with Theo. Sometimes, Siobhan is there, too, an intense and meticulous presence behind the lens, constantly interrupting to change the track of the conversation or adjust the angle of the camera. Most of the time though, Siobhan is with Haina, and it's just her and Theo. He lets the camera run. He lets her talk and talk.

Elly won't admit it even to herself, not yet, but she finds herself engineering additional opportunities to speak to Theo, to be in the same room as him. She's almost always aware of his presence, wherever he is in the house. She's relieved that her offer of the interviews seems to have kept him here, for now, but she doesn't know how long that might last. When she asks herself why she so desperately wants him to stay, she can't answer. She only knows that it has something to do with the softness of his eyes, the way he always asks if she's feeling okay before they start their interviews, if she needs anything. She likes the way his eyes look behind his glasses, a murky river green, a ring of gold around the pupil. The way those eyes look at her – it makes her feel like she's burning. It's almost too intense to be pleasurable, but she aches for the feeling whenever he isn't near her. One day, he gives her a Terry's Chocolate Orange he brought with him, casually and without ceremony, and it's so out of place in the surroundings of Hex House that it feels like a talisman from another time. She cherishes it the same way she would a photograph, taking it out of her bedside table every now and again just to look at it, to run her fingers over the foil, to turn it over and over in her hands. She doesn't eat any herself but gives a piece to Margot, who grins at her through chocolate-coated teeth then closes her eye and lies down on her bed, as if in rapture.

When the camera isn't on, her conversations with Theo meander. They talk about arbitrary, everyday things. Theo tells her that he knows all the lyrics to every song by Green Day, and that his death row meal would be a sausage sandwich made by his mum. He tells her that all his friends think his favourite TV show is *The Sopranos*, but it's actually *The OC*, and he grew up wanting to be like gentle, nerdy Seth. He asks about Elly's dad, and she finds herself telling him about the last collection of sculptures he made before he died, a series of animals in hibernation.

One day, she shows him how to make apple tarte tatin. He messes up the pastry but it still tastes good, and they share it after dinner in the parlour, picking at the syrupy apples until there's nothing left but crumbs. The flavour is so tart, the lights are so dim, and Theo is sitting so close to her that Elly feels bold. Without thinking, she takes one of his sugar-crusted fingers into her mouth, licking off the granules before holding it there on the warmth of her tongue. She watches him watching her, the way his chest rises and falls, faster faster faster; watches his eyes become unfocused and heavy-lidded, until he seems to come back into himself and pulls his hand away.

Sometimes, it makes Elly feel guilty, how much she looks forward to seeing Theo's face over breakfast, the way she listens out for his voice in the hallway whenever she's working in the kitchens, the way she craves the pressure of his body beside hers in bed at night, in the blurry moments before sleep. She wonders what Ethan would think, and she thinks about his baby in her belly. It makes her hate herself. She'd desired Ethan, but it had felt so different. Wanting Ethan had felt like staring into an open mouth and stepping willingly inside. Wanting him had made her feel small, as if she were barely a body at all, only the idea of one. When she thinks about Theo, when she pictures his hands around her hips and his lips on her neck, she feels bigger than herself, bigger than him, bigger than the whole house. It makes her want to stand naked in the sunlight, arch her back, swallow the world. One morning, she greases her wedding finger with warm butter and finally manages to ease the ring up and over the bone. She puts it in her bedside drawer in the dormitory and locks it. After a while, she forgets it's there.

During one interview, in the candlelit refectory late at night, Theo asks her if she still thinks about walking out of Hex House and back into her old life. Elly doesn't know how to explain it to him: how that simply doesn't feel like an option anymore.

"Siobhan said I was on the news," she says. "Before you got here. Did you... did you see me?" *What a ridiculous question to ask*, she chastises herself. *Stop being so self-absorbed*. But still, she watches his face intently as he nods.

"Sometimes I feel guilty," he tells her, "knowing where you are, when all those people are looking for you."

Something twisting and sharp, deep in her belly. "I'm sorry."

"Don't be," he says quickly. "I understand why you ran. Why you couldn't stay with him." He lowers his voice. "None of it is your fault, Elly."

Almost instantly, her eyes start to burn. Because without realising it, she has always believed that the way Ethan treated her *was* her fault, that it had to be, that his behaviour was only a reflection of her inherent weakness. She blames herself for all of it: for going through with the wedding, for being pregnant with a baby whose father she fears, for running, for hiding in Hex House with no clue what to do next. She has always, she realises now, thought herself a coward. Hearing those words out loud – *none of it is your fault* – makes her feel as though her insides have been scraped clean.

She feels unable to continue that particular train of conversation, so instead she asks, "Are you sorry you came here?"

"Maybe." Theo blows air out through his lips, drags a hand through his hair, then says, "No, actually, I don't think I am. I don't know what kind of person that makes me."

"I don't know what kind of a person I am, either."

"Has it changed you? The house?"

Elly thinks about the feathers sprouting from her hands. She thinks about how it felt to be in her hex form, flattening all the world beneath her. "I don't know what it's doing to me," she says, and it's true. She doesn't know why she does it – seconds later she will wish she hadn't – but she reaches out for his hand and pulls him towards her. "I'm glad you're here," she says.

What is it that crosses his face then? Elly senses a pulsing, a longing, in the way his eyes focus on her lips and his body inches forward. But it only lasts a second before he withdraws his hand, leaving hers cold in her lap.

SIOBHAN

NOW

Siobhan and Owen meet for dinner at Wildfire. The restaurant is Owen's suggestion, intimate and low-ceilinged. The menu declares that it's proudly Scottish and is full of things like Shetland Mussels and haggis with Drambuie sauce. Siobhan feels underdressed and hungry. Her scar hasn't stopped throbbing since yesterday. Overnight, it oozed a pale green stain onto the sheets. This morning she plastered it with Sudocrem and a foul-smelling scab fell off into her hands.

Owen is quieter than usual. He greets her with a hug, but he won't quite meet her eye as they take their seats and order a bottle of wine. It's a novel feeling, not entirely unpleasant, to know that he's annoyed with her. Maybe he's an entirely different person than what she thought. Maybe she should have more respect for him; maybe she should put more effort into resisting the temptation to test him, to punish him.

"You seem tired," she says, once they've ordered their food.

Owen's face is half-hidden by his glass of wine. Their waiter merrily fills up their water, oblivious to the tension. "I was out at Melody Blossom last night," he says. "For no particular reason."

"How's Sylvie?"

Owen maintains eye contact, then places his glass down. This is a new side to him. Spiky. It makes his movements quicker and voice lower. Siobhan hadn't thought he had it in him. "Siobhan," he says, and it sounds like a warning. Her belly feels warm and empty. "You need to tell me what's going on, what this obsession with Sylvie is all about. You're putting me in some pretty uncomfortable positions, and I know you know that. You could get me in serious trouble."

"I told you to say hello," Siobhan says. "Nothing nefarious."

"You know what you're doing. I just don't understand why."

"Don't you like Sylvie? There's nothing not to like."

"Of course I like her," Owen snaps back, a little too loudly. Siobhan becomes aware of eyes turning their way. "But why do you care?"

"I'm in control," Siobhan says, and something in her voice makes him pause, look away. He casts a wary eye around the restaurant, as if concerned that they're being watched, that a hidden cameraman is going to jump out at any second and reveal the stitch-up.

"I like you, Siobhan," he says. "But you need to stop this now."

She finishes the dregs of wine in her glass and fills it up. His is empty, too, but she leaves it that way. "Fine. I'll stop."

There's a prickling silence in which Owen looks in

every direction but Siobhan's. It lasts until the starters arrive, and they stare down into bowls of Cullen skink rather than at each other.

"Why is it called Cullen skink?" Siobhan says. "It's just soup."

"It's named after where it's from," Owen says, then seems to run out of steam. "Never mind."

Before the mains arrive, Owen excuses himself to go to the toilet. He leaves his phone unlocked on the table and while he's away, it flashes with the arrival of a new message. Watching the closed door to the toilets, Siobhan edges it towards her so she can read the name of the sender. When she sees 'Sylvie', an electrical current floods her veins. She opens their message history. Sylvie's latest message comes as response to one he sent last night, at thirty minutes past midnight.

Hope this isn't weird, Owen had written, *but it was really great to run into you tonight. Lovely to see you let your hair down. Get home safe! Here's a link to my company. As I said, it's just something to consider. I definitely wouldn't mind having you on board. Maybe we could go for another drink to talk about it?*

A ten-minute pause between messages, and then he'd sent, *You looked really beautiful tonight, too. Hope you don't mind me saying.*

Siobhan wants to jump up from her chair and smash the phone into tiny pieces. She wants to pour the wine all over herself and lick it from her skin. She wants to grab both sides of Owen's face and bring it close to hers and kiss him or spit at him. *I knew it*, she wants to scream, *I always knew what you were.*

She scrolls down to read Sylvie's reply.

Hey! No worries. Thanks for the drink, and the link. Would love to meet up and talk about the job opportunity. So excited that you'd consider me. When works for you? Appreciate the compliment, too. Winky face. Kiss.

Siobhan marks the message as unread and replaces the phone just in time for Owen to come back to the table. She watches him as he picks up the phone and reads the message, studying the blankness of his face, the way it gives absolutely nothing away. He puts the phone back down and their mains arrive. He spears his steak with a knife and Siobhan watches the juices ooze. All she can think is, *Yes. I know exactly who you are now.*

The next day, Siobhan arrives at the Showroom at 5 p.m. Sylvie is already sitting at the box office, inspecting one of her manicured nails. They'll work together for a couple of hours to cover the busy Saturday night shift – some new blockbuster has been released, something about the end of the world and a president held hostage – and then Siobhan will do the close.

"Hey, Sylvie," Siobhan says, taking her seat at the kiosk.

Sylvie gives her a polite nod. She's wearing dangling earrings and a long necklace, a beaded evil eye swinging from a fine gold chain. The blockbuster is halfway through in screen one and the explosions are so loud that they rumble under their feet.

"Good week?" she asks, and Sylvie looks up at her,

frowning. Their brusque snippets of exchanged speech rarely extend to a full conversation.

"It was fine." She doesn't return the question.

"You know," Siobhan begins, not quite knowing where she's going with the words until they're out of her mouth, "I ran into Owen Jameson the other day."

Sylvie looks up. "Oh, yeah?"

"Yeah. We just caught up a little bit, you know. He said you were doing brilliantly. That you're one of his brightest students. He couldn't say enough good things about you. Just thought I'd let you know."

If Sylvie is trying to disguise her wide smile, the hint of colour creeping into her cheeks, she's failing. "That's very flattering," she says. Her soft French accent adorns every word, making it faintly musical.

"I remember you saying he seemed like a bit of a creep, but he seemed fine to me."

Sylvie nods. "Yeah. I had a tutorial with him the other day and he was so generous. He really knows his stuff. I think maybe I got him wrong."

"Maybe you did."

"You know, he even offered me a job. I could be out of here before long."

Siobhan keeps her face straight, implacable. "You don't say."

At that moment, a cluster of customers arrive through the main doors, and there's a steady stream of them until the end of Sylvie's shift. Siobhan watches her as she leaves, wondering where she's going. She wonders if Sylvie ever sits alone in her flat and drinks until her senses burn. In the quiet after closing time, Siobhan cashes up the till and powers down the two computers at the box office. Keith appears, looking harried, though there's not much left to do.

"Can you clean the popcorn machine once you've finished that, Siobhan?"

"Sure."

"Don't forget the grease tray."

Siobhan's mind begins to wander as she scrubs, inhaling the scent of burnt butter and salty corn. She thinks about clawed feet and outstretched wings. She thinks that some people are able to take and take without ever stopping to think about what they're taking. She thinks about the kind of hunger that never goes away.

Edinburgh Waverley is busy and freezing when she arrives the next morning to catch a train to Glasgow. She sends Theo a message. *I'm on my way*. He doesn't reply.

On the train she sits at a table, hemmed in on all sides by three young boys. Two are playing music loudly from their phones, chatting and chewing Starburst, while the other is reading *The Catcher in the Rye*. Every few minutes, the talkers throw a sweet wrapper at the reader. Half of the colourful little balls land in Siobhan's lap. The boys don't seem to realise she's even there.

The train arrives at Queen Street and the passengers all filter out of the barriers and into the city, into their separate lives. The last time Siobhan was in Glasgow was when she had tried to see Theo, only to be turned away and driven back to the station by his flatmate. The fact that she'll see him this time, and more than that, that he's *asked* to see her, makes her feel buoyant as she heads down St Vincent Street. He was working from home today, he'd said, but was pretty back-to-back with meetings. It would be easier just to come to his flat, rather than go out for coffee. Siobhan had been secretly glad – she's keen to soak up the details of his new life. She wants to know the kind of teabags he keeps in the cupboard, the brand of deodorant he buys, all the idiosyncrasies that might help her to know him again.

There's a long wait after Siobhan rings the buzzer. It's so long that Siobhan thinks he's changed his mind and isn't going to let her in at all, but finally, he lets her inside.

He's wearing headphones and talking rapidly about subscriber numbers and follower counts when he opens the door. *I'm on a call*, he mouths. *Five minutes.*

She follows him into the flat. Theo sits down in front of his laptop at a table also covered by empty mugs and an open diary. He says something like, *Sorry, sorry, where was I*, and Siobhan feels like life has skipped forward too fast, that one moment Theo was the scrawny teenager who collected comic books and was too shy to speak to strangers, and now he's this capable, working man, someone who attends conference calls in his living room. *He is an adult now*, she thinks, *he is a real adult, while I am an overgrown child who can't seem to find a way to exist in the world.*

His flat is bright and open plan, the living room, kitchen and dining room all in one large room. She takes a seat on his sofa – soft, tan leather – and looks for signs of the Theo she knows. The flat is very tidy. That's unlike him – unless he cared enough about her visiting to have cleaned beforehand? There are no posters on the walls, only one tastefully framed print of some graphic art, and there's a recipe card for sticky ginger noodles stuck to the front of the fridge by a magnet reading 'Meltwater Summit'. The person who lives here actually thinks about what they might eat. Attends events dedicated to professional development. Often, Siobhan feels as though Hex House's claws have ripped through the thin skin of her life. They barely seem to have touched Theo's.

"Coffee?" Theo asks, and Siobhan realises he's taken his headphones off and is now talking to her. He isn't smiling. She feels, suddenly, like an intruder.

"No thanks." Then, "Got anything stronger?"

Theo shakes his head.

"What, you don't drink now?"

"Not at 1 p.m."

"Suit yourself. Coffee's fine."

Theo busies himself with the kettle and the mugs and the milk and Siobhan stands behind him, leaning against the granite countertop.

"Nice place," she says.

"Thanks."

From where she's standing, she has a view down a narrow hall and into a bedroom at the other end. There is a dressing gown laid over the end of the bed – plum-coloured, made of silk, undoubtedly a woman's.

"I thought you were still living with Joe."

Theo doesn't answer. He carries their mugs through to the living room and places them on the coffee table, each one on top of a coaster. When they're both seated, he says, "I meant it, Shiv. I'm not really interested in catching up."

"It's just a question."

"Yeah, well. I've got plenty of those for you."

"Okay. Ask me anything."

Already, she can feel it: a tightening of those old wires between them, straining and twisting.

"I need to know who you're working with, on this documentary."

"Some woman called Zara Doherty. She's at SunWolf."

"And you're just going to hand over our story, everything we went through, so they can make a decent chunk of change from it?"

"No." Siobhan chews at the inside of her lip. Although, isn't that partly what she is doing? Zara seems to have some moral motive for making the film, some journalistic integrity and commitment to telling the story right. But does it really matter? SunWolf stand to make a profit either way. Rich people getting richer from the stories of broken women, same old story, and Siobhan is making it happen. She thinks about Zara's face when she saw the footage – footage Theo doesn't even know made it out of Hex House. She'd crossed a line, showing that to Zara. There's no going back now. "I'll make sure you're paid," is all she can think to say.

Theo scoffs. "I don't care about the money."

"Yeah, seems like you're doing pretty well for yourself these days." Siobhan hears the accusation in her voice, the obvious note of bitterness, and hates herself for it. She likes that he's doing well, that he's obviously making money, but she can't bring herself to tell him that.

Theo doesn't respond straight away. He sips his coffee then asks, "This Zara – what's her connection to Hex House?"

Siobhan thinks about the strange way Zara talks about the house, all the things that seem to glitter under her tongue that she never gives voice to. "She's just... interested in it. Apparently, she's speaking to someone else who's still there."

"Who?"

"I don't know."

"And she's never been?"

"No. I'm not sure she even believed it was real, not until I..." *Until I showed her*, Siobhan thinks. "Until I told her what happened. Most of it, anyway. Who knows what she makes of it."

Theo shakes his head, not meeting her eye. His face is pale. "So she knows. About the hexing."

When Siobhan nods, Theo stands, running his hands through his hair. He paces the monochrome rug. This, at least, hasn't changed: his need to move whenever he's nervous. "If you're doing this, you need to tell her about Elly."

Siobhan feels her scar throb. "I know," she says.

"You're finally going to own your part in it? In what happened to her?"

A stab of pain behind Siobhan's eyelids. She hasn't had a drink today. She swallows, hard. "Elly made her own choices."

Theo turns to her, eyes wide and thunderous. Evidently, she's said the wrong thing. There's a chime from his laptop, an incoming video call, but he either ignores it or doesn't even hear it.

"See, this is why I can't talk to you," he seethes. "You know *exactly* what you did, how far you pushed her. She wasn't ready. She was vulnerable. And you still can't admit to yourself that all you cared about was the documentary. All you cared about was getting good material."

"That isn't true, Theo."

"It's your fault she's dead," he hisses.

Siobhan goes cold all over. This, she knows, is what's kept him away from her for four years. This is why he can barely look at her.

"And then you wouldn't even do the right thing by her afterwards by telling her family. You've made me live with that, all this time. And now you want to tell the world about it. Why now? To make yourself feel better? Because Haina's dead, so you don't have to be scared of her anymore?"

Siobhan looks at Theo, and he looks back at her, and all she wants to do is say, *Stop it, what the hell are we doing, we only have each other in this.* That might have worked once, but not with this grown man standing in front of her, not with this warped version of Theo who keeps his dishes dry and stacked on the draining board and makes enough money to keep the heating on during the day. She doesn't have the upper hand anymore. Their conversations no longer belong to her, to do with as she pleases.

"I wasn't the only one there, Theo," she says. She can't bring herself to look at him. "You could have said something at any point over the last four years. You're your own person, aren't you? You're my *big brother.* So why did you stay silent?"

A muscle in Theo's jaw is twitching. He looks like he used to when in the grip of a nightmare, grinding his molars in the bed opposite her. "You told me not to," he says. "You made me promise, for all the women still there."

"It's not like I cut your tongue out," Siobhan says. Her voice is flat, lifeless.

Theo stares down at his feet. It's the first time she's seen him look like the Theo she knew – young, unsure. "I kept my word," he whispers.

Siobhan digs her nails into her palms. He *had* kept his promise to her, all these years, and he'd hated her for it with every single second that passed. She could tell him the reason now, now that Haina's dead – the real reason she had to make sure he never told anyone what he knew, but she can't get the words to come. For a long minute, they both stay silent, avoiding each other's eye.

"You were just so *sure* of Haina," Theo says eventually. "Of what she was doing, and the need to protect it. You, and all the other women. It's as though you were under her spell. I never understood it."

There's an odd sound, and it takes a second for Siobhan to realise that it's coming from her, that she's laughing. Theo looks at her strangely, as if she's a wild animal. "Of course you didn't understand it, Theo," she tells him. "For fuck's sake. It was always different for you. You didn't need the house. You could never know what it was like, to feel like it was your only chance of survival. The house never got *inside* you, not like it did for the rest of us."

Theo looks up, eyes sharp. "The rest of us," he says. "You include yourself in that?"

Siobhan shakes her head, feeling fuzzy and lightheaded. She's getting confused.

As her and Theo's time in the house had worn on, she'd found herself spending more and more with Haina. It's what she'd looked forward to when she'd woken up each morning: the warmth of the fire, the softness of the velvet armchair, Haina's intense energy across from her. In all her life, Siobhan had never felt as able to talk as she did during all those hours in the study. It was like a dam had finally been opened. She told Haina about her childhood, the early years before Nora left her dad, how she'd been too young to recall anything but a murky, dread-filled feeling. She told Haina about the shelter, the other women who would stroke her hair but flinch when she tried to hug them. Nora sat at the window each day, watching, watching for *him*, not stopping until he died a year later and she could watch him being lowered into the ground. Siobhan talked about moving into the Leith flat, the happiest years of her life, just her, Theo and Nora. Then, the way Nora started to look at her differently when she became a teenager and started drinking alcopops in parks, started staying out late, started smuggling strong spirits into the house. Normal teenage behaviour, she'd always told herself, nothing her friends weren't doing, too. But Theo and Nora never touched a drop. And while her friends could stick to one or two drinks, Siobhan never could, drinking until she was sick or passed out or forgot where she was, who she was. *Maybe it was my way of knowing him*, Siobhan told Haina. *Of trying to understand who he was and why he did what he did. I didn't have a problem – I don't have a problem. I was just figuring it all out. But Mum looked at me like I was his ghost. Like he'd come back to haunt her.*

All of this, Haina listened to, squeezing Siobhan's hand. Nodding as though, yes, she understood it all. And over time, the lines had started to blur. Siobhan had started to feel not like an outsider, but part of the very fabric of the house. Like a *guest*. That feeling had become, in her mind, inextricably tied to the making of the documentary. She'd begun to truly understand it: how much the guests needed the house, how much they needed Haina, and she'd felt a powerful pull to preserve it all, to capture it and make it tangible. She became single-minded in her focus, in her desire to get it perfect. The documentary would be something special, she knew – it would make her and Theo's careers. But as the weeks rolled on, it became about more than that. Something she couldn't quite give words to: a way to tie herself to the house, to feel closer to it, and to Haina, even once she'd returned home.

If only she'd known then how the house would haunt her, no matter what she did.

Siobhan shakes her head, trying to root herself in the here and now, in the warmth of Theo's flat. "I'm doing the documentary because you were right, Theo," she hears herself saying. "We should have told someone about Hex House, about what Haina was doing, when we left. Haina is gone, and yes, that makes it easier. But we can finally leave it all behind. It's the right thing to do."

Theo is still standing, blocking out the light from the window. "No," he says quietly. "The right thing to do would be to go and talk to her husband, Ethan. And her mum. The right thing to do would be to tell them what happened to Elly so *they* can have some fucking closure, not you."

When Siobhan swallows, it feels as though there are stones in her throat. "I don't know if I can do that."

Theo laughs. It's a cool, hard sound. "I know. That's

231

why I'm going to do it." Siobhan's head snaps up to look at him. "If you're breaking our silence, then so am I."

She finds herself nodding. Haina is dead, what can she do about it now? "Okay," she whispers. "Okay."

Theo sits down again, at the opposite end of the sofa to her this time, his legs so long they slope upwards from the hip when he's seated. "There's one thing I need from you, Shiv," he says. "If you're really going to do it, if you're going to do this documentary and tell the world about Hex House and what Haina did to Elly, then I need you to do something for me. It's the last thing I'll ever ask of you."

Siobhan studies his face carefully, the dark brows, the melancholy eyes. She would do whatever he asked, if it would mean she can be in his life, but she knows that's not the bargain.

When Theo speaks again, his voice is low and rumbling, like the onset of a rainstorm. "I need you to go back to Hex House."

Falling. It feels like she's falling.

Siobhan grips onto the arm of the sofa to steady herself, but it's still as though her centre of gravity is swimming through the air. "What?"

"Haina's gone now, right? You need to find any of those poor women who feel like they need to stay there, for whatever reason, and tell them to go back to their lives." He pauses. His hands are clasped in his lap. "I need you to go and get Elly's baby, so that her family can finally have a piece of her."

The baby. It's the one thing Siobhan has barely let herself think about since that awful day in the woods, the day they ran in the opposite direction from Hex House.

It's the one thing she's never been able to find an escape from, no matter how much she drinks or how many sweaty clubs she abandons herself in.

"I can't go back there," she says, because no other words will come out. Still, they feel wrong on her lips. They rebel against the thing inside her that's whispering, *We could go back. We could really go back.* "Besides. I wouldn't even be able to find the house if I tried now. Haina invited us last time, remember?"

Theo nods gravely, but without surprise, as if he's been expecting this very obstacle. "I've seen you, Siobhan. I've seen how you don't eat and you don't give a shit who you hurt, and don't even kid yourself that I don't know how much you drink. I think you'll find it. I think the house will want you."

"Theo," Siobhan whispers, and it sounds like what it is: a plea. "I can't go back there. Don't make me do that."

Theo's face is cold and hard, his mind made up. "It's the only way you'll ever be able to heal from everything that happened, Shiv. I know you can see that. It's breaking you apart."

Siobhan looks down at her hands. They're shaking. She wants a drink so badly she could scream. She wants to drown in numbness, she wants to know nothing but air in, air out, one step, then another. It is too heavy to carry herself around.

"If you can't do it for you," Theo says, more gently now, "then please. Do it for me."

Half an hour later, Siobhan wanders around Kelvingrove Park. She follows the sweeping arc of the river as it cuts through the parkland. The day is freezing and drizzling but there are still plenty of people around: students on their way from one lecture to another, walkers pulling their dogs away from discarded rubbish, men who smell half-dead bundled on benches. Siobhan tries to figure out how someone would categorise her if they saw her, sipping wine from the bottle and sitting so close to the edge of the river that she could ever so gently roll forward and just let it take her.

Until today, she'd thought everything with Theo could be repaired. She'd rationalised it all in her mind as if it was still under her control, assumed that Theo would be a constant in her life always, like breathing and falling asleep. But she hadn't realised that the cords between them didn't exist anymore, that she'd taken a knife to them the day they walked away from Hex House and she'd asked him to never, ever, breathe a word of the things they'd seen.

I had to, she reminds herself uselessly. *I didn't have a choice.*

She needs to stand up. She needs to get the train back to Edinburgh and slip back into her life, a life that barely makes sense anymore. But all Siobhan can bring herself to do is sit by the river, as if time doesn't matter at all. She wants to drink and drink until the alcohol smothers and destroys each and every thought in her head, one by one.

ELLY

THEN

As autumn unfurls and the days get colder, Elly finds herself craving meat. She wants it bloody and rare; she wants it dripping. In quiet moments she finds her mind wandering, imagining tearing a steak apart with her hands, the fleshy give between her two front teeth. She no longer has porridge for breakfast, but strips of bacon, covered in butter, dipped into jam. She stays long after everyone else has left the table for chores, hoovering up discarded strips of fat and half-eaten sausages. She can no longer fill herself up. Even if she can't fit in another morsel, she still doesn't feel sated. It's as though there's another, secret itch in her belly she can't find a way to scratch. Margot giggles at the desperate way she eats. She catches the drips of grease from Elly's chin with her little finger, lifts them to her own mouth. Grace slaps Elly's hand when she catches her stealing rare cuts of beef from the fridge but also seems quietly pleased.

"I remember it well, that stage," she says almost

wistfully, looking at Elly's stomach, and Elly doesn't know if she's talking about the pregnancy or something else.

Elly wants to talk about hexing more and more. And now that she is one of them, the women seem keen to unravel, to pour their secrets into her. Margot tells Elly that she has never believed in a god, not really, but when she hexes, she feels like she's touching something timeless. Janine says that when she's in her hex form, it's as though her brain is no longer itching. Some of the other women just say they like the way it feels to leave their bodies behind.

The air is growing cooler. The gardens smell of smoke and mulch. When she wakes in the morning, Elly can see her breath. They close the doors in the kitchen while they work to keep the heat in. It's getting harder for Elly to stay on her feet all day – sometimes the pressure in her pelvis is so intense that she squats down on the floor, and Keiko brings her a stool to sit on and a chicken bone to gnaw. Sometimes, when they are alone together in the kitchens, she shows Elly how to sign different words: *hungry, dinner, wine, meat*.

One morning, as they clear up from breakfast, Grace is much quieter than usual. There's no humming old pop songs, no calling out of banal tasks from one side of the kitchen to the other – *watch that butter doesn't burn, chop those leeks a bit finer, check the bread's almost ready* – no swearing outbursts when her hands bother her, though she would always be too proud to admit that as the reason. Aside from her heavy footsteps, she is silent. Elly looks at Keiko, who shrugs. They work on in a heavy sort of quiet, until the door opens and Siobhan comes into the kitchen. She speaks to Grace in a low voice but Elly can just about make out what she's saying.

"Haina would really like us to capture your ceremony tonight." A pause. "If you're comfortable with that."

Siobhan is standing close to Grace and is so tall that she looms over her a little, casts her in shadow. Grace's First Fly had taken place a few days before. Elly hadn't been able to watch as she leapt from the roof, could only think of Lakshmi. But Grace had soared through the sky like a comet; unstoppable, burning bright.

"I don't think I am comfortable with that," Grace says flatly.

Elly watches from the corner of her eye as Siobhan braces her palms behind her and uses them to hoist herself up so that she's sitting on the counter. She's getting flour all over her black jeans, but she doesn't seem to care. Perhaps she meant this position to be casual, non-threatening, but it makes the muscles in Grace's neck tighten. Elly can see them from where she's standing: fat bands of rope under the skin.

"Yeah, I get that. It's really important we get this footage though, for the film. I know how committed you are to the house, so I'm sure you understand."

"I don't really care about the film," Grace says, but not unkindly – there's a sort of blankness to her words. "And you don't know anything about me."

When Elly thinks about it, she doesn't know much about Grace either. She knows that she's an early riser and won't go to bed until after midnight, and only when she can't find a single task to occupy her hands any longer. She knows that she likes a teaspoon of honey in her tea in the morning and that she has cracked sores on her strangely shaped hands from all the kneading and scrubbing and working.

Grace's day-to-day life, Elly could recite by rote, but of what brought her to the house in the first place, she knows far less. They have exchanged scraps of information, now and again, made bold by the tedium of work. Elly knows that Grace comes from Belfast. She knows that she once had a wife and doesn't anymore. She knows that loss carved a ravine deep into her, a space only hard work can fill.

"You said we didn't have to be on camera," Grace is saying, "if we didn't want to be."

"Of course, of course," Siobhan says, waving a hand. "And there's plenty we could do to obscure your identity, if that's what you're worried about. I just think—"

"No," Grace interrupts. The sudden loudness of her voice makes Keiko look up from where she's simmering stock on the range. Her eyes dart to Elly, wide.

Siobhan is shrugging. Elly wonders how many people have said no to her in her life, and how many times Siobhan has accepted that answer. "Fine. I just think it's a bit selfish, is all."

Elly holds her breath. She expects Grace to retaliate, but instead she's laughing. Siobhan jumps down from the counter.

"You think it's *selfish*, do you?" Grace says. "As selfish as using the stories of wounded women for your film? As selfish as invading their private, secret sanctuary and shoving cameras in their faces so that you can get your story?"

"We're trying to celebrate Hex House," says Siobhan. There's a steeliness to her now. "Haina invited us here. She asked us, she asked *me*, to do this. I care about the house as much as you do."

238

But Grace isn't listening anymore. She's returned to her dough, and she starts to hum to herself as if Siobhan isn't even there. Siobhan holds both of her palms up in exaggerated surrender and backs her way out of the kitchen door.

"Back to work, Elly," Grace says without looking up.

Elly hadn't realised she'd been staring. Now, she reaches into a cupboard above her head to bring out the bananas for tonight's dessert. When her fingers touch the skins, she recoils. They've gone black and are leaking brown mush all over the wood. They smell putrid, as if they've been spoiling for a long time.

"When did these arrive?" she asks Keiko.

Frowning, Keiko puts a finger to her cheek and then her shoulder. The sign for *yesterday*.

In the afternoon, as Elly heads to Haina's study for her next session, she tries to remember what she knows about the ceremony. She'd meant to ask about it last time, but before she could, Haina had tied a belt around Elly's neck, tightening the notches until her vision splintered. When she removed the belt, the snowy feathers weren't only covering Elly's hands but her forearms, her biceps, her shoulders. She felt as if she could hear the heartbeats of every creature within a one-mile radius. She felt too enormous for the study. When she looked at the glass window, she knew that she'd be able to break straight through it. Haina had seemed almost giddy, scribbling in her notebook.

"It won't be long for you, Elly," she'd said. "You are *formidable*, my angel."

Elly hadn't had a chance to ask what she meant before there'd been a knock at the door, Margot, waiting to start her session.

Now, Elly knocks and enters the study, nerves fizzing in her stomach, although she can't pin them to anything specific. Haina gestures for her to sit down. She looks tired today, more unkempt – her eyes are puffy and stray hairs are escaping her low bun.

"Last time, you said I wouldn't need long," Elly says, before they can begin. "Did you mean that my ceremony could be soon?"

Haina smiles. "That's right."

Elly looks down at her hands. "But Grace has been here for years. I've only been here for…" She stops. How long *has* she been here? Weeks, months? Her stomach is large now, it stops her from bending down or from sleeping very long at night, but there is no other way to tell how long has passed since the night she ran from the cottage.

"It takes some guests less time than others to truly master their hex," says Haina. "Some women are very unusual, in that their hex has been waiting for a long time to be discovered. That's you, my angel – you are very special. Very special indeed."

Elly feels the words settle over her and tries to believe them. *Special*. Still, anxiety prickles at the underside of her skin. "And what happens?" she asks. "At the ceremony?"

Haina's smile doesn't dim, but it does seem to strain at the edges. "Another simple test. Nothing more. Like the First Fly, only, a little bit more difficult. It might seem strict, all these trials, but I'm sure you can appreciate that I can't let you go until I know you're strong enough."

"Strong enough?"

A muscle in Haina's jaw tenses. "Strong enough to survive. *Out there*."

At dinner, Haina informs them that Grace's ceremony will be taking place out on the lawn after sunset. Some of the guests cheer, others touch Grace on the arm, some of them whisper, *May your hex protect you*. Grace smiles back at them all, but her eyes are dark, faraway. From the other side of the table, Siobhan glowers. Elly eats with a frenzied excitement in her belly, keen for the light to disappear and the ceremony to start. *It won't be long for you, Elly*, Haina had said. *You are formidable*. No one has ever described her in that way before. Sweet, kind, thoughtful – never formidable.

Elly and Keiko bring dessert to the table – blackberry tarts topped with bitter lemon cream – and retake their seats. Elly glances across the table at Theo. He's barely spoken to her since their last interview, when she took his hand in hers and he pulled away. He won't meet her eye. It makes her feel cold, exposed. Perhaps she'd read it all wrong – instead of desiring her in all of her size and strength, desiring her for the unknowable thing she's becoming, maybe he fears it. Worse yet, maybe he just doesn't care.

She's about to say his name when there's a loud sound: a groan that sounds like it's coming from beneath their feet. Then, a shrill whine, like a creature with its leg in a trap. Suddenly, the room is filled with glass. It hurls itself inwards, shards the size of wine bottles raining like bullets from the sky.

Elly is aware of two things happening almost simultaneously: one of those shards falling towards her face, then a strong pressure knocking her sideways, causing the edge of the table to jam into her ribs, right above her belly.

Screams puncture the air. There's a whipping wind and a new cold in the room, uninvited and fierce.

Elly opens her eyes. There's glass everywhere, blood everywhere, though she doesn't know who any of it belongs to. The screaming voices are wild, mad as wolves on the hunt. The sound runs rings around the room. Elly's head feels tight. Her side is throbbing. Distantly, she thinks, *The baby, the baby.* Theo is on top of her, looking down, frantically grabbing her face and holding it to the light.

"Are you hurt?" he demands, his voice like hammered metal. "*Look* at me, Elly. Are you hurt?"

Elly peers down at herself, at the floor, where bowls have been upturned and cutlery dropped. Her body feels numb and faraway, but it's barely marked. The baby tumbles in her belly, pressing its elbows out against the taut skin of her abdomen. *I'm here. I'm here.*

"I don't think so," she says, struggling to get her breath.

Theo helps her to her feet. Tiny shards of smashed glass make a silvery sound as they hit the floor, dropping from the creases in their clothes. The other guests look at each other in bewilderment, at the cuts on each other's faces. And then they look up. There are gaping holes in the refectory roof. The frames which held the panes in place are warped and rusted. Had they always been like that? The panes themselves have fallen out like teeth from loose gums, but it was almost as if they had been blown inwards by a mighty force. As if the house were under attack. For some reason, it makes Elly think of the rotten bananas in the cupboard, the burst pipe in the bathroom. She closes her eyes and sees skeletons sagging, wood rotting. Haina is looking upwards, too, her eyes flashing, fists clenched at her sides. There is something weary about her expression; a tiredness that goes beyond a lack of sleep, the kind of tiredness that reaches deep into the bones. She starts to move around the room, checking each person, putting her fingers to their cuts, dabbing at them with the hem of her dress and staining it dark. Most of the guests are stunned and wide-eyed, but it doesn't seem as if anyone is too badly hurt.

Elly runs her hands over the skin of her upper arms. A spear of glass had been heading straight towards her. What would have happened, if Theo hadn't shoved her to the side? She looks at him now. There's a deep scratch on his forearm. Elly offers him a napkin from the table. He hesitates then accepts, mopping up the beads of blood. Every time someone moves, there's the electric crunch of glass underfoot. If Elly concentrates, she can still hear it: the low rumbling under the house's foundations that had come before the shattered windows.

Siobhan is the first to speak. "What the fuck?" Her voice is hard and loud, cutting through the room.

No one responds. Haina is staring up at the shattered glass panes again. She looks as though she might cry, or maybe scream. Eventually, she says, "This house is very old." She rubs a hand over her face, massaging the features. "And it is very tired." Siobhan opens her mouth to say something else, but before she can, Haina addresses the room. "Let's think of happier things. It's time for the ceremony. We can clean all this up later."

She picks her way across the debris towards the refectory door, and after a moment, the rest of the guests, still slow and bewildered, begin to follow her.

Elly is clammy all over, and there's the strangest sensation inside her stomach, as if she's been travelling too fast, but she's unharmed. "You protected me," she manages to say to Theo.

Theo looks away, uncomfortable. He doesn't answer. Elly becomes aware of someone watching them from further back down the hallway. Siobhan. She isn't smiling.

The lawn stretches between the pond at the back of the house to the treeline at the edge of the woods, a flat expanse of lush green grass framed by colourful borders. Haina holds Grace's arm gently, and together they stand near the treeline while the rest of the guests form a loose crowd around them. At first, Elly can't concentrate on what's about to happen. All she can think about is glass, the noise it made, the ragged holes in the refectory roof. But then Haina starts to talk, and her uneasiness dissolves at the sound of her steady voice.

"My angels, we're here tonight for Grace," Haina says, "to show her how much we love her. And to decide whether or not she's ready to leave us."

Elly swallows thickly. She's been so preoccupied by the particulars of the ceremony, she hadn't paid much mind to what might happen afterwards. The thought of working in the kitchens every day without Grace's calm presence, her tireless energy, her low, melodic voice – it makes her feel empty.

At the front of the crowd, Haina has taken Grace in her arms. The two women embrace, and even from this distance, Elly can see that Haina's cheeks are glistening. Grace's expression doesn't give much away. She looks serious, resigned. Is she thinking of Lakshmi, the way she'd dropped from the sky? Is she thinking of what's waiting for her beyond the woods?

"You have the love of the whole house," Haina says.

This time, Elly is ready to join in with the chorus of voices. *May your hex protect you*, they call into the night. *May your hex protect you, Grace.*

Grace gives a nod, and Haina steps aside. The only light in the garden is the pale illumination of the moon. The evening world is full of noise: buzzards scouring the forest for a meal, toads making their gasping croaks down by the pond. Even so, Elly feels as though she can hear the breathing of every guest standing around her, could pick out their heartbeats by sound alone. These heightened senses are new, she knows. Close by, Theo's pulse is quick but steady. Without his camera, he seems incomplete, at a loss. A few metres away, Siobhan's irritation at not being able to film the ceremony seems to have dissolved into curiosity. She watches Grace closely with her dark eyes.

"I'm ready," Grace whispers, and the crowd begins to shout. Elly had almost forgotten how it felt to become tangled up in that net of cruel words: like being restrained by the kind of twine that cuts the skin.

"It was your fault she died."

"She took her own life because of you."

The words become louder, more insistent. Someone picks up a clod of earth from a nearby border and hurls it at Grace. Grace sees it coming and lets it pelt her full force in the chest. Haina looks on, smiling serenely.

"You'll never be forgiven, no matter how much you hurt yourself."

"Who would look at you now?"

"You should have saved her."

Elly gasps at the realisation that this last cruelty has come from her own mouth. She doesn't know how she knows the cruellest thing it would be possible to shout, but she does; she feels like she can inhabit every inch of Grace's story. Somehow, she knows what will hurt the most.

The ugly words keep flying through the night air, and it doesn't take Grace's body long to respond. Elly had seen Grace's hex at her First Fly, but it shocks her anew now: the lush eider that rashes over every visible inch of Grace's skin, the iridescent specks of gold in her spread wings, the way her fair hair disappears from her head, leaving behind a pate of slicked feathers. The skin around her breasts and stomach remains almost bare, as though it's been pecked. It looks fleshy and pink, raw to the elements.

When Grace's transformation is complete, Elly feels a consuming sense of calm to look at her. She looks almost *more* like herself in this form, truer to the essence and core of what Elly considers to be Grace: the kind, impatient, sturdy heart of her.

Grace's wings begin to beat. Elly feels it on her face: the mighty gust of air, bringing with it the smell of earth, the smell of nests filled with newborn chicks. All at once, the guests grow silent. Her muscular legs take a few, powerful strides forward, as if she's going to run straight into the crowd. All the women fall back together, but there's no need, because Grace never reaches them. Instead, she is suddenly airborne, she is above their heads, she is beyond them and away. The guests begin to cheer as Grace's silhouette grows higher and smaller. From this distance, Elly thinks, she could be an eagle. Anyone looking into the sky now would see nothing more than the large shadow of a night predator. Maybe they would think, *What an impressive-looking thing*, but they probably wouldn't look up long enough to notice.

When all grows silent again, some of the women settle themselves down in the grass. It's a cold night and the lawn crunches with the first suggestions of frost, but they don't seem to mind. They stretch out their limbs, scars shining in the moonlight, backs to the earth and faces to the sky.

"What's happening?" Elly asks Margot. "What are we waiting for?"

Margot had been bobbing up and down on her heels, but now she plops down so that she's cross-legged, as flexible and nimble as a child. "You'll see," she says.

Elly joins her on the grass, tilting onto her side to avoid the uncomfortable pressure on her swollen belly. It's been painful all day, her ribs aching, a low pulsing in her lower abdomen. She wonders why they're out here on the grass rather than on the roof, although part of her is relieved to not be up there again. She can't stand there without thinking of Lakshmi, how she'd given Elly her lipstick on her first day in the house, the way she'd squeezed Elly's hand the night she died. Siobhan and Theo are the last to sit. Only Haina remains standing. She keeps her unreadable face turned to the stars.

How long does it take for them to hear that swooping sound again? One hour, maybe two? Elly is shivering, the wetness from the earth seeping upwards into her clothes and the gaps between muscles, but she forgets all about the discomfort when she looks up at the sky. There is a shape looming, approaching them at speed – lower and faster, lower and faster. It doesn't look like Grace; it's too large, too misshapen, seeming to be composed of two entirely different parts. The guests scramble to their feet. Many are already cheering, stretching their arms high above their heads, as if they might touch the creature carving its way through the night air towards them. Elly can't make sense of the picture until Grace has landed back on the grass. Her feathers are rain-soaked. They bring with them the scent of elsewhere. Her black eyes are wild and roving. She uncurls and reveals what she has brought with her in her enormous claws, her carrion: the limp body of a woman.

Elly staggers backwards, the blood draining from her face. The woman is middle-aged, hair streaked with grey, her body thin and wiry. There are oozing lacerations in her stomach from where Grace's claws have gripped her. She has been carried here from who knows where. Her wounds leak darkly onto the grass at their feet.

Haina's eyes are electric, her skin glowing and vital. She seems to have grown taller and broader in a matter of minutes. "My angel," she says, and her voice is unstable, a train teetering on a track, about to plunge down the mountainside and into rapture, "who have you brought us?"

Grace shakes out her ruffled feathers, throws her head back. The noise she lets out is so loud, so high and deafening, that Elly's legs give out beneath her and she drops to the ground. The noise seemed to gut her from the inside out – she feels void, as though she's been vomiting. She's shaking. But there's another feeling, too: the satisfying cleave of comprehension.

She'd understood Grace's cry.

It wasn't a linear thing like a sentence, or even complete, like an image. Instead, it was a jangling bag of shards, of broken words and meanings.

child killer under the bridge cruel cruel hands and horrible knowledge

only did it because she could

they begged and begged but

she'd do it again

no one will miss the child killer

Haina takes a step towards Grace and holds out a hand so that it brushes the matted softness at her cheek. "You've done well, my angel," she says in a voice so tender it makes something in Elly's stomach loosen. "You deserve your prize."

Grace lets out another sound – shorter and sharper this time. On the ground, the unknown woman twitches and her eyelids flicker. Bile rises in the back of Elly's throat. Because she knows, doesn't she? She knows what is about to happen. A variation of this moment has happened in her dreams every night since her last session with Haina. She recognises the desperation in Grace's face now, the way

249

her claws outstretch in anticipation, her pupils widening with the *finally* of it all.

So when Grace descends on the unconscious woman, when she uses those talons to rip open what's left of her stomach and pull out the intestine like a long, bloodied rope, when she pokes the claws into the eyes to spear them out and pulls the flesh away from the thighs, discarding it on the grass, Elly doesn't take a step back. Instead, she steps forward. There's something dragging her towards the body, meaning she's ripping at it, too, now – she and the rest of the guests. A noise in the back of her throat: she's screaming. A guttural, seething howl. She's screaming, not in fear, but in something closer to ecstasy. Grace grins up at her, and she has never looked so alive.

They dissemble and destroy, they disconnect and dislocate. Elly doesn't know how long it takes, but when the night is at its thickest, there is nothing left of the woman but a single word spelled out on the stained grass, a word made up of skin and muscles and bone.

Hex.

The women all stagger backwards to admire their creation, exhausted and dazed. Grace is still in her hex form, clumsy but somehow luminous, an orb of light in the centre of the garden. The bloody word seems to pulse, to beat. Elly feels as though she has been waiting to look at that word, to understand what it means, all her life.

As the commotion dies down, Grace begins to transform again. Her feathers shrink back into the landscape of her skin, long hair grows from her scalp. She is getting smaller. She becomes the original Grace, the Grace who now seems so defenceless compared to the might of her hex.

There is blood on her face, down her chest and collarbone, covering her bare breasts down to her navel, but she has never looked so clean, so new. She looks to Haina with heavy-lidded eyes.

"Well done, Grace," Haina whispers.

What happens now? Elly wonders. What could possibly follow what she has just seen? How can time just continue to tumble on and on, now that she's been irreversibly changed?

Haina places a hand on Grace's quivering shoulder. "You're free to go, my angel."

Grace bows her head, looking at her bare feet in the grass, as if remembering that they belong to her and that she needs to use them now. Her gaze turns to the crowd. She gives the women a sad, final sort of smile.

"May your hex protect you," she says as she turns. Still naked, she walks into the woods. They swallow her like they're starving.

Some of the guests follow as far as the treeline, where they search the darkness for her. Elly keeps her eyes on the trees, expecting that at any moment, Grace will return, that she'll have changed her mind, that the house won't let her go. But the night remains still. The trees don't move. Elly becomes aware of Haina, disappearing into the house and then re-emerging with a large canvas bag, into which she heaps the woman's remains, humming to herself. Elly wonders what she might do with them, but finds that she doesn't really care. She can only think about Grace. Inside her, the knowledge rings out: Grace is no longer part of the house. Elly knows that when Grace tries to find a main road, a place to take shelter, that she'll find it. The house won't draw her back. Not anymore.

It's when she's looking out at all that blackness, the hopeless infinity of it, that the first pains in Elly's stomach start to make themselves known: the thrumming beginnings of labour.

SIOBHAN

NOW

Siobhan sits in the recording room with Zara, nursing a cooling coffee she'd picked up from the library café. She can't remember the events of the night before too well, only that she'd stayed in Kelvingrove Park for hours alone, drinking. She'd only left when a man in a puffer jacket approached her and asked if he could sit down, then asked her why she didn't want the company, then said, *Right okay fuck off then, frigid bitch.*

Somehow, she'd made it home on the train and into her own bed. She dreamed of Theo. She dreamed of the day the refectory roof caved in and he had the choice of protecting Elly or Siobhan, and had chosen Elly.

Zara seems spaced out this morning, too. It's the first time Siobhan has seen her since she showed her the footage of Lakshmi. She doesn't have any make-up on and looks paler than usual, less remarkable. She's wearing black leggings and an orange jumper that drowns her. As she sets up her recording equipment with her usual meticulousness,

Siobhan notices that her hands are shaking.

"Everything okay?" Siobhan asks.

"Fine," Zara says, then she shakes her head. "Another letter came from Willow yesterday. Now that I know it's all real, I just…" She rubs her eyes. "It's just so heavy. I don't know what to do with all this knowing."

If Siobhan had to describe the feeling that had eaten away at her for the last four years, rotting her brain chemistry and gnawing at her nerves, she wouldn't have been able to put it better than that. *I don't know what to do with all this knowing.*

"She says the house is falling down," Zara says. "She keeps saying that it's *sick* – that's the word she uses, *sick* – and that she's in danger, but she doesn't know where else to go. I think she needs help." Zara takes a deep, shuddering breath. "I think we need to help her."

"What do you mean?"

Zara won't meet Siobhan's eye. "I think we need to try and find it again. The house."

Siobhan stills. "That's not possible," she hears herself say. She tries to block out Theo's voice.

I need you to go back to Hex House.

She wishes those words hadn't made so much sense to her. She wishes they hadn't pulled at something buried deep – a secret, a magnet, something burning.

"But you found it once before, didn't you?" Zara says, leaning forward. Her words gush out, as if she's been holding them in. "Maybe you could find it again. I think we need to, for the documentary. For Willow. And…" She hesitates before continuing. "And for Thomas."

Siobhan stays silent. Tiny little Thomas with his round

eyes and red cheeks. Thomas, clasped in Elly's arms. "So he's still at the house," she manages to choke.

"Willow says so. She says she takes care of him. But I don't know how safe it is there anymore, for either of them."

It was never safe, Siobhan almost says, but doesn't.

"We don't have to decide anything now," Zara says quickly. "I just wanted you to think about it, that's all. Are you still up for doing an interview today?"

Siobhan nods. The words are already itching under her skin, making her squirm, trying to find an escape route through her pores.

Zara breathes deeply, then turns to the camera. "Okay." She gives Siobhan a curt nod to let her know they're recording.

"I want to ask you about the ceremonies." Zara's voice has already regained its cool confidence, its steadiness. All emotion is gone. She is nothing but professional. "In her last letter, Willow told me that the ceremonies were the final step in Haina's 'training', so to speak. That the women could only leave once they'd passed."

"That's right."

"Did you witness a ceremony, during your time in the house?"

"Two."

"Can you talk a little bit about what they involved?"

Siobhan takes a long sip of her coffee. It's cold, strong, bitter. "The women had to prove that they had what it takes to survive on the outside. They had to..." She pauses, clears her throat, then continues more quietly. "They had to transform into their hex. And then they had to bring back a sacrifice."

"And when you say transform, you mean into..." Zara pauses, and Siobhan doesn't miss the way she shudders. She knows she'll be thinking of the creature she saw Lakshmi become on film, a creature that shouldn't exist. "They transform into birds?" The word sounds so surreal, so absurd, that Siobhan laughs. Zara flinches, and Siobhan realises how she must look on camera: delirious, unhinged. "Sorry," Zara says, "into *hexes*?"

Siobhan nods.

Zara's face is blank, giving nothing away. She maintains eye contact from behind the camera. Siobhan is grateful for her practised calmness. It creates a net, a net she can pour it all into. "And by sacrifice," Zara continues, "what do you mean?"

Siobhan feels her lungs expand and contract – once, twice, thrice. Funny how some breaths take so much more effort than others, how some you need to convince your body to take, if only to remind yourself, *I am alive I am alive I am alive.*

"A human sacrifice," she says eventually. "The hexes hunt people who have done harm, done horrible things. Things you can't forgive, that's what Haina said. How she justified it, I suppose. *These people have done things that need to be punished.* But they also had to find someone who wouldn't be missed, see. Rapists. Murderers, loners. They always seemed to know the right ones to take. I don't know how." The words hang in the air. Zara's face blanches. "They rip them apart. Destroy them. Once they've made a sacrifice, they've completed their ceremony. *Then* they're allowed to leave."

Zara looks as though she's going to be sick. She lurches

forward to pause the recording and spends a long few minutes with her head between her thighs, breathing deeply. Siobhan stays where she is, staring at the table. There is a faint buzzing between her ears. She has carried it all for so long, and almost feels too light without it, as if she might simply drift away. She watches as Zara rights herself, wipes the sweat from her forehead and clicks the camera on again.

"I want to talk to you a little bit about Elly Carmichael," she says, voice steady once more. It's impressive, really, how she's able to control herself. "Do you feel ready to talk about her?"

Siobhan's throat is already dry and constricted. But she'd known this moment was coming, so she forces herself to say, "Okay."

"Were you at the house when she gave birth to Thomas?"

Siobhan nods.

"Can you tell us a little bit about that?"

Siobhan can remember it all so clearly, the way they'd all lingered out on the grass after Grace's ceremony. Siobhan had run back to the room to get the camera. With Grace gone, there was no one to stop her recording. The camera panned around the euphoric faces of the guests as they sang together and hollered at the top of their voices, sending swinging cries far out into the night. Siobhan had felt numb to everything she'd witnessed: the writhing woman on the ground, already bleeding out, the dark-eyed guests crowding around her, the way they'd spelled out that word in the grass, the word that seemed to pull everything into its orbit. *Hex*. She'd expected to be disgusted, but instead, she'd felt the release of something in her belly – something uncurling, something responding. She would ask Haina about that, the next time they were alone.

When the camera found Theo, he was staring straight back at her, pale and grim-faced. There was vomit on the side of his mouth. He started to shake his head, to say her name, but another sound interrupted him: a high keening, animal and strange. She'd spun the camera to the source and found Elly on all fours in the grass, one hand clutching at her stomach. Somebody shouted, *The baby*, and Haina was the first to move. She picked Elly up as if she weighed nothing at all and carried her into the house. Strong Haina. Capable Haina. Surely nothing bad could happen to Elly, not while Haina was there holding her.

On a night she can't quite pinpoint in the loose landscape of the last week, Siobhan had found the footage of the birth. She watched it and then replayed it again, starting with the shaky moment she'd followed Haina and Elly into the parlour, where someone had already laid out clean towels and sheets. Siobhan propped the camera up on the table before rushing to help. Later, she would tell Theo that she'd forgotten the camera was rolling, but that was a lie. Even while she held a wet flannel to Elly's forehead, all she could think, with a shocking amount of clarity, was, *This is going to make for great footage*. She left it running all night and only switched it off when the baby arrived, pink and mewling, just before noon. All around its fleshy body had been cracked pieces of shell.

"I haven't seen many newborn babies, but I knew Thomas was beautiful," she tells Zara now.

"How did Haina react? When he was born?"

Siobhan remembers Haina's face – jubilant, sweaty. "She looked at him like he belonged to her," she says. *Isn't it wonderful*, Haina had said to Siobhan later that day, *isn't it wonderful to have some fresh blood in the house?* "Like he belonged to all of us."

Later, in the bath at Owen's house, Siobhan listens to the sounds of him cooking for her in the kitchen: the soft clatter of utensils, the turning on of the extractor fan, the slight resistance of the seal as the fridge is opened and closed again. Like everything in Owen's flat, the bathroom is clean and simple, all white metro tiles on the walls, a thick glass panel bisecting the room to create a shower, a roll-top bath with brass feet. Siobhan's dark hair floats all around her, slightly reddish and mermaid-like. She combs her fingers through it, looking down at her body: her small chest and nipples the colour of conkers, her lean stomach, the way her pelvic bone arches up against the skin like the walls of a cathedral. The colour of her scar has changed again: the skin around it is sallow now. Greenish. She knows it's infected, that the infection will be causing the queasiness and her headaches and the clamminess at the back of her neck. What she needs is a doctor's appointment and a prescription and a little foil packet of oblong pills to be taken with food three times a day. But it all just feels like too big of an ask: the calling up and making an appointment, the sitting in a waiting room looking at the floor, the pointed questions in a room that smells of antiseptic. *And how did you say you got this?*

they'll ask, and she'll say, *I can't tell you, I don't know anymore*. It's her body, she'll let it rot if it wants to.

In the other room, she can now hear Owen's voice. He's on the phone. He speaks softly, as though he doesn't want her to hear. Whoever is on the other end of the line, it's someone he speaks softly to. As quietly as she can, Siobhan rises from the bathtub and creeps naked across the bathroom to put her ear to the door. A small puddle of water forms at her feet. She struggles to decipher the sentences, but the odd thing stands out.

Meeting. Tomorrow. I've been waiting.

When he hangs up, Siobhan wraps herself in a towel and walks out into the kitchen without drying herself. He jumps when he sees her there, dripping onto the tiles, pale and pruned from the bath.

"Feeling better?" he asks.

Siobhan tries to remember turning up at his door but can't. She can't remember if she's been drinking today or if it's the persistent wooziness that's making her forgetful; the half-awake clamour behind her eyes making everything else seem fuzzy and faraway.

"Yes," she says, and he seems pleased with that, though he's still frowning. Siobhan has the vague sense that she's in trouble, that she's said or done something she shouldn't have. Something he feels she should be ashamed of.

"Here." He piles a plate with something gloopy and beige. It smells like spices. "It's Tarka Dhal," he says, and Siobhan can't summon the energy to ask what that means. She takes it to the island and picks at it, scooping up the same few lentils with a fork then putting them down again.

"Was that Sylvie on the phone?"

Owen pauses on his way over to her, holding his own steaming bowl. He's obviously trying to keep all his features neutral, but the slight quirk of his eyebrow shows her all she needs to see.

"It's okay if you're talking to her."

"It was just my niece."

Siobhan looks at the clock above the fridge. It's ten thirty in the evening. "You know, I *want* you to talk to her. It was my idea."

"Siobhan." He sets down his plate. "We can't talk about this. I could... I could get into trouble, you know. I could lose my job."

"Only if you're doing something wrong. Only if you're abusing your position." She meets his eye. "Are you?"

"Siobhan," Owen warns.

Her pulse is a moth, her skin is the light. She keeps her teeth clenched together.

Owen sighs, deflates. He comes over to where she's sitting and places one hand on either side of her face. She flinches – she doesn't like it when he touches her without her touching him first. "I think you're trying to push me away," he says, very gently, as though she's a feral animal. "I want to care about you. I want to be there for you. I wish you'd just let me."

It all sounds so disappointingly innocuous, so banal. You can care about anybody. You can be there for anybody. She holds his eye and can't believe that he can't see her thoughts written across her face. *I want you to do every single little thing that I tell you*, she thinks, tries to think it loud, tries to think it out into the space between them. *I want to own you*. Maybe there has to be a compromise.

261

Maybe she has to listen to what he needs from her, first. She lets her head tilt forward, so that her forehead is resting on his chest, wetting the soft cotton.

"I'm so tired," she says.

He has one hand on the small of her back and the other finds its way behind her knees, so that he can scoop her up. They abandon their full plates in the kitchen and move into the lounge. They are around the same height, so she's surprised at how easily he's able to carry her. The living room is dark. When he sets her down on the sofa she clicks on the lamp, and he doesn't complain. He brings through a dressing gown and she's able to change into it without him seeing her scar. He settles in beside her and she leans her head against his shoulder, lets him put his arm around her and kiss her on the top of the head, lets him make her feel small. *An American in Paris* is showing on an old movie channel and he makes a small grunt of satisfaction. Siobhan feels safe; she feels claimed. She thinks about couples all over the world sitting in this very position, and wonders how many are making concessions, how many are giving away tiny parts of themselves with every second that goes by.

"It could always be this easy," Owen is saying, stroking her wet hair, and Siobhan makes herself nod.

His phone is on the table closest to her, so when the text arrives, she sees it before he does. She picks it up and reads the words, *I can't stop thinking about seeing you tomorrow*, under Sylvie's name. She hands it to him with a smile.

He stares at his screen for a long time before saying, "You really don't mind?"

"I encouraged you," she says simply. Then, with a coy kind of shrug, "I like it."

"But *why*?"

"I don't know." At least that part is honest.

"Because I never meant for this to happen, you know. I didn't want it to. But there's... there's something there. We both feel it, Sylvie and I." He locks his phone screen and turns his torso so that he can fully face her. "You really can't tell anyone about this. You understand that, don't you? How serious it could be?"

Siobhan nods.

"Can I trust you?" He is so raw and vulnerable. The power he places in her hands is so heavy that it almost topples her.

"Of course you can," she whispers. She nuzzles into his neck, drawing her knees up to her chest, fitting into the smallest space possible. "Now text her back." She feels him hold his breath, the sudden stillness of his chest. "Tell her you can't wait either."

Only once she's watched him type out the reply, only once she's watched him hit 'send', does she kiss him fully on the mouth; an enthusiastic, full-blooded reward.

The next day at the Showroom, Siobhan works the morning shift with Sylvie. Sylvie's hair is worn down and straight, ringed with shine from the overhead lights, making her look angelic. Her long fingers are adorned with silver rings and her make-up is simple and classic. She wears red lipstick. *All this for Owen*, Siobhan thinks.

Why did you bother? You are already worth a hundred of him. Throughout the shift, Sylvie taps her boot against the leg of the desk. It ticks and tocks in Siobhan's brain, a timer counting down to noon.

When Sylvie picks up her bag and heads for the cinema door, casting an absent-minded goodbye over her shoulder, Siobhan knows where she's going. She watches her leave and tries to tame the riot in her blood.

ELLY

THEN

The twisting in Elly's stomach is so intense that she feels as though she can't exist inside her own body. With each contraction she tries to escape herself, to rip free of her skin, clawing at her own face and the faces of the women who kneel beside her. They hold her hands, coo comforting words, but Elly can only scream. She makes silent bargains – *Please, I'll do anything* – but she doesn't know what she's asking for, or who she's pleading with. The sensation is so all-encompassing that it near-blinds her; she can't distinguish one woman from another, they are simply a presence, one entity that mops her forehead and massages her back and tells her the baby is coming soon, soon, I promise.

There is pain – so much pain – but this feeling is more than that. She has become mighty, more powerful than she has ever been, perhaps even in her hex form. Her body rides the riptide of each contraction, following an ancient code it has understood all along. Everything inside her works together to bear down, her teeth clamping so tightly she feels something at the back of her mouth crack. The night hours are lost to her. She turns her focus inwards to the soft, quiet world behind her eyelids. She already knows this time is sacred, that she will think of it every day for the rest of her life, and she wants to immerse herself in its truth and brutal beauty. When she's lucid, it's only in snatches. She stores up the small details that make themselves apparent: the red sisters singing their melancholy Gaelic songs; the brush of Margot's curls against her cheek; the way the air smells like candlewax and damp. Theo's panicked voice, further away. *Should it be taking this long?* A sprig of lavender held under her nose. Haina's face, those dark eyes, constellations of obsidian and cinnamon. *You clever, clever girl.* The darkness fading, the sun coming up, milky and weak. *Turn her over. That's it, gently now.*

Finally: a startled cry that doesn't belong to her. The baby. Her baby. A baby that has somehow, miraculously, come out of her body and is now in the room, breathing and crying and stretching out its tiny arms. The gloomy mid-morning is suddenly momentous and strange. A sharp cracking, an erupting, pieces of dark brown shell littering the parlour floor. A warm, slippery body placed on her chest, still attached to the cord.

You, she thinks, looking down at the perfect, swollen face. *Of course it's you.*

She wants to be alone with him. She wants to use her body as a shield to protect him from view, because he is hers, hers alone. Her love is enormous, almost too painful to hold in her body – she gives birth to that, too, and it bursts forth and floods the room. Euphoria makes her shake. She looks down at the boy, her boy, *Mine*, and grips his tiny hand as hard as she dares. She is crying, she realises. He is too precious to be born, too important to be at the mercy of the world.

The placenta is a violent purple when it slips from her body. It looks like a creature that should never see the light, like something pulled up from the bottom of the ocean, like something that has only ever known a life fumbling around in the deep dark.

The women swarm and chatter. They tend to her and the baby with so much tenderness, but Elly barely notices it. All she can see is him. She presses her nose to his forehead, inhales the scent of his skin. She wants to stay like that, the two of them tight together, always.

"I will be worthy of you," she whispers. "I promise."

Elly's body feels different without the baby inside. For days she is sore and limping; excavated, hollow, but before long the strength starts to return as her stomach muscles shrink inwards. She thinks about the birth all the time, the wonder of it, the way it had made her feel close to something greater than herself. It was not dissimilar, she realises, to how it feels to hex.

She begins to remember what it felt like, for her body to be her own. Only, she is changed now. She's a mother, but she is also something else, something the house has made. Something she cannot name. Now her body no longer has a baby to grow, she feels the fullness of it – her every cell buzzes with strength, with potential.

Elly calls the baby Thomas, after her dad. She sees shades of him in his tiny face: the bluntness of the nose, the darkness of his hair. She looks for Ethan there, too, and is relieved not to find him. There is an ache though, an urge she can't ignore. *You have a son*, she wants to tell him. *Look what I did for us, look what I made, even when you were trying to slowly crush me.*

Elly can't be fully sure of the dates, but she thinks that Thomas has arrived early. She hadn't expected to give birth at the house, had always assumed that, somehow, she would be gone by then, although that seems faintly ridiculous now. She hadn't thought about how it would be practically, to bring a baby into the delicate orbit of Hex House, how the other guests would react. But as the days go on, she feels more and more as though she is in a village of women, all of whom seem keen to help her every minute of the day or night. Janine rubs Elly's back at night while she nurses – that odd, wonderful sensation of the milk arriving and passing from her to him, a pearly thread connecting them, magically sustaining his little body. Keiko brings her cinnamon tea and ice cubes for her cracked nipples. It's Margot who seems to love Thomas the most. She takes him so that Elly can sleep, shower, or have her sessions with Haina. She stares down into his tiny face with such intensity that it's as though he's somehow communicating with her, only her.

Sometimes, after a nap, Elly looks out of the dormitory window to see Thomas with the sun on his face, surrounded by all the women who already love him like he's their own. Seeing him so well cared for, her thoughts wander often to her sessions with Haina. In between each, she anticipates the next. She notices things about the house that she didn't before, things that hadn't made sense but now crystallise into perfect clarity. She recognises the deep grooves in the wooden floor of Haina's study as claw marks. She knows the sound of scratching on the roof is the women practising with Haina, wheeling in the air around the house until the sun rises. In some of the women who are almost ready for their ceremony, she senses a new kind of hunger, a restlessness they can't sate.

Elly advances quickly in Haina's sessions. She can find her hex form with barely any prompting, and she knows the shape she is taking is closer and closer to her final hex. One afternoon, Haina brings out a mirror so that she can regard herself and her hex form for the first time. What she sees makes her hold her breath until she's lightheaded. She is double her normal height; she takes up so much space with her layered wings, the colour of fresh snow. Even with her pointed beak and wide-set eyes, always scanning the room, always watching, she looks more like herself than she has ever known. She can feel the power in her clawed feet. She feels how they could crush something, someone, with no effort, no effort at all.

And then there's Theo. Theo, who has been avoiding Elly since before the birth. Whereas before it had made her feel ashamed that she'd so evidently read the situation wrongly, now she no longer feels able to let him ignore her. All her passivity has evaporated, and in its place is nothing but strength, nothing but want. She watches him moving around the house, capable hands hoisting his camera onto his shoulder, the veins in his forearms, the pulse in his neck, and she desires him so much that it's as though her skin is on fire. She has never known lust like it. Now that her body is her own again, she wants to truly inhabit it, to let it not only desire but, finally, have.

One afternoon, Elly feeds Thomas in the dorm. His eyes have been opening more and more, starting to focus on her. He reaches up a searching hand for her face and she presses it to her lips. "Hello, beautiful boy," she whispers.

Margot comes into the dorm, sitting next to Elly and looking down at Thomas.

"Shall I put him down for a nap, Little Mouse?"

Elly nudges into her shoulder. "What would I do without you, Margot?"

Margot beams as Elly passes her Thomas's warm, sleepy body, holding him tightly to her chest. "I don't want him to ever have a nightmare," she whispers to Elly. "I don't want him to ever stub his toe, or feel embarrassed, or be spoken unkindly about. It makes me feel like my heart's breaking."

"I know. Me too."

Margot strokes Thomas's head, where reddish blonde hair has started to grow over the cradle cap. She sings a lullaby in her soft, high voice.

Elly heads downstairs, listening to Margot's singing and Thomas's contented gargling until they're out of earshot, then goes to look for Theo.

She finds him by the wooden bench around the side of the house, the south-facing side that gets the light long into the afternoon. He's filming crisp leaves falling from one of the oak trees fringing the woods. When the gaze of his camera finds her, Elly knows her light knitted dress, the shade of winter berries, will be a shock of colour against all that gentle brown. The days are colder now, but Elly feels warm as he pulls his face away from the camera to look at her.

"I want you to interview me," she says, after a pause.

She senses Theo's hesitation, the way his eyes look everywhere but her, the way he takes a couple of steps away, towards the door. "I think we've got everything," he says coolly. "We shouldn't need any more interviews."

Elly watches him, searching his expression for an explanation. She finds only uncertainty, discomfort. She steps forward and takes the camera from him, placing it on the bench. She makes sure it's recording, and then holds Theo's hand, pulling him backwards so that they're in the shot, then settles herself down in the grass. Theo stutters something incomprehensible, looking from the camera to Elly and then back again.

"Just sit down," she tells him, and there seems to be enough authority in her voice for him to obey. They sit together beneath the oak, in the sight line of the camera. He is unnatural in front of the lens, shifting self-consciously.

"What do you want me to ask you?"

Elly tilts her head to the side. "Anything you want," she says.

He's quiet for a long time before he asks, "Do you think Thomas will meet his father?"

The question feels like a cold, stinging blow across her cheek. She must flinch, because Theo's expression softens. "I'm sorry," he mumbles. "I didn't mean that to sound so harsh. I know it's not as simple as that."

Elly looks up at the dormitory window, where Thomas will be drifting off to sleep. He doesn't know what a dad is yet. But soon he will. And what will she tell him? She hasn't let herself think that far ahead, but the answer feels clear now. *One day.* One day, when she's strong enough, she'll take her son to meet his father.

"What do you think you would say to him?" Theo is asking, more gently now. "To Ethan, if he were here?" It is always a strange kind of thrill to hear Ethan's name from Theo's mouth. It feels like slipping into a bed that isn't hers.

What would she say to Ethan? Maybe, *You were so wrong about me*, or perhaps, *I finally understand that you only loved the idea of me*, but neither of those feel true enough.

"I wish I could show him what I am now," she says instead, and she means it.

"And what are you?"

Elly doesn't think there are any words for that. She wonders, for a second, what he thought of her during Grace's ceremony, when she'd helped rip the unknown woman apart, making her into something both more and less than a body. Then, with a small jolt, she realises that she doesn't care. She isn't willing to shrink it, or change it – this wild thing in her – to be more acceptable to him. She must have been quiet for a while because Theo is looking at her closely, his gaze questioning.

"I want to ask you some questions now," she says.

"Okay." She likes the way he doesn't challenge her, never makes her feel stupid for the things she says or wants. "Shall I stop recording?"

He makes to stand up, but Elly reaches out a hand to

stop him. "No. Keep it rolling." Theo clears his throat, but nods, a reluctant consent. "Do you think Haina chose you and Siobhan for a reason? To make the documentary?"

Theo shrugs. "Shiv said Haina knew about her film, based on the shelter where we used to live. I'm only here because she wouldn't come without me."

"I think it's more than that," Elly says, interrupting him. He looks up, eyebrow quirked, signalling for her to continue. "I don't think she would have picked Shiv, I don't think you ever would have been able to find the house, if she didn't need it, just like the rest of us." She waits, then says, "I think she's in pain, maybe both of you are, and Haina could sense it. I think the pain is buried deep, but it's just as real as the rest of ours."

If she hits a nerve, Theo doesn't show it. "I don't think either of us are in pain," he says simply.

"Maybe not now. But there's something there."

Theo goes silent. He looks as if he might stand up again, then seems to change his mind. There's something different in his expression when he looks at her now, some- thing less guarded. "I was five when we moved into the shelter," he says, so quietly that she has to strain to pick out each word. His eyes avoid the camera; they're firmly on Elly now. "Shiv was three, too young to remember the time before. But I remember everything."

He tells her all of it – more than she could ever have expected. He tells her about how his parents had met when his dad was a high school maths teacher and his mum was a student. How he'd waited for her to finish school – Nora had thought that was so romantic – before asking her to go to dinner. How his mum had felt there was never any other option but yes, and said he'd always seemed to know that. Theo told Elly about his dad – red-cheeked, funny, generous. Then, the kinds of things he'd do to their mum when he'd been drinking: holding her hands under hot water until she screamed, opening the window of their tenement flat and leaning her backwards out of it, a hand around her neck, pulling out hanks of her hair that Theo would find scattered around the house the next day and think were rats. He tells her about how he would lock the door of the bathroom and hold Siobhan in there until the shouting stopped. How sometimes Theo looks at Siobhan and he can't help but hate her, because she reminds him so much of their dad. That she's selfish and brash, the funniest and most confident person he knows. That when she drinks she gets messy and physical, and he can't stand to be around her, because it's like looking at *him*. That maybe she doesn't remember all the things that happened but they seem to be inside her still, trying to claw their way out. He tells Elly these things in a voice so delicate and cracking it's as though he's never said them out loud. He gives it all over to Elly for her to hold in her hands, to cherish or crush. He trusts her, she realises, and for some reason that makes her feel heavy and sad.

"That's why you're here," is all she says. "That's why Siobhan is here. You need the house just as much as we do."

His eyes are soft and wet. He looks down at his hands, at the lines on his palms, as if all the answers are there. There are voices coming from the house, from the kitchen where the women will be preparing dinner, from the study where Haina will be sitting with one of the guests, or maybe Siobhan. These days, it always seems to be Siobhan.

"I have one more question for you," Elly says.

Theo glances up at her, his face a question.

"Did I get it all wrong?" she asks. "I thought you might see me – understand me, like no one else does. But lately, it's as though you can barely look at me."

Theo's teeth are gritted behind closed lips. She sees his jaw pulse. One of his hands seems to be holding the other in place, as if he isn't sure what it might do without an anchor.

"Do you hate me?" she asks, and it comes out so plainly, so loudly, that he flinches. His answer won't change anything, but she still needs to know. "You've seen what I have the power to become. Are you scared of me? Are you revolted?"

Finally, he looks at her, *really* looks at her, and it's with so much intensity that Elly's breath gets trapped in her throat. She's suddenly dizzy.

"You think I'm *revolted* by you?" he hisses fiercely, on a hot exhale. Elly's blood feels riotous under her skin. "For fuck's sake, Elly. You're the only thing I think about, every hour of every day. You're the only thing keeping me here."

Elly holds her breath. She watches him, her eyes on his lips, which are wet now – reddish, as if bitten.

"But what am I supposed to do about it?" he asks, and she hears it in his voice: frustration, months and months of it. His hands are fists in his lap. "You've been through so much. What kind of person would I be, if I tried to…" He trails off. "You need to heal; you need peace. You don't need *me*."

Elly remembers the camera on the bench, recording their every inch of movement, committing it to tape. She knows how the shot will look – the cool crispness of the day with its perfect blue sky and vivid colours; their bodies close but not touching.

"I don't need you, Theo," she whispers. "But I want you."

They unlock something in him, those words. They make something fall away: the last vestiges of his self-control, of his guard. When he grabs at her, it isn't gentle, it isn't polite. It's desperate and searching. He pulls her on top of him and their bodies push backwards into the grass, and all Elly knows is his mouth and his hands and the intensity of his desire, answering the simmering burn of hers. When she kisses him, she doesn't think of Ethan. She thinks only of his mouth on hers and the sound of birdsong, high in the trees.

Later, they dance together in the parlour, surrounded by the other guests as they move and sway in the low light. The song playing on the gramophone is old-timey and slow. It makes Elly think of wartime, of distant bombs being drowned out by music. Theo holds her closely, hand heavy on the small of her back. She grips the curls at the back of his head.

Then, they're in his locked room in the eaves. He pulls the dress from over her shoulders and stands back to look at her. She watches him drink her in, and in his eyes, she sees herself; strong, uncompromising, otherworldly.

Haina suggests she take her First Fly that night. Elly had expected to feel frightened by the idea, but the reality is the opposite – it fills her every cell with hope, with the heady possibility of flight. She tingles with the anticipation of air.

She carries Thomas on their way up to the roof. The sky is greedy with stars and the air smells like bonfires. Elly senses all of the creatures in the woods and longs for the sky. Thomas gazes up at her with his wide, round eyes and she thinks, *You, my boy, are more wonderful than all the stars combined.*

Theo pulls her aside when they get to the roof. "Are you sure?" His expression is pinched, furtive. "You don't have to do this, if you're not ready. You can say no to Haina."

"I'm not Lakshmi," she tells him, because she knows in her bones that the same thing won't happen to her. She knows it in the same way that she knows the wind is blowing southward tonight; that it'll rain all the way from midnight into the light hours.

"I'm so worried about something happening to you," he tells her quietly. "I don't know what I'd do."

She knows that making him feel better isn't up to her. And she doesn't need to, because Siobhan is at his elbow now, looking only at Theo and not at Elly.

"She says she's ready, Theo," Siobhan says, and there's a spikiness to her voice, a vague unpleasantness. She's holding the camera. "It's her choice."

Haina and the rest of the guests are ready and waiting for her. Margot takes Thomas, and he snuggles happily into her chest. Elly is quick to transform. She doesn't even need any provocation from the other guests; she doesn't need their jostling or their cruel words or hand-crafted insults hurled like spears. When her body changes shape, it does so quickly and with a sense of relief, as if it had simply been waiting for permission. She can sense Theo's eyes on her as he holds his breath.

"Fly, my angel," Haina whispers in her ear. "Fly."

Elly is running. She hurtles towards the edge of the roof, the wind a whistle in her ears. A memory returns to her in the seconds before she reaches the wall: the night she found the house, running alone through the woods. She'd been so weak then, so passive – the world and all its horrors happening *to* her. Now, she carves her way through it like a blade. Then she is airborne, and she doesn't think of anything at all.

She can hear everything there is to hear: the shouting and cheering of the guests on the roof, the rapidity of their beating hearts, their hexes lurking inside them pleading, *Let me out, let me join her.* She can hear the soft whirring of Theo's camera. She can hear the slow growing of roots far beneath the soil. The quick, short breaths of her baby, the way they mirror her own, as if their lungs are connected, their bodies are still one entity, split in two.

She can hear the low rumble of Ethan's voice, far, far away.

The treeline comes into sight. She could fly for miles, she knows – there is no need to turn back to the house just yet. Instead, she wheels in the air, turning her feathered belly to the sky. The outstretched branches of the trees caress her wings and her beak and her face. Down there, on the floor of the forest, is a creature: something not long dead. She wants it; she wants it feverishly. Folding her wings to her body, she dives straight downwards and scoops it up into her claws. It is a bird, mauled by a fox, a fox spooked by Elly's shadow looming long across the trees, a fox now hiding in the undergrowth and wondering what she might do with its kill. Elly clutches the still-warm body of the bird then turns so that she's heading back to the house, to the rooftop with all its noises and all its faces, so far from the steely serenity of the forest at night.

When she lands, she drops the bird at Haina's feet.

"Clever girl," Haina whispers. There are tears in her eyes. "My clever girl." She picks up the bird, holds it tight to her chest, then takes it inside.

The days pass by in fevered glimpses. Elly feels more awake in her hex form than her human form. She practises with the other more advanced women on the rooftop at night, flying through the starry hours, returning exhausted and sweaty by morning. She kisses Theo deeply in dark corners.

She is becoming more attuned with the night world than she is with the house. She knows the textures of the sky better than she knows the planes of her own face. She used to think in Google search terms – *how to prevent fruit flies, is cycling healthier than walking, how to make Genoise sponge* – but now she thinks in moon cycles, in bird calls. Sometimes, she lets herself wonder what it all might mean, if her time to leave might really be approaching.

Elly is still tethered enough, however, to realise that the other guests are beginning to worry about the house. As autumn turns to winter, the house's degradation seems to accelerate. Slate tiles slip off the roof and shatter against the patio every morning. The potatoes stocked in the kitchen cupboards sprout wart-like eyes in a matter of hours, turning green and putrid in their hands. In the bathroom, the water comes out the colour and texture of sludge. Whenever anyone plays the piano, the sound is ugly and discordant, no matter how many times they tune it. The mournful notes ring through the house, day and night. The wallpaper peels. The masonry cracks. Elly feels the house's lack in her bones.

Then there's the smell. It rises up from under their feet: bitter, rotting. The smell of something dying.

There are also changes in Haina. She stoops as she walks now, as if her joints are aching. She sits often and for long periods of time, rarely leaving the chair in her study. Her skin seems grey, pallid. Her eyes are dull. She speaks to Siobhan and Theo more than the rest of the guests, and she knows that they're talking about the documentary, and that the documentary is important to Haina, and perhaps to the house itself, in ways that Elly can't even begin to guess at.

Siobhan and Theo have been at the house for months now, and the documentary is almost finished. Soon, they'll be leaving. Elly can't decide how this makes her feel. She isn't as sad as she expected to be.

Because I'll be gone soon, too.

SIOBHAN

NOW

Siobhan has been watching Hex House clips again. Even the ones she wasn't present for are so familiar now that they've started to feel like memories, like they're scored into her grey matter.

She watches the clip of Elly and Theo out in the autumn garden again and again. She watches Elly's face as Theo tells her about their family, their history – their dad and the way Siobhan is his mirror image. All the things he's never said to her, all the things she'd had no idea that he'd ever felt. He just gives it all to Elly, who sits there and says, *I think Siobhan is at the house for a reason*. It makes Siobhan want to scream; it makes her want to smash the laptop screen into nothing. She watches Elly kiss Theo over and over and it makes her queasy to see her brother that way, but it also makes her think that she has never kissed anyone like that, not really, not with so much want and purity and confidence. She wonders if she ever will. It makes her feel hollow, to think about what Theo lost when he lost Elly. She is about to play the clip again when the text from Owen arrives.

Sylvie is coming over tomorrow night, it reads. *Are you happy?*

Siobhan's pulse stammers. Saliva floods her mouth.

Very, she replies.

She goes to the bathroom and clicks on the overhead light, which is pale and sickly. It makes her skin look like it's glowing. She opens her phone's camera and captures her topless torso in the bathroom mirror. Her face, which is sallow and drawn, and her leaking scar, she leaves out. She sends the photo to Owen.

Jesus Christ, he replies. Then, after another minute, *You're so incredible.*

Siobhan goes into the kitchen and makes herself a rum and coke, and then another, and then just a rum. The radio plays thumping bass into the flat. She sways and bounces, knocking over furniture, until someone in the flat below bangs on the ceiling. She jumps up and down on the spot where she hears their banging, trying not to cry.

When she finally falls asleep, she dreams of the tiny mouths of birds. She dreams of them open and wanting. She dreams of Thomas reaching out to her with his fat fists.

Come back to Hex House. Come back.

The next day at the Showroom, when Sylvie reaches into her handbag to pull out a lipstick, Siobhan catches sight of something silky in the bag. A slip with a lace trim. It makes her feel like she's drowning in something rich and delicious, though she is so feverish today she thinks she might actually be sick. Her scar feels as though it's been seared into her skin with a hot iron.

"What are you doing tonight?" Siobhan asks, towards the end of Sylvie's shift. She knows exactly what Sylvie is doing. She knows the smooth feel of the buzzer she'll press to be let into Owen's apartment; she knows the expensive smell of his lobby and the clean scratch of his sheets.

Sylvie shrugs. "Not much," she says, "just drinks with a friend. A good friend." This last part she says with a smile that makes Siobhan's scar ache and her eyes water.

Siobhan tells Keith she has a headache so that she can leave the Showroom before Sylvie. He frowns. There is a white smear on his collar that looks like toothpaste, and she focuses on that rather than his peering eyes. "You can go," he says, "but let's not have it happen again."

She pulls on her coat over her polo and heads straight to Owen's. He doesn't sound surprised to hear her voice snaking down the intercom. When he greets her at the door, he looks nice, polished, in his white shirt and dark green chinos. He's wearing shoes in his own house, and he smells like spice and citrus. There's another smell coming from the kitchen: butter and garlic. He's making fettuccine Alfredo. It's almost six thirty. Sylvie will arrive in half an hour. Before Owen can speak, Siobhan smashes her mouth to his.

"I'm going to be in the bathroom," she tells him when she pulls away. "I want to hear you with her."

Owen stutters something in protest, and Siobhan knows this is too far, that he's dangerously close to telling her to leave. She keeps a hand on his arm.

"I'll just hide in the airing cupboard if she comes into the bathroom," she says. "She won't see me. And I'll reward you after, I promise."

He moves to one side, like she's given him the answer to a riddle, and she steps into the flat. Siobhan heads straight for the bathroom, catching a glimpse of Owen's worried face before closing the door. Siobhan looks at herself in the medicine cabinet. It's bigger than the one she has at home, so she can see herself more clearly. The face looking back at her doesn't feel like her own. It's too strange, the cheekbones too prominent and the lips pale and chapped. She's wearing a V-neck T-shirt, and if she looks closely, she can see that there's a new mottling to the skin along her collarbones, a change in texture that makes her stomach twist. Suddenly, she wants rid of all of her clothes; she can no longer stand the feel of fabric on skin. She kicks off her shoes then peels off her T-shirt and leggings, her skin clammy and too warm, then pads across the room to the bath and climbs inside. The porcelain is cool. Her legs are almost too long for the tub, so she props her feet up by the brass taps, twisting one forwards and backwards with her big toe so that the cold water starts and stops again in spurts. She can't look at her scar. She won't. It feels like a black hole sucking everything else into it. It feels like it's eating her from the inside. When she closes her eyes, she can see black shapes moving through the air, gliding, graceful and predatory.

Owen knocks on the door, asks if she's okay. She doesn't answer. Then there's the sound of the buzzer ringing and Owen moving away from the bathroom door to answer it. Siobhan pretends she is deep under water, as far away as possible from the sky and all the things it's filled with.

Sylvie's voice drifts into the flat and Siobhan's body tightens at the proximity, though, of course, they sat even closer together earlier in the day. It is impossible to hear her properly from in here; her voice is too quiet and liquidy. It's more impossible still that Siobhan has made all of this happen. She can hear them in the kitchen: Owen taking her coat, telling her he hopes she loves fettuccine Alfredo, that he's thrilled she's accepted the job at his production company. *I just want to get to know you a bit better.*

It is these things that tell Siobhan that her instinct is right, that she had been right about Owen since that first night she'd run into him at the cinema. She'd almost been able to smell it – that unshakeable belief in himself that, yes, he is a good person, a good *man*, whatever that means, while all the time being just one push away from his true nature. From just taking whatever he wants, whenever he wants it, never even stopping to think of the powers and privileges he's using to get it. There are worse men than Owen, she knows this. But somehow, this only makes it worse. It's the insidiousness that she can't take, the way his rotten parts have slipped in to sit so easily alongside all his goodness. *He just can't help himself*, she thinks. *He is a magpie, and she is so shiny.*

"I don't want to pressure you into anything," she hears him saying. "This can be anything you want. It's all under your control."

When Siobhan closes her eyes, she can see herself pulling Owen away from Sylvie and her perfect skin and her bright future, with hands that aren't hands at all, but sharp claws. She can see herself ripping into him – how good it would feel to undo all of his completeness, to muddy his perfect shirt with blood – picking at the flesh underneath his ribs. The heat from her scar has travelled upwards and outwards, consuming her whole body. Something has erupted from beneath the scar tissue.

When she opens her eyes, she is changed.

And in that second, Siobhan knows for the first time what she really is – what she has been all this time, what's been lurking inside her since she left Hex House. The thing she couldn't even admit to herself, let alone Theo. She is the thing that Haina had known she could be, had told her she could be, all those long afternoons in her study.

Hex, she whispers now, into the echoing quiet of the bathroom. *Hex*.

Only, there is an incompleteness to her; she feels lumpen, misshapen. She isn't in her final form, then, not yet. As she rises from the bathtub, she watches black feathers shivering along her forearms. Her clawed feet click on the tiles. They are twisted and knobbly, agony to walk on, but she drags herself to the bathroom door and pushes it open. Her vision is fractured now – pinpoint sharp, black and white.

Siobhan is silent as she moves through the flat. Owen and Sylvie are still in the kitchen. She can see them through the open doorway. Sylvie is seated on a stool at the island and Owen is standing over her. He has one hand cupped under her chin, raising it. They are kissing. Both of their eyes are closed. They don't see her. Siobhan goes instead into the lounge, low-lit by lamps, a candle flickering on the coffee table, making the room smell like smoke and vanilla. She stands near the sofa, and then with one sharp talon, tough as bone and the colour of old teeth, rips open one of the leather cushions so that the stuffing comes spilling out. She drags that same claw along the perfect wood of the coffee table, leaving a deep, pale mark, thinking about the scratches on the floor in Haina's study.

"What's that noise?" Sylvie says from the kitchen.

Siobhan can hear Owen's heartbeat. It speeds up – *thud thud thud* – as if he is only now remembering what lurks in the house with them.

"Nothing," he tells her.

With her long, pointed beak, Siobhan smashes one picture frame after another, sending the shattered glass falling to the floor.

The voices in the kitchen stop.

"Don't move," Owen says.

Siobhan stalks back out into the hallway and into the kitchen. Owen sees her first; he'd been on his way into the hall, to apprehend her. *Big, brave man.* That thought makes her laugh, a wet, hacking sound that causes both Owen's and Sylvie's eyes to widen. With what? What do they see when they look at her? Siobhan imagines herself – mouth dripping with thick saliva, feathers obsidian and outspread. She must look like a nightmare. Like a reckoning. Owen's mouth falls open. Sylvie starts to scream.

Siobhan opens her mouth to say something – she isn't sure what – but all that comes out is a splintering kind of cry. Owen and Sylvie cover their ears, as if the sound causes them physical pain. Owen sags against the countertop, immobilised, but Sylvie is running. *Good for you*, Siobhan thinks. *You're so much stronger than him.* Sylvie wrenches open the door to the main flat and then is gone. Siobhan can still smell the sweetness of her perfume on the air, can hear her making her way down the stairs and out into the night.

Good girl, Siobhan thinks. *Run, and keep on running.*

Siobhan stops wailing. Owen takes his hands from his ears. It is quiet in the flat now. There's nothing but their breathing. His, short and fast. Hers, measured and slow. What should she do to him? Scalpel-sharp images in her head: Owen's body, rearranged into a new shape, the shape of a single word, sprays of blood on the pretty kitchen tile. But no, she can't pull him apart like the women did with their sacrifices, because what would that mean? What would that make her?

But, still. He needs to be punished.

Does he know that it's her, when he looks up into her face? Can he still find her in the features of this thing she has become? From the way his eyes glimmer, from the way they flicker to the open bathroom door and back again, Siobhan thinks that yes, he does. Maybe he knows that it's her who scoops him in her powerful arms and takes him across the kitchen to the window, the window that shows them the whole of the city sprawled out at their feet.

Maybe he knew it would end this way all along, that somehow, she would bring everything crashing down, because he doesn't resist. He doesn't resist even when she holds his body close to hers, so close and tight that she hears a bone crack; even when she opens that old window and lets him fall seven storeys from it. The sound of him hitting the pavement is a short, sharp shock, and then the night is quiet.

When Siobhan wakes up in the morning, naked in bed, soles of her feet dirty and a hoarseness in her throat like she's been screaming for hours, it's impossible to tell what's real. Her fever's broken – she's no longer clammy and hot, and her head feels clearer than it has in days. Her scar still looks awful, but the inflammation has calmed down. It's red, rather than green and weeping. Beside her bed is an empty packet of ibuprofen and a bottle of tequila, only an inch of liquid left at the bottom.

She sits up in bed. Cool light streams in from the open window. She hadn't shut the curtains last night. Where had she been? The evening appears to her all out of order: outstretched wings, cold bathtub, the sharpness of claws, the Showroom, smashed picture frames. Sylvie running from the flat. Owen's peaceful face before she let him fall, fall, fall.

Siobhan lurches to one side and vomits over the side of the bed, straight onto the carpet. What comes out is black, like old blood, like tar. It can't be real. None of it can be real. She's not well, she had a fever – she'd dreamed the whole thing, here in bed. She grabs her phone from the bedside table. It has 2% battery left.

Can I see you today, she writes to Owen. *Please.*

The pressure in her head is building. It's almost unbearable. She grips her phone in her fist and smashes it into her forehead, as if that'll create a hole and let it all come leaking out. She puts her fingers to the skin there and they come away bloodied. *What are you?* she thinks to herself, swallowing down more vomit. *What have you done?*

But of course, it isn't true. It can't be – because she isn't like the women at Hex House, no matter what she saw or learned there. No matter what Haina told her. She's put so much distance between that person and this one, spent so much time trying to forget. It was just her infection, she tells herself over and over, willing it to be the truth. Last night, she watched Hex House clips and drank until she passed out. That's what feels real, that's what feels right, despite how vivid her dreams were. Exhaling shakily, she puts her hands to her face to find that her cheeks are wet. She feels like she's scrambled from a train track in the nick of time.

I'm sorry for everything, she writes to Owen. *I'll leave you alone now.*

Her phone dies before he can reply, but it doesn't matter, because she's sure of it now, that she imagined it all: her transformation, her violence, Owen falling like a bird shot from the sky. It had felt so real, all of it – she had wanted it so badly that she can still feel that want shaking in her bones. That want had almost undone her.

She sits in bed, the world spinning around her, filled with impossibility. She doesn't know how she fits into it anymore. The only thing she can do is get up. She'll shower, and then she'll see if she can piece herself back together, see if there's anything left to fix.

Siobhan only sees them when she throws back the duvet to get out of bed. All around her on the mattress are feathers: thick, wet, and dark.

ELLY

THEN

Haina isn't at breakfast for two days in a row. The door to her study stays locked, only Siobhan permitted to go in and out. Elly asks Theo what's wrong, but he just shrugs. *Shiv won't tell me.* There's a bite to the way he says it, a bitterness.

The guests whisper amongst themselves, exchanging worried glances across the table. Barely anyone eats. Margot chews one of her curls in her mouth, replacing it with another when it becomes sopping wet.

"This isn't good," she whispers. "Something bad is going to happen, Little Mouse. I know it."

No one has ever seen Haina like this before. Elly can feel the sickness in every fibre of the house, the carpets, the threadbare cushions, the rattling table legs. The sky is gloomy and overcast. The smell, the smell of rot that no one can pinpoint or eradicate, is everywhere. It feels as though it's closing in on them. Elly wonders if it's coming from her own skin.

One morning, Siobhan appears at Elly's shoulder.

"She wants to speak to you," she says.

Elly follows Siobhan down the hallway and into the study, feeling eyeballs on her back. The curtains have been drawn and it's sour in here, like bad breath, like unwashed bodies. It takes Elly's eyes a long time to get used to the gloom, but when they do, she can see that Haina is slumped in her armchair. She is so thin, her clavicles jutting like a pair of bike handles from her chest. Her cheekbones look like they could cut clean through the skin.

"Come and sit down, my angel," she says, her voice a rattle.

Elly does. She remembers all the other times she's sat in this very chair, when she was the one who'd felt frail and fragile, sitting across from a Haina who was vital and urgent and powerful. She has the sense of something ending, or of something huge approaching, but she can't stand back far enough to recognise its shape.

"Have you enjoyed your time with us?" Haina asks.

The hairs on Elly's forearms prickle. "You've changed my life," she hears herself say. "You've changed *me*."

Haina smiles. Siobhan is hovering by the door, silent. "That's good," Haina says. "I'm so glad. Because I've been thinking about your ceremony, and I think that it should be tonight."

Elly's mouth goes dry. "Tonight?"

Haina coughs, her body wracked by the force, as if it'll split her in two. "You're ready," she says eventually, once she's recovered enough to speak. "Aren't you?"

Elly sits on her hands to stop them shaking. She's been flying nightly for weeks now, and feels more at home in the air than she does on the ground. But the thought of what she needs to do to pass her ceremony, and the thought of walking free of the house and never coming back, makes her feel sick with fear. "I don't know," she says.

"It's the final scene Theo and Siobhan need for their film," Haina says, and there's a new desperation to her voice now, an urgency. "We have to get this film into the world, Elly. We have to bring more people to this house, don't you see?" When Elly doesn't answer, she says, "*Please*, my angel. You're the only one who's ready."

Elly watches her, and so badly wants to say yes. She wants to give her what she needs – she wants to be pleasing and obedient. The first time she'd met Haina, she'd felt with an iron conviction that she should never say no to her, and she feels the reverberation of that now, clanging and insistent. It would be easy to say yes, she thinks. And yet, she can't, because deep in her belly, she knows that while she's almost ready, she needs more time. To do her ceremony tonight – it could be dangerous. And for the first time in her life, she feels enough steel in her blood to refuse.

"I'm sorry, Haina," she says. "I can't."

She can sense Siobhan's eyes boring into her back. "We really need that scene," Siobhan says, her voice hard and cold. "Then we're done."

"I just need more time. A few days."

Haina coughs again, doubling forward with the effort. Siobhan rushes to her side, but Haina waves her away. Elly swallows, feeling as though there are rocks in her mouth. It's so stark that she can't believe she didn't see it before. Haina is dying. They might not be able to wait days.

Somehow, she realises, her ceremony could save Haina. She doesn't know how that can be true, and wishes she had all the puzzle pieces in order to see the whole.

"What's happening, Haina?" she hears herself whisper. "To you? To the house?"

Haina lifts her head, her breaths ragged and slow. Her eyes land on Elly's. They flash like coins in the gloom. "You can help, Elly," she whispers. "You're the only one who can."

That feeling again – a resistance, a knowing, deep in her bones, that something isn't right. "I can't," she says, but her voice is quieter this time.

"Because you're scared?" Siobhan says, and it's not cruel, but close. "Don't you want to show everyone that you're not weak? Don't you want to show Thomas?"

Haina says nothing. She sits very still in her chair, watching.

Elly bites down hard on her lip. She holds it all in her hands: the documentary, Haina, the house, all of it. It's so heavy, but at the same time so sharp. It needles its way into her body, into her mouth. She knows she should still say no, that something about this is very, very wrong, but then she thinks of Thomas. Those tiny hands, those eyes she feels like she's always known. He deserves a mother who is strong, who is brave. And hasn't she been making excuses all her life? Isn't this new form she now inhabits capable of feeling fear and still surging forward?

"Tonight," she whispers, and in the half-dark, Haina smiles.

Elly spends the day with Thomas. If she passes her ceremony, she'll take him with her, but it still somehow feels necessary to soak up the details of him, to memorise the slight upturn of his nose, the wrinkles between his forearms and his elbows, the way he seems to look past her and then suddenly focus, peering at her with so much knowing that it makes her eyes water. At first, she had wanted to pretend that there was nothing of Ethan in Thomas, to pretend, even, that he'd come to her in some other, unearthly way. He was a gift to her for being strong, for being good. But now when she looks at him, she sees Ethan in the way Thomas's thin covering of hair shines auburn only when the light hits it directly; the way his eyes are beginning to turn a warm hazel, the colour of a woodland in autumn. It's not as painful as she expected to see these things – instead, it makes her almost miss Ethan, makes her miss the pieces of him that she had loved fiercely. There'd been plenty. When he blushed, it would travel all the way up from his neck to his forehead. In sleep, he made quiet, content noises, like a puppy. There was an unguardedness to the way he laughed, throwing his head back so you could see all the way into his mouth. She aches for him, sometimes. Thomas feels like all of Ethan's most wonderful parts, redelivered to her as a second chance.

She keeps Thomas close to her chest while she walks the grounds of the house, and when he reaches out to touch something – a dangling tree branch, a drooping strip of wallpaper – she lets him. She has all the patience in the world for him. At dinner, Margot offers to hold him while Elly eats, but she keeps him on her lap instead, bouncing him as she chews on strips of rare steak. She lets him pull on her hair and bunch it in his tiny fists. His every move is miraculous to her, an unlikely wonder. She wants more time, but before long, night starts to close in on the house, turning the sky a milky lavender, and she knows that it's time for her ceremony.

The night air is harsh and unforgiving when they step outside. The guests wrap layers of clothing around themselves, teeth chattering. Elly barely feels the cold. She is barefoot, wearing only a black slip dress and a hairband Margot had made for her out of intertwined ribbon. She'd given it to Elly the night before, cheeks flushed with pride.

"Thank you for being my friend, Little Mouse," she'd whispered into Elly's ear.

"I might not pass, Margot. Maybe I'll stay right here, with you."

Margot had smiled sadly. "Maybe."

Now, Margot holds Thomas at the front of the loose crowd of guests, and Elly stands alone by the treeline. Some of the women come up to kiss her and squeeze her arm before resuming their places in the throng. When Theo approaches, he's frowning.

"You don't have to do this," he says. "I know Siobhan has been pushing you, for the film, but don't let them pressure you into it."

Elly reaches out a hand and pushes one of his curls from his face. "I'll come and find you," she says, "out there." He bites his lip, drawing a fat bead of blood, but he rejoins the crowd.

When Haina appears in the doorway of the house and begins to limp towards them, everyone turns. It strikes Elly again how broken she looks, especially away from

296

the safe cocoon of her study. There is a bone-white streak through her hair that wasn't there this morning. When she takes Elly in her arms, Elly can feel each and every rib through the skin of her back. She thinks she hears them creak with effort.

"Are you ready, my angel?" Haina whispers in her ear.

Elly thinks about what it would mean to leave, tonight. To wander naked through the forest with Thomas, back towards the life she knew. Only, she won't go back to the village, or Edinburgh – that thought is already forming in her mind. When she tries to picture where she will go, she can't quite see it, can't see herself anywhere else in the world. She remembers what the woman had told her, all those months ago in the bathroom at her wedding. *It's the woods you need. Just keep going and don't stop.* She can only hope that the woods will come through for her a second time, that they'll show her the way forward again.

"I'm ready," she tells Haina, who pulls away from her. She feels very lonely, all of a sudden, standing solitary in front of the waiting crowd.

"You have the love of the whole house," Haina says. Her thin voice is barely loud enough to hear.

"*May your hex protect you,*" the crowd responds, their words a warm balm on her skin.

Elly knows what comes next, and she steels herself for the barbs and the cruelty, the insults designed to accelerate her change. She doesn't need them, but it's part of the ceremony, she knows, and they don't hurt any less when they do come.

"You're weak."

"You're pathetic."

"You made it so easy for him to break you."

"Thomas is better off without you as a mother."

It's the last one that tips her over the edge, that makes her shoulder blades burn, the skin screaming as the feathers break free. That precise cloud of vision takes over once more, sharpening her focus, dialling up her hunger. Only, this time feels different to all the others; there's an extremity to it. A finality.

The crowd is cheering now. She can't make out any individual faces but Theo's, which is frowning, concerned, afraid. As her hex, she doesn't care. She wants to leave them all behind. Haina gives her a nod, and already something about her has changed, something has woken up to replenish her waxy complexion. Elly holds her eye for a long second, then she starts to run. It only takes two or three strides for her to build up enough momentum to jump up and tuck her legs beneath her, to let the air and the wind propel her forward, towards the trees, towards the forest.

Everything is so much calmer up here, away from the others with their noise and their feelings. The sky is swirled purple, huge and swallowing. She forgets that it's her ceremony. For a blissful minute or two, Elly simply glides.

But then there is the thing she's barely let herself think about: what she needs to do to complete her ceremony, to walk free. And she craves it; she craves it in a way that's unignorable and deadly.

There are a thousand scents on the air, more – the creatures living and breathing and sleeping and procreating in the world beneath her. She can smell them now: all those who mean harm, who plan to spend their nights inflicting pain. The desperate, lonely souls with no one left. She could take any of these back to the house, she knows, and pass. But she isn't interested in them. There is one scent that picks itself out amongst all the rest, drawing her closer.

Soon, the woods give way to quiet country roads, the occasional car spearing the darkness with twin headlights the colour of cat's eyes. She follows them through clusters of tiny towns. She's above her own village – look, there's the church with the toppled gravestones on the lawn – then she's heading towards the brighter lights of the city, towards Edinburgh Castle, looming like a sentinel over the Old Town, the buried tunnels and worlds beneath. Now, here she is in the New Town with its immaculate buildings and expensive flats. Quiet, empty streets mean she can hover nearer the ground. She is so close to him now that his scent brings tears to her eyes.

Ethan's flat – not hers anymore, if it ever had been – is on the ground floor. Elly lands in the alley between his building and the next. When she touches earth, she is herself again – her vision has regained its full colour, and she feels the cold, wet earth through the skin of her feet, not her claws. She is naked and shivering, but no one can see her down here. She has a few minutes, at least, to peer into the kitchen window. It's a jolt, to see it all again – the pristine marble countertops, the stainless-steel fridge, the empty fruit bowl. She used to think this flat was incredible, modern and expensive-looking, so different from the little cottage she'd grown up in. Now, it only seems cold. It's like putting on an old jacket, only to find it no longer fits, and that it never actually suited you. The kitchen is empty, but the lights are on. Ethan must be home. Of course he's home – she'd smelled him, fifty miles away.

When she'd first moved in, Ethan had encouraged Elly to use the kitchen for her baking. He proudly showed her a drawer and a cupboard he'd kept clear for all her equipment. And so, Elly had spent nights dusting the countertops with flour and rolling out her dough, making loaves of rye studded with seeds for breakfast, creamy pear and ginger tarts for dessert. After a month, Ethan started commenting on the mess. After two months, Elly packed her baking things away and never got them out again.

Here he is now, Ethan, walking into the kitchen with an empty wine glass in his hand. All the air leaves Elly's body, and she leans against the cold stonework for support. This is a different Ethan to the one she'd imagined when prompted by Haina. This Ethan looks as if the last months have sliced at the core of him, leaving him scarred. He's put on noticeable weight, mostly around his chin and stomach, which protrudes slightly over his leather belt. His eyes have a sunkenness about them, like they're retreating further back into his face, and his hair is longer, more unkempt. He's still wearing his wedding ring. He plays with it now, rotating it absent-mindedly.

Elly had always thought that she was a thing Ethan could pick up and set down whenever he wished, that nothing about her actually broke the surface of him. But looking at him now, she can see the clear consequences of herself and what she's done. All the ways she's unravelled him.

If she went back to him, would it be different? Now that he's had a chance to miss her, to see clearly all the ways he'd been cruel? She could put Thomas in his arms and say, *Look at all the good we did together.* He would grin and kiss her and they would still be married, and maybe then they could carry on, they could have a life together. But there's a hollowness to the scene, and she can't get herself to picture his eyes – she can't picture them looking relieved or grateful. Everything would change, but nothing would.

Elly watches Ethan lean against the countertop and pinch the bridge of his nose between his fingers. He looks up at the wall opposite, and when she cranes her neck, she can see that the wall-mounted TV is on, turned to the news channel. It's uncanny at first, to see Ethan's face on the screen as well as in front of her. The doubling makes her dizzy. She can't hear the TV, but she can see the words underneath the news reporter, who speaks grim-faced into the camera.

Elly Carmichael – husband admits to physical altercation on night of disappearance

Elly's hand reflexively touches the back of her head, the slight ridge that's formed where her head made contact with the cottage wall all those many nights ago. She can still see Ethan's eyes in the seconds after, the fear there, the intensity of his regret. Ethan is crying now, his shoulders sagged forward. He looks like a frightened little boy. She wonders what broke him, what made him admit to the violence in the cottage – or whether the facts were just too heavy for him to carry any longer. Maybe he even thinks he killed her, that he hit her head harder than he thought, that she'd wandered out of the cottage and bled out in some lonely, forgotten place.

Elly moves an inch closer to the window and touches her fingers lightly to the glass. If only she could touch him, rest her head on the broad expanse of his chest like she used to, the place that used to feel like the safest in the world. She wants to tell him that she forgives him, because she no longer fears him, no longer needs him. She only wants him to turn and look at her, to see her framed in the window, naked and cold but so, so strong.

Why has she come here tonight? Maybe at one point she believed she could do it, what she knows Haina expects of her, but she knows now that she won't. The man she's looking at is suffering in a way she could never inflict with physical pain.

When she turns her back to the window, there's a stillness in her belly that's something like peace. And when she returns to Hex House, she returns empty-handed.

SIOBHAN

NOW

Siobhan is walking quickly towards the New Town, barely breathing, buoyed along by fear. Her backpack is heavy – she'd stuffed her laptop inside before leaving the flat and not bothered to lock the door. Her phone is still dead in her pocket. She couldn't bring herself to charge it.

When she reaches Owen's street, it isn't a surprise to see the police cordon, the vans parked around the front of his building, the uniformed officers peering down at the pavement then up again to the open window, high above. She sees it all and her body responds with a heavy kind of knowing. Of course she did it. She was going to do it from the day she met him. It had all been inevitable, because she's never been as far from Hex House as she thought. It had stayed right there in her bones, waiting. The seeds had been planted a long time ago, and now they're sprouting their ugly heads above the soil. All those afternoons in the study with Haina.

There's something inside you, Siobhan. You're not ready yet.

But you will be.

Siobhan stays frozen where she is, lurking by the park a hundred or so yards away from Owen's building. Bile rises in her mouth.

Then she's running, running faster than she can ever remember, barging roughly into the shoulders of passersby, curse words following in her wake. She can't slow down – if she slows down, she'll think, and she can't afford to do that. Not now. At first, she doesn't know where she's going, but gradually it occurs to her that she's following a scent: the scent of coffee, citrus and pine. *How is that possible?* But of course, she knows the answer. All of her senses are sharpened knives now.

Siobhan only stops when she reaches a tall, old building on Rankeillor Street, sitting in the shadow of Arthur's Seat. The hill was once a volcano, but now it's a popular walking spot, all granite and gorse. Hardy hikers holding water bottles and wearing waterproofs pass her and say *Good morning*, their smiles drooping when she leers back at them. Someone is coming out of the building, and they hold the door open for her. Siobhan slips inside. She follows the scent up to the second floor and rings the bell.

When Zara sees her, her mouth falls open and her hands drop to her sides. Siobhan pushes past Zara and into the flat, ignoring her protestations of, "Wait, how did you…"

"I need to talk to you," Siobhan says. She walks straight into a small living room, then stops, breath short in her throat.

The flat is nothing like how she expected. There are no comfy sofas to sink into or art prints on the walls, no purring cat or meticulously tended house plants. The room is stark, almost bare. The only pieces of furniture are two armchairs and a coffee table, and they're surrounded by boxes, taped tightly shut.

"I'm moving," Zara explains. She sounds tired, as if her voice is a heavy thing to carry. "They sacked me. At SunWolf."

"What?" Siobhan blinks, trying to get the scene to make sense, trying to root herself in the present. "Why?"

Zara sighs and slumps down into one of the armchairs. "I haven't been completely honest with you, Siobhan. I guess there's no reason not to tell you now. They never..." She trails off, blows air out through her lips, then continues. "They never backed the Hex House documentary. I pitched it, but they never wanted it. I've been using company resources and equipment anyway. They finally rumbled me."

Siobhan walks over to the second armchair, sits down. She feels dizzy from running so far. For a second, she forgets about Owen, the sound his body had made when it hit the pavement. Zara's words make certain things slide into focus – why Siobhan never met anyone else at SunWolf, why they always did their interviews at the library and not the office. "But why didn't you just drop it?" she asks.

Zara's eyes shift to the coffee table, and Siobhan sees now that it's covered completely with pieces of paper and photographs, like Zara's been trying to patch something together from disparate pieces. Siobhan's eyes snag on one of the photos. Dark curls. Pale skin. A single, staring eye.

"I'm sorry I lied," Zara's saying quietly. It sounds like all the air has left her body. "I just needed you to trust me."

"Why do you have all of these pictures of Margot?"

Siobhan asks. She picks up the one closest to her. Margot, much younger than when Siobhan met her at the house. She's pregnant, and she has both eyes. She's standing in front of Edinburgh Castle, beaming into the camera. There's a taller, older girl next to her. Her hair wasn't yet dyed that bright, artificial red – it's the same coal-black as Margot's. It's only the open, earnest expression that Siobhan recognises as Zara.

"I've been looking for my sister for a really long time," Zara says, sighing sadly. "I didn't expect it to happen like this."

Siobhan feels pieces of information clicking into place, keys into locks, sending doors swinging open. "Willow."

Zara nods. She drags her hands down her face. Her eyes are shifting from left to right, as if she's rapidly calculating how much she should give away. She reaches for a bottle on the coffee table and hands it to Siobhan. It's whisky – strong, bitter. Siobhan's hand shakes around the bottle, the liquid inside trembling.

"We were obsessed with Hex House, growing up," Zara says. "Margot especially. She always believed it existed, but then, she was just like that. Kind of... whimsical. She wanted fantasies and fairytales to be real. It's no wonder, really, that she rebelled against our parents the way she did." Zara laughs. It's a humourless bark, reverberating in the almost empty room. Siobhan remembers one of their first conversations over chow mein at her flat. *I had kind of an intense childhood. Me and my sister moved up here as soon as we could, but she... she didn't last long.*

"Margot went missing seven years ago," Zara says. Her voice has regained its polish, its professional sheen, as if she's talking about just another story she's covered. "It's been a cold case for most of that time. No leads, no sightings, no evidence. Then, six months ago, the letters started. Willow, she signed them. At first she was pretending to be someone else. It took me a while to make the connection, to figure out it was her, and even then, I still didn't believe she was *actually* at Hex House. I thought maybe she was just confused and unwell, or she wasn't ready for me to find her. But it was *something*, a way for me to get closer to her somehow. I started doing my research, found the HexHeads forum, pitched the documentary, followed her lead to you. And then you showed me that footage." Zara shivers. "And I knew then that it was all real. That Margot had been telling me the truth. I knew exactly where my sister was, and it was one place I could never go."

Siobhan listens, eyes scanning the pictures on the table. In one of the photos, Margot and Zara are teenagers, both wearing school uniforms: grey skirts and dark green blazers. One of Margot's socks has fallen down and she points her tongue into the camera. Zara is looking at her, frowning, her uniform immaculate.

"She wants to come home, Siobhan," Zara says, her voice cracking. "I've been trying to get her out, her and Thomas, but Haina won't let them leave."

The air in the flat feels still. Cold. Siobhan closes her eyes, lets the realisation come flooding in. It feels like icy water up to her neck, stealing her breath.

"Haina isn't dead, is she?" she whispers.

"No, Siobhan," Zara says, very quietly. "She's waiting for you, at the house. She... she wants you back."

Siobhan grips onto the corner of the armchair, feeling weightless. Of course, it would come to this. She understands now. She was always going to go back. The pull of the house, the pull of Haina – it's been dragging her backwards since the second she left.

You're ready now, a voice chimes, and she doesn't know if it's her own, or Zara's, or even Haina's. It barely matters. She already feels like her body is elsewhere: in the wilds, in the woods, searching for the door.

"She's been using Margot, using me, to get to you," Zara is saying. "The documentary. I thought it would be the best way to persuade you to go back, and help me get to the house. Margot said if you thought Haina was dead, then you might…" She trails off again. Her face is pale, pained. "I'm so sorry I couldn't tell you. I'm just trying to help Margot. I have to get her out, Haina's not well, she's—"

"What does she want with me?" Siobhan interrupts.

Zara is quiet for a long moment, raking a hand through her hair. "She says you're part of the house," she murmurs eventually. "That you need it. That it needs you. That it's where you belong."

A bristling at her fingertips. Feathers are waiting underneath, waiting to spring forth and consume her skin. Siobhan screws her knuckles into fists and closes her eyes. How many times, during those long, meandering conversations, had Haina told Siobhan how important she was for the house? How she was *meant* to be there. Back then, Siobhan had assumed she'd been talking about the documentary.

"Please, Siobhan," Zara begs. "You have to help me find Margot. You need to help me find Hex House."

Siobhan tries to block it out, to ignore it, but it's so strong now that she can feel it tugging at her bones: the siren song of Hex House, calling her home.

Two hours later, Siobhan and Zara stand in Edinburgh Waverley train station. It's 5 p.m. on a Thursday, rush hour, and the station concourse is bustling with people and suitcases, announcements and platform changes ringing out every few seconds from the Tannoy. It's almost laughable to Siobhan that she was supposed to be at work today, but that instead of sitting behind the box office with its smeared glass and ancient till, she's here, on her way to the one place she said she'd never go back.

Zara is quiet and pale as they make their way to the platform. She grips her bag of recording equipment with white knuckles.

"Do you really think we'll be able to find it?" she asks, as their small train rumbles into Waverley. "The house?"

Siobhan breathes deeply, feeling the air push at the outlines of her lungs. She hasn't had a drink in twelve hours now, and a damp sweat is plastering her hair to her forehead. She feels shaky, unreal, can't stop herself from seeing Owen's face in the seconds before she let him fall. Her hex, releasing his body to the night – the part of the house that never left her. "I'm sure," she says.

Their train is busy with commuters talking on their phones, standing guard next to their Brompton bikes and eating bags of Pret crisps, but with each station that takes them away from Edinburgh and deeper into the countryside, it gets quieter and quieter. Zara and Siobhan sit at a table, looking out of the window.

"Tell me about her," Siobhan says eventually. "Tell me about Margot."

Zara smiles. "What do you want to know?"

"Anything you want to tell me." The Margot that Siobhan remembers always had a strange, haunted quality. She'd seemed brooding and immature but also somehow nurturing – Siobhan could never figure out whether she was a lost child looking for a mother, or a mother looking for a lost child.

"Margot had a bad childhood," Zara is saying. She keeps staring out of the window, at the fields and farms passing by, rather than at Siobhan. "I guess we both did. Our parents were pious. Strict. Physical with their punishments. I look back on it now and think, *Fuck*, but we just didn't know any different. I could have tolerated it my whole life, I suppose – I didn't have much imagination. Margot, though…" Zara makes a little noise in the back of her throat. "Ever since she was tiny, she just couldn't pretend, like the rest of us could. She didn't know how to be like everyone else. She asked questions and she was loud and she broke rules. My parents were ashamed of that, I think, the way she saw colour while everyone else only saw black and white. They'd hide her away. Forbid her from doing things. It was probably the worst thing they could have done."

The train stops and the last passengers from their carriage disembark, leaving them in the quiet.

Zara shrugs. "She was so stifled and unstimulated that it should have surprised no one when she got pregnant.

Some local boy, I still don't know who. She was fifteen, and she was bored, so I didn't blame her for any of it. I blamed myself. It was my job to look after her and I failed. I failed her so badly, Siobhan."

The ticket officer arrives to check their tickets and Zara stops abruptly, her words hanging in the air. She waits until he's left the carriage to continue.

"I knew Mum and Dad would make her have the baby, but she just wasn't ready, you know, in her mind, and our parents would have made her life hell. I just wanted to do what I could for her. So, we ran away together, we came to Scotland. It was all my idea. At first, we were only going to come so we could figure out what to do. But we loved it here. I was eighteen, so I got a job to provide for us both. Our parents didn't even look for us. I found out from a friend that they told the community they'd sent us away on a charitable mission. It made me realise that maybe their strictness wasn't because they cared about us, like I'd always thought. It was only about how we made them look. And the longer time went on, the more obvious it became that Margot was going to keep the baby. I think she'd gotten the idea of it in her head by that point. Being a mother. We felt free, for a while. We were happy."

Siobhan remembers the picture of Margot and Zara standing in front of the castle, Margot heavily pregnant, her eyes twinkling. "She never mentioned a baby," Siobhan says.

Zara shakes her head. She looks down and Siobhan pretends not to see the tear she wipes away with her sleeve. "We called her Willow. You should have seen her. God, she was so beautiful. And we were okay for a while. We were.

But being a mother – it was all too much for Margot. She was so young, and Willow wasn't an easy baby. She'd cry for days on end, she wouldn't eat. We never slept. One day, Margot disappeared with Willow and when she came back she was alone. I screamed at her and shook her but she'd never tell me where she'd taken her. And she was never the same after that. Not really."

Siobhan thinks about the Margot she'd met at the house, her intense fractiousness, her roving eye. It had felt as though something were always simmering under the surface of her skin, about to boil over.

Zara rubs roughly at her cheek. "She couldn't cope with what she'd done, I don't think. But she'd never talk about Willow. She never wanted to speak to me at all. She started coming home less and less. Sometimes I wouldn't see her for days on end. She started hanging out with a group of guys she'd met down the local pub. Horrible guys. It was them that got her hooked on it."

Siobhan doesn't ask on what. It barely matters.

"Of course she couldn't afford it. We barely had anything. Everything I made she stole to pay them, until there was no money left to steal." Zara takes a deep, trembling breath. "That's why they took her eye. Payment. Punishment."

Siobhan feels cold suddenly. She wraps her arms around herself as Zara continues.

"I should have tried harder to keep her in line. I was her sister, for god's sake, I was the one who'd brought her up here and then everything just went to shit. But you've got to know, Siobhan, she was so *difficult*." Zara leans over the table, her eyes crackling with something fierce. "She didn't make anything easy. She'd hiss at me like a cat and bite me so hard she broke the skin. She'd set fire to things and leave them in my bed while I was sleeping. She'd take every pill in the cupboard just to see what it felt like. At first, when she went missing, I was relieved. I'm not even ashamed to say it anymore. I was." She holds Siobhan's gaze for a moment before looking away. "I only started looking for her when it had been two weeks. Obviously, the police didn't want to know. She'd turned eighteen by that time, so she was legally an adult, and she'd run away plenty of times before. The police already knew her, because of the drugs. They started an investigation but it was half-arsed and there were no leads. They didn't give a shit. It feels like no one has ever given a shit about Margot. They told me she'd turn up." Zara grimaces. "I guess, eventually, she did."

"How is she getting those letters to you?" Siobhan asks. "From inside the house?"

Zara is staring into the middle distance. "She told me about a kind of network of women, on the outside. She'd memorised my address, and when things started getting... bad, with Haina, she wrote letters and left them at the treeline. When they started disappearing, she just had to hope one of the women was collecting them, that they were getting to me. She just kept writing and writing. Of course, I can't write back to her, so for all she knows, I never got any of them. She won't know I'm coming for her."

There's a strange feeling in the pit of Siobhan's stomach, tossing and tumultuous. She pictures the treeline, where the manicured gardens of Hex House give way to the darkness of the woods. The invisible threshold there, the boundary between one world and another.

"I have to bring her home," Zara says. "She isn't safe, I know that much. Haina intercepted the letters." She pauses, swallows. "I pushed the documentary so hard because I thought it was my only way to find Margot. But it turns out *you* were, Siobhan."

"What do you mean?" Siobhan asks flatly. She needs a drink so badly that her stomach is churning, her hands shaking.

Zara keeps her level gaze fixed on Siobhan. "When she found out about those letters, Haina must have been so happy. They gave her all the information she needed: that Margot was my sister, that I was in Edinburgh, that I was a journalist. Margot was Haina's way to get to me. And I was her way to get to *you*."

The view changes again, becoming a long stretch of lush countryside as the train rumbles on.

"She could have gotten to me herself, if she'd wanted to," Siobhan says, almost too quietly for Zara to hear. "Sent her women after me. Made me come back."

Zara leans forward. Siobhan hadn't noticed the purple rings around her eyes until now. "But that's just what I've been trying to tell you, Siobhan," she hisses. "She isn't the same Haina she was when you left. The women on the outside don't listen to her, not anymore."

When they finally terminate, they are amongst the only ones left on the train. The station they pull into is small, old, sleepy. Without looking back, Siobhan heads away from the empty car park and towards the overgrown path that runs alongside the track. It's lined with dead brambles.

"Is this the right way?" Zara asks, tripping over a half-empty beer can. It's almost completely dark now. There are hooded figures on the path up ahead, smoking – teenage boys that stop their conversation as the women approach and only continue again once they've passed. "How do you know where to go?"

"It's the woods you need," Siobhan hears herself say. "Just keep going and don't stop."

Before long, they find the woods, or the woods find them, and the darkness is almost absolute. They can just about see the outline of the three hills, silhouetted against the completeness of the sky. There's a waxing moon, pale and sad, helping to light their way.

"Can we stop for a while?" Zara asks after they've been walking for a couple of hours.

Siobhan shakes her head. She isn't sure how she knows, but this time is different to the last, when she'd been invited to the house by Haina. They'll only find the house when they're starving and desperate, when they're freezing and falling asleep on their feet. But with every step she feels it getting closer – feels something inside her calming, quelling.

So, they walk. Blisters bloom and burst inside her trainers. Zara keeps pace with her, silent, every so often peering through the trees for a sight of golden windows and smoking chimneys. At one point she brings out a camera and turns it on herself. The sight makes Siobhan giddy. She'd held a camera in these woods herself all those years ago, trying to find the house. It feels faintly ridiculous now.

"It's almost midnight, and the temperature is below zero," Zara says, her exhales forming clouds of mist as she speaks. "I think we might be lost."

Siobhan wonders if they are, in fact, lost. It's true that she has no idea where they are, and yet, she knows they're going in the right direction. And when, half-dead with tiredness, she trips over a root and stumbles forward, when a nearby tree twists and falls, revealing a house behind it, a house of honey stone with pink roses climbing improbably up the walls around its door, she doesn't feel frightened, and she isn't tired anymore.

All she can think is, *Finally*.

ELLY

THEN

From the moment Elly lands back in the garden at Hex House, her powerful claws clutching at nothing but air, she knows what it means. She has failed her ceremony, and she won't be permitted to leave the house. The thought doesn't bother her – she hadn't felt ready to leave, relishes the idea of having more time – but she knows that, somehow, her failure means much more than that. By failing her ceremony, she has also failed Haina. She has failed the whole house in a way that she can't yet understand or put into words. As she changes back, her hex dissolving into her exhausted, aching woman form, and as Theo rushes forward to wrap her naked body in his jacket, she feels a crushing sense of sadness that's echoed in the faces of all the women around her. They are downcast, pale – some are even crying. Haina herself stands immovable, so still that she looks like a photograph. The transformation and the flight have taken everything out of Elly. She can barely stand.

"I'm sorry, Haina," she whispers. "I'm so sorry."

But Haina is shaking her head, holding up a hand to stop her talking. "Come and rest a while in my office," she says slowly, as if each word costs her something. "Then we'll talk about it."

Elly tries to follow her inside but her every muscle is lead. She falls to the floor, on her knees in the wet grass. Her vision is blurring, fracturing. She's aware of arms around her body, lifting her, carrying her inside. Theo's face is above her, smiling in a way that's both reassuring and worrying. He lays her down on the sofa in Haina's study, where she sinks down deep into the cushions, barely aware of the boundary between the fabric and her body. "I can stay with her," she hears Theo say to Haina. "I'd like to stay with her."

"Go back outside, Theo."

Why does Haina's voice sound like that? So harsh and clear, like cold Arctic water?

They exchange a few tense words Elly can't make out, but then Theo is gone, the study door is closed, and Haina and Elly are alone.

The study is dim, lit only by a couple of candles on Haina's desk, flickering low. Haina has poured them both a cup of steaming cinnamon tea, but Elly doesn't even have the strength in her body to sit up and drink it. Haina sits next to her on the sofa, gently lifting Elly's head so that it rests in her lap. She fans her fingertips over Elly's forehead, each touch light as a whisper. It reminds her of her first night in the house, sitting in this very study, the way Haina's comfort had felt like a warm blanket after a long night of stumbling through the cold. Elly closes her eyes and pictures her mum. Her dad. She thinks of Thomas, somewhere out there in the cold garden, being clutched to another woman's chest.

"I tried, Haina," she hears herself say. "I couldn't do it."

When Haina speaks, her voice is soft and velvety – honeyed, as it had been on the first night, when Haina asked if she would like to come inside. "Why not, my angel?"

Elly had thought about this on the long flight back to the house. Because she had *dreamed* of hurting Ethan. So much of her had wanted to. She'd fantasised about all the ways she could now inflict pain. But seeing him there in the kitchen – tired and pale and defeated – none of it had seemed worth it anymore. "I don't think he deserved it," she whispers.

Haina moves to the side so quickly that Elly's head jerks, falling back against the sofa cushion. Then Haina is kneeling on the floor, her face directly level with Elly's. Her eyes are alight and crackling. "Of course he *deserved* it," she hisses. Her face is so close to Elly's that it appears she's been split in two – that she is two heads coming from one body. "After what he did to you? You had *one* chance to show him how strong you are. One chance to punish him, to bring him to us, and you just wasted it. And do you know what that makes me think, Elly? It makes me think that perhaps you aren't strong enough after all. That there's nothing more I can teach you. The day I let you go, even if you don't go running back to Ethan – which you will – you'll just let someone else break you all over again."

Elly lets the words wash over her, each one heavier than the last, as if they're pushing her deeper and deeper, burying her under the waves. She wishes she had an ounce of energy to sit up, to speak, but there's nothing left.

"Do you understand, Elly?" There are tears in Haina's eyes now, fat tears that overspill her eyelids and stain her cheeks. "Do you understand why I can't let you go?"

The room suddenly feels colder. Elly is shivering. Haina stands, and at first, Elly thinks she is going to fetch the blanket from the armchair to drape over her. But instead, she's pulling at the heavy rug in the centre of the room, hauling it off to one side. Underneath, built into the hardwood floor, is a small square outline with a metal handle. A trapdoor.

How many times has Elly sat in this room, in this very chair, never knowing that door was just beneath her feet?

"What are you doing?" She's so delirious that she's not even sure whether or not she's spoken out loud. Either way, Haina isn't listening. She loops a finger around the metal handle and pulls it open. She turns to Elly, her face expressionless, voice flat.

"Can you walk, Elly?" she asks. "I need you to walk now, my angel."

Elly is about to say that no, sorry, she can't walk, she barely has the energy to blink, but her body has different ideas. It hauls her up and off the sofa, as if Haina's command brought it to life, and walks her into the centre of the room.

"Down," Haina tells her, and Elly's feet find the lip of the trapdoor, the first rung of a ladder that leads deep down into the darkness. A smell rises up to meet her: dust, damp, something else, something awful: like decaying meat. It's the smell that's been permeating the house in recent months, seeping into their clothes and climbing its way up through the plugholes. She doesn't know how her legs carry her, but somehow, they do – ten rungs down, twenty, thirty. Haina is up ahead of her, pulling the trapdoor shut above their heads and plunging them into blackness. Elly freezes, her body pressed so close to the ladder that her lips touch the wooden rung.

"Keep going," Haina instructs. One of her boots comes down onto Elly's fingers.

Elly screams and wrenches them away, keeps on climbing down, powerless to resist. After fifty-five rungs, her feet hit a solid stone floor. Her heart is a mean fist against her chest cavity.

It is cold down here, so cold. The air feels old and undisturbed. All around her, above and below, is darkness. She can barely see her hand in front of her face.

What is this place? And why is she down here? She registers, distantly, that she might be in some kind of danger, real danger, but she can't make herself care. She is too tired to feel anything at all. She thinks of Thomas, of his tiny fists balling and relaxing in sleep, and her heartbeat begins to slow. But even Thomas feels far away now, like a thought she can just watch go by.

Haina has appeared beside her. She has a hand on Elly's shoulder. "I hope you can understand," she says in a voice that makes Elly shiver, "that this is the only way it can be. I tried, Elly. But you just wouldn't listen."

A scratch, a flare, a match held out into the dark, and the scene around them carves itself into life.

They stand inside a cavernous underground chamber. The ceiling is vaulted by a network of stone arches, stretching further away than the light from the match will let her see, creating a network of segmented little rooms.

It looks like honeycomb, or a rotten apple filled with wormholes. And those arches, there's something strange about them – as Elly peers closer, she sees that they are more detailed than she'd first thought. The stone is covered with little ridges and grooves, and that's when Elly realises that they're not stone at all.

They're bone.

Close to the bottom of the pillars, she can make out elegant, swooping femurs and two-pronged tibias, long, thin ulnas and pelvises stretched open like flowers, tiny toe bones filling in all the gaps. As the columns climb, they're replaced by thick shoulder blades, sternums and undulating clavicles. Finally, when she looks properly at the central arch that sweeps left to right directly over their heads, she realises that it's made of skulls. Thousands and thousands of skulls, their grinning teeth and empty eye sockets looking down on her.

Elly vomits then, and the sickness is violent and tugging, as if she's trying to escape this awful room from the inside of herself. Everything about it feels wrong: the darkness, the smell, like something long rotted, the feeling of being so far underground. It is the opposite of being in the sky, of being free, and everything inside her is recoiling. She wants to turn back to the ladder and scramble up towards the light. She wants to fly, she wants to forget about this place – this place lurking underneath the beautiful house and the bountiful gardens, this place that has existed unbeknownst beneath her feet ever since she entered the house and who knows how many centuries before that – but she can't. Haina's hand is on her shoulder, urging her forward, and all she can do is obey.

"Why are we down here?" she manages to whisper. The stench in the air is growing stronger, thicker. There's a presence here, a deep presence she understands now that she has always sensed, the pulsing of something living, something that exists at the root of everything the house is. She feels it more strongly with every step. It drags her towards it, hungry, insatiable.

Haina's voice is a low hum, as if it's vibrating, and it echoes around the corners of the underground room. She's walking behind Elly, so she can't see her face. "Do you understand why I can't let you go, my angel? Do you understand that you've proven that you're not strong enough to face the world and all its teeth, despite the lessons I've given you? Despite the *gift* of your hex?"

They walk further and further into the darkness. Elly's legs feel numb beneath her, but still, they keep on carrying her onwards.

"I'll try again," she finds herself pleading now. Anything to make Haina stop pushing her forward, anything that might make Haina allow her to turn back, anything to forget all about this terrible subterranean world and what it might mean. Because she's started to hear sounds now, awful sounds, the cries of dying birds, the screams of women in deep, unending pain. "I'll do better next time. I promise."

"But it's too late for that, Elly," Haina tells her. "Yours is a different fate, and I promise you it's no less worthwhile. You're not fit to survive out there. You've shown us all that. No – *your* purpose is to make sure that this house stays standing, so that it can do for other women what it so almost did for you."

Elly opens her mouth to protest, to ask questions, to scream – but there's no point, because they've reached their destination now, and there's nothing else to be done. Her legs buckle. She sinks to her knees, and Haina lets her.

"You can stay at the house forever, my angel," Haina says, and she says it so desperately and thirstily, as if she's been wandering the desert for days and has finally found water. "Isn't that so beautiful?"

Before them is a great, yawning pit, the diameter larger than three men laid lengthways. It's the colour of blood, fleshy and bulging, rippling in constant motion. The stench is incredible, putrid, and it seems to stick to every inch of Elly's skin. It burrows down deep under her fingernails. It coats the back of her throat. It fights its way to the back of her eyeballs. It claims her, complete and unwilling. There are flaps at the entrance to the pit – they open and close in a steady rhythm. As if it's living. As if it's *breathing*. And with every shuddering inhale, those flaps open, and they reveal a sour darkness inside. The darkness isn't complete – Elly can make out shapes inside it. Gleaming eyes, reaching hands. Lastly, and with a sickening lurch that steals her breath, Elly recognises the once-graceful spray of wings, hundreds of wings, chewed up and mashed into a feathery pulp.

"You're going to kill me," Elly states simply. Her body doesn't feel like her own, as though there's no life left in it, as though it simply wants to fold and fall, all the way down into the pit. No, not a pit, she thinks. A *mouth*. "You're going to feed me to the house." *Like you do with all the sacrifices, and all the other women who don't make it out. Like you did with Lakshmi.*

Haina is on her knees next to Elly, clutching her chin,

pulling it upwards so that they're eye to eye. The whites of hers have turned gravestone grey. "It is such an honourable thing," she whispers, revealing a mouth gapped by missing teeth, "to sacrifice yourself so that this house might continue. It's what you were always meant for, Elly. *Out there*, there would always be someone who'd sniff out the weakness in you, who'd make it their mission to break you. And they would get such satisfaction from the process. In here, you will always be protected. Isn't it wonderful, that you can save us all?" There are tears in her eyes now, a manic euphoria to her voice. "Elly, the house is so hungry. We are so, so hungry."

Elly can't get her thoughts to stay in a straight line. They're firing off in a hundred directions – she thinks of Ethan, gutted by his own cruelty. She thinks of all the women upstairs, ignorant of this horrible crypt beneath their feet. She thinks of Thomas. His bright eyes. His tiny lips. She suddenly, fiercely, wants him away from here, as far from Hex House as he can possibly get.

"It's wrong," she manages to choke out. "It's all so wrong."

Haina recoils, as if Elly has slapped her.

"Wrong?" she spits. "Was it *wrong* when you discovered your hex in the room right above our heads? Was it wrong when you glided through the air, the whole world at your feet? Was it wrong when you saw what the house, what *I* do for these broken women, how we keep them safe in a sanctuary no one else can find? No, of course not. It is the house that has given you all those things, let you feed from its life force. No one ever stops to think where this house's power comes from, they're just so willing to take and take and take from it. They never think about the price." She pinches her fingers hard around Elly's chin, then yanks it to the side so that she's staring down into the awful, gaping hole at their feet. "You see it now, don't you? The price you have to pay."

The screams from inside the pit are so loud that neither Elly nor Haina hear the creaking of the ladder behind them, or the footsteps of two people approaching. One is running, an arm outstretched, shouting something impossible to make out. The other is following more slowly behind, holding a camera.

Theo and Siobhan are seconds too late to stop Haina from bringing her head close to Elly's and whispering, *"You have the love of the whole house."* They're seconds too late to stop Haina's other hand from finding the small of Elly's back and pushing, lightly. That gentle push sends Elly tumbling downwards into the black, into the house's waiting, starving mouth.

For Elly, there is a long moment of nothingness, of silence, of respite from fear and noise. Then, an all-over glow, a blissfulness, because she knows her wings are at her back, that her feet are now claws that can rip flesh, that her taut belly is rounded and feathered. She feels it, when the house takes her, when it melts the flesh from her bones. It isn't horrible, it isn't painful – it is euphoric. She feels everything that she is, all her strength and her fear and her memories and her love and her anger and her passion. It all leaks outwards into the walls around her, into the bricks and mortar, into the floor above her head, into Haina's body. She feels it fortify, give life, preserve the house for whoever might come next.

But it's more than that. Her death will be important, she knows, for reasons she can't even guess at. She can sense it though, and she has never felt so needed. She has never felt so strong.

Her last thought is of Thomas.

My boy, she thinks. *I'm finally worthy of you.*

SIOBHAN

NOW

Siobhan and Zara stand on the doorstep of Hex House. They are soaked through, shivering. Siobhan has lost the feeling in the tips of her fingers, but she can't bring herself to care.

"I can't believe we're really here," Zara says shakily. She looks up at the house with trepidation, as if at any moment, arms might sprout from the walls and grab her. "Do we... do we knock?"

Siobhan turns to her. Zara is still holding her camera, pointing it at the door. She understands now, for the first time, how jarring it must have been for the women when she and Theo arrived bearing cameras and microphones and equipment; how it must have felt like the seams of their lives were torn wide open.

"No one is going to invite us in this time," Siobhan says. "But Haina will know we're here."

The old handle is cold and wet under Siobhan's hand. She pushes it down and the door swings open. At the sight of the hallway, she holds her breath. This is a different house to the one she'd entered four years ago. Back then, it had been warm, welcoming, bathed in a glow from table lamps, the floors freshly scrubbed. This house looks as though no one has used it in a very long time: there are no rugs anymore, revealing dangerous-looking holes in the floorboards. There's a single bulb overhead, fizzing and flickering. The picture frames on the walls are smashed and hanging askew. The whole place smells like mould, like rot. It is so, so quiet.

"Jesus," whispers Zara. Then, "Margot? Are you here?"

There's no one in the parlour, where a jagged crack splits the grand piano in two and stuffing is leaking from the sofa cushions, or the kitchen either, where the cupboards are bare and cockroaches scuttle by their feet. As they walk quietly through the house, Zara's camera records it all. Siobhan knows how sad and ruined it'll all look on film. *It isn't supposed to be like this*, she thinks, *it wasn't always*.

They pause at the closed door to Haina's study. Zara starts to move towards it, but Siobhan puts a hand on her arm. "Not yet," she says. Instead, they head up the staircase, careful to avoid the places where the wood beneath their feet has softened and fallen away. With every step, the house seems to groan in protest, as if even the pressure of their footsteps is painful. They walk along the landing towards the dormitory. Siobhan remembers there being forty or so beds in here, but now there is only one. The curtains are drawn, so the room seethes in a moody, sour-smelling glow. It's freezing, many of the windowpanes cracked and jagged, the curtains flailing in the wind. Siobhan thinks the room is empty, until someone whispers, "Zara?"

They approach the bed slowly to find two small figures curled up under a blanket. Margot, impossibly thin and pale, her eye shining in the dark, and a small boy with reddish brown hair and freckles across his nose.

"Margot?" Zara's voice is fragile and small. "My god, Margot."

She rushes towards the bed and scoops Margot into her chest, crying quietly, whispering words Siobhan can't hear. The little boy watches with wide-eyed curiosity, then he looks up at Siobhan. She feels every hair on her body stand on end. He looks so much like Elly: he has the same questioning look, the same uncertainty Elly always seemed to carry with her, as if she were never quite sure that she was welcome or wanted, as if she didn't have the same right to take up as much space as anyone else. As if she were always waiting to be punished.

I'm so sorry, Elly, Siobhan almost says out loud. *But I've found him now. I'm going to make sure that he's safe.*

"You're so big, Thomas," she says. Thomas clings to Margot, flinching away from Siobhan's attention.

"Go away," he says quietly.

Zara pulls away from Margot finally, and Margot turns to Siobhan.

"You came," she says. "I didn't think that you would."

Zara grips Margot's hand. The camera has been propped on the bedside table, still recording. "It's going to be okay now," she says, smoothing down Margot's hair. "You can come home."

Something flickers across Margot's face – something

terse, frightened. She shakes her head, bundles Thomas close into her. "She wouldn't let us go," she hisses. "Not unless I brought *her* back."

Zara and Margot both stare at Siobhan, standing at the foot of the bed.

"Where are the others?" Siobhan asks, and her voice doesn't sound like her own.

Margot looks away. "Long gone. All started when you left. When Elly disappeared. Haina said she didn't survive her ceremony, but we knew that wasn't the truth. You'd run off in the night like that, and we knew then that Haina *did* something to her, something that made the house feel well again, just for a little while. Turns out, all she did was lie, lie, lie." Margot wipes at her nose with her sleeve, and Zara holds her closer. "The flock stopped bringing food. The women started leaving, and Haina just... let them go. She knew we didn't trust her anymore, do you understand? One by one, they all left. But Haina never let them take Thomas. *I need his young blood in this house*, that's what she said. And I just... I just couldn't leave him. I've tried to leave but we just keep finding the house, over and over. She won't let us go." Margot's whole body shudders. "She'll never let us go."

Siobhan looks around the desolate room, remembering it bright and teeming with life. She thinks of Elly, looking at herself in the full-length mirror, admiring the size of her bump. Siobhan feels calm, truly calm, for the first time in months, even years. All around her, the house groans, and her bones seem to answer in the way they become heavy and dull. For the first time, maybe in her life, she is exactly where she needs to be.

"I'm going to stay," Siobhan hears herself say. Her voice is firm and low. "I'll be her blood. You can go now, Margot. She'll let you go. Thomas, too."

There's a sound from downstairs: a deep, guttural moaning. It sounds like something giving way. It sounds like a woman's voice, calling out in pain. It's stronger than ever now, the pull inside Siobhan, dragging her down, down, down.

"You have to leave," Siobhan whispers. "Now."

Zara and Margot rise from the bed, Thomas carried on Margot's hip, his face pressed into her hair. Together, they walk silently down the old stairs. The noise is getting louder. Siobhan's flesh is tingling all over – impatient, something surging inside to break free. *Not yet*, she tells it. *Not yet.*

At the front door, Margot pulls Siobhan close. She smells like sweat, dirt, unwashed clothes. Her mouth finds Siobhan's ear, her breath hot and urgent. "Haina only wanted to protect us," she whispers. "She only ever wanted to be our mother. That's why she did it."

"I know," Siobhan whispers. Margot pulls away, and Zara takes Siobhan's hand in the doorway.

"Do you know what you're doing?" she asks. "Maybe we can all leave, together. Maybe Haina's given up, maybe she's..."

"I have to stay," Siobhan whispers. What she doesn't say is, *I killed a man. I can't go home. This is the only place that'll have me now.*

"Do you need us to go and get help?" Zara is asking.

Siobhan shakes her head again. She makes herself smile. "Just stay at the treeline for a little while," she says.

"Keep the camera recording. You'll know when to stop."

Zara stares at her, frowning, but she nods. Siobhan watches as Zara, Margot and Thomas make their way towards the treeline, away from the house. She watches them step over the boundary from garden to forest, and she feels the house cry out, a wrangling screech. The ceiling above her head sags dangerously. There is barely any blood left, no energy to feed it, nothing to keep it standing. Through the gloom of the trees, Siobhan feels Thomas's eyes on her, staring. Then, she closes the front door, and she is alone. Except, she isn't – there's a presence behind the study door, waiting for her. A presence that's been waiting for her to return since the night she ran from the house. That night returns to her now in achingly clear detail as she makes her way for the final time down the hallway towards Haina's study.

Haina's hand on Elly's back, pushing her down into that awful pit. The horrible seconds after, Haina turning, inexplicably stronger-looking, more vital, eyes like lava. Theo, scrambling at the edge of the pit as if he'd hurl himself right in after Elly.

"She jumped, didn't you see?" Haina said, hands on her chest. "The people who come to this house are so broken, so fragile, my angel. She sacrificed herself. She did it for us, to feed the house."

Siobhan hadn't said anything at all. She was still recording. She couldn't make herself stop. She was horrified to find that she was relieved, relieved that Haina looked better, that somehow, the house would stay standing.

"Where is she?" Theo screamed, launching himself at Haina. He had her by the shoulders and was shaking her

333

so hard that Haina's head snapped back and forth. She offered no resistance. "What did you do to her?"

"She's at peace now, Theo," is all Haina said. "She's saved us all."

Theo's eyes had widened, as if she'd sent an electric shock through his skin. "You're sick," he whispered, and Siobhan had never heard his voice laced with so much venom. "You're a murderer."

Haina's expression changed then, the smile disappearing. Siobhan noticed it before Theo did, the way her eyes were flickering and darkening, the way her fingers were extending into horrible, pointed claws.

"Theo," she screamed. She flung herself at him and tried to pull him backwards, away from Haina, away from that horrible pit. At first, Haina resisted, but then Siobhan felt her let him go, and they both went stumbling onto the cold stone floor. Haina towered above them, still growing, still changing. Her hex was mightier than any of the other women's. She was huge, her feathers the colour of fire. She was mesmerising. She was ruination.

"Run, Theo," Siobhan whispered, pushing him towards the ladder with every ounce of energy she had. Then they were both on their feet and running, pulling each other along. Theo reached the ladder first, started to scramble upwards towards the light. Before Siobhan's foot hit the first rung, she felt something grab her shoulder, drag her back, spin her around. She stood, face to face with Haina, with her hex, everything Haina had always been, something ancient and unknown and powerful beyond measure, something that had created the house around them through sheer will, something that had fed it year after year, done what she needed to do to keep it standing.

She was screeching – an awful, animal screech – but Siobhan could still make out the words.

"Why do you think I brought you here?" When Siobhan didn't answer, Haina screamed it again. "Think about it, Siobhan. Why are you *here*?"

"To make the documentary," Siobhan said feebly, struggling against Haina's grip. "To show the world what Hex House is."

Haina threw her head back, and it took a few seconds for Siobhan to realise that she was laughing. The sound was like nails dragged across metal. When she looked back at Siobhan, her eyes were burning. "You really thought I brought you here to make a fucking *movie*?"

Those words were ice water down her spine. She couldn't move – couldn't do anything but stare at Haina, at the monstrosity of her, the majesty. "No. You're special, Siobhan. My *angel*. It had to be you, don't you see? The itch inside you. The ache. Here is the answer: this house is your home. It can't go on without you."

Siobhan looked desperately up the ladder, Theo's feet disappearing as he reached the study above.

"This house passes hands," Haina was saying. "It has to, to survive. It wasn't always mine, do you understand?" Another wrenching cry, then, "Soon, it'll be *yours*."

Siobhan staggered back, every nerve ending burning. *No, no no.* From the top of the ladder, Theo screamed her name down into the darkness.

"What about Theo?" she asked Haina in a small voice. "Why did you bring him here, if it's me you want?"

"Well." A wry flickering across Haina's face. If she was

still in her human form, Siobhan would have called it a smile. "I've always wanted a pet to play with."

Then her claw tightened around the camera in Siobhan's hand, squeezing until the plastic cracked, until the metal innards showed. "It was fun, for a while, watching you make your little film. But surely you knew I'd never let you leave with that footage?" As the broken pieces of camera fell to the ground, Haina brought her mouth down to Siobhan's ear. "I will keep this house standing for you until you're ready to come home. And you will keep its secrets. You will make sure *he* does, too. If you don't, I'll find him. I'll gut him and leave him for the crows." Siobhan felt an intense pressure below her belly button, a ripping open, a gushing of blood as Haina dragged her claw against the skin. "Don't forget."

Then she released her, and Siobhan was scrambling up the ladder, desperately striving towards the light, screaming in pain. In the seconds before she reached the study, before she took Theo's outstretched hand, she heard Haina's voice a final time beneath her.

"You'll come home soon, my angel." A musical sound, almost like laughter, echoing off all the old stone. "You need this house now, and it needs you, more than anyone. You'll see."

Then Theo and Siobhan were running. Through the house, past the open-mouthed guests, through the gardens. He kept trying to turn back, but Siobhan pulled Theo towards the treeline, grabbing at him, covering him with her blood. Agony was rippling from her abdomen but she knew that they had to keep running. They ran until their legs were plastered with mud, until they could barely breathe, until there was no choice but to fall down in the dirt. When Siobhan looked at Theo, she realised he was crying.

"We have to go back," he sobbed quietly, when he could breathe again. "My god, we have to get help. Elly, she..."

Siobhan screwed her eyes shut, trying to understand what she'd seen. Elly, sacrificed to keep the house standing, to feed it, to allow it to continue being a safe sanctuary for all the women under its roof. The other women who *needed* the house, who had nothing else. She'd seen it for months, the way it transformed broken people into something else entirely, something powerful, something unnameable. She'd felt it herself – the tempting tease of strength, *power*, in her veins. She didn't know what she was about to say until she said it, her voice trembling. "We can't go back, Theo. And we can never tell anyone about Elly, about what we've seen."

"What?" Theo was incredulous, on his feet now, challenging her. "Are you *insane*?"

"You've seen what it does for them. The women. We can't take that away from them. The house... it has to keep going. Women have to keep finding it." *And I can't lose you*, she thinks. *I can't let her take you from me.*

"Siobhan. You were there. She *killed* Elly, she..." His voice broke. They stood in thick silence, a horrible stalemate.

"Elly sacrificed herself," Siobhan heard herself say, hating herself for it, hating herself more than she ever had. But there was no other way. Theo wouldn't care about Haina's threat. She had to find another way to keep him quiet. "Elly did it for the good of the house. For Thomas. She wasn't strong enough to leave."

Theo was shaking his head. He looked young, defeated, and tired. So tired. "You don't believe that, Shiv. You saw what happened. You *filmed* it." At that moment, he seemed to realise the absence of the camera in Siobhan's hand.

"It's all gone," she said dully. "The camera – she crushed it. All the other footage is back at the house."

"Then we have to go *back*."

"No, Theo," Siobhan growled, and he flinched away from her. Haina's words rung in her ears, haunting her. *You will keep this house's secrets. You will make sure he does, too. If you don't, I'll find him. I'll gut him and leave him for the crows.* "Please. We just have to walk away from here. We have to forget. You can't take the house away from those women." *And you can't take the house away from me*, a second, smaller voice inside her chimed. She smothered it, pushed it down deep. "Besides," she whispered. "It's too late. We've already left. Do you really think we'll ever find it again?"

Theo had looked defeated then, his whole body sagging inwards. "I'm going to the police," he said weakly.

Siobhan wiped a single tear from her cheek. "And what do you think they'll do?" Her words hung in the quiet. "Nothing. Besides maybe lock you up."

Theo sank to his knees in the dirt, and Siobhan knew she'd won. Still, she remembers now that it took her hours to get him to agree to the deal that's been in place ever since: that Theo would stay silent, but he would never speak to her again, the deal that was a lightning strike through the centre of their relationship. She knows that when he walked away from her, he spent hours, maybe days, trying to find the house again. So did she, but it was no longer theirs to find. Not yet. It was only when she stumbled out onto a quiet country lane, only when she thrust a hand into her pocket to find money or anything she might use to get her home, that she found the memory stick. The memory stick onto which she'd downloaded all of their footage a couple of days before, just in case. The memory stick she would never, and could never, tell Theo about.

Now, she stands alone in front of Haina's study. Behind her, one of the ancient oak beams falls from the ceiling and crashes into the floorboards, barely missing her. She doesn't even flinch. Siobhan turns the handle, and steps inside.

Like the rest of the house, the study is in disarray, a nightmarish, twisted version of the room Siobhan had known. The torn curtains are drawn, papers strewn around the room, dirty and ripped. Siobhan's eyes land on names she knows, *Keiko*, *Janine*, *Isla*, notes about their hexes, their progress. The fire is not lit, the window is smashed. It is deathly cold. The rug in the centre of the study has been left rolled up, the trapdoor underneath open and gaping. There are stains on the woodwork surrounding the door – dark, blotchy.

"Haina," Siobhan hears herself say. The sound of her voice sends birds flapping from the tree outside the window in fright. "I'm here. I've come back to you, just like you said I would."

She peers down into the blackness beneath her feet. Haina is down there, in the crypt, Siobhan knows. Down in that awful place where she feeds the house what it needs to be what it is. She stands next to the opening, but she can't make herself go down there, not again.

She doesn't have to. There's a noise coming from below

now, getting louder with every second. Someone – something – is making its way up the ladder.

Siobhan hears Haina before she sees her, hears that harrowing gasping sound, a hoarse, struggling wheeze, the noise of something dying. Then, a single hand, pale and impossibly bony, appearing out of the darkness and bracing itself on the floorboards. Siobhan staggers backwards as Haina, or what was once Haina, emerges: her body covered with skin that hangs from the bones, like a loose sack. Her eyelids sag beneath her eyeballs, making it seem as if her eyes might, at any second, finally give up and fall to the floor. She has little hair left – only a few straggling grey strands on a bald scalp. It seems to take everything she has to haul herself from the top rung of the ladder and onto the floor of the study, where she trembles on all fours, a spindly, wretched creature. As if in response, the walls around them cry out and a thick section of plaster crumbles and falls, sending up plumes of dust. Siobhan meets Haina's eyes. Despite her physical ruin, they are still unmistakably Haina's, dark and burning and fierce. To Siobhan's surprise, she holds out one of those wasted hands. In a rattling voice, she says, "Help me. Please help me."

Siobhan freezes, but then holds out her hand to Haina's, half-carrying her broken body over to the armchairs by the desk. They sit down, and if Siobhan closes her eyes, she could almost be back in this study four years ago, sitting across from Haina, her own hex only just beginning to simmer in her blood. She hadn't known it then, what was happening – that something was waking up in her. She didn't know that it would never sleep again. Siobhan and Haina stay silent for a long moment, looking at each other.

"Knew. You'd. Return," Haina says finally, sadly, each word a struggle.

One of the candles on the desk gutters and goes out. Siobhan shivers. "How many of them did you kill, to keep this house alive? To keep yourself alive?"

"Wrong question," Haina splutters, and Siobhan thinks the strange twist to her thin lips might be a smile. "How many did I *help*?" Another wracking cough. "Broken women. Nowhere else to go."

"It wasn't your choice to make," Siobhan whispers, voice shaking, "to take their lives away."

"All gone now, anyway," Haina whispers. "After... everything. But you." She meets Siobhan's eye, and there's still something bright in the ruined socket, something furious and alive. "My angel. Knew you wouldn't abandon me." She stares closer at Siobhan, so close that Siobhan can see the fine rings of yellow around Haina's pupils. "Do you see it now? Do you understand?"

The room is so cold that Siobhan can't feel the tips of her fingers. A tremor threads its way all the way through her, because yes, finally, she understands.

Haina's smile is wide, revealing a mouth of black gums, missing teeth. With great effort, she stands, holding her arms out towards Siobhan. Siobhan stands, too. She allows Haina to embrace her, to pull her into a body that's barely anything but bone.

Siobhan can feel her every synapse sizzling and burning, the locked part of her brain waking up, the furious part, the part she's forever trying to drown with wine and whisky and sex and anything else that numbs it just for a second. Anger – an anger that's lived inside of her since she can remember, watching her mum cower from every touch and flinch at the sound of a phone ringing. Now, it takes over, it spreads out over the skin like water, it claims her completely, rippling out from the scar on her stomach. Siobhan's eyes snap open. When she looks down at herself, she already knows what she will see. Feather. Claw. Pimpled bird flesh. Feathers, the colour of deepest night. There is no hesitation this time, no pain.

Here is her hex, in all of its horrible, incredible glory. She feels as though she could scream the sky down.

Haina pulls away, just slightly, so she can look at Siobhan.

"My angel," she whispers. "How beautiful you are."

Siobhan breathes raggedly. She is angry. She is so, so angry.

"It's yours now," hisses Haina. "All of it."

Siobhan has been angry all of her life. It's finally time for her to unleash it.

When she slices her beak into Haina's neck, Haina doesn't resist. She doesn't fight back. She lets Siobhan tear into her, she lets her separate muscle from skeleton, she lets her pull out each sickly, failing organ. She smiles, and then she begins to laugh.

The house is rumbling, shaking. Around them, the plaster falls away from the walls, as if it were only ever a facade, hiding the house's true nature. Underneath is tightly woven straw, pieces of twig and branch, dry, rotting leaves. The foundations of a nest.

"You have the love of the whole house," Haina screams.

Siobhan feels Haina's spine snap under her fingertips, falls with her to the ground.

"*May your hex protect you,*" Haina whispers in her ear, and then Siobhan pulls her heart out of her chest. She watches it until it stops throbbing in her hands.

Finally, Siobhan is calm. She is sated; her fury is satisfied. The house is quiet for only a moment before it begins to fall, with a sigh, as if it has been waiting to do so for a very long time. The bricks dissolve to dust, the wood buckles and splinters, the windows shatter. As the rubble comes down, threatening to bury her, Siobhan thinks of Zara, standing safe beyond the treeline, filming it all. She thinks of how the camera will see it: the way the house seemed to be nothing more than straw and mulch when it fell. The way it left nothing behind, no clues as to what it once was, no beds, no furniture, no bodies. The way that, in the very last second before the final pieces hit the floor, it had looked almost like something were taking flight into the sky above it. In the smoke, the fanned outline of wings.

ZARA

AFTER

Zara pushes herself back from her desk and rubs her eyes. Her hands come away covered with black smears from where she's smudged her eyeliner. It's almost 4 a.m. and she's been working for hours, fuelled only by coffee and the occasional biscuit brought over and force-fed to her by Margot. Outside the window, the world is turning a hazy pink. It's spring – the mornings finally getting lighter, the days warmer. Her vision is blurry and her muscles ache, but three months after bringing Margot and Thomas home from Hex House, she's finally finished. The film is done. Everything Siobhan and Theo captured four years ago – found on the laptop that Siobhan brought to her flat and left there before they returned to the house – everything she compiled over the last year: all of the interviews with Margot and Siobhan, the footage she got from Hex House itself, that final day. She's been working on the film for so long that she no longer knows what story it tells. The story of a house. The story of broken people looking for a home. The story of a woman who convinced herself that was what she was providing.

Zara stands, stretching her neck to the left and right so it lets out a satisfying click. Margot comes into the study, little Thomas trailing behind, rubbing his eyes, wearing pyjamas covered with colourful tractors and trucks. He's thrived in the months he's been with them, slowly adapting to life outside the house, filling out and growing taller, though he sometimes still asks about Haina. Zara doesn't know what to tell him, only that he's safe now. When she tells him that he never has to go back there again, that he'll be with his real family soon, he pulls a face, a face that makes Zara's stomach lurch. Multiple times a day she has to stop, breathe, tell herself, *You did the right thing. You're doing the right thing.*

"Can I have a biscuit, Auntie Margot?" he chirps quietly.

"Shhh, Little Mouse, it's the middle of the night." Margot leads him back to bed. When she comes back into the study, it's with a cup of tea for Zara. She settles herself into the sofa across from the desk and studies Zara's expression.

"Finished, is it?" she asks.

"It's finished."

Margot nods, smoothing back her curls from her face. "Good. That's good." They sit in silence for a long minute before she asks, "What now?"

"I don't know," Zara says. Every inch of her body feels heavy. It's a question she's wrestled with since they left the house, since the moment she stopped searching in the house's rubble for Siobhan because there was no more

Siobhan left to find. So many times, she almost stopped working on the documentary, almost hit delete on the whole folder of footage. But something keeps her going. She can never know how the truth will be received; she knows only now that it's her responsibility to share it.

Somehow, rumours about the documentary are already circling – on the HexHeads forum, on social media. She's been receiving messages. Some are encouraging and positive, others are ridiculing, calling her a fantasist, a conspiracy theorist. One or two have been threatening. They're icy and detailed, so detailed they could only have come from previous guests. *Leave it alone*, they warn. *Keep the house's secrets*.

So much of her wants to bury the documentary, just as Siobhan did, to pretend she knew nothing about Hex House and Haina and all the things that happened there. But then she thinks about what doing just that did to Siobhan, and it hardens her resolve.

Zara, with Theo's help, has been painstakingly hunting down women who'd been at the house. Some were easy – Keiko, Janine, both living in Edinburgh now – others proved more elusive. Some she's still hunting for. She wants their permission before she does anything with the film, so she has to keep looking, has to keep searching for people who don't want to be found. She needs to tell Theo that she's finally finished, that the documentary is fit to honour Siobhan's memory. And there is someone else's permission she needs, too, someone she's been delaying going to see for three long months as she's pieced together everything that happened. It's almost time, she thinks, but not yet. There's time to rest first.

In bed, she falls into a heavy, syrupy sleep, head fuzzing with static. Next to her, Margot sleeps soundly. She rarely screams in her sleep anymore, but when she does, Zara rolls over to hold her, to whisper into her curls, *You're safe, you're with me, you're safe now.* At 6 a.m., Thomas climbs into bed between them, presses his warm, sleepy body into Zara's. When she wakes, he is watching her. His eyes are so like Elly's – the eyes she's seen peering curiously into the camera in so many of Siobhan and Theo's clips – that it sometimes steals her breath.

"Shhh, Little Mouse, not yet," Margot soothes from the other side of him, but Thomas is awake and wriggling now.

"Is today the day we go and find Granny?" he asks, and Zara senses Margot's body stiffen. It's a day they've both dreaded, but there's no more putting it off now.

"Yes," Zara whispers, pushing a russet lock of hair from his forehead. "That's today."

When it's time to leave, Margot doesn't want to go. She stalks quietly around the flat like a pale ghost. She says she won't come because she's going to meet Keiko, but Zara knows it's really because she can't face the thought of being parted with Thomas. Zara has struggled with the idea, too, but of all the decisions she's had to make, she knows for sure that this is the right one. Before they leave, Margot holds him close, so close that he laughs and squirms away. She turns before he can see her cry.

Zara packs a bag for Thomas – a few changes of clothes and his favourite toys just in case – and also brings her laptop with a version of the finished documentary on it. They're on a train from Edinburgh Waverley by midday. She orders Thomas a babyccino from the coffee shop at the station, and he sips at it, like a tiny man on his way to work, a foamy moustache forming on his upper lip. He asks her questions as their train pulls its way through the sleepy towns. He's always been so curious, but never so much so as today. So Granny is Mummy's mum? *Yes, she is.* And I've never met her before? *No, you haven't.* What if she doesn't like me? *She will love the very bones of you.*

When they get to the final station, they hop on a bus and ten minutes later, they are in Elly's village. Zara grips Thomas's hand tightly. It's just as Elly had described it on tape – there's the church where she married Ethan. There's the bakery where she worked, open today, the smell of bread just noticeable on the air. There's the place where the high street branches off to a smaller path that leads into the woods, the path Elly must have taken all those years ago, pregnant and still wearing her wedding dress. Somewhere close, she knows, is the cottage she ran from on the night she found the house. And closer still, the house where her mum still lives.

"Come on," Zara says to Thomas, who grips her hand and follows her obediently. He can't know how significant this place is, not really, but she thinks he can sense it. They walk down the high street, past the chemist and the corner shop and the post office. When they come to a small white stone cottage on the corner, they pause outside the gate. Zara stares down the path to the door, which is slightly ajar. In the front garden, there's a trowel and some gardening gloves by the rose bush. She can hear the radio from inside. Zara waits, suspended between one moment and the next, knowing Elly's mum is just a shout away. That Theo has already been to see her, given her all the details he could bear to, told her that Zara will be coming. Ethan, he's had less luck finding.

Zara feels almost unworthy of the power she knows she has. Holding her hand is a grandson this woman has never met. In her bag are the answers to everything that happened to her missing daughter. It's almost too much. Zara almost turns around. But then the cottage door opens fully, and a woman appears holding a half-full mug of tea, her forearms streaked with soil. She pauses in the doorway when she notices Zara and Thomas standing at the gate, her brow furrowed. Her eyes land on Thomas, and Zara knows that she can see Elly in his mouth and his nose and his eyes. Those wide eyes that are careful, so careful. She knows in the way that only a mother knows. She sinks to her knees and opens her arms out wide.

It's the woods you need.
Just keep going and don't stop.

If you listen closely,
you might hear something stirring.

There's a woman in the woods. She's tall and thin
with a serious face and a scar across her belly.
She's been away for a while,
but now her feet are on the ground,
and she's building a house.
She's building a home.

She's trying to be better than what
came before, to honour the memory of
someone who deserved better.

Maybe things can be different, this time.

If you go looking, maybe you'll find her.
She'll be waiting for you in a golden doorway.
If you listen closely, very closely,
you might hear her ask:

Would you like to come inside?

ACKNOWLEDGEMENTS

In its own way, a book is a house, and so many people have poured their hard work and dedication into the building of this one.

I'd like to thank my wonderful agent, Marilia Savvides, for being the fiercest cheerleader and friend a writer could ever ask for. Your incisive brilliance transformed this book. A huge thank you to my editor, Daniel Carpenter, for so kindly and expertly guiding me through this process, and for believing in *Hex House*. I'd also like to thank Charlotte Kelly and the rest of the Titan team for doing such a beautiful job in bringing it to life and getting it out into the world.

Thank you to Creative Scotland, whose generous support made the writing of this novel possible. Also, to New Writing North and Word Factory – winning the Northern Apprentice Award and receiving mentorship from the brilliant Catherine Menon was a real turning point for me and my writing. Thank you to the Bridport Prize for boosting my confidence, and for tirelessly platforming emerging writers.

Having dedicated time and peaceful places to write is

both a privilege and a blessing. Thank you to the Mairtín Crawford Award, through which I was very generously gifted a stay at the idyllic River Mill Writers' Retreat in 2022, where sections of *Hex House* were written. Much of the novel was also written at the wonderful Gladstones Library. Thank you for the quiet, safe oasis you provide for writers.

I'd like to thank Sue Vice, Adam Piette and Laura Joyce for your support and encouragement during my PhD at the University of Sheffield. A massive thank you also to the Creative Writing department at York St John University. The incredible year I spent studying for my MA taught me who I wanted to be as a writer and gave me the invaluable gift of friends for life. Amy, Rose and Matthew – you are forever my Golden Girls. I can't imagine life without you.

Thank you to my very talented writing group – Alicia, Nick and Neil – for all the prompts, feedback and good times chatting writing over pints. You guys keep me in my good habits. Thank you to (Dr!) Lizzie, who inspired me to follow my niche interests to PhD level and who helped me solve one of the key plot-holes in this book over tapas. Thank you to my soul sister Georgie, for always understanding, for being weird with me, and for all the nights in the Winning Post. To Laura, Pez, Hannah, Ellen, Fran, Megan, Anna and Cat for being there from the beginning – you are all extraordinary. Bazmuir forever.

To my parents, for supporting me every step of the way and never laughing when I said I wanted to write stories for a living. That is no small thing. Thank you. To my big sisters, Jen and Sarah. Our sisterhood is magical and one of the great joys of my life. Pop, you're the strongest person I know – thank you for always lighting the way. Pepita, thank you for the incredible character artwork, and for being the reason I write in the first place. I am so proud of you both. 'Should you need us.'

I'm lucky enough to have married into a pretty amazing family (Lesley, Charlotte, Rich, Evie, Teddy, Kate, Tim, Iris, Jude, Phil, Chris, Alex and Bella – I hope you know you're all getting a box of books for Christmas for the foreseeable future!). A very special thanks to Lesley Jones. Your encouragement and kindness mean so much to me.

And finally, to my little family. Philip – my North Star, my steady anchor, my very best friend. None of this would have been possible without your unwavering belief and unquestioning support. I'm fairly certain your heart is made from pure gold, and I am grateful for you every single day.

Dylan. You are the reason for everything I do. I wrote *Hex House* while pregnant with you, but while it's a bit dark and twisty, you are the brightest and most joyful beam of sunlight I've ever known. Just promise you won't read this book until you're a little older, okay?

ABOUT THE AUTHOR

AMY JANE STEWART grew up in Yorkshire and Edinburgh, and now lives in the Scottish Borders with her husband and son. Her short stories have won the New Writing North and Word Factory Northern Apprentice Award and the Mairtín Crawford Award for Short Story. Her work has also been widely published, including in New Writing Scotland and *Test Signal*, an anthology of northern writing. She has an MA in Creative Writing from York St John University and is currently studying for a PhD at the University of Sheffield, exploring the transgressive nature of winged women, from angels to circus artists. *Hex House* is her first novel.

Instagram: @amyjanestewart
amyjanestewart.co.uk

For more fantastic fiction, author events,
exclusive excerpts, competitions, limited editions and more

VISIT OUR WEBSITE
titanbooks.com

LIKE US ON FACEBOOK
facebook.com/titanbooks

FOLLOW US ON TWITTER AND INSTAGRAM
@TitanBooks

EMAIL US
readerfeedback@titanemail.com